REA

In the Slipstream

In the Slipstream:
An FC2 Reader

edited by Ronald Sukenick
and Curtis White

Normal/Tallahassee

Published by FC2 with support provided by Florida State University, the
Unit for Contemporary Literature of the Department of English at Illinois
State University, and the Illinois Arts Council.

Address all inquiries to: Fiction Collective Two, Florida State University, c/o
English Department, Tallahassee, FL 32306-1580

ISBN: Paper, 1-57366-080-9

Library of Congress Cataloging-in-Publication Data
In the slipstream: an FC2 reader / edited by Ronald Sukenick and Curtis
White. -- 1st ed.
    p. cm.
  ISBN 1-57366-080-9 (alk. paper)
   1. American fiction--20th century. 2. United States--Social life and
customs--20th century--Fiction. 3. Short stories, American.
I. Sukenick, Ronald. II. White, Curtis, 1951- . III. Fiction Collective
Two (U.S.)
PS659.I54 1999
813'.0108--dc21   99-36266
                                    CIP

Cover Design: Todd Michael Bushman
Book Design: Brian Monday

The editors would like to thank Martin Riker for his editorial assistance in
this project

Produced and printed in the United States of America
Printed on recycled paper with soy ink

Illinois ARTS Council
AN AGENCY OF
THE STATE OF ILLINOIS

This program is
partially sponsored
by a grant from the
Illinois Arts Council

CONTENTS

Fiction Collective Two

Black Ice Books

The Nilon Award

Who Do They Think They Are?
A Personal History of the Fiction Collective

Jonathan Baumbach

1

I got into my only publishing venture not for idealistic reasons (not at the beginning) and not for business considerations (least of all for that), but out of desperation. *Reruns*, my third and—at the time of its completion—best novel was rejected thirty-two times over a period of three and half years. It was circulated by Candida Donadio, a literary agent of the highest reputation, and so had every chance to find acceptance. During the years that *Reruns* was almost, if not quite, making connection, I had difficulty getting into another novel. My first two novels had been taken by major publishing houses on first and third tries, and had had their share of favorable attention. I had been spoiled in a modest way. *Reruns* may have been a departure from the first two books but it was also an outgrowth of what I had been doing, the inescapable, if not so obvious, next step. It was a breakthrough book, I supposed, a leap beyond where I had been and I had, fair to say, an excessive (and perhaps obsessive) attachment to it.

I began to talk to other writers whose work I admired about alternative means of publishing fiction, starting out with my friend and colleague in the Brooklyn College MFA Program, Peter Spielberg. This was in 1973, a time when there were exceedingly few small press outlets for booklength fiction, and certainly none capable of appealing to more than a handful of readers. It was not our idea to create another marginalized small press. Our aspirations were naive and inflated with quixotic enthusiasm. We wanted no less than to publish the best new fiction around and have it acknowledged as such in the media and carried in book stores virtually everywhere. We hoped to create something comparable to the wide-reaching writers' cooperatives in Sweden and England, although there had been no tradition for it in the U.S. In our unguarded expectations, we saw ourselves becoming (for innovative fiction) the New Directions of our time.

At our early meetings, we analyzed the commercial publishing scene by sharing negative anecdotes. In addition to the old horror stories of how our books were not properly marketed (were not in bookstores when reviews appeared) were new ones about editors admiring manuscripts, keeping them on ice for five or six months (I certainly knew about that), and then turning them back because the writer had a "poor track record," or because the book was perceived to have limited sales potential or, with all good will, the house didn't know how to present it to the marketplace. Sometimes books were accepted only to have that acceptance revoked at a higher level. And then there were books that had been published and had gotten a positive reception that were out of print (nowhere to be found) a year or so after coming to life. Fiction that redefined the rules, innovative and experimental work, was having the most trouble finding a home in what was clearly (though unacknowledged) a publishing establishment increasingly attuned to the bottom line. The writers I talked to tended to believe there was an audience out there for their books that had not been sufficiently tapped. Since we understood the appeal of what we had written (or thought we did), we supposed we had a better chance than the publishing houses of reaching that audience. A group of us, some eight or ten fiction writers mostly based in New York, began to meet at my place or someone else's to explore the idea of a novelists' publishing cooperative. We were in broad agreement on the necessity of taking the authority of publication into our own hands, although objections kept surfacing. It was more difficult to publish books and distribute them and sell them than we imagined, was one. Running a publishing house, even if we shared the labors, was prohibitively time-consuming, was another. Our business after all was writing books, and there was barely enough time to do that. The more sensible among us warned of the need for capitalization if only to get the enterprise into motion. And we were aware—we made ourselves aware—that without a distribution agreement we were history without ever having had one, dead as it were before we began.

We meditated on the death before life that was our present circumstance, persuaded ourselves against hope. Urgency kept us going, a sense of irony. Who would have thought, having done nothing yet, that we had gotten as far as we had.

Between meetings, between exhilaration and despair (and the sometime inability to distinguish one from the other), Peter Spielberg and I sought advice and information, went around together—each too diffident to do it alone—talking to printers and distributors, representatives of foundations, anyone who seemed to know something about the publication of books. We met with explicit encouragement for our idea and unspoken skepticism about its ever coming to pass. In the evenings, the two of us spent hours talking with each other on the phone (to the exasperation of our wives), sorting and analyzing information, reviewing alternatives, trading off anxieties, holding on as if the only thing that sustained our ephemeral project was the other's voice at the end of the line.

At some point, Spielberg and I went to see the Provost at Brooklyn College and suggested the Fiction Collective—the name our group had selected from other homely and unmemorable choices—as a forerunner perhaps of a Brooklyn College press. The provost was sympathetic to our idea, though vague about what he could do for us. Funds were out of the question. Space, he said, might be provided, some mailing privileges, and official connection with the MFA Program in Creative Writing (of which I was co-director). It would take time, eight months or more, to codify arrangements.

The talk at our meetings, now that we had a name to validate our existence, took a new turn. There had been a feeling in the room, inchoate and embarrassing to admit, that our collective authority lacked symbolic weight. The ritual of a publisher's acceptance offered the satisfaction of official sanction while our own improvised ritual—majority vote of writer-members—couldn't, didn't. For a sense of our worth, we were dependent (some of us at least) on an editor's approval. The more we denied the sway of establishment culture, the more we seemed to be confessing it. The enemy, if there could be said to be one, was as much within as without, whispering what was to become a familiar reproof: Who do they think they are?

Who in fact did we think we were?

In addition to the New York group that was meeting regularly in my Brooklyn house, which also included writers from neighboring states and upstate New York, there were fellow collectivists in California and Colorado and New Hampshire who kept in touch by mail and sometimes phone. I remember Ron Sukenick, with whom I had been exchanging letters almost daily, writing from California—"No one tells me what's going on." As if anything were going on beyond the rehashing of the same problems and objections. I remember someone, perhaps in a subversive mood, suggesting we do novels in throwaway editions, and someone else saying, "Isn't the transience of commercial publishing the very thing we're resisting?"

Well, let's do something, I remember saying, sometimes to myself, sometimes out loud, concerned that the seemingly endless series of meetings was becoming counter-effective.

Finally, we decided unanimously—objections spoken under our breath—to do an anthology of new short fiction to be called "Statements," and on the strength of that to apply for grants to do individual novels. The anthology, by dint of its breadth—a wide range of prominent writers supported the project—would announce us as a collective.

A few weeks later, during one of our daily phone conversations, Spielberg said he was worried that by the time we got the anthology together—six months to do it right—the impetus we had to go ahead would have dissipated. We had already, in his opinion, been talking too long. After each of our meetings there seemed to be less enthusiasm for going ahead than before.

After consulting with the others, we decided to postpone the anthology, which was after all an advertisement for the collective and not the main event, and instead do the first series of novels for our opening publication. It seemed the only thing to do—the manuscripts had been ready to go into production for some time—if we were ever going to do anything.

The plan was to do six books a year and bring them out in groups of three approximately every six months. The first series, the first three manuscripts that were accepted and ready to go, were *Twiddledum Twaddledum* by Peter Spielberg, *Museum* by B. H. Friedman and *Reruns*. We broke the editing chores down in an informal way. Spielberg would edit *Reruns*; B. H. Friedman would do *Twiddledum Twaddledum*; I would do *Museum*. The only clear principle was to avoid reciprocity—that is, to avoid the potential conflict of interest in editing a book by the person who was editing yours.

At some time—so much was happening at once it's hard to keep the chronology in place—B. H. Friedman asked a young artist he knew to devise a uniform format for the series, something that would suggest a collaborative effort. One of his ideas, the one we decided on by majority vote, was to have the cover made up of a montage of faces, all in photographic negative except for the author of the particular book, who would be highlighted in positive. The format was used only for the first series (in the following series, each writer designed his own cover—Donald Barthelme, in fact, designed the cover of Mark Mirsky's *The Secret Table*), though it has been picked up in dimunition and used as an identifying symbol on the back cover of later books.

The more you have to do, it's always seemed to me, the more time you have to do still more. While editing *Museum*, while analyzing printing estimates, while making last minute revisions on *Reruns*, I went around with Spielberg (and sometimes with Mark Mirsky and Jerome Charyn) interviewing potential distributors. The head of one distinguished publishing house, initially interested in the possibility of distributing our books, woke up one morning (so it was reported to us) furious at the idea of the Fiction Collective. "Who do they think they are?" he said, or was reported to have said. "We publish all the good fiction that comes our way. There isn't any worthy fiction not getting published." It was an attitude we would encounter, directly and through oblique report, again and again.

To inspire such anger gave us a sense of weight and importance. We dreamed ourselves benign and reasonable and woke to find ourselves a menace to the business of literature.

The first publishing house to offer us distribution services was the small independent publisher, George Braziller. Two larger houses were hanging fire at the time, procrastinating in their fashion, but we accepted Braziller's forthright offer without waiting to hear from the others. It occured to us that the offer might be used as leverage to induce action elsewhere, but we were for the moment inured to temptation. George Braziller, Inc. announced our first series in the centerfold of their catalogue.

We had a mutually satisfying relationship with Braziller for something like seven years. Since one of Braziller's strengths was the European novel and in particular the nouveau roman, our list of innovative American fiction seemed a perfect complement to his. {A tax law requiring publishers to pay taxes on warehouse stock eventually made it unfeasible for Braziller to continue distributing our books.} In its moment, the arrangement with Braziller was a turning point in our fortunes. The Braziller connection gave us immediate credibility, got us into bookstores, put us on the map.

While the distribution arrangements were being made, before and after—the Collective obsessing us like a difficult love affair—Spielberg and I were checking out printers, comparing costs for various sizes of press run, evaluating reliability and convenience factors. A large printer in Michigan (with a sales office in New York City) gave us the lowest overall production bids and we decided, a last minute decision, to have the whole job done by them: typesetting, pages, binding, etc. We would use ten-point type for the first series, allowing forty-two lines (thirty-five is average) to a page—an austere choice. Austerity was our most persistent vice, but since we had no capitalization we felt obliged to make self-effacing choices. An attendant irony: the reviewer in *The New York Times Book Review* would reprove us for having an excess of blank space in our books.

When a writer has a novel come out, I've discovered (a discovery underlined by doing a book with the Collective), a variety of primitive feelings that have little to do with the nature of the work itself rise to the surface. A novel is sometimes, perhaps at some level always, an act of aggression toward the world at large. Unacceptable feelings toward parents, lovers, friends, adversaries are revealed in, as it seems to the writer, transparent code. Such aggression engenders guilt. The childish association between wishes and deeds comes to the fore. On top of that (or on bottom), there's the murderous ambition of the writer to succeed, no small hostility in itself.

A publishing house mediates between the novelist and the rest of the world, serves (among other services, of course) as a symbolic protector. A publisher (or editor—I use the words interchangeably here) shares a writer's potency, takes it on himself by doing the writer's book, and at the same time shares responsibility for the murderous implication of that potency. A needful relationship on both sides, though traditionally rife with real and symbolic betrayals.

We were offering the writer—and I doubt that we understood it ourselves at the time—a new and less sanctifying relationship with his publisher. We were asking him to stand in for himself, to become (in the metaphoric sense I've been using all along) his own father.

2

Making ourselves known, getting press, was easier than we anticipated. We were news, the first open-ended fiction writers cooperative in America. The stories we read about ourselves were our own story returned to us through a variety of distorting mirrors.

We had books almost five months before publication date,

and so we sent out paperbacks (we published in both cloth and paper simultaneously) in lieu of bound galleys as advance copies. It turned out that almost everyone who reviewed us—one of the mysteries of our experience—asked for books to be sent to them again.

By now the second series had been accepted—*98.6* by Ronald Sukenick, *The Secret Table* by Mark Mirsky and *Searching for Survivors* by Russell Banks—and was being edited. Anyone who had a book accepted for publication by the collective automatically became a member. And anyone who was a member could and did read manuscripts. It took 4 Yes votes out of a possible 7 readings to get a manuscript accepted.

Our promise to the writer, which we've held to in all our various manifestations, was to keep all books in print for the life of the collective.

The first piece to appear about the Fiction Collective was in "Scenes" in *The Village Voice* (July 4, 1974). The representation was not notably inaccurate, was in fact sympathetic and encouraging, yet its publication embarrassed me. It was as if our private fantasies had been broadcast. The piece announced our presence on the scene, but it was disturbing to see my words, not always used as I had meant them, stare back reproachfully from the page.

Next the reviews came in—the prepublication reviews—from *Publishers' Weekly* and *Kirkus* services, sent to us in photocopy from Braziller. On the whole, we were treated respectfully and in the *Kirkus* reviews with more than passing perception. It was just like, I remember thinking (another small irony), bringing out a book with a publisher.

On September 15, Ronald Sukenick presented in the "Guest Word" of *The New York Times Book Review* something of a Fiction Collective manifesto, which caused a small uproar among those already piqued by our existence. Sukenick had presumed to say that the Collective was publishing (or would publish) quality innovative fiction—first-rate serious work—that was being "starved out" by the publishing industry. According to the establishment, such fiction was either not being written or was already being published in abundance.

Conventional wisdom had it that a good novel, no matter its uniqueness or difficulty, would ultimately find a publisher. It was impolitic to call conventional wisdom a liar.

What we wanted of course was not only to have the best overall list of serious fiction around, as Robert Coover said about us some years later, but to jostle the publishing establishment into taking more chances with innovative fiction. I couldn't imagine us going on indefinitely. When would we find the time to write our books? We were, I wanted to believe, a stopgap action in a period of emergency.

The period of emergency has been as long running and persistent as the Collective itself.

Reviews of the Collective's books—and the obvious thing was to review the series together—tended to set up invidious comparisons among them, playing them off against one another for rhetorical convenience. We had to remind ourselves that we were not in competition, as no writer really, outside the contrived arena of media, is competing with any other.

Most of the attention we received was generous. The Quality Paperback Club, just starting out, presented our first series as a Special Selection. The *New Republic* ran a long and highly favorable review of all three novels in the Fall Book Issue. Insightful, affirmative pieces appeared in *Newsweek*, *The Village Voice*, *The Los Angeles Times*, *The Chicago Tribune Book World* and *The American Poetry Review* among others. *The New York Times* reviewed the series both in the daily and Sunday Book Review. Something like forty-five periodicals throughout the country either covered Fiction Collective as a news story or reviewed the books or both. The *Washington Post* listed *Reruns* as one of the notable books of the year. The first printing of all three novels sold out before publication date. The following series did equally well, but each succeeding series on the average sold slightly less than the one before. Much of the publicity we received was dependent on our novelty and that of course faded with time. The books are still in print, however, and continue to sell, are taught (some of them) now and then in American Fiction courses in colleges around the country.

Shortly after the first series of novels was published, we

received a grant from the New York State Council for the Arts to hire a Coordinator (a combination managing editor and publicist). The following year, the NYSCA grant was renewed and the National Endowment for the Arts gave us funds to subsidize, in large part, eight new works of fiction.

Spielberg and I co-directed FC for five years, supervising the publication of thirty books plus *Statements* (published by Braziller), and *Statements II* (subsidized by Brooklyn College), a longer running commitment of time and energy and exhausted hope than I anticipated. Raymond Federman and Carol Sturm Smith co-directed for the next year or so and then Thomas Glynn and Harold Jaffe took over. Even after I stepped down as co-director, I continued on the board of directors and remained closer to the operation of things than was good for my own work. And eventually, Spielberg and I took over again as co-directors for a second term. Our second term was much shorter than our first. As our grants started to dry up, survival became increasingly problematic. It was necessary to invent the Collective a second time—I'm talking about the emergence of FC2—to give it renewed life.

It is hard (when you have no money) to sustain the publishing of original fiction in the U.S. and virtually impossible to sell books in significant number without the wherewithall to advertise. Media is a system of mirrors that tends to discover and honor whatever it offered for discovery and honor in the first place. We are a culture in which the perception of something counts for more than the thing itself. I have long since stopped imagining that we can play our game on the main stage, but we have for a long time continued to play. No one has made any money. All the time that's been given has been given for its own sake. This has been a sometimes grudging labor of desperation and vain hope. We may have produced a number of distinctive books in the last quarter of this waning century—it is not my part to say—but I suspect our greatest achievement is our prolonged survival when there's never been any hope for us, as we should have known all along from the very start. Who would have thought, having lasted sometimes invisibly for twenty-five years, that we had gotten as far as we had.

Introduction

Ronald Sukenick and Curtis White

Jonathan Baumbach's comments on the Fiction Collective bring us up to 1988-89. At this time, the Collective was directed by Mark Leyner, Rachel Salazar, and Curt White. The involvement of the University of Colorado, Boulder, was growing through its Nilon Prize for Excellence in Minority Fiction, as was the participation of Illinois State University through its National Fiction Competition. And yet things were not well. The Fiction Collective had reached a point where it had exhausted most of the collectivist energies of its origins. The people upon whom most of the responsibilities fell were becoming more frustrated with their lack of any real authority. Beyond the contests, the Fiction Collective had essentially ceased to exist. It had certainly ceased to exist as something that could be said to "matter."

It was within this context that we (Ronald Sukenick and Curt White) decided to inform the membership that unless we were allowed to re-organize, re-energize and administer the Collective, we would depart, taking the resources with us, and start a new press. In Jonathan Baumbach's words, "We were threatening to take our football and go home if we couldn't be quarterbacks."

More or less.

In the winter of 1989, a small group of writers including

Curtis White, Ronald Sukenick, Mark Leyner, Jonathan
Baumbach, B. H. Friedman and Peter Spielberg met in Peter's
Brooklyn apartment to hash out the future. There were, under-
standably, some misgivings and resentments, but the final decision was that our constitution would be rewritten giving White
and Sukenick dominant control over all aspects of the press.
To signal this break with our own past, we agreed to call this
new organization Fiction Collective Two or, as we have come
to be known, FC2.

Our first problem was to begin to professionalize the organization, that is, have real distribution, marketing, promo-
tion and professional-quality design for our books. Most of
this was handled ably, under impoverished circumstances, by
Don Laing, our business manager at Boulder and former Director of the American Booksellers Association. We divided
responsibilities between our two offices at the University of
Colorado and Illinois State thus creating a model for collaborative organization which we would later expand by engaging
Northwestern University Press as our distributor.

Editorially, our first great project was the creation of an
imprint, Black Ice Books. Black Ice was to be modeled on the
successful Autonomedia Foreign Agents series which had in-
troduced radical European thinkers like Jean Baudrillard and
Paul Virilio to a lot of North American graduate students in
the early eighties. Black Ice Books were to be short, cheap,
radical and hip. We also imagined—and Larry McCaffery was
largely responsible for this—a merging of the avant garde with
the popular. Hence, avant pop. We sought out the radicals of
form and content in "genre" fiction and discovered books like
John Shirley's *New Noir* and Samuel Delany's *Hogg*.

Thanks to a series of NEA grants, the gradual streamlin-
ing of our organization and production practices, and the considerable success of our Black Ice Books, the early nineties
were stable and exciting. FC2 succeeded in foregrounding the
original Fiction Collective's unique purpose to be a showcase
for the nonconventional in the context of an aggressive inde-
pendence from mainstream publishing. At this time, we were
enjoying the success not only of Black Ice but of a series of

triumphant Nilon winners (including, among others, Diane Glancy's *Trigger Dance*, Yvonne Sapia's *Valentino's Hair*, and Ricardo Cortez Cruz's *Straight Outta Compton*) which received enthusiastic national reviews, impressive sales and "Best of Year" acknowledgments from *Publisher's Weekly* (Sapia) and *The Nation* (Cruz). We were also vicariously enjoying the meteoric success of Mark Leyner's commercial career with a book originally accepted by the Collective, *My Cousin, My Gastroenterologist*. Gerald Vizenor's *Griever: An American Monkey King in China* established him as one of the leading—and most iconoclastic—Native American voices.

A by now familiar if not chronic problem reoccurred in 1994 when our distributor, the Talman Company, began falling behind in payments. We decided it was time to move on, and we were very fortunate to find Northwestern University Press. In an all day meeting at the "Orphanage" home of Curt White in Normal, Illinois, the Board of Directors (Ron, Curt, Richard Grossman and Cris Mazza) hammered out a deal with Nick Weir-Williams and Kim Maselli of Northwestern, including a $15,000 bridge loan. FC2 finally had stable and dependable distribution, marketing and fulfillment.

Things went well with Northwestern at first. Sales popped up 25-50% across the board. Our books were reliably in stores where they hadn't been seen for years. We had a presence at the American Booksellers Association Convention again.

But beginning in the fall of 1994 a series of events deepened our understanding of the difficulties of being a small nonprofit in a world created for multi-nationals. First, the University of Colorado decided to shut down the publishing program including a phase out of the Nilon Award. The reasons for this decision were almost entirely political, self-destructive and familiar to anyone who has spent much time among university administrators. Fortunately, the Normal office was able to absorb most of the new responsibilities and shift some to Northwestern.

Then, in the fall of 1996, FC2 was clobbered along with every other publisher in North America by a series of returns from Barnes and Noble so massive and extensive that books one had imagined "sold" as much as five years earlier suddenly showed up back in the warehouse in the thousands. FC2's sales for that fall were wiped out, and yet somehow we had to pay nearly $30,000 in printing bills. Fortunately, we received an NEA grant for that year that made it just possible to survive. So, you see, the NEA has done good. But that's just the beginning of that story.

As is commonly known, that NEA grant of 1995-96 was a mixed blessing. In the spring of 1997 we were used as the stick with which Congressional Right Wingers like Pete Hoekstra (R—of course—MI) could beat the NEA. Curt White spent most of that Spring working with staff at the NEA to minimize the damage. But FC2 authors Cris Mazza, D.N. Stuefloten, Jeffrey DeShell and Doug Rice all were labeled pornographers. (A label they wore with good humor and some pride, given its origin.) Doug Rice's *Blood of Mugwump* was even waved about on the Senate floor by none less than Jesse Helms, who decried the effects of Rice's work on his innocent young staffers who had been obliged to read it. Never mind that the book rewrites equally bloody and disturbing work from Greek mythology and William Faulkner. The development of poor Tiresius' mixed sexual condition was found by congressional saints to be an assault on fundamental American values! That it was also a confirmation of a certain congressional will-to-stupidity goes without saying.

Before vanishing in the way that all scandals must, Congressperson Tom Ewing of Illinois, Curt White's so-called representative, actually visited the president of Illinois State University to ask for White's head, or some other "decent" part of his anatomy. We are happy to report that it is still possible to just say no to the little men and women on Capitol Hill.

On the positive side, this fracas with bureaucrats, politicians, and Donald Wildman's Council for Family Values (they who had earlier attacked Maplethorpe and Wojnarowicz) did get FC2 back in the foreground of national literary discussion. We reclaimed our role as bad boys/girls (and sometimes boygirls) of North American fiction and helped to re-energize the idea that fiction can still matter both as art and as cogent social antagonist.

Conflict and dissent, however, were not merely external to FC2. But the main grounds for infighting were literary. Let no one think it was an easy process approving a book for publication. This was perhaps not surprising since FC2 by this point consisted of a sampling of writers from all parts of the country and many different literary backgrounds. There were many struggles over manuscripts, and there were ever-shifting factions of literary taste to be reconciled before a manuscript was accepted. Thanks to our independent editorial panels, many of FC2's oldest and best known members had books rejected, not excluding the directors of the organization. On the other hand, this made more room on our list for younger writers new to FC2, who were eagerly sought out by those same directors. During these years a very large proportion of the writers had never published with FC2 before, and many of them had never published books anywhere before. Women and minority writers were especially welcome.

But our strongest memory from the last ten years of contrarian publishing is of course the satisfaction we have found in doing what the Fiction Collective/FC2/Black Ice Books have always done: find worthy fiction outside of the impoverished commercial tastes of mainstream publishing and give it an opportunity. We've found this work in "the slipstream."

In the process, we hope we have given our culture a life it would not otherwise have had. Read these "greatest hits" from our first quarter century, then re-discover Baumbach's *Babble*, Sukenick's *98.6*, Federman's *Take It or Leave It*, Katz's *Stolen Stories*, Leyner's *I Smell Esther Williams*, Mazza's *Is It Sexual Harassment Yet?*, Dara's *Lost Scrapbook*, Grossman's *Alphabet Man* and see if we aren't still, as Robert Coover said of us back in our earliest days, "the best list in town."

——*The Fiction Collective*——

Raymond Federman

In the early days of FC—I'm talking some 25 years ago—when a book was accepted the author had to come up with a certain sum of money for production of the book which was matched by the NEA grant. Eventually, when the book sold a certain number of copies the author would be reimbursed. These were the good old days.

When *Take It or Leave It* was accepted I had to come up with 3500 bucks—it was a big book and the typography presented some extra cost. Now in 1975 when the book was accepted [it appeared in 76] I didn't have 3500 bucks to see my book published. I wasn't yet the Distinguished Melodia E. Jones Professor. On top of that I had a daughter in college and another in a private school. I could have sold one of the daughters but it was not practical. I could have sold my Beckett collection but it would have brought tears to my eyes. What to do?

My lovely wife came up with a brilliant idea. Let's go to our bank and borrow the dough. You're kidding, I said. To publish a book? We could tell them we are renovating the house, my lovely wife said. We borrowed from the bank last year for that purpose. Let's try anyway.

So here we are with the manager of M & T Bank. Don't tell me you're renovating your house again, he said, with a banker's grin on his face.

I couldn't resist. No, I said, we need 3500 dollars to publish a book.

At first he looked dumbfounded, but then I pulled out a copy of the manuscript of *Take It or Leave It* and put it on his desk. He looked at it, flipped a few pages, and asked: How much you need?

3500.

He took out some papers out of his desk, looked at them, and said: No problem. In fact, I'm going to give you the best rate I can. On one condition. I want a copy of the book when it comes out.

Well, the rest is history. But my Banker now own a signed copy of *TIOLI* which one of these days he might be able to sell for a fortune. So it goes.

V
Cyrano of the Regiment

YESYES BUTBUT . . . ? [Deep voice with a tone of slight discouragement]

Yes but what!   [Ah you guys are still here I thought you'd left]

Ah you guys are fed up with these disgusting details
fed up up with these exaggerations
up with these explanations
with these digressions
these preambles

Ok—agreed! <u>The 82nd it can go fly a kite</u>!   But
Nonetheless that's how he landed in that outfit and like it or not
(LADIES & GENTLEMEN) he has 27 jumps behind him!
27 parachute jumps!   That's something!   Isn't it?
A bit scared at first but it's normal in the beginning.
You get used to it!
You hang on in spite of the pain @@@@@@@@@@@
the fear §§§§§§§§§§§§§§§§§§§§
and the butterflies @@@@@@@@@@@ But
then there is the training. Ah what tremendous training! Just in
case I suppose! Ah what preparation! Just in case there is a war.
But now finished! It was all over. He had it—above and beyond
the head he had it—up to here—(and MOINOUS too of course)!
Yet it was not that bad (after all) if one considers

if one reflects a bit on all the advantages of this kind of   E
                                                                X
                                                                I
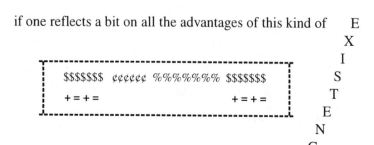
                                                                S
                                                                T
                                                                E
                                                                N
                                                                C
this kind of careless   E X I S T E N C E
where others think for you / where others decide for you /
where others / in fact / protect you (and let us be fair and not
forget the free board & room & the free uniforms)!   And so
we took advantage of all that of all those advantages in other
words—MOINOUS and I—but especially ME (*He hardly
dared admit it*) I took advantage of my eduction: I wrote love
letters for all the guys in my barrack [Company C / Third Pla-
toon] voilà!

I wrote love letters for all the jerks in my barrack who couldn't
do it alone Love letters to all the guys' little broads in all the
corners of America For all the ignorants in my barrack to all the
little hicktowns of Texas Kentucky Alabama Tennessee Geor-
gia Louisiana Mississippi and even as far north as Ohio which
in those days I pronounced OYO because of the difficulty I had
with the H in the middle question of background and experience I suppose In fact there was one guy whose girlfriend lived
in Alaska therefore I even wrote some love letters as far away as
Alaska I'm not kidding Took two weeks for the replies!
nnnnnnnnnnnnnnnnnnnnnnnnnnnnnnnnnnnnnnnnnnnnnnnnnnnnnnnnn

nnnnnnnnnnnnnnnnnnnnnnnnnnnnnnnnnnnnnnnnnnnnnnnnnnnnnnnnnnn
Five bucks a letter that was my price (TAKE IT OR LEAVE
IT) and no one really bitched about it. Therefore Wow would I
bang that loving stuff away (I had a beat-up old Underwood
portable in those days)! Fabulous dreams. Unbreakable vows
of all types. Uncontrolled promises. Endless resolutions. Lan-
guishing memories based (as it should be) on minimal details

furnished by the crums in my barrack prior to the creative outburst. Weeping descriptions of Nature in local colors. Wild erotic situations of surrealistic denseness whose filaria of suggestiveness was certainly enough to corrupt even the most perverse kind of minds. Positions and contortions that would require for correct execution and proper results the acrobatic talents of the entire population of a zoo or tiergarten. And in the margins of the writing paper which of course the guys would furnish with envelopes and stamps (AIR MAIL) dirty little drawings and doodles drawn with a set of color pencils. Ah what ORGIES! I invented on the spot! What ROMANTICISM! I created in those moments of epistolary passion sitting on the floor like an Indian chief typing away madly on my footlocker! I wrote approximately twelve letters per week (4 to 6 pages each), with a few extra ones for the holidays. I would read them aloud to all the jerks in the barrack before sending them off in bundles. And the answers (unbelievable if you can imagine!) we would get. I was THE CYRANO OF THAT REGIMENT. All them sweet little cunts in all them corners of America—including remote parts of Alaska—were madly in love with me without suspecting of course that the guy who was writing to them was not their official boyfriend.

I was the love-hack, the love-dispatcher of the 82nd AIRBORNE DIVISION. And as soon as the replies would arrive, in a continuous stream, the guys would make me read them, immediately on the spot, even before they themselves were allowed to open the letters, but, of course, some of them would cheat behind my back, they couldn't wait those dumb bastards to read how much their little broads adored them and how they reacted to my poetic delivery, but those who were caught opening a letter before me, the cheaters (two or three guys were spying for him), they had to pay off a fine, the next letter would cost them one dollar more and they were not permitted to hear the next public reading I gave, once a week, of all the replies that had arrived in the course of the week, that

would, indeed, teach them in no time that I meant
business, teach them a moral lesson!

Ah, did I have fun writing those letters, full speed, and
without the least apprehension, with two fingers, on
that beat-up old portable typewriter of mine, without
thinking much about what I wrote, in those days form
and content I must confess didn't mean much to me,
nor the questions of

style and meaning
I simply accumulated words any old way

I simply piled up the words as fast as

I could
up & down
&
sideways

metaphors
upon
contradictions   metaphors
on
top of contradictions

I exaggerated full blast
I played with words
with double meaning &
triple meaning &

without any respect (I must confess) for grammar
syntax   style   spelling
logic   disposition   order

punctuation   meaning

it was just a matter of filling up space
PAGES
&
PAGES

(approximately a buck a page I kept

telling myself
as I flipped them over)   and so
when I ran out of stuff to say

I would simply copy   borrow steal
plagiarize   all
over
I would   the damn place
simply open a book
any book
(usually romantic novels)
(or classical tragedies!)
and copy whole passages   *verbatim et litteratim*
throwing in a few foreign expressions   here and there
(Latin Spanish Italian German or just French)
those guys didn't know the difference
that's for sure   and the more I gave them the more they loved
it
Ah what creativity   what spirit of creativity I was
in   in those days
what inspirations
banging every
night on my old beat-up Underwood   (with two fingers)
sometimes telling one broad what I was supposed to say to
another one
sometimes even getting the letters all confused
the names all mixed up
sometimes sending a letter that was supposed to go to a girl in a
little
hicktown in Nebraska
to a girl in a little
hicktown in Arkansas
but who cared
who gave a shit
it kept going (full blast) and they loved me for it   both
the jerks in my outfit
and all the little cunts in all the hicktowns of AMERICA

» » »

HERE IN FACT LET ME GIVE YOU AN EXAMPLE
(AMONG MANY) OF THE TYPE OF LOVE LETTERS I
WROTE IN THOSE DAYS—OF COURSE I'M ONLY
QUOTING THE GOOD SEXY PASSAGES—AND I'M
SOMEWHAT CORRECTING EDITING EXPURGATING
CENSURING (IF I MAY) THE KIND OF ENGLISH I USED
IN THOSE DAYS—PURIFYING (IN A SENSE) THE KIND
OF LANGUAGE I WROTE IN THOSE DAYS—IMPROV-
ING SOMEWHAT THE TONE STYLE GRAMMAR SYN-
TAX—THE   PRESENTATION   ALSO—AND   OF
COURSE—THIS GOES WITHOUT SAYING—CORRECT-
ING THE ABOMINABLE PRONUNCIATION I HAD THEN
(AND STILL QUITE IMPERFECT) WITHOUT HOW-
EVER ATTEMPTING TO DEFORM THE ORIGINAL

Fort Bragg, Fayetteville, N.C.
(Let us say), January 15, 1951

My Darling, My Treasure, My Lovely Adorable Juicy Peach, My Dear
M*******

You cannot imagine how much I thought of you, last night,
under my lonely khaki blankets, alone, in my narrow military
bed, surrounded by the heavy oppressive solitude of life in the
army. I felt, in me, through my flesh torn by the pain of your
absence, a suffering of indefinable nature. The inner empti-
ness of my soul rang with shrieks and groans, it was as though
needles and knives of fire were piercing my body.

Unable to endure this atrocious suffering, I took my private
member in my hands, and feeling it palpitating savagely like a
lost animal, no a giant fruit rather, an enormous banana which
was pulsating there outside my own body, I began to shake it,
to handle it, to squeeze it with all the furor of my desire, and

suddenly I felt flowing, full blast, Woosh, a delicious juice that I wanted to transmit immediately to your essential organs. Ah my dearest reservoir, how much I wanted to feel, at that moment, the wild sugars of my fruit flow in you like a torrent. How I wanted to hear them burst inside of you like a gun, like a cannon (a 75 millimeters), no, like a volcano, in the deepest parts of you, in your most secret, tender, rare and unexplored regions.

Ah! if only you knew, my golden treasure, how much I missed you (how much we missed each other) last night, when, alone, naked and vibrant under my military blankets, at the most solitary moment of night in North Carolina my eyes closed, I saw the image of your sweet and soft body sneak next to mine inside my cot. Ah! dear feathery chicken, adorable pitless peach of tender flesh, smooth and rosy body of such lovely round contours, velvety like a mushroom without tail, little sugared snail, landscape of my inner dreams, if only I could make you feel, yes, how much I wanted (last night but also every night) to penetrate you, with what endless passion, what a huge desire I wanted to rush towards you beyond the mountains, beyond the valleys, beyond the rivers and the canals from under my khaki blankets of loneliness, then you would have known the dimensions of my love, depth of my pool of pleasure, despair of my trembling tools, sources of my frantic appetite and frustration. I see in my dreams your voluptuous greedy hips and your adventurous thighs, hardly ripe, avidly opened to receive, there in that moist furry meadow of yours, the harvest of my nocturnal cultivation.

Ah! do I worry, do I WORRY to know that you are alone so far away in your little Missouri Hicktown. But . . . are you ALONE? Here comes doubt in my mind. I fear the thought that, perhaps, at this very moment some son of a bitch of another guy (OH! do I tremble) is holding you in his tottering skinny arms, while my muscular arms, my PARATROOPER arms, my arms, splendidly fortified by thousands and thousands of pushups cannot hold cannot squeeze you tight to make you feel (despite the distance) with what madly power, what energy, what vitality, what frenzy I would like to grab those lovely contours of yours and squeeze them out of their last drop of love!

Here life is sad without you, and I find myself absentmindedly carving at random your initials on all the tree trunks in the forest of my solitude. But otherwise everything is fine, except for the disgusting grub. If you have by any chance a bit of money saved could you (DARLING) be nice to me as you've always been and send me a billet doux? I adore you passionately madly and desperately with my entire soul and body. Give your saintly Mom a BIG kiss for me (but not your Dad) and think of THINK OF ME dear love as much as you can.

Your BIG and SAD Carrot, J***K*****

LET ME GIVE YOU NOW (BRIEFLY!) AN EXAMPLE OF THE RESPONSES MY LOVE LETTERS WOULD OCCASION IT IS (I THINK) A RATHER GOOD TYPICAL EXAMPLE BUT OF COURSE (I NEED NOT EMPHASIZE) THE BROADS DIDN'T HAVE MUCH IMAGINATION NOR A GREAT DEAL OF TALENT FOR THOSE SORTS OF THINGS NONETHELESS (LET US BE FAIR) THEY TRIED THEIR BEST AND WOULD PUT ALL THEIR HEARTS INTO IT AND MAKE UNUSUALLY VALIANT EFFORTS TO COME UP WITH DECENT REPLIES NO DOUBT I INSPIRED THEM IN A WAY BECAUSE FROM TIME TO TIME WE WOULD GET SOME TOUCHING AND DELIRIOUSLY HILARIOUS LETTERS HARD TO BELIEVE SOME OF THEM WILD ENOUGH TO DRIVE YOU UP THE WALL BUT WHAT STYLE WOW WHAT GRAMMAR WHAT ATROCIOUS ORTHOGRAPHY (QUITE INCREDIBLE) MOST OF THAT STUFF PURE HILLBILLY JARGON (OBVIOUSLY THOSE DUMB LITTLE FARM GIRLS WERE ILLITERATE [*LIKE THEIR BOYFRIENDS*] AND COULD HARDLY READ OR WRITE OR JUST

ENOUGH TO SCRIBBLE THEIR ANSWERS) THERE-
FORE ONCE AND AGAIN WE ARE FORCED TO COR-
RECT SOMEWHAT HERE AND THERE IN ORDER TO
IMPROVE THEIR REPLIES (OR AT LEAST THE ONE
EXAMPLE WE ARE PRESENTING HERE) AND IN
ORDER TO RENDER THEM MORE READABLE
MORE COMPREHENSIBLE MORE ACCEPTABLE
BUT (PLEASE) DO NOT IMAGINE FOR A MOMENT
THAT WE ARE INVENTING THIS REPLY THIS RE-
MARKABLE REPLY ABSOLUTELY NOT THIS IS A
REAL PEARL AN ORIGINAL A GENUINE FULLY
GUARANTEED AND OFFICIALLY AUTHENTICATED
VERSION AS WRITTEN BY ONE OF THE GIRLS
(*WHOSE NAME OF COURSE SHALL REMAIN ANONY-
MOUS*) AS DELIVERED TO US ONE DAY ENCLOSED
IN A PINK PERFUMED ENVELOPE VIA AIR MAIL
SPECIAL DELIVERY

This example is chosen at random from among a stock of more
than four or five hundred.

Kirksville, Missouri
(Approximately)
January 23, 1951

*My BIG Dear Turnip, My SAD Muscular Paratrooper, My Lonely
Prune, Dear J****,*

*I reread your last letter at least two hundred times since it
came and it is with tears in my eyes, dearly adored carrot, that
I'm writing you today, for me too I feel inside of me, in my
most secret regions, as you say so well my creamy one, in my
most private parts, that immense void, which you ALONE can
fill so well! Yesterday, me too, nude and trembling under my
soft warm pink blankets, I felt those huge needles and knives
of your absence (Oh delicious heavy artillery of yours!) softly
penetrate my inner landscape devastated by the sadness and*

boredom of civilian life in Missouri where nothing—NOTH-ING (I swear to you) ever happens, ever comes to fulfill me, to replenish me, to sweeten me with the sugars of love.

My legs timidly spread apart, my eyes tightly closed, my breasts raised shyly and lovingly towards you out there in the direction of North Carolina, in a pleading manner, I suddenly imagined you had returned to lie next to me in my empty couch. Your solid and vigorous hands were voyaging all over my sad body, circulating back and forth over my palpitating contours, rediscovering at once the boundaries of your property which, I swear to you on my mother's beloved soul, my dear brave paratrooper, has not been touched since you departed so heroically more than six months ago!

As my hands, shivering with desire, followed the traces of yours along those contours of my body you describe so poetically, a strict, severe, monotonous voice, deep down inside of me, kept whispering that I should not do such unspeakable gestures, not let myself be tempted by those movements of weakness and despair, that I should not harvest in the darkness of my solitude, especially without the proper tools, the golden wheat that belongs to you. This deep voice (no doubt the voice of reason, of religion, of morality, of Law & Order) grew louder and louder as I pursued (in my mind only) the image, that magnificent image, of your giant fruit, your sweet banana, enormous, nervous and probing, as it wriggled deep inside of me in search of love. But, it is finally with empty hands (empty and humid hands, ALAS) that I came back BACK TO MYSELF, alone, weeping of sadness in my lonely bed, still knowing how you must want me, out there, far away, beyond the meadows, beyond the plains and the deserts, beyond the dark clouds, beyond the highways and the throughways and the superhighways. Oh! my darling prune, how I love to hear those juicy words you speak so tenderly, that rich and poetic vocabulary you know how to dispatch so well in my direction with such waves of eloquence.

Ah, my dearest ferocious monkey how well you know how to climb the trees and branches of our love to hurl yourself (like TARZAN) into the voluptuous jungle of our passion. My precious apricot do not doubt of me, do not worry, I am yours, do not be jealous, for I am yours alone, for ever and evermore! I am of those who remain faithful until death doth us part in the flesh and in the soul. I am waiting for you, you are there in my skin, bones, nerves and organs like a Dainty Deity whom I sacralize, whom I divinize. Come back, oh how I miss you. I can't stand it any more.

My mother tells me that I am crazy to love you so much, crazy to adore a man like you because you are not worth it, because you are a GOOD-FOR-NOTHING, a miserable, lazy creature, but me I know, yes I know that it is not true, and I am convinced that you are GOOD-FOR-SOMETHING, and that it is not your damn fault if you are the way you are. Me, I know that you are good, real, beautiful, gorgeous, enormous, vibrant like a stallion. If I didn't know you as much as I do, would I stop to inscribe your name lovingly with my fingers in the fresh cow-dungs I encounter in the pasture where I wander aimlessly as I nostagically search those secret places where we used to cultivate our love? So, I beg of you, brave adorable paratrooper, continue to do all your training and your PUSH UPS, solidly, regularly, and stubbornly (in spite of those mean sergeants) so that when you come back to me (SOON!) you will be in full shape, strong and ready to grab me and crush me in your fortified arms.

Here the weather is bad. Rains all the time. I'm sad and depressed. Everybody is sad and unfriendly. I spend my time watching television, or playing my record player. Yes, the days, the weeks, the months pass so slowly in my solitude. If I can manage to save a little cash (without my dear Mom noticing it) from the money she gives me to do the shopping, I'll send you a nice TEN dollar bill AIR MAIL & SPECIAL DELIVERY for the anniversary (I do hope you remember!) of our first encounter at the State Fair as we proudly watched the black

Angus parade in the corral, and of our first passionate and secret embraces in the back seat of your brand new Chevrolet. Good Bye! Good Bye dearest love, my brutal and manly para-trooper. I send you thousands and thousands of French kisses XXXXXXXXXXXXXXX!

> *Your BIG Juicy Apple, SAD and Desperate Without You But Faithful and Devoted, Your One and Only Peachy M****

@@@@@@@@@@@@@@@@@@@@@@@@@@@
Other examples of such love letters are available (at reduced rate) either from the publisher or directly from the author of this exaggerated tale. Discretion guaranteed. Money back if not satisfied!
@@@@@@@@@@@@@@@@@@@@@@@@@@@

Steve Katz

This piece, as are all pieces, is dedicated as well to Thelonius Monk, Fats Navarro, John Coltrane, Billie Holiday, Charlie Parker, Bud Powell, Lester Young, Milt Jackson, Lee Konitz, Cecil Taylor, Eric Dolphy, Ornette Coleman, Lennie Tristano and so many others who through their music opened for all of us the American art forms. Herein, specifically, we never intended to effect the death of the band, but it happened, just as it does in American imagination, American experience, American art. After experiencing this, all we could do was submerge, and remain down here, restless but wary. Occasionally, out through the pervasive Marsalis of things these days, we send up a light probe, some kind of snout.

Death of the Band

«for Philip Glass»

He felt two small hits as he listened to the music from the bandshell, as if he had been struck by some pebbles; in fact, if he hadn't glanced at his shoulder and noticed the blood that was seeping through his t-shirt he wouldn't have paid any attention. Now he had two wounds.

One listener behind him tapped on the back of a bench with his umbrella, one slept. A scantily dressed girl turned away when he caught her eye. There was no one else on the benches. Then he saw the composer, cradled in the lowest branch of a large maple, aiming his gun. He gestured for Arnold to move aside. Arnold moved, embarrassed to be in the line of fire. A parabola of dusty light suddenly filled part of the hollow in back of the musicians, then clouds covered the sun again and the composer commenced firing rapidly into the bandshell.

The gun had a silencer, but the audience could hear the shells ricocheting inside the music. The effect was thrilling Americana. Then the musicians began to fall. It was in their contracts that each of them keep playing until he is hit in the head, which happened on the count of seven for some, three for others. Once all the players had fallen, the performance was over. It was then that Arnold, who had got out of the way, began to feel guilty for the death of the band.

Peter leaned back against the tree trunk and cradled the weapon in his lap. This was the first piece he had written following strictly his ideas of irreversible subtraction. The performance had been exquisite, as good as his music could be played.

The instrumentation, the live performance, the composer as performer: everything was coming together. A nice surprise was the role the audience took on its own, like a tragic chorus. This was a dramatic dimension he couldn't have predicted. Peter himself had worn the maple tree as if it were a mask. It had become more than drama. It was a ritual, and he was the shaman. How interesting. No way to predict it. It was worth all the psychic hernias that one got dealing with the art world in the seventies, just to make these few discoveries about one's own music. He sat in the maple tree mask and enjoyed the little applause and fondled the instrument he had played so well. It was just a 22. Everything had become the music, even Rumi, his sound man, backing a van to the stage to get the equipment. They had to get out fast. The bandshell was to be used again that evening for a free performance of the Pro Musica Antiqua.

Arnold passed through the zoo to the south end of the park pressing one of his wounds. The hit on the shoulder had just scored the flesh, but the one that had pierced his back was still bleeding. He could touch the little slug lodged between his ribs where the flesh had stopped it. If he took it to the hospital that would involve the police, and endless explanations, and put his favorite young composer through a lot of paralyzing legal rigamarole. And he might have to explain about the band. He didn't know how to deal yet with his responsibility in that regard. He had moved out of the way. Would the band still be alive if he had stayed put? How to answer that one? He propped himself against the park wall and slowly slid to the west side. Maybe now he had become just part of the music, turned loose in the city. Now he didn't regret skipping work, because he had got to witness a rare performance of the music he loved, a premiere performance, that had moved him greatly, that had become a part of him in these two wounds that complicated his response, a slug lodged in his ribs like a dangerous bit of information. But he hadn't figured it out yet, just how he felt about the death of the band.

The Detective touched the bodies with the toe of his wing-tip shoe. Eight of them, all longhairs, each hit in the head by a small caliber bullet. It was neat, the work of a skilled marksman, so clean, very little blood spilled. He didn't want to flatter anybody, but this was good work. He knew right then that this one would go unsolved. He'd do the paper work, but no arrests here. It would blow his statistics. His rate of convictions was already too high. He was becoming a better detective, but he didn't want them to expect too much of him. They'd start to push him. They'd want to make him a Lieutenant. He couldn't take that. Out of respect for professionalism he'd let this one go unsolved. The hitters he ran into these days all had long hair, so either way this was some kind of low-life snuffed. He pulled out a pad to write down the number 8, and noticed that an enormous crowd had gathered. "The turkeys are gathering," he muttered, his voice amplified by the bandshell. The audience applauded. "Bullshit." He turned his back on them. He didn't like this kind of caper, where he ended up on a bandstand. He hated the public eye. He liked the old-fashioned idea, so hard to come by in the seventies, of a murder in a boudoir.

They came from the rowboats, from Bethesda fountain, from the merry-go-round, from the zoo, and they kept coming, climbing down over the rocks, busting through the bushes. This was amusing. This was human interest. This was the biggest crowd the bandshell had seen in years. "Everywhere is punks," said The Detective, scanning the audience. They applauded and cheered and whistled. Ice cream wagons, hot dogs. Pretzels. Balloons six feet long. Sparkling yo-yos. The networks arrived. Camera buffs by the dozens joined the police photographer, calling out f-stops and shutter speeds.

The Detective knew it was time to leave it with his men in blue. He scrutinized the bodies draped over the music stands one last time. One thing he had learned for sure from the spiritual practices he pursued to help ease his mind in this tough line of work was that none of these deaths meant anything at all. That was something of which he was convinced. Not even a drop in the cosmic bucket. He couldn't worry about individuals any more. They were a lot of skin stuffed with punks as far as he understood it. That was why he was becoming a better detective.

Arnold still had the key to Betsy's apartment, though they rarely saw each other any more. He let himself in. Betsy was a Pisces and a liberal, full of cloying displays of generosity that he found tiresome; but at this point the prospect of Betsy wiping his brow and loving him a little was the only good possibility he had. Her apartment was sloppy as usual, dishes piled in the sink, soiled clothes on top of everything. He put his finger on the lump between his ribs. The bleeding had almost stopped and the pain was down to a dull ache. He scrubbed out one of her pots and boiled up her French paring knives. He felt remarkably clear, and unafraid of what had to be done. He wished there was someone with a video port-a-pack to record his excellent moves. He ripped an old sheet into strips and boiled them, found Hydrogen Peroxide in the medicine cabinet, laid the strips of bandage over the bathtub, and sat down on the toilet seat with a paring knife. Betsy's knives always had a surgical edge. He thrust out his rib-cage, keeping a finger on the lump of lead, and then touched the point of the blade to his flesh, punctured, opened himself between the ribs. The slug squirted out over the bathmat as if it had been waiting to complete its trajectory. He felt as if he had suddenly shed twenty-five pounds. The stinging of the peroxide was wonderful. He rose with it as if from dream to dream. He hadn't needed a hospital. He didn't have to tell anyone about the death of the band. He could hang on to the wonderful feeling Peter Glucks' concert had given him.

He went to Betsy's bedroom, messed up as usual, vaginal cream open on the night table, applicator fallen into yesterday's underwear on the floor. He sat on the bed and thought about telling her everything, because Betsy would understand, because at one time the deepest bond between them was a mutual love for the new American music. He leaned back on the pillow as the pain struck him, and he passed out.

"You people are as prejudiced about us as we are with you. You better believe it. You don't have to be so condescending with me," the Detective told the girl who had joined him at a table in the museum cafeteria. Betsy blushed. He was probably right. She had no business asking if he was a cop. She touched his sleeve. "I'm sorry. Sometimes I don't think before I speak." He sure looked like a cop, but sort of attractive.

"I don't want to implicate you as a hippy, but you ought to be aware that hippies have their own prejudices." Since he had started occasionally snacking at these museums he had been getting a lot more ass, and that made him a better detective.

"I'm sure that's true," said Betsy. "The hardest thing to see sometimes is yourself" She detected a surprising sensitivity in this man, and he was alive, tuned in, not like those people she usually spent time with, bored, stoned or frightened. This man was refreshing.

"People find out I'm a detective and they right away have some ideas like 'Excitement,' they think. 'French Connection.' Like I found eight musicians, or something, shot through the head in the bandshell this morning and I bet you instantly think, 'Heavy. Adventure.' "

"Eight musicians?"

"I don't know musicians from toll collectors. Maybe they were joggers. But they were all shot through the head, and what that means for me is another long boring routine. A routine. A good detective has to appreciate a routine. I am in love with boredom. Here." He takes Betsy's hand and presses it to the gun under his jacket. "What do you think that means? Anything?"

"I think it's horrible to have to live with a gun all the time."

"It's a routine. It's like your tampax. I use it once a month. Most of my work is paper work. I file reports."

"There were really eight musicians killed in the park this afternoon?"

"It's a new American hobby. Mass murders. You're lucky it isn't California. Eight is a drop in the bucket there. What's your name?"

"I'm Hilda," said Betsy. She didn't think it would be cool to give a detective her real name. She liked the strong, thick hands on the table, the cleft jaw like two small boulders.

"You live around here, Hilda?"

"I live across the park."

"I don't like to beat around the bush, Hilda. I got a tight schedule. Let's go over there now. You know what I mean."

Betsy looked away, as if she needed a moment to decide, but her mind was already made up. It was a thrilling and slightly kinky idea. The Detective got up. "No offense meant. If you don't want it I'll understand. But let me pay for your Tab." She let him do it, the first time in years she had let a man pay her bill. She slipped her arm in his as they left. No one had any idea who she was. This was the strangest thing she had done since she was a teenager. "I don't know if those guys were musicians or not. They could have been parkies . . . interns . . . foreigners . . . She pressed close to his body. They left the museum through a display of South Sea artifacts.

"In most places they won't let you hunt with a cross-bow," said the salesman.

"I'm not going to hunt," said Peter Glucks. The instrument was fiberglass, very fancy, fitted with a brass sight and trigger, and a small brass winch to draw the string back; but it wasn't what Peter had visualized.

"Where do you intend to use this weapon?"

"I'm not sure it's really what I want," said Peter. "Do you have anything made of wood, like polished cherry or birch?"

"I haven't seen one made out of wood for years. It's not practical. Where will you use this weapon?"

It was something more medieval that he had in mind, something carved and elegant. "It'll just be a small hall," he said. "No more than three hundred people." The piece was scored for viola da gamba, harpsichord, recorders and hunting horn, all of them amplified. It needed a special environment.

"I'm sorry," said the salesman. He took the crossbow away from Peter Glucks. He wasn't going to be the one who sold a deadly weapon to a madman. "I don't think we have what you want."

Peter didn't protest. This was the kind of resistance to his art he faced wherever he turned. He was used to it. Things would work out. When the time came to perform the piece he'd have his instrument. He would face more troublesome problems when he returned from his European tour. He had a recording session then, and that was infinitely more problematic with his new music than a 'live' performance. He was thinking about videotapes, recording the new work on videocassettes. That would make his new music a star. He left the Sporting Goods store. The crossbow idea wasn't so touchy. A more delicate problem was his piece for koto, piccolo, and blow-gun.

"Shit," said Rumi, when Peter got back to the van.

"What's wrong?"

"We got another damned ticket."

"Well," said the composer, philosophically. "I suppose we'd better pay this one."

Betsy gasped when she saw Arnold lying in the mess in her bed. He had grabbed the tube of contraceptive cream as he was passing out, and had squeezed it all over the sheets. "I'm not the neatest person," she told The Detective, who was snooping in every corner. She slapped Arnold's face. He was really out.

"I'm meticulous," said The Detective.

"Are you casing my joint, or something?"

The Detective stopped at the foot of the bed. "Is this the junkie you live with?"

"This is Arnold. He's a good friend."

"I deduced as much,'" said The Detective. "But does Arnold stay or do I go or what?"

Betsy lifted the bedsheet and saw the dry blood. "He's been hurt," she said.

"We've all been hurt," said The Detective.

"Get some cold water," she said, feeling Arnold's pulse. "I wonder what happened." The Detective shrugged and went for water.

"Your kitchen is for pigs," he said, returning with a bowl. She swabbed Arnold's forehead with a wet rag. "Look, Hilda honey, either he's out of here in ten minutes or I'm leaving."

"Come on. Have a heart. The man's hurt."

"Sweetheart, a little blood is no new thing from my point of view. He looks okay. He moves."

Arnold opened his eyes. "Betsy," he said, touching her face, leaving a smear of contraceptive cream on her cheek.

"What are you doing in my apartment, Arnold?"

"Dying," he smiled.

"Who shot you?" she glanced at The Detective.

"Not interested," he said. "I'm off duty. This isn't my precinct." He went back to the kitchen.

"Peter Glucks," Arnold told her.

"The composer?"

"It was part of the music, the way he ended the piece.

"Shooting you was music?"

"It wasn't like that, like it was me he shot. I was between him and the band, and he was shooting the band. I don't know if I was part of the music or part of the audience. But I moved out of the line of fire and then he shot the band. He shot it in the head. It was wonderful."

"What did it sound like?"

"I mean it was horrible, but you felt that it was some important music, and I was involved in it. I mean I was morally involved. That is a real innovation. It was my choice to move or not . . ."

"He shot everyone in the band?"

"What's all this Liptons?" shouted the detective from the kitchen? "Haven't you got any good tea?"

"Who is that?" asked Arnold.

"He's a detective. I brought him here, we were going to ball, but I didn't expect you . . ."

"Don't tell him anything. Nothing. Don't say I'm here."

"He knows you're here. What can I say to him?"

"Say I was bit by a dog. Say I was in a fight. This music is very important to me, Betsy. It's turned me around. I can't explain it yet but my whole attitude to myself and music is different. I'm . . . I don't know."

"Arnold, this detective found eight musicians dead in the Central Park bandshell today."

"I know, Betsy, and I'm trying to understand if it was my fault."

"How is it your fault?"

"Betsy, I moved out of the way after Glucks hit me. The band might still be alive if I hadn't moved, I think. Maybe not.

But I have to figure it out."

"O Arnold," said Betsy, wiping up the vaginal cream. "Only a Jewish person would worry about that. You had a Jewish mother."

"What difference does that make? I even took the bullet out by myself. Look." He exposed his wounds as Betsy headed for the kitchen.

"He's really been shot," she said to The Detective, who had finished looking in all her cupboards.

"I don't want to hear his story. All I know is you don't have a decent cookie in the place. And you buy this gummy peanut butter."

"He says he was shot at the concert in the bandshell. By the composer. By Peter Glucks." She enunciated very carefully, with great solemnity. "Doesn't that ring a bell?"

"Honey, everything rings a bell in this city. Nobody's to blame. Nothing's wrong. Everything's wrong. Everyone's to blame. Everything happens here and we don't need an explanation. It's all criminal activity. Nothing causes anything. Everything causes everything. That's the rules. Now why would a girl like you fill her breadbox with Wonder Bread? That's murder. That's suicide. You're just lucky I'm off duty."

Arnold stood in the door of the kitchen as straight as he could. He was white as a slice of bread. The wounds throbbed a little but he felt okay. "I . . . I think I'm going to leave. You guys want to use the bed, so go ahead. I'll go home. I feel pretty good. I just want to talk to Betsy for a minute." He took Betsy's hand and led her out of the kitchen. "I'm sorry, Betsy," he whispered, "that I've driven you into bed with detectives." Betsy was touched. She and Arnold once had a very intense thing going. Tears dampened the corners of her eyes. "Relationships. Fuck them. I'll always love you somehow, Arnold," she said. "It's all so impossible," he said, and went out the door.

"Aren't you going to do something?" she asked The Detective as he stepped out of the kitchen.

"Just shut up. It's not your business." He came at her down the hallway. "Shut your woman's mouth." He twisted her arm and pushed her against the wall. He grabbed her head and dug his thumb in just under the jaw. No one had ever hurt her like this before. She could feel his fist in the small of her back. "Look, I know now your name is Betsy, not Hilda, but I'll let that go. You're lucky I'm not on duty. Just stay out of my business and stop trying to make this into a movie. Now do your little trick for me."

She believed she hated him, but there was nothing else she could do. Her hand grazed his cock as she turned. It wasn't even erect. That made him more dangerous. She knew she'd better do it with him now, even though Arnold had wasted all her birth control. At least she'd learned from this experiment that her prejudices about such men as The Detective had some foundation. She'd never make a move like this again, but for now it was too risky not to fuck. One consolation was that if it did happen to her, abortions now were cheap and easy.

After that day time passed at a certain pace for everyone: endless for Arnold who was going through the deepest changes; frantic for Betsy who cursed her luck when she missed two periods; for Peter Glucks time seemed not to pass at all; and The Detective put time aside and monotonously assembled evidence.

Arnold never left his room. Once he had consumed all the food in his cupboard he started a long fast. He had a sense of purpose; there was something he needed to do. That concert had changed his life, a great compliment to the young composer. His two wounds became two scars, a permanent inspiration to Arnold. He turned his friends away at the door. When his office called he hung up. His longest phone conversation was with Betsy, who for three quarters of an hour described her abortion to him. "Is that all," he asked, as soon as she stopped talking. He wanted to remain alone and silent. "Yes, but I . . ." He hung up. After that Betsy changed the lock on her door. She realized that for her Arnold was a lost cause. He was getting thinner, contracting around his two ripening scars. They were the fulcrum of his new understanding, a petroglyph incised in his flesh. They held like amulets the special charms of his new understanding, that the music was something outside the mastery of an instrument, or knowledge of harmony and counterpoint. He was reaching for a new, ineffable reality where art and experience coincide. He practiced the guitar every day. He hadn't played for years because he hated to hear himself. He had always been lousy, and a worse singer; but now it pleased him even to sing. And so what? He'd get through it. He was still terrible, and the hours of practice didn't help. So what? He realized now that the art wasn't in the guitar or the ordering of the sound or the invention; it was somewhere else, somewhere he was grinding himself to go, somewhere he had first been given a glimpse of when he witnessed, even participated in, the death of the band.

The Detective continued to piece it all together, just for the exercise, for the art of it. It wasn't happening too slow, and it wasn't happening too fast. His mixture of indifference and devotion made him a better detective. Long hours got him home late and he fell asleep with his service revolver on. When he woke up his mind was full of thoughts. Were they true? Were they false? He was being led to several inevitable conclusions. Did they matter? He was glad to be alone. He took off the revolver and the clothes and put on some pale gold pajamas. He set a cushion on the floor in the center of his living room and lit a Joss stick. "Fuck the lotus position," he said and crossed his legs. Almost as if he had flicked a switch he emptied his mind of thoughts, erasing a whole week's work. His lids floated down, his pupils floated up. Men and women. Good and evil. What the fuck? Hot and cold. Colors sifted through and stabilized as pure white light in his skull. It was all the same. He had a job to do. Work and play. Guilty and innocent. A clear pleasant bell began to tinkle in the void he was attending. It entered his position through the left ear.

His new music made Peter Gluck's life more complicated, and most of what he spent his time doing had nothing to do with making music. The hassle of booking concerts, setting up tours, arranging accomodations, all fell on him since he wasn't popular enough yet to afford a manager. His work was classified, unfortunately, as 'serious' music, and serious music didn't make bucks. So the chores were his, and he actually enjoyed it, even shopping for the peculiar instruments. Now he had a wonderful old crossbow, with quarrels made of ebony and brass. More complicated was that he had to continually rehearse new musicians. He never thought he would find players enough willing to perform his new music, considering the consequences; but that wasn't the case. Every week at least two or three would show up at his loft with a viola or a clarinet and ask to be in the band. They all knew what that meant, but they wanted to learn the music, and as one older player said, "It's safer than walking the streets in the city these days." And everyone played the music with enthusiasm and dedication. A whole new breed of exciting young musicians was finishing their careers playing his music. It was thrilling for Peter, and only his sure sense of priorities prevented him from turning it into a power trip. "No. No thank you," said a very talented flautist when Peter offered, as always felt obliged to do, to buy the man dinner before performance. "I'm fasting today, anyway."

He had finally found the bass clarinetist he needed to complete the band for his Chicago concert: two electric pianos, an amplified violin, a trumpet, a singer, and the bass clarinet. The voice was a new notion. It didn't totally work yet, but there was something very rich about it. The fall of a singer might make the performance a little too much like tragedy. That wouldn't work. It had to be a delicate balance. But it was only February 14, and he had till April to get it right. The singer was really good, and good looking. She had been a model once, and had studied voice for years, had specialized in lieder. And there was something about her that touched him personally, but he couldn't let himself get involved. He had too many plans. It would be unprofessional.

The singer answered the doorbell. Arnold was there, dressed in his fatigues. He hesitated a moment, squinting into the light, and then stepped inside. "Is this Peter Glucks?" His voice quavered slightly, as if too finely tuned. "Right," said someone sitting at the piano. Arnold set his instrument case on the floor. That he was moving very slowly made everyone pay attention to him. There was something new about Arnold's manner, something fine and ascetic, a pure glow. He could be someone you almost feared, but someone you also aspired to be.

"I want to audition for the band," said Arnold.

"That's weird," Peter said. "You're number eight today."

Arnold looked at the singer. "What's your instrument?"

The way he said it made her blush. "I si

ng with the band," she said.

"I love you," said Arnold. "I want you to help me."

"This thing is growing so fast it's scary," said Peter Glucks. He pointed at Arnold's instrument case. "If that's a guitar, man, I'm sorry. I've never really written a piece for guitar. There's the pop-country-folk stigma that keeps me away from it. I know that's just in my own head, but I haven't really dealt with it. But I really do appreciate that you came to see me." The composer laid his arm somewhat patronizingly on Arnold's shoulder. "I really have no use for guitar, but leave your address in case I write something."

Arnold slipped the composer's arm off his shoulder and stepped back. He unbuttoned his shirt and slowly opened it to reveal the two gleaming scars. "Do you recognize these?"

The band closed in for a took. Peter Glucks ran his finger down the scars. "O how strange," said the composer. "I almost forgot that piece. You were in the bandshell. You were heavier. Weird. There was something in that first piece that I still . . . wow."

"It's lovely," said the singer, kissing both scars.

"Thank you for coming by, man. I'd almost forgot how that piece worked." He ran the backs of his fingers up the piano keys. "The music never ends. ideas just grow one out of the other." He tapped his forehead. "I can't believe how fantastic."

"Do you want to hear me play my instrument?"

"Of course, man. I'd really dig to. I might do a piece for guitar. Who knows. I'm open to anything. Go ahead."

In the fluorescent light everyone seemed made of enameled steel. Arnold unsnapped his case. "I don't sing very well," he said to the singer. "Can you come and sing with me?" She smiled and crossed the room to stand next to him. He lifted his instrument out of the case. As soon as she saw it the singer sang. Arnold stepped in front of her and put the butt of his instrument to his shoulder. The singer burst into her own rendition of East Side/West Side. Arnold opened fire. "All around the town," sang the singer. There wasn't time for the composer to even sit in on crossbow. The whole ensemble fell in every direction as they were lunging for their instruments. It wasn't the greatest performance, but it was Arnold's first, and he played as well as he could. The responsibility for the death of the band could now unequivocally be laid on, him. He embraced the singer and they backed out the door. She was still singing and he lightly patted the beat on her arm. Something special had happened between them. They were a new duo, a direction of their own in the new music. The elation made them laugh when they hit the street and lost their voices to the traffic, thrilled with their discovery of each other; and they skipped away to Chinatown, singing and holding hands.

Mark Leyner

To do my greatest work, the optimal psychological condition is to feel alternately, from instant to instant, like an abject fraud and a Nietzchean aristocrat. I oscillate between these two poles, which are separated by a nanometer. I dance in that tiny synapse. Music? Arnold Schoenberg. The singles—the old 78s. Venue? IKEA. I sit at a fake computer keyboard in one of the simulated home offices, contemplating various disastrous trajectories for my career, as shoppers jostle me, checking dimensions with plastic tape measures.

Huxley said in *Beyond the Mexican Bay* that "the natural rhythm of human life is routine punctuated by orgies." I suppose that the natural rhythm of the author's life is writing punctuated by book tours. Frankly, I'd prefer just orgies. Just give me unpunctuated orgies. That's why I'm writing for television now. Orgies, scotch, candy corn . . . That's the life I want.

He had one of those aroooooooga horns on his car

«for Elizabeth Ross»

Aroooooooga! Aroooooooga!

"Carla, he's here!"
"I'll be right down!"
"What did you do with the laundry tickets—I've got to go by there later?"

Aroooooooga! Aroooooooga!

"What were you reading about Vilas?"
"What about Vilas?" she says, leafing through the paper. The kitchen looks nice. It's suffused with the cheerful sunlight.
"The thing about Vilas . . . you just read it to me."

Aroooooooga! Aroooooooga!

"Oh, oh . . . 'At last Vilas lunches on the clubhouse terrace'?"
"No," he says, wiping soft-boiled egg from his chin.
"This, 'Vilas passes jogging. He has planes to catch and no time for conversation. He must be in Copenhagen tonight, and in Tokyo a few hours after that'?"
"Yeah . . . yeah."

Arooooooga! Arooooooga!

"Carla!!"

"I've got . . ." The rest of her sentence can't be heard because of the dishwasher.

"What's wrong with the dishwasher?"

"I think something's caught in the blade."

"What blade?"

"If you'd come over here and look you'd see what blade."

"What's caught?"

"Probably one of those idiotic ceramic-handled hors d'oeuvre knives I've told you a million times not to put in the dishwasher."

Arooooooga! Arooooooga!

"Does Carla know he's here?"

"You heard me screaming at her."

"Maybe she doesn't know he's here."

"I've been screaming at the top of my lungs."

"Maybe she didn't hear you."

"She answered . . . she said she'd be right down."

"Maybe she just meant that in a routine way."

Arooooooga! Arooooooga!

He almost knocks the salt and pepper shakers and the bottle of vitamins over, reaching for the ashtray.

"If you're going to the laundry, take the stuff I've got."

"What stuff?"

"It's in a pile next to the hamper."

"Do you want that velour thing cleaned?"

"No, leave it. I might want to wear it if I go help Norman with the car tonight."

"His Fiat?"

"No, Barbara's Malibu."

"What happened to it?"

"Steven had a little accident with it or something."

"Why can't he just . . ."
"The trunk's just jammed."

Aroooooga! Aroooooga!

"I think I hear her coming."
"Carla?!"
"Carla!" they both yell.
There are no pets in the house. At least none have ventured into the kitchen and one would imagine the smell of breakfast to be a pungent animal attractant.
"Where was Vilas going to be before Tokyo?"

Aroooooga! Aroooooga!

"What?"
"Where did it say Vilas was going to be before Tokyo?"
She leafs back through the paper, "Copenhagen."
"I knew something reminded me of Danny Kaye."
"What's that got to do with Danny Kaye?"
"He sang that song 'Wonderful Wonderful Copenhagen' in that film about Hans Christian Andersen."
"Norway seems like it would be nice."
"Copenhagen's Denmark."
"I know, I meant Norway."

Aroooooga! Aroooooga!

"Are you going to call Marilyn about the house this summer or should I?"
"This week's very bad for me," he says, lighting a True Menthol.
"What's so bad?"
"Busy. I've got that thing in Morris County coming to trial Thursday—Friday if we're lucky. And I've got that crazy business with your brother-in-law's doctor . . ."
"Carla only wants to come for half this summer if we go."
"It's up to her."

"I'll call then."

"Ask her about something closer to the beach this time."

"The other one wasn't that far."

"It was a twenty minute walk."

Arooooooga! Arooooooga!

"Carla!!" she yells.

He counts his change and yells too, "Carla!"

"What's she doing?"

"Is she in the bathroom?"

"She might be in there."

"Do you have quarters?"

"Wait . . . yeah. When Marilyn talked to . . ."

"I need quarters now for the lot. I owe them sixty cents from a few weeks ago anyway."

"You should park in the lot near your father's old store."

"That's a fifteen minute walk."

"Isn't it free?"

"It's not even so near that store—it's about two blocks . . . it's nearer to the Stanley than to the store."

"It's first come first serve anyway . . . you could see a movie on the way."

"They're all Spanish."

"You never took Spanish in . . ."

"There's no Spanish there now anyway—it's all Indian now."

" . . . there's Indonesian, Indian . . ."

"There's about eight Indian groceries."

"You should get me some curry."

"You can get curry at the supermarket—I bet it's cheaper."

"You think that would be cheap?"

"Cheaper."

"If it's cheaper here, no one would shop there, never mind open eight groceries."

"They live there—they shop there. It's got nothing to do with saving a few pennies. It's neighborhood stores . . ."

"If it's a few pennies, you could just as easily pick me up

some things."

"Like what things?"

"Like curry powder."

"I'm not even parking near there. I owe the other lot about sixty cents so I have to go there anyway."

"I don't have time to fool with that anyway this week. We'll have franks tonight—on the grill or something . . . maybe just a cold salad. I have my hands full this week. I have about three months of late planning to do in one week . . ."

Aroooooooga! Aroooooooga!

"What are you doing?"

"Counting the months till July."

"On your fingers? It's three months."

"You don't even know when you're taking your month. How can I make any arrangements?"

"I told you . . . Make arrangements and I'll work around them."

"Alright then, I'll plan for July . . . and it's four months."

"What four months? There's a week and a half left this month."

"Two weeks—and if I have to put down a deposit or sign something, it matters."

"It doesn't matter. If there's a deposit—there's a deposit. But call me before you do anything."

"I thought Art's girl got married and left."

"She did."

"I thought she answered yesterday when I called."

"That must have been Susan."

"Who's Susan?"

"Susan's a new secretary."

"Whose?"

"No one's yet. We're getting one more girl and then rearranging the whole thing."

"You're not going to have Fran anymore?"

"No, no, Fran's staying with me."

"Who else left?"

"Frank Tarrant's girl."

"She already . . ."

"She didn't leave—she was fired. She was incompetent."

"How's your penis today?"

"Redder."

"All European men must have red penises then."

"If they wear tiny mesh underpants they have red penises."

"You said European . . ."

"I said European cut, not mesh frankfurter skins."

Aroooooooga! Aroooooooga!

She leaves and returns with a stack of magazines. "What's that?" he says rubbing his eye. "Cynthia . . ."

"My eye itches like crazy . . . Cynthia what?"

"Cynthia Hayden asked for these when I was done."

"Cynthia Hayden wants decorator magazines?"

"She asked for them when I was done so I said fine. Don't rub it—it's getting all red."

"Do we have any Visine?"

"No."

"Are you sure?"

"Positive. Why don't you rinse it a little with some cool water."

"It's alright."

"Did you see the picture of Carter with the Indian head-dress?"

"Where?"

She folds the paper and hands it to him.

"What's that for?"

"It has something to do with that commercial where the Indian cries about pollution."

"He reminds me of Anthony Quinn at the end of 'Requiem For A Heavyweight.'"

"Is that . . . is that where Bogart does publicity for . . ."

"That's not 'Requiem . . .'"

"Let me finish."

"I know what you're talking about."

"What?"

"That's not 'Requiem For A Heavyweight.' That's 'The Harder They Fall.' Bogart's a sports writer and becomes a press agent for this mob's fighter stable . . . no, for this mob-owned giant South American fighter who can't fight. He's a giant dumb fighter—the 'Bull of the Pampas' or something—and they let him get slaughtered and don't pay him and he's got poor parents and everything and finally at the end Bogart pays him out of his own pocket and writes a big exposé with his wife leaning over the typewriter."

"Do you want a match?"

"No . . . wait . . . yeah, yeah—I thought I had one more in here."

She reaches into a drawer across from the table.

"Here."

He lights a True Menthol with a kitchen match.

"When you spoke to your father last, what did he say about your mother's surgery?"

"What about it?"

"Does she need it or not or what?"

"Probably. She's got an appointment this week or next week with a man in New York."

"With Larry's cousin?"

"Not Larry's cousin—with a gastroenterologist."

"At Mount Sinai?"

"Not at Mount Sinai—at his office."

"She's upset?"

"She's probably upset. It's not serious really."

"What do you mean it's not serious?"

"It's not serious—she'll probably need it done every once in a while from now on. It's annoying and uncomfortable—but it's not serious."

"What's serious to you?"

"A blood clot is serious, a broken hip is serious at her age, a heart attack is serious, a stroke . . ."

Marianne Hauser

4/20/99

Dear Martin,

Marianne Hauser asked me to make a copy of these pages of *The Talking Room* for the FC2 Anthology.

Marianne (now 88) is busy finishing another book. So I did that for one of the great FC writers—make sure the piece gets in the anthology.

Email me if you have problems.

Best,
Raymond Federman

P.S. Marianne has no anecdote to contribute she said.

from *The Talking Room*

Whenever mom was gone from the house which was always, Aunt V would check the hospital wards and the city morgue, though first of all she would check BANGS of course. I myself once tried to look for mom there, but the bouncer wouldn't let me through the door, though the door was open long enough for me to spy mom's face liquid in the steamed mirror behind the bar.

B for BULIMIA, BANGS, or BOMBS. A firecracker explodes in the night or is it a cherry bomb, though it is not the 4th of J else we would be in granny-anny's hills, with me and Olli balling in the weeds behind the garbage dump under a cluster of stars dripping honey.

A fire engine shrieks through the rain. It comes to a sudden halt and I wonder did a real bomb explode on the pier and blow it up, all the way up to the moon? The moon is littered with bits of rotted wood and chunks of cement. What place is there left for me to meet Uncle D in the sunset?

We met at BANGS, but that was years ago and by sheer accident, Aunt V says to mom into the roaring night. Since then much water has passed under Queensborough Bridge, and how often haven't you promised me since that never would you set foot into that vile bar again?

No answer from mom.

Aunt V coughs noisily—to wake her up? For mom might

well be asleep. Aunt V claps her hands and says, you've broken your promise time and again—how many times have you lied?

No answer from mom.

A teakettle whistles. Aunt V must be brewing herself a pot of strong tea. For she is weary to the bone, having searched for mom in every low bar, though none, she says, is quite as low as BANGS which is the lower depth. You can't sink lower.

Funnybone china clatter of cup against saucer. Tuning fork ping of teaspoon and sugar tongs. Aunt V plays hostess to herself. She pours. How many lumps? No lemon, honey. Maybe a drop of rum.

You keep asking, she says (though mom has asked nothing of course) why I ventured into BANGS at all that wet afternoon of our fatal encounter. Frankly I don't remember. I may have wanted to get out of the rain. Naturally I had *heard* of BANGS as who hasn't? It's been raided often enough. No, love, I wouldn't say I expected a classy joint like the Plaza but I certainly wasn't prepared for a whorehouse either, I mean the absolute vulgarity of the place, black tablecloths full of cigarette burns, moth-chewed velvet drapes and filthy carpets and plaster statues of naked nymphos inscribed with such obscene graffitti even you, J, would blush if you bothered to read them though of course the place is so poorly lighted you can't even read the menu. I dare say, B—I take it she is Mrs. Bangs—doesn't enrich Con Ed.

Another teeny weeny drop of rum, sweetie? Say when. WHEN!

Wow! Musta spilled half a pint into the low, low décolleté of my tea rose frou-frou taffeta tea gown from Dallas Texas.

Dear me. What a mess, says Aunt V, drying herself with wads of pink toilet paper. No, no, a hundred times no, J, BANGS never could be my cup of tea, the fems there are either terribly low class or chronically nympho—present company excluded, J—and as for the middle-aged johns at the bar, the less said the better, they pay through the nose for watered-down booze to watch you and your likes carry on, jesus, I know those commuting family men, I've sold them property in Chappaqua, they masturbate under the car coat, and then they drive off to the Union Club to tell the boys how we women abuse our right to vote.

Aunt V takes a deep breath and kicks the wad of toilet paper into the fire. No, J, you wouldn't get your jollies from them, no, it's the repulsive waitresses you are after, the table-hopping hepped-up broads in their jump suits, dear christ, figures like jellyfish, the fattest one, the one with acne, how she pushed her behind against you when she stomped into the girls room like a stormtrooper out for blood. But let some guy complain of the cockroach in his manhattan and she screams him down like the whore she is: DUMKOPF! WHY DIDNTYA SAY YA WANTED A CHERRY! I almost threw up. And the smell! A decent fellow wouldn't touch that creature if you paid him for it. But you, J, you touched her, and don't you dare lie to me! I saw you! I saw you make it with her in the girls room.

Aunt V must have jumped up from the oriental divan and sent the cushions flying and the tea wagon spinning into eternity. She moans oh why won't mom be happy unless she wallows in depravity? Surely it was god's will that brought them together that faraway afternoon at BANGS in the rain. Then mom was the desperate one. She cried on her shoulder then, Aunt V remembers with a moan as sad as the wind.

My J, my terrible angel, why are you set on destroying us both?

No answer from mom. Perhaps she is asleep on the floor, on the bear rug. Perhaps she is not in the house at all.

City pigeons trip over prickly shadows. We are taking another detour through trampled grass. That way we'll never make it in time to watch the wild beasts at their bloody feast, digging into the raw meat, gorging themselves on the government inspected carcass of some old cow. That cow died in Olli's pasture. I'd like to see the feast and yet I don't. I have two minds. And Uncle D would get sick if he watched.

His checks, forever waiting to be slapped, are burning with a steady fever. Break that silence, papa, hit your son! But old man river, his or mine, is dead. I wish Aunt V and mom would give each other the silent treatment, but they won't, their fights flood the night, spill over into the sewer, the river, and cross my heart Uncle D, I'd rather not ever go back again to the noise house.

Domestic squabbles are normal enough and you mustn't let them get you down, says Uncle D. Two adults rubbing shoulders under one roof: the very mechanics of such a union spell friction. Noise can't be avoided under the circumstances and the big ears of the little pitcher are bound to hear more than is there. That's why I have, at least so far, preferred to live alone, with no one listening to my solitude, not even Jessie.

The prancing pigeons have taken on the shimmer of peacock feathers, of scoured steel pots. Swirls of rainbows. Let me share your solitude, Uncle D. I'll be your homing pigeon. I've taken off my shoes and socks and my toes curl pink in the grass.

The city fathers, he says, scanning the headlines in the striped sky, are searching for a final solution to exterminate the pigeons—a sanitary measure, they pretend. Soon we may have to embark for Venice to see a live pigeon.

But Venice, a one-time haven for honeymooners, is rapidly sinking into the ground, so Uncle D or my little transistor informs me. San Marco doomed. The singing Campanile sighs and sinks. The squirrel scampers off, the pigeons vanish as the good humor man, B's best friend, comes tinkling out of the green bush. When I was still little (but already very fat) I used to gobble up his stuff by the dozen, stick, paper and all.

The popsickle & icicle
eloped on a red tricycle

Lipstick-red raspberry sherbet all over my face. Already I am feeling ten pounds younger. You must have been a darling baby boy.

I was, he says, excepting fits of tiger tantrums, a reasonably well adjusted tyke. I honored papa, loved mama, and if sister Phoebe got under my skin it was because she always threatened to drag me off with her on a blind date. We were a well assimilated family in the magnolias, respected by both gentile and colored folks. I was suckled and weaned at the ample breast of pitch-black Penelope. Shut your eyes and suck the fruit. What we don't see don't hurt. I was a blind reader.

Scrawny little D in knee-length breeches got lost in the slave quarters one breathless almond-sweet late afternoon ante bellum. Penny was washing herself in the wooden tub, a black stark naked dream. Get out of here, you little devil! she yelled through the steam and pitched a cake of soap at him. He ran like the devil. The silken twilight was a honeymoon blanket tufted with almond tree blossoms. But he thought he was going blind with the soap in his eyes.

Yes, I say yes, I think of mom, fish-tailed, a dripping dream in the mermaid tub. Oh yes, I take his hand out of his pocket and hold it to my lips, it's soft and smooth like wet rubber, I kiss it (the almond soap smell!) and with my chin I guide his hand to touch my breast under the poppy dress.

I'm sorry! He jumps away from me as though stung by a bee. There is no bee under my poppied bodice. He flexes his arm and the dial of his shockproof wrist watch flashes green. Just when exactly does your mother expect you home, my dear girl?

Never. She's disappeared again, don't you remember? She split and Aunt V will be hunting for her through the night, with the police in tow. Every precinct has been alerted. May we have her photo, ma'm? But none exists. Aunt V snapped her once on the sly in the tumbleweeds, but mom smashed the camera. If you must have a likeness, sir, look for it in the mirror. However, a brief description should help: 5'6". White skin tanned brown, brown hair died blond, eyes nondescript. J jeans, T shirt, Q sneakers. No hat. No purse. Walks with a slouch. Almond-shaped mole on left buttock. Thank you for your patience, officer. The drinks are on me.

I'd rather spend the night in the zoo than go back to the screaming house on the stinking alley. I won't be missed. Mom's on the missing persons list. Besides, I've got my dummy tucked away in my bed, with the radio playing an eagle scout program under the crazy quilt. They can have my dummy. So don't you leave me, daddy-o, if you do I'll throw myself to the lions, I swear. I'm crazy for you.

Crazy. He studies me through thick-lensed glasses, a mustached Christ in a safari coat. Growing pains, he says. Or puppy love. I don't quite hear him. I am thunderstruck by the sudden apparition of one lioness. For having taken another detour we have made a short cut and find ourselves with the beasts he had hoped to avoid.

But feeding time is over. The lion has retired to his cave. His queen, her majesty of suns and sands, is lying stretched out on the cement of her cage, digesting, dreaming desert dreams of terraced make-believe cities. No leftover bones on her stone couch. No blood on her whiskers. Uncle D can contemplate her through the bars without nausea. She's carved from yellow sandstone. A quiver (dream of bloody meat?) runs through her rib cage and mine. Eat me. I wish I could shrink like A in WL, squeeze through the bars into the cage and put my head with hers on the huge paws and sleep.

May I stay overnight at your place?

I should have added please. Aunt V says never hesitate to ask favors as long as you observe the civil code of general amenities laid down in ETIQUETTE FOR TINY SCREAMERS, rev. ed. Curtsying should be revived as a sign of respect as there is nothing prettier, she says, than the blush of little girl lost dropping a curtsy with the appropriate no sir, and yes madam do. Uncle D's exquisite manners should teach mom and me a lesson. No cuss words from his lips. His cultured speech allows you to ignore some of his less desirable habits, such as keeping his hands in his pockets or picking his nose. He did it when he appeared at her office to inquire about some tenement up for sale on Lex and 111th. Forgive me, madam, may I take up a minute or two of your valuable time?

What charm. Only the deal fell through because the tenement caved in before they got there to look it over. No casualties worth mentioning. A minor disaster, sir. Junkies and junk. I doubt the neighborhood would be your cup of tea. May I drop you some place?

V&D taking tea in the lamplight twilight parlor an hour or so before feeding time. He in big daddy's chair, legs crossed, one hand in his pocket. She reclining à la Récamier on the

chaiselongue bleu in her bell flower blue bell-bottom loung-
ing pj's. What big strong hands you have, madam! His eyes
under glass were swimming into the froth of her ruffled cuff.
Those hands, monsieur, have labored hard for bread! You'd
have thought they had marriage in mind, the way they faced
each other across the painted porcelain dish of sugared al-
monds, conversing on mutual comfort, southern funds, the
generation gap. What fun it would be, said Aunt V, if our B
were a deb, come out with the rest of the lovely young flowers, I watched them in New Orleans, they were presented to
society, I watched from the gallery, their bare shoulders, the
cleavage as they curtsied all the way down to the floor in genuine dacron. Of course our B wouldn't quite make it, too heavy,
besides her mother lacks what it takes to make the social redge.
It's no picnic, I swear, those girls have to go through umpty
FBI screenings and dress rehearsals for one big curtsy. It is
quite a trick to get back on your feet again once you are all the
way down.

Down on Bourbon St. with the rest of the strippers, said
mom, appearing fresh out of the shower, hair wringing wet,
old greasy bathrobe hanging open. Her body in the mirror lion
yellow, smooth like rubbed stone. Excuse me, madam, she
minced, breaking wind. I didn't know you had the colonel vis-
iting. Don't let me interrupt you, ladies.

Please, Uncle D, keep me, don't leave me, colonel! I bend
one knee under the poppies though not enough for him to see.
I roll my eyes and fold my hands. Genuflect. Should I tell him
of my southern blood? Granny-anny came from southern
Croatia. Down she'd go on her knees in front of the altar, the
silver ikons black with time. Black mother and child in the
altar cage. No father present.

Daddy butchered, cooked and eaten. Will they make soup
of my bones?

I can't, he says, shaking his head at the lioness, entertain
you in my bachelor quarters unchaperoned. Your aunt would
not consider it proper and she is absolutely right.

None of her g.d. business, I'm 13, give a little take a
little, bursting with life inside out!

But he says I don't understand, that's just the point and Aunt V is not the only stumbling block. For there is his doorman.

The d-man, what's he got to do with it?

Everything, says Uncle D. He is my conscience, please don't ask why. It must be an obsession as I hardly know the fellow except from sight. He's never said a word to me. He merely opens the plate glass door, tall and accusing in his uniform up to the cleft chin, silent authority, the mere suggestion of his Roman eyes, unblinking under the vizor, cows me and more than once have I sneaked in behind his back to escape detection while he was busy at the curb with one of our co-op wheelchair cases or poodles. One night he caught me in the act. I'll never forget his accusing eyes in the shadow of the vizor in the wall to wall hall mirror. I felt like a thief on my own premises, so abjectly guilty I apologized and slipped him a 10. 10 days it took me before I dared leave my co-op and face him again.

Please ten times please equals love. I won't stay more than 10 minutes, cross my poppies. Am not cowed by your D man. Shall tell him you are my dad.

But the answer still zero. O no. No guest has entered his apartment for he could not endure the sense of loss once the visitor has departed again to leave him with nothing except himself and his library alphabetically arranged up to the ceiling.

Yuriy Tarnawsky

tokyo dog
an fc dream

Here's a dream I had the other night. I am sure it has something to do with FC in general and my book in particular.

I'm in the middle of a barren landscape that I know is Tokyo suburbs. It's dusk or dawn, or perhaps the first day of nuclear winter. I don't see myself but see everything as if I were a camera.

There's a dog running through the landscape, carrying a severed human hand. He's running determined like a robot and seems not to be aware of anything although he runs around obstacles such as trees, fences, houses, etc. The houses are few and far apart. There's light in them, as if people were just getting up or getting ready for bed. Life inside them seems to be teeming like maggots in a rotting body.

The dog runs on and on, stiffly, the hand shaking in his teeth as if trying to reach something in vain. He's passed all the houses. The landscape now is completely barren with hills on the horizon flat like vomit that has dried up. He comes to a spot, puts the hand down on the ground, and starts digging with his paws. He uncovers the face of a man. The man looks in his thirties, has black hair, and features that could be European or Japanese, as sometimes happens with Japanese people. The man's glassy eyes stare into the sky and lumps of earth on them look like insects on water. The dog takes the hand in his teeth and lays it next to the man's face. It nestles close to it and looks as if it were growing straight out of the man's cheek. It's as if the man were a thalidomide baby, except the worst case imaginable.

Having done this, the dog remains sitting on the ground looking around bored as dogs do when they're just killing time.

White Plains, NY
May 3, 1999

Out of Chemnitz's Biography II
(Chemnitz Gets Raped)

The following happened shortly after Chemnitz went to live alone. She had an apartment of her own. It was in a tenement building. The building was old. It was run down. Chemnitz's apartment was on the second floor. It was early spring. It was late afternoon. It'd been very cold so far that year. This was the first warm day. Chemnitz was at home. She was alone. She was in the living room. The window in the room was open. It faced the street. Chemnitz was leaning out the window. She watched the people in the street. The sun had already sunken down behind the buildings. The street was completely in their shadow. There was a feeling of spring in the air. The air smelled like freshly plowed fields. It seemed there was open country nearby. This wasn't true however. At one point Chemnitz noticed a man. He walked on the other side of the street. He walked on the sidewalk. He came from the right. He was tall. He was slender. He looked strong however. He walked with a springy gait. It was distinctive. The man's hair was long. It was blond. It was wavy. It looked nice. The man had a few days' stubble on his cheeks. It glittered like gold dust. Chemnitz could see it even at that distance. The man wore a shirt, jeans, and shoes. The shirt was made from a thick material. The material was checkered. It was red and black. The shirt was unbuttoned at the collar. Its sleeves were partly rolled up. The man's jeans were worn. His shoes went up above the ankles. They were laced. They had rubber soles. The shoes were yellow. Their soles were white. The shoes looked new. Chemnitz thought the man was probably an artist. She found him very attractive. She remarked she wouldn't mind having intercourse with him. The man must have felt Chemnitz looking at him. He turned his head in her direction on passing the window. He also must have sensed Chemnitz's feelings. He gave her a big smile. His eyes were pale blue. Chemnitz thought them extremely beautiful. They made her feel a little strange about the man however. They looked unnatural. It was as if the man wasn't quite normal. Chemnitz was embarrassed by the man's smiling at her. She was also a little angry at him for his having sensed her feelings. She didn't smile back. She turned her head right. She didn't turn the head back for a long time. She did look in the man's direction a few minutes later however. By then the man was in the next block. He walked as before. He was partly hidden by other people. Chemnitz could barely see him. She could recognize him by his gait however. At that point she'd forgotten her anger toward the man. Her original feeling for him returned. She was glad to have seen him. She felt glad to have stood at the window. She felt relaxed. She couldn't remember when she'd enjoyed herself so much last. She couldn't remember when she'd looked out the window like that last. She felt she should do it more often. She planned to do it again very soon. She felt she'd spent enough time at the window however. She decided to go back into the apartment. She had a lot of house chores to do. She went ahead with this. The chores took her a couple of hours. Chemnitz then fixed her supper. She ate it. She did the dishes. She cleaned up in the kitchen. She took a long bath. By then it was about nine. Chemnitz put on a nightgown. She went to bed. She took a book along. She proceeded reading in it. She'd read for about half an hour. She lay on her back. The book rested on her chest. She held the book upright with both her hands. The bedroom door was open. Chemnitz felt she'd seen something stir in the door. She in turn remembered having heard some noises a few minutes earlier. She'd assumed they'd come from outside the apartment. She realized now however this wasn't so.

She realized they'd come from somewhere in the apartment. She then finally realized there was someone in her apartment. She realized the person had just appeared in the door. She gave out a shriek. It was pathetically weak. It seemed a dead bird that'd flown out of Chemnitz's mouth and fallen onto the floor. Chemnitz lifted her eyes. She looked in terror at the door. There was a man standing there in fact. He was the man Chemnitz had seen in the street that afternoon. He wore the same clothes as then. The sleeves of his shirt were rolled down now however. The man leaned on the door post. He had a sarcastic smile on his lips. He held a knife in his right hand. It was a switchblade knife. It was open. The man was running the thumb of his right hand over the blade. He straightened up when Chemnitz looked at him. He said for Chemnitz not to scream. He said he wasn't going to rob or hurt her. He said he wanted to have intercourse with her. He said he had a feeling she wouldn't be adverse to the idea from the way she'd looked at him that afternoon. Chemnitz had completely forgotten her original feeling toward the man. She was terrified. She barely understood what the man was saying. She didn't speak. She didn't move. She just followed the man with her eyes. The man came up to the bed. There was a night table next to it. The man put the knife on the table. He took off his clothes. He threw them over the foot of the bed. He put his shoes under the bed. He took the book away from Chemnitz. He put it next to the knife. He got into bed. He warned Chemnitz not to do anything silly. He said the knife was within his reach. He forced her to have intercourse with him. Chemnitz didn't resist the man. She continued being terrified. The man stayed in bed after the intercourse. He got a pack of cigarettes and a book of matches out of his pants. He offered Chemnitz a cigarette. She refused it. She didn't smoke. She obviously would have refused the man's offer anyway however. The man lit a cigarette for himself. He put out the match. He put the match, cigarettes, and book of matches next to the knife and the book. He proceeded to smoke. He threw the ashes on the night table. He lay on his back. He talked. He talked about some of the more noteworthy current events. He obviously wanted Chemnitz to talk with him. She didn't do this however. She merely said "yes" and "no" when she absolutely had to. She continued feeling terrified. She probably wouldn't have talked anyway however. The man finished the cigarette. He put the butt out with his fingers. He put the butt with the ashes. He forced Chemnitz to have intercourse with him again. Chemnitz again didn't resist the man. She continued feeling terrified. The man got up after the intercourse. He got dressed. He took the cigarettes, book of matches, and knife. He said good-by to Chemnitz. He then left. Chemnitz continued feeling terrified for a few minutes after the man had left. She then got furious. She was furious at the man for his arrogance. She considered his calmness a sign of arrogance. She was also furious at herself. She felt she should have resisted the man. She didn't know how she could have resisted him however. She felt he would have overwhelmed her no matter what she'd tried to do. She felt nonetheless she should have done something. She didn't enjoy having intercourse with the man at all. She'd hated it. This was the first time she'd really hated having intercourse. She got up. She went to the outside door. She checked it. It was locked. Chemnitz knew the man had come in through the door. She knew this from remembering the sounds he'd made. He knew he'd forced the lock. She wanted to see how he'd done it. She decided to look at the door from the outside. Momentarily she was afraid to open the door. She was afraid the man was outside. She remembered her anger however. She overcame her fear. She opened the door. The man naturally wasn't outside. Chemnitz checked the lock. It looked normal. Chemnitz then realized the man had forced the lock by slipping the blade of his knife in the crack in the door post. He'd then pushed back the bolt of the lock. Chemnitz locked the door. She felt filthy. She wanted to get rid of all the traces of the man. First of all she wanted to be rid of the man's semen out of her vagina. She took a shower. She douched herself out. She put on a new nightgown. She cleaned off the bedside table. She threw the burnt match, butt, and ashes in the toilet bowl. She flushed the toilet. She finally changed the linen on the bed. She tried to go to sleep after that. She had trouble doing it however. Every time she'd doze off she'd dream the man was standing in the door. She'd then wake up. A few times she woke up with a shriek. She went to sleep only at dawn. Chemnitz was afraid the man would come the next night. She decided to call the police then. The door was in the hallway. Chemnitz pushed the kitchen table against the door. She planned to call the police while the man was trying to push the kitchen table out of the way. She went to bed again at about nine. She didn't take a book along however. She just lay in bed with the light on. She lay again on her back. She looked at the door. She listened carefully for any noises. She was stiff with tension. Along about the same time as the previous night she heard noises coming from the front door. It sounded like the man had started fumbling at the lock. Chemnitz's heart started beating violently. She decided to call the police. The phone was on the night table. Chemnitz reached for it. She then heard footsteps in the apartment. She couldn't understand how the man got past the table so quickly. The footsteps were loud. They were fast. In a few seconds the man stood in the door. Chemnitz had managed only to touch the phone with her hand by then. She lay back on seeing the man. She felt helpless. The man wore a jacket in addition to the clothes of the previous day. The jacket was denim. It was worn as the jeans. The man had the knife in his hand. He looked angry. He came up to the bed. He said it was stupid of Chemnitz to think the table was going to keep him away. He also told her it was stupid of her to try calling anybody. He said she was stupid to think anyone would come to her help. He said this included the police. He said it'd take the police an hour to get to her place. He said he could rape her ten times and get away by then. He also said he could kill her if he wanted. He said he could get away without anyone catching him. He told her to stop being silly. He said she'd obviously liked him when she saw him in the street the day before. He also said she hadn't been a virgin when he had intercourse with her the first time. He said he therefore didn't understand why she was making so much fuss. He came up to the bed. He again forced Chemnitz to have intercourse with him. He behaved this time practically the same as the previous night. After the intercourse he asked Chemnitz if she had anything to drink. She said she didn't. She said she didn't drink alcohol. This was true. It nonetheless gave Chemnitz pleasure to say this. The man then got out his cigarettes and matches. He again offered Chemnitz a cigarette. She again refused it. This time she also told the man she didn't smoke. It also gave her pleasure to say this. The man then asked Chemnitz if she had an ashtray. She again said she didn't. This was also true. It also finally however gave Chemnitz pleasure to say this. The man then got up. Chemnitz began losing her fear at about this time. She thought of doing something while the man was away. She thought of calling the police. She also thought of taking the man's knife. Before she had a chance to do anything however the man came back. He brought a plate along. He put the plate on the night table. He used the plate as an ashtray. After that he again behaved as the night before. He again forced Chemnitz to have intercourse with him. Chemnitz was completely rid of her fear when the man left. She got up immediately. She wasn't furious with herself this time. She knew there was nothing she could have done to resist the man. She knew it would have been futile and dangerous to resist. She was glad she hadn't tried to do anything while the man was in the kitchen. She decided however to get a latch for the door the next day. She decided to call the police when the man was at the door. She hated the man with a passion now. She especially hated his eyes. This was because of them being so blue. The man looked crazy to Chemnitz. She felt he was crazy. She felt this was the reason for his behavior. She didn't bother looking at the door and changing the linen or her nightgown this time. She did take a shower, douched herself out, and cleaned off the plate however. She got a latch for the door early the next day. She didn't have a screw driver. She therefore got one too. She put up the latch as soon as she got home. She latched the door. She felt safe. She felt she could resist the man now. She expected him to come that night again. She waited that night the same as the night before. She waited till midnight. The man didn't show up however. Chemnitz fell asleep about then. She fell asleep with the light on. The light stayed on the whole night. Chemnitz began to think the man would not show up again. She felt relieved. She also almost felt sorry however. She would have loved to see the man get caught. She was still waiting for him the next night however. She lay in bed as the previous two nights. Along about nine-thirty she again heard noises coming from the front door of the apartment. She quickly picked up the phone. She started dialing the police number. She dialed the number. The phone started ringing. Chemnitz then heard a loud crashing noise from the front door. After that she heard footsteps in the apartment. They again were loud. They were again very fast. Chemnitz realized the man was in the apartment. The phone kept ringing. It wasn't being answered. Chemnitz got terrified again. She didn't want the man to see her making the call. As a consequence she hung up. She then quickly lay back. She waited for the man. He appeared in the door a few seconds later. He wore the same clothes as the last time. He again carried his knife. He also carried a six-pack of beer. He stopped in the door. He shook his head. He said Chemnitz was even stupider than he'd thought. He said he'd barely noticed the latch. He said he gave the door just a little push. He said the latch came off right away. He said the wood was all rotten in the door. He said it was no use her trying to resist him. He said if he wanted he could always come in through the window. He said he could also kidnap her in the street. He told her to get it out of her head she could escape him. He said he'd have intercourse with her whenever he wanted. He then went into the kitchen. He put the beer in the refrigerator. He came back with a plate. He put the knife and the plate on the night table. He then behaved as on the previous two occasions. After the intercourse the man got up. He asked if Chemnitz wanted a beer. Chemnitz said she didn't. She didn't bother reminding the man she didn't drink. The man then went into the kitchen. He got a bottle of beer out of the refrigerator. He came back. He opened the bottle with his knife. He threw the cap on the plate. He took a swig out of the bottle. He got his cigarettes. He lit one. He got back into bed. He proceeded drinking, smoking, and talking. As was said the man's appearance in the apartment had terrified Chemnitz. Along about this time the fear had left her again. She was actually finding the situation funny. She thought the man was so arrogant it was funny. She suspected he'd be very gullible because of that. She decided to trick him. She decided to try pretending she liked him. She planned to arrange for him to come the following day. She planned to notify the police. She planned to have the police arrest him then. She then proceeded carrying out her plan. She cuddled up to the man. She said it was silly for them to go on this way. She said there was no reason for her to resist him since she liked him. She said she just didn't like to be forced to do anything. She said they should become lovers. The man said this was exactly what he'd been saying. He said he was glad she'd finally come to her senses. Chemnitz then decided to go further than she'd planned. She decided to try finding out the man's name. She planned to tell him her name. She hoped the man would then tell her his. She wasn't sure he'd do it. She felt however he might. She felt he was that arrogant. She went ahead and told the man her first and last names. She asked him what he was called. He behaved as she'd hoped. He told her his first and last names. At least he gave her a first and a last name. He did this without any hesitation. It was clear they were at least his common aliases. Chemnitz made sure she wouldn't forget the names. Momentarily she wanted to ask the man where he lived. She then checked herself however. She felt the man might get suspicious. She was afraid she'd get too careful after that. She felt she didn't need the address anyway. She felt catching the man in her apartment was better. She suspected that was the only thing to do in order to have a case against him. Chemnitz then talked with the man. Having finished the beer and the cigarette the man had intercourse with Chemnitz again. After that he stayed in bed for a while. He and Chemnitz talked some more. The man then got dressed. Chemnitz got up to see the man out. She walked with him to the front door. She asked when she should expect him. The man said he wouldn't be able to come the next night. He said he'd probably come the night after that. Chemnitz and the man kissed. The man left then.

Chemnitz went to the police the next day. She told them the story. They showed themselves willing to cooperate with her. The night after the next two policemen came to her apartment. They were going to stay in the bedroom. They told Chemnitz to let the man in. They told her not to talk to him. They said it should look as if they weren't friends. The policemen told her to bring the man to the bedroom. They said they'd arrest him there. Chemnitz was very excited. She was hoping the man would come. She was afraid he wouldn't come however. She was afraid he'd guessed her plans. She was afraid he'd kill her then. It got to be the time the man used to come. He didn't show up however. Chemnitz then began to be really worried. She was sure she was done for. She was sure the man had found out she'd gone to the police. She asked the policemen what they should do. The policemen said they should wait a little longer. Then along about ten o'clock there was a knock on the door. Chemnitz thought her heart would jump out of her chest. The policemen had been with her in the kitchen. They quickly ran into the bedroom. They ran on tiptoes. Chemnitz went to the front door. She opened it. It was the man. He came in. He kissed Chemnitz. He greeted her. Chemnitz didn't answer him. She was so weak with fear she couldn't have if she'd wanted to. She was afraid the man would guess the situation from her behavior. She locked the door. She led the man into the bedroom. The policemen then jumped the man. They put handcuffs on him. The man didn't offer any resistance. He laughed at the policemen. He said he and Chemnitz were lovers. He said they'd had a quarrel. He said Chemnitz was trying to get back at him. He said the proof of this was the beer in the refrigerator. He said he'd brought it two days ago. He said what brand it was. He said he'd drunk only one bottle. He said the beer was still there if Chemnitz hadn't thrown it away. The policemen however didn't believe the man. Chemnitz had already told them about the beer. They insisted on arresting the man. They took him to the police station. They asked Chemnitz to go along. They wanted her to bring charges against the man. They wanted the man to be arraigned. They took him to the magistrate on duty. The man proved himself clever however. He insisted on calling his lawyer. He apparently had one. He called the lawyer. The lawyer came very soon. He was at the station in less than half an hour. He asked the magistrate to let the man go in his custody. The magistrate agreed to do this. He set a date for a hearing. The man and his lawyer then left. The man's names turned out to be correct. The man however turned out not to be an artist. He was a laborer. He was unemployed at the time. He'd been convicted for burglary three times. He'd also had four charges of rape brought against him. The charges had all been dismissed however. This was because of there not being enough evidence against the man. The magistrate talked to Chemnitz after the man and his lawyer had left. He apparently sympathized with Chemnitz. He suggested Chemnitz get herself a lawyer. He said she'd most probably be sued for libel by the man. He also said the case was going to be tough. He wished Chemnitz luck. Chemnitz talked to the two policemen after talking with the magistrate. They apparently also sympathized with Chemnitz. They talked to her for a long time. They said the man had proven himself too clever. They said had he resisted them or betrayed himself by talking while being arrested the case could have been much easier. But given the circumstances it looked pretty hopeless. The policemen said that just about the only way to have anyone convicted of rape these days was to catch him in the act. But they said going through the trial couldn't hurt anything. They said the man's record would definitely be against him. They also said the man would almost definitely get something for the possession of the switchblade knife. While talking to the magistrate Chemnitz began to fear the case was hopeless. Now she was sure it was. She couldn't understand why the police had gone along with her plan under the circumstances. This was in spite of them having given her the reason. Chemnitz barely listened to the policemen. She wanted to get away from them as soon as possible. She wanted to be out of the station. She said good-by to the policemen at the first convenient moment. The policemen offered to take her home in their car. Chemnitz refused the offer however. She wanted to be alone. The policemen then offered to get a taxi for her.

Chemnitz refused this too. She said she'd get one herself. She however didn't plan to take a taxi. She didn't want to go home. She didn't know where to go. She just wanted to get out of the station. The policemen then asked Chemnitz if she was alright. She assured them she was. She then left the station. There were steps leading from the door of the station down to the sidewalk. There were about a dozen of them. Chemnitz walked down the steps. She turned left on reaching the sidewalk. She continued walking. This was in the direction opposite from her apartment. Chemnitz walked slowly. The station was about in the middle of the block. The block was long. Chemnitz walked to about halfway between the station and the end of the block. She then heard a strange noise. It sounded primitive. It seemed to have been made by an animal. The animal seemed wild. Chemnitz was surprised by the noise. She didn't know where it came from. She then heard it again. This time she realized it came from her chest. She realized she was crying. She continued walking. She had difficulty doing this however. Her body shook. This was especially true of her face. Her lower jaw kept jumping up and down. Her teeth kept chattering. They sounded like china. It seemed they'd break. It also seemed as though her jaw would detach itself from her face and fall down to the ground. It seemed an object on a table jumping up and down during an earthquake threatening to fall down. It seemed it'd do it. It seemed fragile It seemed it'd break. Chemnitz really seemed to feel this would happen to her jaw. She seemed to feel she'd never be able to put it together and attach it to her face again. She seemed to feel this would be her end. She tried to keep her mouth closed. She couldn't do it however. She pressed her hands to her face. She tried to keep her mouth closed this way. She still couldn't do it. She was desperate. She really felt as though her end was near. It was past midnight. There was a lot of traffic in the street however. The traffic moved in one direction. Chemnitz walked against the traffic. Her eyes were full of tears. Tears also flowed down her cheeks. She saw the headlights of the cars through them. They seemed huge. They seemed to rush at her. They seemed to drown in her tears. They seemed to dissolve there. They seemed then to flow in currents down her cheeks.

Peter Spielberg

The Author's Posture

One of the many hazards of fiction writing is that one may be taken at one's words. Despite the standard disclaimer, "Any resemblance to reality, living or dead, is purely coincidental," readers continue to mistake fiction for truth, *Dictung* for *Wahrheit*. A stronger caution is needed. "Warning! It's been determined that fiction reading may be dangerous to your sense of reality."

All serious artists, aspiring or fulfilled,— painters, composers, authors—are witnesses, eyes pressed to the keyhole. As a writer, I stand as a witness against my time. "Against" is the key word. For "time" one could substitute self, ethnic origin, country of domicile, religion, gender, class, or similar affiliation.

In Flight

Although a veteran of a number of trans-Atlantic flights and accustomed to the authoritarian ways of air carrier personnel, I fight the safety belt which cuts into my stomach and reminds me that, lately, I've been putting on excess weight. It seems to me that we've been strapped down for an unreasonably long time. Our jumbo jet is safely airborne, has already climbed above the smog clouds, must be miles out over the ocean, but still the first officer won't release us from captivity.

Perhaps the "belts-on" treatment is part of the newfangled therapy—an eight-day wonder cure—for which I've signed up. This is no ordinary flight, but a chartered planeload of recently divorced, over-the-hill men, heading for a weeklong retreat at the Human Rehabilitation Center in Le Conquet, a tiny Brittany seaside town some twenty kilometers South of Brest.

As I look around at my companions (they don't appear to be bothered by being kept tied in their seats) doubts about having allowed myself to be bamboozled into joining their group well up once again. I came close to balking in the airport's departure lounge when the reality of having to spend a week in an all male camp faced me. If I hadn't been over tired from a month of insomnia and too zonked on Valium to walk straight, I would have refused to board the plane.

At least the flight attendants are female, but that's small comfort since the rehab center's brochure makes a point of the necessity for strict sexual segregation during the therapy period proper. The retreat is to be a total one. Nothing to distract us from the work ahead...

Yet I can't help having doubts. I've never had much faith in quick remedies. The faces of the men around me don't inspire confidence; judging by their vacant expressions, one might take them for a bunch of salesmen off on a junket to the fleshpots of Paris. Do they know what they are in for? Or are they, like me, blindly winging toward martyrdom at a better than five-hundred-miles per hour clip?

The six hours and twenty minutes of idleness to come, the estimated flying time, won't be easy to live through, not unless I can get potted first. I keep my finger on the service wanted button, but neither cabin attendant nor drinks are in sight.

Maybe it's intentional—keeping us waiting in our seats like patients at the dentist's office, keeping us drinkless and bored, the first tricky step of the program which is to assist us in adjusting to the single state: the equivalent of a working day in limbo to soften us up. Nothing to do but thumb through magazines (though no magazines are distributed) or mull over the years of self-deception that brought us here. The last thing I want to do! I've been over that ground too many times before and gotten nowhere. That's why I joined the group—to learn to slough off past failures, to cut my losses and invest any remaining assets in a new—if limited—life.

The captain's voice—unmistakably female (as are all the other crew members on this special flight, from pilot down to baggage handlers)—lilts over the intercom to give us the customary make-yourself-comfortable spiel, as well as to apprise us of our estimated flight time and the weather conditions facing us. "This is Captain Earhart. Welcome aboard Flight 101. Your jumbo jet, we call her 'The Spirit of New York,' is equipped with the most sophisticated instrumentation ever, including an auto-pilot that is capable of executing an impeccable three-point landing if need be..." Blah, blah, blah.

"To avoid turbulence caused by unseasonably strong head winds," she concludes, "we'll be cruising at higher than our usual altitude of thirty-four thousand feet. If any of you feel discomforted, don't hesitate to employ the oxygen masks which are at your disposal. Flight attendants will be happy to assist you with this procedure. And please leave your safety belts on while seated."

I'm not fazed by the news, though my neighbor looks troubled. He sits ramrod straight, belt buckled as per instructions. By the time the refreshment trolley rolls up the aisle from the rear of the plane, I'm more than ready for my second drink.

"Saved by Lady Bountiful!" I greet the lady in navy-blue and notice that the blouse of her uniform reveals a pleasing double bulge, the approximate center of each hemisphere marked by a dart-like knurl. Her breasts seem to be burgeoning before my very eyes! "Make it a double will you. My whistle's gone dry," I gasp.

She hands me my ration of mother's milk with her left hand, using the right to support the weight of her swelling bosom in an erotic, albeit awkward, fashion. I reach out to aid her, grab the tumbler from her left hand so that she'll have both hands free to tend to her mammary burden.

She shows her appreciation with a hint of a smile, but doesn't take advantage of my having freed her second hand. Instead of taking a breather, that is, stopping for half a moment to counter gravity by lending each heavy breast individual support—right hand under right, left hand under left–as I expected (or in a criss-cross pattern, as I fantasized, right hand cupping left hemisphere, left cupping right), or simply pausing to adjust the straps of her bra ... instead, she carries on as before: using the back of her right hand and part of her right forearm to buttress the whole works as she left-handedly delivers a can of Coca-Cola to my tight-lipped neighbor.

I observe the operation with a friendly though critical eye. Definitely a clumsy way of handling the situation, and not particularly efficient either. At this rate we'll be halfway across the Atlantic before everyone is served.

She answers my unspoken criticism by offering what I at first take to be an apology, being unable to follow the technical part of her explanation.

"Cellular tumescence is a nuisance at this height above sea level. Though we understand the causal factor and the general formula—plasma membranes expand in reverse proportion to specific density—no one has, to date, come up with effective countermeasures. We are, of course, able to control the problem to some degree; otherwise we couldn't long tolerate heavier-than-air levitation, could we?"

"No, we couldn't," I agree.

"All part of a day's work." She bites her plump lower lip as she scoops ice into a plastic glass.

I click my tongue politely, though I'm no longer sure with what it is I'm commiserating. Has she offered me an explanation for the remarkable waxing of her boobs or an excuse for serving me with her left hand?

"I realize you're doing the best you can," I add for want of anything better to say.

"We *all* are!" With a shake of her blonde head, she directs my gaze to the other side of the aircraft where her top-heavy double, dressed in a baby-blue uniform, is valiantly serving refreshments while discreetly battling the same phenomenon. "It has something to do with pressurization, you see. But we've learned to accept it. Nothing to be done about it. I hope you'll bear with us."

"Perfectly all right. I'm beginning to enjoy the flight."

Then, realizing that she might misinterpret my remark as a cheap pass, I make an attempt at deflating the tension by asking a dumb question: "Will we be climbing any higher?"

The question is dumb, not because every other passenger must be bothering her with similar twaddle but because it touches on the sore point which is causing our mutual embarrassment: if the extraordinary dilation of her (their) breasts is, in fact, linked to the altitude of the flight, any further ascent will undoubtedly cause further distention! Her blouse can't possibly contain another cubic inch of stuffing. The mother-of-pearl buttons are already strained to capacity. They'll explode like shotgun pellets. Her blouse will burst open, her naked bust spill out like an overinflated inner tube through a gash in a bicycle tire.

"I don't believe so, sir." Her tone seems cooler as she recites a pre-recorded reply: "Not unless we encounter unexpected turbulence."

"That's a relief."

"Please don't worry about it. The oxygen masks drop automatically. I'll be right here to help if needed."

The inertial force of another burst of acceleration glues us to our seats. No wonder! If that crazy bitch at the controls hasn't taken the aircraft a couple thousand feet further up! The *no smoking* sign is flashing 'Mayday!' for all it's worth. "Douse all cigarettes," the public address system screams. "Masks on! Keep calm!"

With a popping sound, similar to a champagne bottle being decorked, the threatened oxygen masks drop from their overhead niches. They dangle before our faces from pinkish rubber hoses.

"Time for an intravenous feeding. What do you say, brother?" I make a last effort to contact the zombie to my right. "You don't agree, eh? ... Maybe you're right. What would you say to a floating enema bag? Nope? Could that there be the umbilical cord?"

No response. He dutifully slips the mask over his snout.

"Scum bag!"

I'm not far off. The translucent, near transparent masks look more and more like condoms, the ultra-thin, supersensitive variety. The taut rubber skins covering the pouting lips and quavering nostrils of my companions-in-separation (every man jack has donned the breathing aid) expand and contract, pulsate to their labored breathing.

The flight attendants have dropped all pretense of decorum. They dash from row to row to help fit the bags—roll them over jutting chins, snap the elasticized edges tight over pug noses, force unruly beards under. They untangle fouled lines and adjust the flow of pure air. No longer able to work with one hand at a time, they are, perforce, unable to cover up. As I foresaw, neither bras nor blouses, can withstand the further drop in pressurization. Their surging flesh overflows its containers, rising like yeast dough...

One small mercy: the conventional laws of physics appear to be suspended. The weight of the women's glands has *not* increased in proportion to their growth. Just the opposite. Once freed from the halters and straps, they spring up and bob in the breeze like those helium-filled balloons I used to buy the kids at the Central Park Zoo. The stewardesses float effortlessly up and down the aisles with grace reminiscent of the underwater ballet in an Esther Williams film.

I'd like to settle back and enjoy the pneumatic display, but this is no movie, nor are we innocent spectators. Retribution is swift at this altitude.

It's now the males' turn to suffer. Not only do we experience difficulty in getting the right mixture of oxygen (it's either too rich or too thin; our lips turn red and then blue, while the females breathe with ease) but the discomfort in the region of our groins can no longer be ignored.

The pain there though dull, though more of a tenderness than anything as specific as pain, forces me to focus on my own problem. My underdrawers are choking me. I loosen the belt of my pants, unzip my fly, pull in my gut, take deep breaths. Nothing helps.

Oh my aching balls! Their sack can't possibly sustain the pressure; the skin is stretched to the breaking point.

I'm not the only one who's in distress. One of my comrades, a tough-looking type in blue jeans and leather vest, heads for the toilet, staggering like a bowlegged cowboy after a hard day in the saddle. He's followed by a dude with a full Afro in a double-knit suit whose breeches bulge as if Renaissance codpieces have come back into fashion. The man in the aisle seat across from me has slipped his trousers down to his knees. His jockey shorts look as if he's stuffed the pouch with wads of absorbent cotton. The stiff on my right, his face turned beet red under its rubber covering, strains as if he's about to lay an egg. He's pushed himself up by his elbows, rear end raised six inches above the seat. Serves him right, I chuckle, trying to wrest a little satisfaction from the thought that he, like the rest of us two-fisted mortals, is afflicted with what, for the want of a more scientific diagnosis, I'll label a mild case of elephantiasis.

Perhaps not so mild. Before it gets better, the tumescence reaches ludicrous proportions, and I'm climbing up on the arm-rests of my seat to take the weight off my swelling scrotum.

What a sight it must be for the stewardesses—a jumbo jet jampacked with obscenely deformed males, bottom-heavy baboons. What a unique chance to play turnabout.

They give our bloated breeches the once-over, then do a double-take. "Need a wheelbarrow, daddy-o?"

I decline her offer and drag myself to the comfort station. Which brings none. I can barely squeeze out a couple of drops though I feel waterlogged, feel like what I imagine a lactating mother whose colicky baby won't suck must feel like.

Taking advantage of my minute of privacy, I verify the extent of the inflammation. My nuts—normally of average size (so I've been advised) and shape (though the left one is larger by half than the right)—my twin jewels are swollen to thrice their optimum size. Fortunately my prime member is not. Otherwise I would never be able to pack my belongings back into my pants. As it is, it takes some doing before I get things tucked away. All the while, some incontinent geezer is rattling the doorknob. No way I can zip up again. I do my best to cover up, hitch my pants with my left hand while lending support to my ponderous testes with the right.

My predicament does not escape comment from the ladies in blue. "It must be jelly, 'cause jam don't shake like that!" they wolf-whistle.

"Poetic justice," my heretofore silent neighbor makes a pronouncement. His voice, filtered through the oxygen mask, sounds like a short-wave radio broadcast, complete with humming, drifting, and static. "You guys never learn until it's too late, do you? All your adult lives you've been leering like naughty school boys at my sister's secondary sexual characteristics, humiliating her, forcing her to run the gauntlet of your passes as if she were a performer in a 42nd Street peepshow. But now the shoe's on the other foot. You're the mutant, the sport of nature!"

"Sorry, doc, if I had known that the lady with the super knockers was your sister..."

"Don't act the fool with me. You know what I mean. Every woman is my sister."

"And every man your brother. Amen!" I feel like kicking the holier-than-thou scout master square in his engorged dumplings. "But I notice that you're not exempt from the punishment—if that's what it is that's being dished out to us—are you?"

"The difference between us is greater than the similarity," he sputters. "Of course, I'm also troubled...to some degree."

Judging by the size of his furuncles, I can't see the difference, and tell him so.

"I've acknowledged my guilt and am the better man for it," his unctuous voice suddenly comes through loud and clear. "My name is Bruno, by the way. And yours?"

"Charles. Friends call me Chuck."

"How do you do, Chuck."

"Not so well at the moment, if you want the truth, doc. You see I'm bothered by this swelling of my you-know-whats, and..."

"If you can be serious for a moment, I'll be happy to explain things. It may help you to accept the situation, *Chuck.*" He underlines my name to indicate his friendship, I suppose. "I've made this trip before, you see. This is my third retreat."

"Are you telling me that you knew all along what was in store for us?"

"Not the specifics...but the general course of the treatment, yes."

"So this," I point at my lap, "this acromegaly or whatever you want to call it is the first lesson?"

"Just the beginning," he pontificates, "a reminder of the grossness of our animal nature—so that we can appreciate the danger of being governed by that which should be beneath contempt. It's a form of shock treatment, if you like, Eastern style, adopted from the Zen masters."

"Are you a monk or something?" It dawns on me that his bald crown may be a tonsure.

"No," he swears. "I'm a sinner like all men, a liar and ex-fornicator. But I've seen the way, Chuck. Dimly, I admit, but with time and patience..."

My patience has about run out, but so have his words. Without as much as a parting wave, he reverts to his trancelike state, and I'm left sitting there, high and sore, not much wiser than before. Certainly more worried, for if I heard him right, what's waiting for us at the rehabilitation camp is bound to be worse than what we've so far experienced.

What a jackass I was to have allowed myself to be talked into going! And I've barely swallowed the first dose of the bitter medicine called "Mortification." Yes, what's happening to us is no accident, but part and parcel of the indoctrination process. Our twin glands swelling to hideous dimensions is meant to mirror our obsession with female curves and protrusions, to mock our hang-up with tits and ass.

"So you go for well-stacked dames? Well, we swinging ladies like our men well-hung too," they're as good as telling us. "The bigger the better. Get a load of that equipment! Wow, I'd like to get my hands on those juicy coconuts!...Disgusting, isn't it? Debasing—to have your worth measured by the size of your private—now no longer so private—parts!"

And to make sure we got the point of the analogy, they sucked us in by first inviting us to ogle them, playing Circe to our piggishness. Only *after* we had shown our all too human inclinations (not an Odysseus among us, unless it's the ex-fornicator on my right) did the weightlessness begin to affect our bodies. Beautiful timing.

"Snicker at our melons all you like, boys," the Anita Ekberg type flashes her teeth, "but now it's our turn to laugh at those crazy blisters between your legs. You need a good jockstrap to hold up that meat, fella. Better get it custom-made. Your ordinary boxer shorts just won't do for the fullsize man."

"All right!" I'm ready to admit the error of my ways. "No need to rub my nose in it. You've made your meaning clear, 'Ogle not lest ye be ogled!'" Yet at the same time I suspect that I haven't as yet fully grasped the implication of what's happening. We're being shown *more* than the degradation of sexual exploitation. That's only part of the message on the billboard.

Hold on! Let's not ignore the obvious. Literally, this gross distortion of human anatomy, it feels as if two air-cushions have been grafted to my groin, makes it impossible—physically impossible—for men to know women, or for women to receive men. Thus we are being reminded, in a particularly nasty way, of the impasse in our love lives. Isn't that why we're divorced from our spouses? Aren't we all ex-husbands who cannot know our wives?

On the other hand, the skyrocketing of our glands should not be taken solely on the literal level. Rather, it's to be interpreted as a parable of our metaphysical condition. Having neglected the spiritual aspect of life, having denied the soul, we are prisoners of the body. That's the kick of the metaphor, crude but right on target: look what happens when you inflate the value of the ephemeral!

My seat-mate opens his eyes for a second and nods his grizzled head as if seconding my reading. Having taken a tentative step on the road to enlightenment, I follow his example and lower my eyelids, better to be able to ponder the consequences of my diagnosis.

Although I'm ill-fitted for the role of penitent and have always mistrusted eleventh-hour turnabouts, I am overcome by a longing to make peace, to reach out toward my companions in pain. For that's what we are—male and female alike—poor creatures longing for a respite from loneliness, but driven by vanity, plagued by the burden of our flesh, mocked by signs of our mortality! I'm at the point of weeping. I'd like to rip the mask from my face and ask their pardon, but no longer have the strength.

Fanny Howe

When I submitted the manuscript of *Holy Smoke* to the Fiction Collective, I hadn't the slightest hope that it would be received by anyone anywhere. And in fact it vanished into stones and silence for many months. When it finally was acknowledged and accepted, I was mystified by the process but happily designed the book with pictures by Colleen McCallion in someone's Lower East Side apartment. My editor was a woman. I never met the guys in the Collective and never really knew who read or accepted it.

So it is difficult to be anecdotal about a situation that was unlocatable in the years when my novels were published—by them, it, us? There were the names—already mythic in the seventies—Sukenick, Baumbach, Mirsky, et al—and masculine. And there was the city—Manhattan—"man" again—and the exhilerating belief that an eccentro-poetics of story-writing might be allowed to exist after all.

Fanny Howe

My anecdote is more like antidote—the story
of something slow, efficient and ultimately
productive—something that in its mercurial
form became a standard for resistance. Despite the fact that my novel was slaughtered
by James Wolcott in the *Voice* who wrote a
venomous attack on the Fiction Collective,
using *Holy Smoke* as an example of all that
was wrong with the Collective, they (we, it?)
published another novel of mine *In the Middle
of Nowhere*. Once again, I never knew who did
what or why—and remain ignorant to this day.

from *Holy Smoke*

Naked feet, rocky torso,
These from my black man;
Pupils of antarctic glass,
These from my white man!

"That's by Nicholas Guillèn," said Selwyn. Then he
suggested we return to the States via Canada. We're on the
same wavelength, I said.

"I just want to see something."

If North is close to Paradise?

"Sort of, although I doubt it," he said with his
disarming smile.

I hear life is good in Canada.

"I've been there many times myself," he said,
"and at first it does seem to be a metaphor
for Heaven. But *comme toujours*, there's a worm
in the ointment."

A worm? In the ointment?

"Well, let me explain."

Can I tape you?

"Go right ahead."

We were in his hotel room and he had a very fancy tape
recorder, which had been used on Castro that same day. He
got everything ready to roll, lit up a smoke and leaned back
to speak. This is what Selwyn said:

» » »

When you cross the border, everything is French—French birds, French trees, French restaurants, French kisses, French toast, French people. There is a glaze of ice (or *glace*) over the asphalt, but if you keep at it, you reach the Palais Royale, where you always wanted to be. In fact, it's a hotel overlooking the most lethal river in human history: sixteen tons of ice float along its surface daily, the banks of the river are sheer, as on the upper Hudson. The Palais Royale is modern, clean, though a family of roaches lives under glass (or *glace)* in a room behind the main kitchen. You don't have to make your bed or sweep your own floor. The rooms are clear as glass. At night you see the Northern Lights in the sky and stars bursting out all over—red ones, blue ones, gold and green ones. Your breakfast is served on a silver tray—French toast, maple syrup, fruit juice and *café* in a large silver pot. The children in your bed drink *café* too, strongly diluted with milk. After their breakfast, the children are dressed and taken off to an excellent school where they can honestly feel that work is play. A large area is kept green as a meadow so they can run around. You have, in the meantime, worked at your craft or art all day, free to take walks, pick at French fries or to converse whenever you felt the inclination. The worm in the ointment turns out to be that river which walls you in. You can't cross it and you certainly don't want to cross the border south and return to the problems you left behind. A certain loneliness in your spacial position affects your moods You don't let your children, if you have them, within one foot of the French windows the first day, then within one and a half the second day, and so on, by halves, until you find yourself, and them, living in bed, waiting for service!

Imagine that, I said and switched off the tape recorder.
    "I am more afraid of corruption than I am of
    death," said Selwyn.
There is more corruption than death in your profession.

"In all professions," he said, "there is. But who
cares about that? The main thing is, you can't
even think straight in this world."
You sound like the Virgin Mary.

"I know I do. And I think she goes beyond
faith, in her message. That is, she implies that
faith itself is corrupt."
If you aspire to sainthood, you're setting yourself apart from
others.

"And if you, nobly, say I won't do such a thing,
you are assuming that the Creator will appreciate
your self-sacrifice and save you on the spot."
Well, then, what.

"Let's fly Air Canada tomorrow," he said.
And then?

"We'll fly from Montreal to Kennedy Airport."
We were both drinking up a storm. We felt we had accom-
plished what we came for. This was a celebration.

"You will have a hangover," he said.
And you?

"I don't get them. But I have some Alka-Seltzer—for
my friends."
Kindness comes when least expected and demands nothing
in return. But as he shook out the Alka-Seltzer for me, I felt
I must express my appreciation for his friendship. I told him
I loved to fly. Not in a jumbo jet, but in a 707, beside the
window.

"Will you hold my hand? I get scared."
That was what I was going to suggest.

"You see," he said, "we're meant for each other."

Robert Steiner

In the cluttered attic of the old cupboard house,
during one of my most immemorial seasons,
I was led to a stack of manuscripts ashen with
dust, like Egypt. These, said Ron Sukenick
that December afternoon, might be a place to
start. Thinking backward, he hefted the bottom book—first come, first served. It was my
first day on board, I was still youngish, merely
twice divorced, and enjoyed Ron's unflagging
energy for the cause and the future and the
cause's future. The present, Himalayan,
loomed from the filigree ceiling downward.
The day faded, I pulled the weak sun's chain,
then cozied into a dangerously splayed armchair with smokes, scotch and a shaky gentle
lamp for friendship. I was alone until midnight, when the blizzard began. The first script
I read I admired and heartily recommended;
the author, we later discovered, had died of
old age two years before. The next manuscript
I read dated from four years previous and,
while its author was happily alive, struck me
as execrable, which by now he surely knew,
hence no threatening correspondence filled out
the big box that comprised his 'file.' So it went,
weekend after weekend, clearing the room of
sad sexy stories too often and badly told, a
few well and never quite told before, some

not really stories at all, others stories not really told so much as promulgated, until together but in separate digs RS and RS combed out maybe four small scripts from the hundred or so that not only had been unattended but by now read as though they had been unattended: resentfully, insecurely, with chips on their shoulders. So, said Ron at the end of our labors, over big big lobsters (it was Mayday), how's it feeling to be cutting edge? Good, I said, the lobster's good. Seventeen years later, or so I have been told, no one else has died before being accepted. Commercial houses can't make that claim.

from *Broadway Melody*

Recently arrived from a nameless castle in the gloamy depths of eastern Europe, the uninvited guest stood shyly in a corner of the ballroom. When a butler approached he accepted champagne, careful to hold the flute far from his tuxedo. Few in the room suspected his identity; these scrupulously shunned him. He remained aloof in the huge ballroom, listening to the orchestra, holding his champagne without sipping, and intently watching dancing couples, when a young woman threw her arms about his neck, laughed drunkenly and vanished in the grip of her partner. The pair foxtrotted off. It was some seconds before he regained his composure to notice the streaks of champagne soiling his tuxedo. He felt more aloof as a result. Yet years later he would be able to recall the melody the orchestra was playing. It was

Munchkins littered the yellow brick road, none of them a victim of an automobile accident, but dead nonetheless. Pumpkin-shaped skulls split vertically, limbs strewn like tree trimmings, munchkins, gathering flies, peppered the land of Oz.

The monster lived a nether life of stagnant canals, medieval aqueducts, ships docking at midnight, fog, mysterious smoky cafes. From continent to continent he sought refuge

in manors, chateaus, castles, and grand hotels. Whether
dressed in a cape, a greatcoat, a wide brim or fedora hat, he
prowled the least traveled streets, among the disenfran-
chised, for his victims. He preferred, however, victims of
class and great wealth, not because he viewed himself as a
provocateur but because these victims reminded him of
himself and his origins. It was more difficult as the centuries
passed to include himself among the beautiful and wealthy if
only because, while their number increased, fewer and fewer
retained or respected the aura of antiquity origins like his
represented. He appreciated wealth while despising its
accumulation, yet more often than not the potential victims
he would encounter spoke of nothing so much as how much
wealth they had accumulated and how they had done so.
This was why when he had met Mina in London she had
seemed to him already the ghost of a vanished race. He had
desired her for his bride and, for a time, she reciprocated,
though her passion required on his part no small effort at
hypnosis. When now he touched Mina's wrist as she lay
dying in the hospital with the blue star on its roof, her
fingers closed around his hand with such slow deliberation
he thought she must be awake. Her grip was enormously
powerful, that of an eagle. Her knuckles bleached, the bones
white enough to break her skin, a nearest chair far across the
room, the porcelain alarm resting like a spider beside her ear
on the pillow, the monster stood uncertain what to do next.
What was killing her, how she could both be one of his
brides and be dying, he could not fathom. Forcing her grip
loose, he hurried to the open window at the sound of physi-
cians near the door. He flew. The snow fell harder, the sky
heavy and cold against his wings. Below, the only traffic lay
in the direction of the theatre, the theatre itself was as bright
and busy as a burning castle. Burning castles the monster
had left far behind. Or so he thought.

When Esmeralda the Gypsy danced, the hunchback slavered,
swinging from one grinning gargoyle to another. So it
should come as no surprise that when Esmeralda the Gypsy

was led into the square by a rope the hunchback went wild, wringing his hairy hands, slamming his hump against the cathedral bells, hurling gobs of spittle down onto the gathered citizens. He flew from bell to bell until he had set them into a sway that rang of misery across the bleak Paris sky. With his one good eye — the other diseased and half concealed by a flap of pink skin — the hunchback witnessed the awful spectacle that drew thieves from the Court of Miracles, merchants from the Marais, drunkards out of Ile-St. Louis, the fishmongers of Pigalle, whores from Montmartre and Les Halle. Two hundred feet below him priests, courtiers and poets recited, jeered, hissed, and swooned with the pressing crowd. With travelers gathered as well, the mob drank, bargained, gossiped, gambled, fell in and out of lust. Some were grizzled, wizened and old, others red and beefy, few with more than a few teeth and most with sexual disease. Many carried lame children on their shoulders. Ceremoniously, as though to resurrect an ancient deity, the Gypsy's black-eyed goat was hanged first, its hooves knotted by hemp, its tail and penis hacked off by sword, its evil eye gouged by the thumbs of a young priest. Afterward the exposed belly was sliced open and dogs let loose on the gibbet, hounds that burrowed so fiercely the goat's flesh was stripped and the carcass, still in the jaws of a dozen curs, plummeted to the ground ten feet below. Blood and fur spattered the crowd five deep. People who did not cheer danced, imitating the goat's gambol. Ragged children washed the gibbet clean with buckets from the river, slipping and sliding as if skating an icy street. Then, with the crowd hushed, it was Esmeralda's turn to mount the steps.

The monster flies. He glides the night air. He suffers snow on his thin bony wingspan. He encounters turbulence. His bat-eyes burn in the wind. He evades a jumbo jet. He lets the wind carry him. He spies a shooting star. He chases a duck late heading south. He is nearly drawn up into the beam of an alien spaceship. He is a little bit lost because of the weather, the traffic. He flies, musing on the skies he has

flown for hundreds of years on nights like this. He appreci-
ates the earth's horizon as he executes a ninety degree turn.
He banks, peeing as he goes.

He's not sure where he is or why or how he got there or
what it is he's supposed to do now that he's arrived — the
room is small, appointed as a Victorian parlor — so he
stands bewildered before a divan on the edge of which sit a
young couple holding hands and gazing into each other's
eyes. Around the young man's hips the tails of a tuxedo hang
like dog ears, around the woman's the folds of a gown
gather as though she's hiding a dwarf. Above them against
the wall, lovers in a salon are painted clasping hands,
leaning toward one another about to speak. Can you remember, asks the young man, when this feeling came over you?
For an instant it isn't clear to the monster who should
answer, the woman on the divan or himself. Suddenly
everything seems strange, the woman replies only an instant
before the monster is about to say the same thing. I'm in a
fog, she adds, and he realizes he is too, trying to step forward but floating instead. My flesh is crawling, the woman
continues. Even though I'm holding your fingers? the young
man wonders aloud. At that she turns her face, staring as at a
great distance but in fact at the monster, only a short one,
who smiles. Either she can't see him or won't acknowledge
that she can, her vision passing through him, beyond his
intrusive presence into the past, future or at the fog she feels
she's in, no one in the salon seems to know. The monster
waves gaunt fingers in her direction, noticing only then that
his hand itself is in fact nothing but fog. He glances down at
his chest, his trousers and shoes, all of which are white
plumes of vapor that swirl when he moves. Holy smoke! he
thinks wafting in the woman's proximity, staring at her
green eyes which are far apart, misted, glassy. He brushes
her cheek with the back of his hand, such as it is, and she
shivers, removing her palm from the man's, who takes it up
again to rub away the chill. She withdraws it, he retrieves it,
she yanks it from him, he grabs it back, petulantly refusing

to release it until the monster intervenes with his own and the others, in unison, jump. You feel it too, the woman remarks. At the edge of a bodice her cleavage heaves, pinching her breasts into taut curves that want to explode from the gown. Of course not, the man lies with a stammer. His eyes widen though, casting furtively through the room for an open window (there is none) or a stir of the drapery (it's as still as the boutonniere in his lapel). As he moves to pour champagne from a bottle in an ice bucket before them, the young man feels pressure at his throat, fingers forcing off air, a fierce grip squeezing his windpipe until he is speechless, gagging, until the whites of his eyes purple and swell. See, I told you, the woman says, taking the opportunity to recover her hand, our love is haunted and doomed. With his newly free hand the young man struggles at his throat against an invisible talon, gasping and choking while he tries to tear the unseen enemy away. Meanwhile the woman talks on, remarking that their situation is utterly hopeless. Hers is the subdued voice of fatalism rather than experience — she is not wrong, perhaps, but she doesn't know why. By now her lover is on one knee, as if to propose to her, wrestling with the invisible strangler, face red as a tomato, tugging at his shirt collar. Sweat runs from his forehead to pool under his eyes. Perhaps, the young woman concludes, we shan't see one another again. The young man's face is like a plum and spittle ropes to the plush carpet. This isn't happening, the boyfriend manages to groan. But it is! the woman replies. That's the whole point! It is! Feeling as if he were about to lose consciousness, the boyfriend remembers the fifth grade, the third, the second, and recognizes that he has lost memory of the fourth, so great is the loss of oxygen. His entire body grows cold and clammy while his girlfriend continues to explain the futility of their love.

The opera house, located at the city's center, not far from the river, was founded twenty years before the most recent century turned. Incorporating architectural features from

Covent Garden, the Paris Opera and La Scala, the chief
designer created a monstrosity of taste as a monument to the
nation's wealthiest socialites. Acoustics however, as well as
vision of the proscenium, remained both in plan and execution still more execrable. In an effort to avoid garishness the
interior, red and gold, was muted by the ivory inlays prevail-
ing on the abundant woodwork. The sunburst chandelier
overhanging the center of the auditorium, while unknown
elsewhere in the world, tended to sway and chime amid the
crossdrafts generated by doors leading to boxes on one side
and private calons on the other. A painting of Apollo that
crowned the proscenium arch began to peel almost immediately so that when the great fire occurred ten years after the
opening (*Faust*), great wings of flaming myth flew through
the theatre like phoenixes, igniting draperies, carpets and
deep velvet cushions. Rebuilt, the palatial house was fes-
tooned with smilax, electric lights and maroon parterres. The
acoustics, unfortunately, remained the same.

Here is a good opportunity to reconnoiter the monster's
emotional life, without which he would be of little interest to
anyone. As we shall see, his emotional life consists entirely
of women, more from out of the past than in the present. It
was not that in his history he had been unfaithful to the
women he loved but that he had tried to love several women
at once. A glandular science fiction, one might conclude. At
an early century in his life, before he was really aware of it,
he had dissolved serious threads to other males and never
invested much vigor in his passage with them, though
attempting to know women well was not only difficult and
at times futile but exhausting. Even if he now and again
had to simplify the differences between women and
himself by thinking I feel this, she doesn't, they don't feel
it either, he still found that women provided more illustra-
tive experiences. Males, after all, had proven too much like
himself. Even so, it's worth noting that women, Mina for
example, tended to die in his proximity, though rarely from
natural causes and never, until Mina's case, from old age.

Some were burned to death, some rent in the heart by stakes, still others decapitated. But it is also noteworthy that not all the women he has loved are dead — some are merely very ill, others light years distant. What is most important concerning the monster's emotional life is that once he realized he would remain defined and identified largely by his relations with women of numerous ages, races and languages, he felt awesomely responsible for the ideas, remarks and glances that might be exchanged in a room or across a table. Often the anxiety made him dizzy, vulnerable and occasionally even shallow. In the midst of his therefore tenuous existence he required cheering, unfettered pleasure to distract from the inherent morbidity. He loved parties, the bigger the better, and holiday festivities most of all, like others this xmas eve are attending.

Munchkins littered the yellow brick road, none of them a victim of an automobile accident, but dead nonetheless. Pumpkin-shaped skulls split vertically, limbs strewn like tree trimmings, munchkins, gathering flies, peppered the land of Oz. The cowardly lion's skin lay stretched across the great door of the wicked witch's dark castle, though inside the castle the witch herself was a puddle of hair, proclaiming her innocence of at least this vile crime by her own murder.

The Phantom, living five cellars below the stage of the opera, adjacent to the sewers and near enough to the river that day and night he can hear water lapping at stone steps, carries the body to his sleeping room with more a sense of curiosity than vexation. Studying the unconscious man's face, the Phantom wonders not only at the costume but at the slick pomaded hair, the errant shaggy eyebrows, the curling tufts of nose feather, the knifeblades of ruby lip, the untrimmed mustachios, the long spiky eyelashes, the thick odiferous facial cosmetic, the protruding and purple scar on the forehead, the dagger-like fingernails, the innumerable liverspots big as nickels — and yet the overwhelming weightlessness of the body. A man so utterly at death's door that he looks as if

he's been rehearsing it most of his life. A man so ostenta-
tiously foreign he looks like someone trying very hard to look
foreign. This figure the Phantom lugs across the stone steps,
through the parlors of his hidden domicile and into his
sleeping room. The Phantom would be content to watch the
body for a while, to invent an existence for it that might have
led to this bombastic ruin, were it not for the barely percep-
tible rumbling overhead that signals the applause commenc-
ing the performance. Still, with one final glance at the morbid
face, whose skin is more parched and crepey than rice paper,
he almost feels himself fortunate to be living his own concealed nether-life and to be hiding his disfigurement behind a
mask. But philosophy will have to wait because now the
Phantom must go to work spooking the audience with appearances here and there in the house, inspiring terror with his
admittedly cheap theatrics and B-movie murders that will
send patrons screaming into the night. And while he expects
the unconscious old man to die before he returns, his only
thought is where, among the scores of corpses already piled in
the sewers, he will find a place for this one.

Jonathan Harker removed from his greatcoat a map of the
world, heavily marked, faded and dog-eared. Though in the
blizzard it was difficult to see, he note-took. He moistened a
pencil point and drew lines of thought across the face of his
map. Corpse to corpse the lines grew, from the Carpathians
to London and back again, to Germany, France, Asia,
angling along the great rivers of the world, the great capitals
of great nations, the fetid jungles of tropical hells, moving
from dot to dot to dot until the lines met in this city this
xmas eve. Harker shuddered, wiping snowflakes from his
spectacles with his necktie. Dr. Van Helsing peered over his
shoulder; together they renewed their commitment to the
cause that had led them over every continent during the
horrible course of their long lives. The monster, they realized at the same moment, was once more at hand. They
lifted their faces to the night sky, raised their fists, crying
Death to the undead! Death to the vampire!

Gerald Vizenor

Griever, the character in my novel, is a presence, not an absence, a marvelous trickster in the modern rush of native stories. He was conceived in griever meditation, as you know, a tricky practice his mother established on the reservation. Griever traveled with me to teach at Tianjin University in the People's Republic of China.

I had not planned to write about my experiences there, but changed my mind at a performance of the Monkey King. I was transformed by the episodic scenes of the opera "Havoc of Heaven." The Chinese Monkey King and the Anishinaabe trickster Naanabozho are distant cousins, and they come to mind in a contradiction, the authoritarian politics of a university.

"Griever: An American Monkey King in China" was written the year after my return from China, and a year later Curtis White called me with the good news, that my novel had won the Fiction Collective Award. The following year "Griever" won the American Book Award.

The Monkey King performance, more than a decade ago, and the production of "Griever" are even closer now in my stories. All so pleasant a memory, to be associated with the Fiction Collective.

Obo Island

Shuishang Water Park bears a horde of tourists, seven wild animals, three birds in a mesh, and dead water; tired pandas thumb the stone walls, tigers wheeze over the children at the posterns, sullen eagles hack the narrow bamboo beams with their wicked beaks, and keels dissolve on the dark blue shores.

Griever rowed a rented plastic boat close to shore in the thick water. The oars screeched in the rusted locks; he drifted in silence under an arched wooden bridge. Overhead, tourists paused on the rail to chatter, hand over hand, and watch the cock high in the bow of the boat. The boards rattled when the tourists crossed over. On the underside, rats roamed in the shadows with bits of steamed *mantou* and other morsels to their colonies on the islet bandstand.

"Mao lives," the trickster announced to the tourists and the rats as he passed under. He raised an oar to tease the slower rodents on the curved support beams.

"*Lao shu, lao shu, 'rats, rats,*'" a man warned from behind the trees on the other end of the bridge. He crouched with a rifle, aimed, and fired three times.

Sandie, a name he had earned from a comic opera, the most sincere character in the stories about the mind monkey, was a government rat hunter. When he raised his rifle, the trickster ducked his head, lost his balance on the second shot, and tumbled into the shallow water. At the same time, two dead rats dropped from the beam; one bounced on the boat near the rooster.

"Asshole, you missed one," shouted the trickster as he sloshed close to shore. Blood splashed when the second rat hit the water.

"*Zhua zhu lao shu*," said the hunter. He shouldered his rifle and waded into the water to hold the boat and retrieve the rats he had shot.

Matteo Ricci, perched on the bow with his wings drawn, pecked at the rodent and the hunter. The cock shivered, raised his beak, and danced down the bloodied plastic gunwales.

"English, asshole," the trickster complained.

"Catch the rats, asshole," the hunter translated with a wild uneven smile. His neck and arms were thick, but his shins were lank, tapered like blades, and his feet were too narrow to walk in water.

"Mao lives," repeated the trickster and raised one rat from the water. Shattered bone and brain marbled the blue mud on shore. "No head here to mount."

"Sorry about that," said the hunter, "no harm intended." He hauled the boat to shore; overhead, the tourists applauded the wild hunter.

"Too much for two rodents."

"Rats are worth more than chickens."

"Dead or alive?"

"Rat steaks and hides," said the hunter.

"Steaks?"

"Dim sum at the guest house."

"Never."

"Rat stroganoff at Maxim's de Beijing."

"Now that sounds right."

"Designer shoes, no less."

"No less," mocked the trickster.

"Berkeley."

"What about Berkeley?"

"You were about to ask me," said the hunter, "where in the world did you learn how to speak with such ease, and the answer is simple. . . ."

"University of California."

"Political science and economics," said the hunter, eager to please an audience, "but these are peculiar times."

"No shit?"

"No shit about the rat steaks and the shoes either," he said, "but listen, your clothes are wet, so come with me now."

"Where?"

"Obo Island on the other side of the water park," he said and pointed with his blunt forehead. He stacked the rats in the bow with thirteen others from an earlier hunt and pushed the plastic boat back into the thick dark water.

"Wait, this is a rented boat."

"Mister Griever," he responded, "never mind now, you are with a government rat hunter and the rent on the boat is of no concern."

"How did you know my name?"

Sandie moved an ovine smile from one side of his face to the other as he rowed; the oars screeched in the locks. The trickster was silent, perched at the stern in wet clothes; his shoes and his trousers from the waist down were stained blue from the lake muck.

The Pavilion of Beautiful Views, painted on an islet in the middle of the west lake, overlooks the whole water park. Tourists cross the bridge for the view and the rats slide between the lattice in search of morsels under the pavilion porch.

"Rat islet to me," said the hunter.

"Why rats?"

"The government cadre offered me pigs, rats, or plastics," he said between slow rows, "so, be honest with me now, what would you choose?"

"Economics."

"Listen, fine shoes for children come from these hides, and we marinate the meat in ginger, pepper, and brine, and then the meat is pressed, dried, and recooked with sesame seed oil. Some of the pancake vendors on the street serve barbecued rat."

"Rattail economics."

"Pigs eat the rest," he said and rowed to the western side

of the water park. Sandie tied the boat to a small pavilion near shore, shouldered his rifle and the blood soaked bundle of rats, and waddled over a low embankment.

Griever, mottled with blood and blue mud, followed the rat hunter into the trees. He folded his right ear, turned a strand of hair, and watched the animals wheedled behind the moist bushes; thousands of white moths lifted from broad leaves and lightened his volant shadow. Small birds healed the wild air he breathed, and wild flowers tousled on the paths to the golden pavilions. There, on a natural mount, a cleared circle in the polished trees, the hunter dressed the rats and spread the narrow hides on fine rosewood frames that enclosed brick hearth. The trickster undressed down to his holster and underwear and spread his clothes on the same frames; then he followed the hunter to a narrow levee over a wide moat.

Matteo Ricci scratched the hard berm.

Obo Island bears three maidenhair trees, one white willow, four small brick houses, a concrete water ditch, a stone shrine and red banner near the levee, five humans, seventeen sows, three breeder boars, one wide barrow, several unnamed shoats and runners and a basketball court.

Obo, a tribal word that means "cairn," a tribal place where shamans gather and dream, is shaped the same as the nation, sheared and cleaved on two mounts. The narrow levee is a stem connected to the curved base of the island. The trees and houses are enclosed in a greater wall and the wall separates the swine from the shaded courts on the eastern shore where the moat widens and pours into a deep lake. When the moon is new, the dark cold water heaves back the voices of dead miners, voices from an old lode that flooded at the end of the revolution.

Shitou, the stone man, was one of the few survivors when the dike collapsed and flooded the mine. Too old to find a new work place he made the island his home. Others, lost and dissociated in the revolution, curious and nonesuch wanderers, arrived and declared a new sericulture, swine, stone, birth control, and rat production unit, named Minus Number One.

Pigsie, denounced as a bourgeois nuisance, crossed the levee with two Hampshire gilts and a Spotted Poland China boar.

Several months later he traded one Seghers, a new lean breed, for three common Yorkshires; then an agribusiness consult- ant, secret agent and swine runner, traded a smart Duroc, which he named China Red, and one American Landrace for numer- ous concessions on the island. Nothing was conceded, how- ever, because the runner was detained for bestialities. Communist cadres discovered the island and demanded a share of the swine herd for their silence and protection.

Kangmei circled the island in her prairie schooner for several weeks with moth seeds in small bundles under her arms; she watched the stone man break stones into laughter and the herder teach the swine to shoot baskets. The island, she de- cided, would be her place because it turned the revolution and the state into wild comedies. She crossed the levee with Yaba Gezi, the mute pigeon, late one winter night when the snow was pale blue.

Sandie, the most earnest and courteous of the wander- ers, was the last to muster the swine on the island. He delivers rat hides to the government, barters the marinated meat at the free market, and attends stone breaks and silk worms in the summer.

Griever held his breath on the levee to beat the smell of swine urine; he broke from the cloud of white moths at one end of the chine and burned his nostrils at the other end near the stone cairns. The trickster was silent and curious; he wan- dered over the island, down the greater wall, over the mounts, bowed, smiled, courted a cat and some mongrels, and shunned the torrid insects near a basketball court where he encoun- tered the last character from the comic opera.

Pigsie, the lascivious peasant with huge golden hands, dribbled a basketball in a wide circle and then pitched it to the trickster at the back of the court. The athlete wore red shoes, loose shorts, knee pads, and a white mask to filter the dust raised by the swine.

Griever held the ball in silence and scratched the nubs with his thumbnails; a thin patch of mud broke and scattered. Swine urine burned his cheeks, ears, the thin skin on the back of his knees, and inner thighs. He bounced the ball once, twice, three times, and moved closer to the basket, which had been lowered for the swine. When three sows and a barrow snorted and wheeled in his direction, he leaped clean over the cairn into a vegetable garden that bordered the court and the greater wall.

"Pass ball, yes," cried Pigsie.

"Sooeeee," the trickster intoned and pitched the ball to the eager swine at the side of the court. *Rawrk, rawrk,* sounded a sow and nosed the ball down the sidelines; she thrust her wet snout high and bounced the ball to a boar near the basket. The swine had the same common character painted on their hams, tender loins, and picnic shoulders.

Matteo Ricci bounced on the back of the boar.

Pigsie blocked the pass, turned, dribbled low, and hooked a basket. *Waaagghh, waaagghh,* the boar warned at the back court. The eager shoats imitated the wild sound and the cock crowed with pleasure.

"What do those characters mean?"

"Names, yes."

"Pig, hog, what?"

"No, no, Horse, Horse," said the herder.

"Wait a minute," said the trickster with his thumb on his ear, "the common character on the ass of that sow means 'horse'?"

"Yes, yes, *ma* means 'horse.'"

"Translate the other characters then."

"Little one named Ant," the swine herder explained, "*ma yi* means 'ant,' *ma* tones change, yes?" He smiled, pitched the ball to an eager shoat, and then faced the trickster.

"Name that one over there."

"Sacrifice."

"What kind of name is that?"

"Two characters mean 'horse' and 'omen,' yes."

"What about the sow under the basket?" The trickster pointed with one hand and then the other. "One character means 'horse,' what does the other character mean?"

"Jade."

"So, how does that translate then?"

"China Red named Agate, yes."

"Horse and jade make an agate," said the trickster, and he pointed to a couchant barrow in the center of the court. "No horse character on that one, no *ma* tone there, what is his name?"

"Mao Zedong."

"No shit, and a barrow no less."

"Communist cadres eat leader," he said, and then explained that the name was painted on the hams of those swine demanded by the cadres each month as tribute.

"What do you eat then?"

"Chicken."

"Lin Biao capon?"

"No, no, rooster," said Pigsie. He pinched the ball with his huge hands, dribbled around Mao Zedong, leaped over the barrow and shot a basket.

"Where clothes?"

"Muddied."

"Sandie, he rat man here."

"Where is here?"

"Obo hai dao, 'cairn island,'" he said and then bounced the ball to the boar with the blue ears. and narrow rooter. The boar snouted the ball, *hummphhh, hummphhh*, from the back court and swished a basket, but the herder called a foul.

"Obo where?"

"Obo hai dao China."

"Hog heaven," Griever moaned and rolled his head from side to side. China Red and the shoats turned and stared at the naked trickster over the cairn. The fouled boar sat tight under the basket with his ears turned forward.

"Me live Albuquerque?"

"New Mexico?"

"Me live Albuquerque," said the cumbrous swine herder near the basket. The shoats faced the same direction, minded the boar, the ball, and the cock on the run.

"You were a student then?"

"America big tits," said the herder and passed the ball to the boar but a sow with butterflies painted on her ears intercepted with her snout high and made a basket.

"That she does," responded the trickster over the cairn. The manure on the garden parched his bare feet but he smiled and applauded the score.

"Studied aeronautic engineer."

"Albuquerque?"

"Balloons, little planes over desert, yes," he explained with a smile. His mouth spread like a marine animal, twice as wide as the words he practiced; his teeth were even, clean, and enormous. The herder summoned forbearance with his wide mouth, huge hands, feral toes, brows, and hunched shoulders; and he teased women to understand his unwonted burdens, the billow of his stout penis under denim.

"Ultralights?"

"Yes, yes, ultralights."

"Well, an ultralight was shipped to me here," said the trickster with his hands packed under the elastic band of his underwear. "So, when the plane is delivered, no more crowded train stations for me."

Pigsie told the trickster that basketball carried him from the rice brigades to teams in the cities, and then he was selected to be educated overseas in the operation of ultralight airplanes. Five months later, however, his student visa was withdrawn because, the investigation revealed, he touched the breasts of nineteen women at the International Adobe Basketball tournament: ten blondes, three were exposed. There, he pleaded, breasts were advertised, over-sized, nurtured in the sun, oiled on the side, boosted on the seams; and pushed into common conversations, even on the run, and so, the athlete said, "So, so, bounced big tits on bleachers, yes."

"From ultralights to pigs?"

"Too much tits, so cadres said, pigs, rats, or plastics," he said and leaped over the cairn into the tomatoes and green beans. "So, which one you me choose?"

"Tits," cried the trickster.

"Pigs, no more tits."

"Rats were taken, right?"

"Right."

"Who has plastics"

"Shitou."

"The stone man is here?"

"Right, right, right," he repeated over and over, stuck on a word that he seldom heard on the island. "Stone man, you meet him where, when he live in California?"

"When did he live there?"

"Build railroad," said the herder, "stone man build cold mountain railroad with hands down." He pushed the white mask back on his head, brushed the dust from his shoes, and wiped his hands on his shorts.

"Gold mountain, but he's not that old."

"Yes, cold," said the herder with a smile, and then he roamed with the swine down to the mount and the greater wall that enclosed the stone houses.

Shitou hunkered over mah jongg moves in the shadow of the maidenhair trees. The stone man turned a bamboo tile, and the trickster trod on the broken stones closer to the game. Three others shared the board and turned the seasons in silence.

Yaba Gezi, the mute pigeon, hovered in blue light.

Kangmei, the moth walker, was shrouded in silk.

Sandie matched a wind tile and cleaned his teeth with a blunt stick; he leaned to the side on the barrel of his rifle. Pleased with chance, he broke the silence and proposed that the faces of rats and bourgeois tourists become the suits. The trickster laughed but no one else was amused.

Matteo Ricci cracked maidenhair seeds.

Griever hesitated on the stone breaks that lined the path to the table beneath the trees; uncertain, he leaned back on his bare heels and bounced his toes together but the scene in the shadows outrode his imagination. He remembered blue bones, the prairie schooner, the black opal, and the birchbark manuscript. He twisted a wild hair on his right temple to catch the reason but the smell of swine urine rent the center of his dreams; his nose burned, he sneezed and lost his balance on the stones.

"Griever needs a mirror," said Sandie.

"No, no, but where are my clothes?"

"Your clothes are on the rosewood frames with the rat skins, remember?" Sandie clicked two red dragons, honor tiles, and explained to the trickster that his clothes, at least, would smell less of swine when he returned to the guest house with his stories.

Matteo Ricci strutted on the table.

Shitou leaned forward in silence, his back to the swine court and the levee. The greater wall ascended from the water like a stone serpent, a tribute to the dead miners, and widened near the mount. The stone man tended the bamboo and character suits; he smiled when the trickster moved closer on the breaks.

"Shitou, break me a stone."

"Shitou, *mo shu*," said the stone man.

"Stone what?"

"He said *mo shu*, 'magic,'" said Kangmei.

"Teach me the stone tricks," he pleaded on the new breaks, "show me how to shatter stone, like you did at the free market." The trickster tiptoed under the maidenhair trees.

"Sun Wukong, *mafan, mafan*," said the stone man. His wide simian ears beckoned when he moved his mouth; he whispered to the cock and smiled at the trickster.

"Mind monkey, what else?"

"Trouble, trouble," Kangmei translated.

"Trouble, no one would be here without trouble," said the trickster. He leaned back on a maidenhair tree, unholstered his scroll, and outlined parts of the swine islanders on the rough paper. The stone man was an ear, the moth walker a cocoon, the swine herder a penis, the rat hunter a mouth, and the mute pigeon a blue stone. In scenes that followed, these faces and other features became stones in the greater wall at the mount. He traced enormous fish beached on the levee; moths, with wild silk banners raised over the blue stones, touched the earlier scenes in the water park where the panda masturbated, and soldiers bound their feet.

"Deep inside the stone is a bird and humor," said the stone man to the trickster. He moved a bench closer to the maidenhair tree and placed one round stone on the rim. "Dream that your hand moves back in time to when the stone was formed," he said with his right hand poised over the stone. "Dream that your hand moves to block the cold, the cold that comes to the stone and laughter, and release that little bird with the break." The trickster mocked the stone man, hacked the stone twice, and bruised his hand.

"Show me the trick," said the trickster.

"Breath, hold that bird on your breath," said the stone man with his hands on his smooth round stomach. He leaned closer to the bench and broke two more slivers from the stone.

"Bird breath, there, how is that?"

"Stomach, not your chest."

"Right, bird breath, stomach," mocked the trickster.

"*Dan tian*, 'inhale,' remember the bird."

"Concentrate, right?"

"*Yeren*," muttered the stone man.

"What was that?"

"Wildman," said the moth walker.

The mute pigeon appeared with two round mirrors, one in each hand. He circled the trickster several times and reined his image closer to the stone; his nose wobbled in the mirrors and turned blue. The greater wall, the trees, the cock, the swine behind the Mount, the bird on his breath, reeled in blue.

Griever remembered his dream in the shaman mirrors, the heat, stubborn mosquitoes on the balcony, and the pictures of swine and blue bones. "Listen," he said as he turned to blue stone in the mirrors, "who was that man behind the evil mask, the one who held the blue bones?"

"Egas Zhang," whispered the moth walker.

"Egas Zhang," the others repeated, and the mute pigeon moved in silence. The mirrors trembled and the trickster lost his image.

"He was never, never my father," cried the moth walker. She lowered the shroud and pitched her head to the side, an instinctive gesture. Under the silk burnoose, she wore a thick turtleneck, the color of cedar bark, and loose pleated trousers that were open at the crotch like those of a child.

"No shit, and blond hair to prove it," said the trickster, closer to familiar seams and testaments. He winked twice, inhaled the noisome scent of swine, spread his chest, and strutted toward the mah jongg table. He wore nothing more than white underwear stained with blue mud on the crotch and his leather holster.

"Battle Wilson," she said through her clean hands, "he was my real father, born in the mountains." She crouched behind the table and twisted her slender waist to the right when she listened. She wore cloth shoes and bound her ankles with silk ribbons.

"Cold mountain?"

"Oklahoma."

"Did he give you an ancient manuscript?"

"Mountain View, Oklahoma."

"Tell me," the trickster crooned, "what did the scroll tell about the future, how can we live forever?" Griever planted his elbows on the table and studied the seasons, the winds, and the dragons. He leaned closer and waited to learn the secrets of the immortal bears from the mountains.

Kangmei turned to the side; she listened to the trickster and studied the puckers and wild creases on his cheeks when he smiled, but she would never answer his questions. Vital energies, she learned from the blind woman in the park, breed and mature in silence.

Yaba Gezi moved the mirrors and his mouth; he turned several words over in silence. The trickster leaned closer, listened to his breath, admired his own brows in the mirrors, and then he demanded a total translation of the silence.

"Nothing," said the moth walker to the mirrors.

"There, he made the same words."

"Children in the pond," she translated.

"What does that mean?"

"Blue bones are children in the pond," she said.

"Crosstalkers," said the trickster, bored with the silence and the translation. The tiles wobbled and the winds turned when he crossed his bare legs and hit the table with his hands.

Pigsie, meanwhile, donned a wide peasant hat and packed four sucklings in the wicker baskets on the rear of his bicycle, two on each side, and pedaled once around the trees.

"Birth control," said Sandie.

"So what," answered the trickster.

"You were about to ask me about the sucklings."

"Birth control?"

"Women who nurse seldom get pregnant," the rat hunter explained, "and, so, the little swine get fed at the same time."

"Hard on nipples."

"We pull their teeth, perfect suckers."

"But why the pigs?"

"China is a one-child nation."

"Pigsie could suck, we could suck."

"Never," said Sandie.

"Our teeth?"

"No, we would get too fat."

"Chinese pragmatists in wicker baskets," the trickster said. "Listen, we could share the best tits on the route," he tendered, "and we might share much more than that and have a no-child nation, how about that?"

"Pigsie, remember, had too much tit."

"Leave the tits to me then," said the trickster.

"There was a teacher who tried that once," the rat hunter related, "he watched the suckers and snorted at women in his classes. Then he gave his clothes away, sucked several breasts for favors, the ultimate spiritual pollution, and was reeducated at a mental hospital."

"Porcine pollution."

"Our mental doctors never see sex as a problem here," the rat hunter construed, "so the poor man had to invent four new critical modernizations before he was released."

"Rats, pigs, plastics, and what else?"

"No, he proclaimed that transportation was limousinized, food was banquetized, clothes were westernized, and the nation was pavilionized."

The mute pigeon wheeled two hand mirrors from the shadows inside the stone house. Wild blue lights bucked the trickster over the threshold, pale spheres and nooses bounced on the back walls and ceiling. The room was decorated with old armor and hand weapons. Mao masks and several manikins held the margins of the room; and one papier-mâché monster loomed alone near a narrow window.

"Egas Zhang," shouted the trickster.

"We made his face with toilet paper," said the stone man when he removed the round mask from the monster. The paper face had been skewered and one ear was broken.

Matteo Ricci shivered at the window.

Griever marched closer to the monster; nose to nose, he reached to touch the blue bones when a light burst from the mute pigeon, circled the room, and the bones vanished. Bewildered, the trickster punched the evil monster hard in the stomach, two inches below the navel, and cracked the toilet paper and plaster cast.

Chinese hand weapons, hammers, battle axes, halberds and swords were stacked on crude museum tables. Spears with bright plumes and tassel ornaments were mounted on the back wall. Breastplates and rhinoceros hide armor covered the manikins in the corners. Outside, at the back of the stone house, there were ballistae and a cloud ladder near the narrow swine houses.

Griever climbed the ladder, whistled to the swine on the other side of the greater wall, and then he returned to the museum. He wielded each weapon on the museum tables, admired a jade mace, an axe ead, and then, in a sudden ritual maneuver, he raised a broad sword, roared, and cleaved the monster down the middle. Egas separated and stood on plastic shoes for a few seconds; then the parts, paper nostrils, narrow chest, and hollow testicles, toppled over. Crepe paper funeral flowers, the core of the monster, eased open on the cold concrete.

"Egas Zhang the eunuch," cried the moth walker.

"Pig feed."

"No swine would have him," she cursed.

"Shit paper then," said the trickster near the window. He wiped the blade clean, returned the sword to the table, and picked a bouquet of flowers from the remains.

Kangmei leaned over from the waist to break parts from the head of the monster. Her rich blond hair brushed the broken chest and paper head as she turned. When the others returned to mah jongg, the trickster moved closer to the moth walker, to the swell of her thighs; he thrust his hand between the pleats in her trousers and touched her moist crotch. She struggled to escape his wild hands. His penis leaped from his underwear and bounced on her bare buttocks; she lost her balance and tumbled forward on the divided monster. The trickster lost flesh and bruised his penis on the broken cast.

————Constance Pierce————

When I learned that the Fiction Collective would publish *When Things Get Back to Normal*, I immediately began to rewrite it. Curt White had made insightful suggestions, and I myself saw the work in a much different light once it was suddenly (and at last) to be public. Driven by my mantra—Build it to last!—I worked to some unanticipated ends: one story grew into a novella, another got the boot altogether. This was almost fifteen years ago. When I pick up the book these days and read a story, I'm gratified and relieved to see that it seems to have lasted. Which is to say that, by now, I hardly recognize it as my own work. It seems itself, with its own integrity, its own convictions. "Chez les petits suisses"—a take on global economy and the smug "neutrality" of the Swiss—seems more contemporary than when it was written, now that Holocaust survivors are suing Swiss banks; a cracked field of study—Psychological History—invented by the narrator of "What I Did for Aunt Berthe," probably wouldn't seem cracked to even the most somnolent reader these days. Which is just to say that old stories can sometimes resonate with subsequent events in the real world, a good incentive to build fiction to last, along with the practical recognition that the moment of its public presentation is brief and often not much remarked. One has to trust in an "aftermarket"—as (thankfully) the Collective must, in keeping our books in print.

The Gourmand

MONSIEUR MAURICE RAMBEAU, the self-styled connoisseur from Poitiers, was having a heart attack.

He had been walking along the street of an obscure village in the Touraine after a very unsatisfactory lunch in a bistro that had been especially recommended to him by the best wine merchant in Tours several days earlier. The lunch had turned out to be ordinary in every detail and in no way worth the extravagant excursion to this place of no distinction, he'd been thinking, when suddenly he had felt his steps slow to a shuffle. He had sagged against the piebald trunk of a sycamore whose limbs had been amputated to a dozen stumps, thinking it was the heat that was doing him in, cursing the primitive village habit of lopping off the natural leaves and branches that might have provided charm to an otherwise charmless spot, camouflage of a depressing emptiness—at least, some relief from the sun. Then a great pain had run through his own substantial trunk, down his own stubby limbs, and he had understood.

Just as his knees were collapsing, he dragged himself onto a mound of grass leading up to a copse, a small park where red canna lilies were growing in a raucous profusion in front of the thick shade of trees that were mercifully untrimmed. But here he sank down, still in the sun. The trees above the mound were just out of his reach, like a distant heaven. He lay silent and livid, staring up at the horrible blue of a too-close sky.

Soon a crowd gathered. Someone tucked a white-papered parcel of laundry under his head, someone else ran for the doctor. A covey of pigeons, that had been huddled among the lilies until the assault of Rambeau on their territory, moved out and began to walk around, eyeing the little man. He could see them pecking at the air, traversing the outline of his body, their neck-feathers undulating in a slow iridescence. Even in his delirium, all he could think of was that he would like to wring their spastic necks, one by one.

It wasn't clear to him why he was so angry at these birds, and he didn't trouble himself to wonder, tangled as he was in his desire to kill them and the secondary matter of the heart attack and all it might come to mean. But the violence of this emotion was profound and eventually obsessive, distracting him from everything else that was going on within him, and much that was going on outside, as the strange villagers moved up and stood very near, their legs seeming a kind of a fence between him and the trees, before he lost sight of everything in his fever for the birds.

Yes, he could see these birds: headless, plucked and trussed, lying all in a row in a huge roasting pan. The breasts would be plumping up, the skin pale and naked even of pin-feathers. Then there would be their succulent well-turned legs, bound together, but one would know about the dark mysterious caverns underneath. . . .

Suddenly, the little man was blazing with passion. He lay half-paralyzed, mouth agape, the eyes loose and rolling out of his control, but there was an unmistakable commotion deep in his baggy trousers. Far away, he was sure he heard a woman titter.

Quickly, with an extraordinary surge of will under the circumstances, he moved his mind along, produced the corpses slathered innocently in honey, sputtering in their own grease. A tumble of raisins now obscured the caverns that had provoked him, crossing some internal wires. Bringing on him the mortifying laughter of a faceless woman that he would give ten years, if he had ten left, to thrash and throttle. Yes, yes—out of the oven and onto a platter of cress, he thought, burning in his haze.

All in a row, all in a row, there: brown and steaming, a spray of fresh orange slices to the side. And between the carcasses, what? Carrots? No, too much like oranges—something more. . . . Leeks! Oh, leeks! Piles and piles of baby, buttery leeks separating the miserable creatures, all on a bed of nice rice, a little fennel dusted over. . . .

This *tour de force* was broken into by some shuffling in the crowd at the arrival of the doctor, a cherubic man in black with very red cheeks. He knelt and began to fumble with M. Rambeau's shirt front, the nervous fingers freezing the patient's will, serving him up to his fury and terror at last.

A few moments later, there was an ambulance, a wild race through the streets, the alarms honking like geese. Inside the vehicle, alone and finally out of the sun, M. Rambeau had an *aperçu* of what the meal had cost him. Outside, a little like a ceremonial guard on either side, the pigeons flew, banking and rolling in a playful formation.

Judy Lopatin

It was the best of times and it was the worst of times: In the fall of 1986 the Fiction Collective published my first book, and the reviews were good; but I also lost my job (as a legal proofreader) and was threatened with a lawsuit. The claimant, a lawyer who thought he was a character in one of my stories and was thus legally defamed, demanded that the Fiction Collective destroy all copies of my book, the short story collection MODERN RO-MANCES. Luckily, the FC stood by me; we even lined up the law firm of the legendary, and at the time living, trial lawyer Louis Nizer to defend us, *pro bono*, if necessary.

Well, was I guilty? I plead innocent. The story in question, "Our Perfect Partners," is a satire with surreal overtones. The day of my firing was equally surreal: I arrived to find my office all a-jumble. It turned out that Xeroxes of the story had been circulated throughout the firm (so much for inviting paralegals to your book party); that a partners meeting had been convened to discuss my perfidy and my firing (only one nay—what a guy!); that my office had been ransacked for incriminating evidence (and thus it was that, though indemnified, our distributors were too scared to put the book in bookstores at pub date). I also heard about how various females at the firm, who took exception to the (fictional) portrayal of a secretary, wanted to dunk my head in the ladies room toilet; but also, from another secretary, how the story had done some good— that it had opened the eyes of everybody at the firm.

The *New York Law Journal* heard about the flap, and a reporter called me, but I pleaded no comment. Too bad; I might have become famous. In the mid-1980s short story collections were in vogue, and young writers were too; and if a lawsuit had ensued, I probably would have won—probably. When I registered for unemployment, I thought it judicious to leave out the fact that I had just had a book published; and so the counselor looked at the path of my dead-end jobs and concluded, sadly, "There isn't much direction here."

It is only coincidence that I have worked for a legal magazine for more than ten years. But here is the end of this story: The litigation department of the firm convinced the injured party that a lawsuit would not be a good idea; the firm later merged, then dissolved; the man who thought he was Mickey Plotnick is, I believe, flourishing at another firm; and, though for many years I felt a certain chill in the air, I am still writing.

Our Perfect Partners

"KEN GRABBER! Oh, that guy's a nymphomaniac," he said disparagingly. I had never heard a man described as a nymphomaniac before. But semantics could wait. I wanted to know more details. The women he had rushed into bed with, and why. But all Guy could tell me was that Ken Grabber thought about women day and night, and talked about them a good deal too. In fact during any conversation—whether about law or otherwise, for Ken and Guy are both lawyers—Ken Grabber would see fit to introduce the subject of women. Women he had dated and who would not, for the most part, sleep with him. "Oh," I said, "then it doesn't sound as if he really is a nymphomaniac after all." Nymphomaniacs get their man, or in this case, their woman. "And anyway," I corrected Guy, "men can't be nymphomaniacs."

Although oversexed Southerners are not my type, I was secretly disappointed that Ken Grabber had not, so to speak, made a grab for me. But that's a cheap joke. His name is not Grabber any more than mine is. Something completely different. Something that shall remain secret.

The law is an open book, but the workings of a law firm are usually secretive. Prospective employees have to sign a release, before they are hired. A release like a promise, a promise of fidelity and obedience. No private gain to be had from privy knowledge, and so forth. At the root of it all is money,

I guess, but from money and its concerns, morality is made. The secret reason that in our law firm (as in all law firms) liaisons between lawyers and non-lawyers are frowned upon (if not actually outlawed) is that the partners are afraid that some financial secret might be spilled upon the pillow during . . . pillow talk.

Ken Grabber has not, to my knowledge, made a play for any of the non-legal (as they call us, as if we were criminal) personnel at the firm; but he has, reportedly, made certain off-color remarks to a young female lawyer—a good-looker, but a stuffy one, just another in a line of Ken Grabber's non-conquests.

Meanwhile, unbeknownst to most, most certainly to his six children, Mickey Plotnick, boy-wonder partner, trafficker in movie-company deals, lives a secret life. . . .

Sidney, my partner—not a partner in the law firm, but my proofreading partner—dreams of proofreading food. Not surprising, since he likes to eat. In one of his former jobs, he claims, a secret room was filled to the ceiling with Pepperidge Farm cookies. Cookies of all descriptions and nationalities, all produced by Pepperidge Farm, which was this law firm's client. In this Pepperidge Farm paradise Sidney gained ten pounds. But Sidney did not get sweeter. That process is reserved for the coming of maturity, or a really neat blonde girlfriend.

No love is lost between Sidney and the lawyers. Hatred is too strong a word to use. There is just no love lost, no love to be wasted. Everybody minds his own business. Mickey Plotnick, for example, does not waste his time greeting Sidney, nor has he ever so much as inclined his head in greeting to me, though we have passed each other in the halls for a year and a half. In his small hooded eyes I have sometimes detected a gleam of recognition, but perhaps I am mistaken. . . . In any case it is not a benevolent gleam. But Mickey must love some-body, he must love his kids, or why else would he let them run wild in the halls of our office? They are a nuisance to every-body, but Mickey Plotnick loves them.

Mickey Plotnick's office is cluttered with photographs of his six kids. He is a little man, always on the go. You have to be on the go to be in the movie business, however marginally. Mickey Plotnick is only in it marginally; he has something to do with a bank that finances motion pictures, and most of them are not even major—a lot of them are horror flicks. (Production was held up on one movie because the producers could not obtain enough bats.) Nevertheless Mickey Plotnick reaps certain rewards; he gets a lot of tickets to screenings. If the movies are innocent enough, and not too horrific, he lets his six kids come along. Does he ever think that the halls of our office are not innocent enough for his kids to frolic in? Of course not. Ken Grabber sits on another floor, and besides, he is not interested in children.

Sidney likes to reminisce about the law firms he used to work at; he is particularly fond of the place where all the word processors were fat, save one. You would think Sidney might have liked the non-fat one, but no. Sidney likes a certain amount of heft on his women, perhaps so they will not criticize the heft on Sidney. Otherwise, though, he wants a woman who is exactly not like his mother; he wants a Protestant with blonde hair who will find Sidney exotic enough to go to bed with.

Has Ken Grabber gone to bed with Mickey Plotnick's wife? Is Mickey's secret life that of cuckold? That is impossible, just as it is impossible (technically) for Ken Grabber to be a nymphomaniac. *Mickey Plotnick lives a secret life.* That is the premise. That requires an active plot, or at least an active imagination. To be cuckolded is hardly a way of life; it is not a lifestyle, it is nothing to be lived or not lived; it is just a passive state, a non-event, like Ken Grabber's seductions, which do not take place.

Mergers, takeovers, ship bankruptcies: these are the dramas of the law office, maybe not the stuff of life or gossip, but still pretty interesting, to those who know what the secrets are. . . . On the high seas several ships were seized by their creditors. The lawyers searched far and wide to get those ships for their clients. They traveled to distant countries, lay low in foreign ports. In the dead of night they stole aboard the ships while the sailors were sleeping. Sleeping innocently. . . . Or sleeping with each other?

» » »

There is a secret relation between Ed, the supply-room clerk, and Vladimir, the messenger. Of course Ed and Vladimir are not their real names. Would I besmirch the reputations of these young men by my off-color remarks? Yes, but I would not use their real names.

Vladimir is called Vladimir because I believe he, or his recent ancestors, came from a Slavic country. I once heard him speaking a foreign tongue. He is a young man with a bad complexion, but he has his youth, which is saying something, because he works with messengers who have lost their youth, their health, their dignity, and sometimes their sense. One messenger shakes, another loses his way and ends up in Boston when he is supposed to be in Philadelphia. Or is this the same messenger? Vladimir, on the other hand, has a sardonic sense of humor and a facility at two languages, English and whatever the other one is. It is even possible that given these natural advantages he earns a better salary than the other messengers, who are out of the running of life but may have made a good living in the past; Sidney thinks at least three of them may once have owned delis.

And Ed, what about him? Ed is called Ed because he reminds the casual observer of Mr. Ed, the talking horse. He is long and lean, and he leans his long head (a Slavic head) out of the corral, or rather over the demi-door of the supply room. Ed has a sense of humor. He doesn't mind when I walk by humming "A horse is a horse." He also has two kids and a wife, and he is just twenty-two, and he only makes about ten thousand dollars a year, if that much.

But Mr. Ed has just walked off his job. He is no longer with us. And that is how I found out about the secret relation between Ed and Vladimir. Ed is gone but not dead, and I know that because somebody told me that Ed has been seen, alive and well, in Vladimir's apartment building. He's been seen there because he lives there, and he lives there because Vladimir is his brother-in-law, something I never knew until Ed was gone and buried, or rather out to pasture, but if you look in the company phone book you can see the truth, or part of it—no mention of their being brothers-in-law, but they do indeed live at the same number on the same street in the same city. Jersey City, New Jersey.

Ken Grabber will soon be going South to see his family; he is soon to attend his cousin's wedding. What makes Ken dread this normally happy event is that his cousin's wedding happens to be the same day as his fortieth birthday, and he is afraid that all his old aunts will question him about his bachelor status. Ken Grabber perhaps suspects his old aunts of evil thoughts. Little do they know of all the women he has bedded, or at least desired to bed; so perhaps they think he is a bachelor because he prefers the company of men. In some sense they are right. Ken Grabber does not seem very comfortable in the company of women. He is a jokester; one of the secretaries at the firm thinks he is "corny," although Ken no doubt thinks he is a great wit. I can imagine Ken Grabber on a date: he makes jokes all through dinner, he won't shut up during the movie, afterwards he has too much to drink and grabs a knee to test the waters; and then when the evening winds to a close he tries to disarm his date into going to bed with him. He makes a lot of corny/witty jokes and says absurd things just to see where it will lead him, even though he knows quite well where it will lead; by this time his date thinks he is a drunk, silly little boy, not at all suitable for marriage, which is a shame since he earns a decent salary. I could explain all this to Ken Grabber's aunts, but I have not been invited to the wedding— Ken Grabber has not even invited me out for dinner.

Now Ken has left the firm, and so has Guy. They are leaving in droves. Both Ken and Guy plan to do "creative projects"—Ken, for example, wants to take pictures. Guy is going to write books—a common lawyer's secret desire. But not all lawyers actually leave to write them. And if they do leave, the lawyers do not generally leave under a cloud like Mr. Ed did, or like one of our old messengers did, a few months ago, when he disappeared on his way to the bank with $7,000 of company money. It was his job to deposit that money. I presumed the poor old guy dead too until somebody told me he'd been discovered in Las Vegas, gambling the last of his life away and losing it all, the money anyway. He came back to New York and turned himself in. No longer does he live the life of a gambler; it has been decided that he must pay back (to the partners) every last cent of the money he first stole, then lost, even if it takes him the rest of his life, even if the rest of his life isn't long enough. One wonders what will become of his meager estate; will his grandchildren be plunged into debt? But that is a question for our trusts-and-estates department, and of course our ex-messenger could never afford their services, which is a shame, since he will probably die soon and in debt. Guy, on the other hand, has at least thirty good years to go, and he gave a month's notice to the firm, and so everything is, for him, correct and on schedule. The only mystery is, why did our messenger leave for Las Vegas when he had $7,000 in his pocket, and not $20,000, as he'd had in his pocket the week before?

Was it art, or money, or girl trouble, that caused Guy to leave the law firm for greener pastures? But no, the pastures belong to Mr. Ed, not Guy. Guy is now (from nine to five; in the evening he is devoted to his new word processor) in the happy world of advertising. His job is to decide whether or not the ads that the creative people in the agency create will get anybody into trouble. Since Guy never gets into any trouble himself, but wishes he would, this job is a dream come true. Now he can look for trouble, for off-color remarks, under the cover of a respectable well-paying job. Off-color remarks are sometimes okay, of course, in this advertising age, as long as you don't cast aspersions on your competitors, your rivals. . . . It is totally unfair of me to cast aspersions on Mickey Plotnick's wife, who is almost certainly not unfaithful, who hardly exists so far except as the mother of his six children, and who would probably have little time to cuckold Mickey even if she wanted to. (Even *when* she wanted to.) Six children are a handful, especially these particular children. When they are not running around the halls of our office—and to be truthful, that only occurs a few times a year, during school holidays—they must be running around the halls of school, and the halls of the Plotnick house. They must be running rings around Mickey Plotnick's wife. It is not surprising that she looks at Mickey and doesn't really see him, that she is blind to Mickey's secret life.

A secret life demands a plot; but it is going to take a convoluted plot to get Mickey, Guy, Ken, Ed and Vladimir, and Sidney in the same room. It is true that they have all walked the halls of the same building, day after day, but a building is a big place. Our law firm occupies three floors, and even though all but Ken Grabber have worked on the same floor (an amazing coincidence; less amazing when you know that it is also my floor), nobody knows anybody else. Except Ed and Vladimir, of course, who are related by marriage, and Ken and Guy, who are more or less on the same level, if not the same floor (though it seems Guy's knowledge of Ken consists only of his reputation for nymphomania).

Otherwise, it is remarkable how little any of these people have to do with each other. Guy does not remember Ed or Vladimir at all, and though he laughed long and hard at the description of Mickey (and Mickey's annoying kids), he has never worked with Mickey; it is all just a superficial impression. Ed and Vladimir have no doubt heard of Guy, Ken, and Mickey, but in their roles as supply-clerk and messenger, respectively, they have kept their respectful distance. And Mickey, for his part, as partner, is certain to have no clear idea who anybody is. (Not every partner is so undemocratic; one charming old gentleman, who resembles Fred Astaire, tips his hat—so to speak—to all who cross his path.) Of course, Guy, Mr. Ed, and Ken Grabber have all since left the premises, and in their cases Mickey has an excuse—out of sight, out of mind. But there is still Vladimir, and as far as Vladimir goes—well, from all appearances, Vladimir does not exist as far as Mickey is concerned. He is there but not noticed, like the furniture, or the proofreaders, or the pictures of old whaling ships. Get me a messenger! Mickey might command Theresa, his sullen Irish secretary; and it is all the same to Mickey Plotnick whether the messenger is the young wisecracking Vladimir, or one of the old ex-deli-owners.

Still, Mickey is smart; you don't get to be a boy-wonder partner if you're not smart, and maybe Mickey has heard the story of the messenger who ended up in the wrong city; Mickey would not like to entrust his important movie-deal documents to this messenger. If he were smart he would recognize Vladimir and value him for his youth, wit, and energy. But if he were smart would he let his esteem for Vladimir show? Mickey is no Fred Astaire; he does not have the credentials to be charming in that old-fashioned noblesse-oblige way. To impress his elders Mickey has to be a mogul—not a movie mogul, but a legal beagle, sharp and ruthless. He has to make them a lot of money, to prove the gamble they took on him was worth it. He does not want to spend the rest of his life paying them back (like the old messenger has to); a few more years, a few more dollars should do it. Then maybe Mickey will relax enough to reveal his secret. It might be anything his fellow-partners would disapprove of: liaisons with Vladimir, or with Ed, or with Vladimir and Ed and Ed's wife, who is Vladimir's sister; or just with Vladimir's sister, who is Slavic too. Or perhaps the secret is only that Mickey is related, by blood or marriage, to one or more of the old messengers; maybe all of the ex-deli-owners are his uncles. . . .

Whatever Mickey's secret is, Theresa has nothing to do with it. Nobody, in my wildest imagination, could bark out "Theresa!" to his mistress, and no mistress would ever answer back "What?" with such a marked lack of interest. Theresa, Mickey Plotnick's sullen but efficient Irish secretary, does tease him sometimes, she even talks back to him, but she always calls him Mr. Plotnick; she doesn't dare call him Mickey. Theresa strikes me as a girl with no future. I wonder about her sometimes, but not too much.

Theresa, to my knowledge, is unmarried, but she would never consider dating Sidney, Ken, or Guy, those three bachelors on the loose. Sidney is too eccentric, Ken too corny, Guy too broken-hearted. And anyway Theresa's taste probably runs to cops. That is no doubt unfair of me, but since I hardly know Theresa (she is as sullen to me as she is to Mickey), I cannot resist putting her in a category. From all appearances, however, Theresa does not seem to be the perfect partner for any of the bachelors. Sidney would find her blonde enough, and even though she is Catholic he would forgive her (he seems to think only Protestants are cool enough to balance his mania); but in the end Theresa is not Sidney's type any more than Sidney is Theresa's. She would not appreciate Sidney's wit and artistry, at the way he can magically transform himself (during a dull session proofreading a revolving credit agreement) into a canasta-playing matriarch who has decided to leave her husband and her meat loaf and rejoin the working world. Nor could she appreciate Ken Grabber's wit, which revolves around the world of popular music and popular electronics; Theresa likes to discuss pets and needlepoint. Does this make her a perfect partner for a cop? Not at all, no more than it makes her an ideal date for Guy, who, though dull, would secretly think Theresa much duller. He wouldn't take her to a jazz club or out to dinner, but he might put her into his next mystery novel, if it is a police procedural—perhaps as a cop's wife.

Mickey, Ed, Vladimir, et al. . . . Why does Mickey always come first? Is it because his private life (unlike Ed's, or Vladimir's, or Guy's, or Ken's, or Sidney's) is as yet unrevealed, ripe with possibilities, rife with danger and mystery? Is it because Mickey is a partner of the firm and therefore entitled to our respect? Or is it because, speculation about his messenger-uncles notwithstanding, Mickey has no relation to anybody in the office? Sidney, Guy, and Ken Grabber are the three searching bachelors; Ed and Vladimir are brothers-in-law; but Mickey is a loner. None of the other partners are Mickey's pal. Is that because none of them do movie deals, or because Mickey is just too rude? What the other partners think of Mickey is secret; but the bottom line is that Mickey has nobody to chat with at the office, except Theresa, and Mickey can only talk to her in the most mechanical, artificial way. Get me this, get me that, Theresa; it is no wonder that Theresa is sullen. Is he so commanding with his wife? It is hard to imagine Mickey outside the office; he might be a much better person, or he might be much worse. It's a shame that Mrs. Plotnick is not more visible; I have never seen her on the premises of the law firm, ever. I've seen the children, of course, those six pretty brats, but although they do have Mickey's energy, they don't look anything like him. Mickey does have connections in the movie business; maybe he hires child actors to run around at holiday-time, pretending to be his, so that nobody will suspect what a horror Mickey Plotnick really is.

Everybody knows what Ken Grabber is; he is a nymphomaniac, even though technically male nymphomaniacs do not exist. In Guy's imagination (an ordinary-guy imagination) Ken Grabber is a nymphomaniac, and that is the important thing, to Guy at least. But it is also important to know that Guy has a crush on that goodlooking stuffy female lawyer Ken once unwisely made a pass at. To punish Ken Grabber, Guy spread the news far and wide of Ken Grabber's nymphomania, and like most at the law firm I believed the worst; but for some reason the rumor remained a secret to Ken Grabber for quite a while. Maybe nobody at the firm talks to Ken Grabber much. But one night I talked too much. Ken and I accidentally found ourselves at the same non-company party; when I ambled up to him and destroyed his in-progress seduction in an instant ("I hear you're a nymphomaniac, Ken," I said genially), Ken was both surprised and hurt. It was then that I realized that never should you always believe everything you hear.

Ken Grabber was, in fact, so disgruntled with me for destroying his reputation, his pride, and his would-be seduction, that now he will never ask me to dinner. I know this with certainty; nevertheless, the other night I could not help dreaming about him. We were going out to dinner, and despite my fears Ken refrained from making corny jokes; he was a perfectly charming and delightful dinner companion. After dinner, we took in a movie, and though in the dark I rather wished

Ken would steal his arm around my shoulder, schoolboy-style, he didn't; he was a perfect gentleman. Nor did he, during the movie, chatter away; he was so silent I was not the least distracted from my dreams. After the movie, we had a cappuccino in a quaint café (something I had never imagined Ken Grabber doing—another surprise); and then he was about to put me in a cab, when I surprised myself by inviting myself to his apartment—which was, conveniently, located nearby. Ken graciously acquiesced. His apartment was furnished with none of the standard accoutrements of the desperate bachelor; it was instead a tasteful, if somewhat bland, setting, a testimony to Ken's mild and gallant temperament. The man would surely someday make partner. . . . But perhaps that was the foreshadowing of the horror to come. As Ken finally, passionately stole his arm around me (we were sitting on a sofa which might at any moment become a sofa bed), and muffled his mouth into the folds of my neck, I screamed. Ken had disappeared! Or— if I really looked at who was biting my neck—he had suddenly turned into Mickey Plotnick—

But Mickey is not the perfect partner; he is hardly typical. Except for Mickey Plotnick, who is known as one sharp lawyer, and illustrates this with energy and volubility (too much volubility, is the secret opinion of many), our lawyers quietly go about their business. Their progress down our carpeted halls is almost somnambulistic. They are ostensibly in search of something, a document from word-processing or a cup of coffee or a partner, but at all times they are all business. In their hands they carry sheaves of papers, and their eyes study the ceiling, the baseboards, or (in those areas our visitors are most likely to see) our expensive Oriental rugs. (My own office is bare, spare, utilitarian, and hidden in a corner; that is its charm.) Everything else is invisible. The tradition for this well-bred reticence goes back to the nineteenth century, as does our law firm. Along with our pictures of whaling ships, and maps of Olde New York before the firm existed, we have several memorials to well-bred, reticent, well-paid men. On the wall opposite my out-of-the-way office, for example, hangs a row of portraits of famous men. I believe they are all former Supreme Court justices, although one of them is also a former President. It is possible, but not probable, that these dead men were also once exemplary members of the firm.

Since Ken Grabber and Guy have both left us before they became partners, their pictures will never grace the firm's walls; in due time they will be forgotten. But neither of them loses any sleep over this. They plan to become famous, which will insure their immortality (in any case their pictures will appear in the newspaper). In the meantime they might practice a little law, here and there, but . . . it's not as if the law is in their blood. . . .

The law is in Mickey Plotnick's blood, but so are the movies. Is that why Mickey is the way he is, does he live in a dream world? . . . When Mickey was a kid he used to go to matinees; he skipped school and sat in the dark and dreamed. But one day he woke up and began to apply himself. He wanted to make his mother proud. Like Sidney, he loved his mother though he pretended to hate her, and luckily when he looked for a wife he found somebody just like his mother, only blonder and prettier. (That is probably why Mickey's kids are prettier than he is.) He thought he could have his cake and eat it too— but no, I am confusing Mickey with Sidney; Sidney is the one that likes cookies, and cake too—Mickey thought he could *reasonably accommodate* all his dreams at the same time. He could have a woman who was like his mother and yet not like his mother; he could make money and have fun too. He would become an entertainment lawyer! A dream of a job, and dreams on the job too. At least that was what Mickey thought. He didn't know he couldn't just turn down the lights in his office and pretend he was someplace else. He didn't realize that banks would want to finance so many horror movies. His dreams died, and so did Mickey; but nobody noticed, not even Mickey.

The foregoing is the kind of poetic nonsense Guy might write, when he is not trying to make a quick buck writing mystery novels. Police procedurals are not Guy's forte; his last mystery had a faulty plot; Guy is really a poet. It would be just like him to endow Mickey's life with a pathos that does not exist; he would like to think of Mickey as a failed poet, or a failed genius, or at the very least as a failed movie-mogul. Or even, if he stretched his imagination to include the non-pretty in this category, as a failed movie star. But Guy is more interested in the nymphomaniacal Ken Grabber than he is in Mickey Plotnick; his imaginings would not do Mickey justice. Mickey is not a failure at anything; he is too ruthless. And while Mickey is not exactly a movie star, he does have an important role in a movie, and this is part of his secret.

Of course there have been very few clues, up to this point, that would logically lead you to this conclusion. But can you expect clues when a plot does not exist? You can only expect facts. You know that Mickey helps to finance movie deals, horror flicks, and that production on one of these flicks was held up due to a shortage of bats. That might be funny, but it is also serious. Time is money. Money is important. In the end, the flick was finished.

Aha! you might think. Somewhere they came up with more bats. In your imagination you see Mrs. Plotnick. She is the dark horse. Nobody has seen the old bat. She is blind to Mickey's doings, blind as a bat. Mrs. Plotnick is a bat; Mickey's secret is that he is married to a bat.

But your imagination is wrong. Mrs. Plotnick is not a dark horse; she is a red herring. Mickey is the bat. Not only is he a bat; he is a vampire, that species of bat that feeds on the blood of others. Yes, yes, of course, you may be saying; all lawyers are vampires. But not all lawyers snub you in the hall; not all lawyers get parts as extras in Chase Manhattan's latest horror flick. You persist in disbelief: why insist that Mickey Plotnick is a bat, when there is a horror lurking in everything? There is horror in Ken Grabber's nymphomania; there is something horrifying about Sidney's cold-blooded search for a blonde Protestant; there is something horrible about proofreading, and messengering, and advertising, and law, and any number of gainful occupations. And then you might think about Ed and Vladimir, and try to shift the blame onto these two innocents, simply because you recall that they are Slavic, and that in Romania, a semi-Slavic country, there exists a province called Transylvania.

But all this is abstract, poetic thinking. Mickey Plotnick really is a bat; take my word for it, or take a look at him. Those gimlet eyes only really see in the dark. But he's never asleep on the job. When production was held up on the horror flick because the producers were short of bats, Mickey secretly volunteered his services; he arranged that filming of the scene would take place at night, and he duly showed up on the set. He had his moment of glory, or fifteen minutes of fame, if you want to be exact about it—the bats were a fairly important part of the picture. Mickey was too modest to dream of stardom (Guy would say); he never thought he might someday be a character in a story; so he just played himself, in the movies, and got paid handsomely for it.

Mickey's out for blood, but what of it? Sidney likes cookies, and Ken Grabber drinks too much, and for all we know Mr. Ed is a horse addict. All of these are lonely occupations. But Mickey—dead if not buried, bereft of the imaginary Mrs. Plotnick and the sham children—Mickey is always in search of his perfect partner. His energy, his power depend on it; so does any remaining resemblance to the boy he once was. . . . For all we know Mickey might like the blood of a poet, or a nymphomaniac, or an innocent. Guy and Ken Grabber think they have escaped in time, but bats can easily fly from building to building. . . . Mickey's secret life is a nocturnal one; you never know whom he might visit, while they are sleeping, innocently. It is a nocturnal life, and therefore illogical; you never know when Mickey might wake up and see something, or someone, he's never really seen before; you never know when he might realize how much he desires the life of that stranger; you never know what secrets, or tears, might be spilled upon the pillow, along with a certain necessary amount of blood.

Clarence Major

Emergency Exit is a book about language and the imagination. I think of it as a prose poem. I had a lot of fun writing *Emergency Exit*. Looking at it today, I see that it is still ambitious and playful looking.

But how much fun readers have with it, I can't say. I knew a few critics who loved it at one time. But time changes us all.

The Fiction Collective was probably the only publisher in America that would have published *Emergency Exit* in 1979. Therefore, I was grateful for the presence of the Collective.

This is an excellent selection from the book because it gives an overview, and a sense of the way it's made.

Scattered thoughts about the rest of the book:

On page 11 there is a photograph of myself in a ditch with a bunch of cows at the fence. They thought I was the man coming to feed them.

On page 23, an abstract painting that says everything is composition.

On page 49 Edvard Munch speaks to me in the form of a sickroom. I understood. My own grandfather was my first death—and it was a big death. It filled up my life that year at age six. This was about that.

Page 76, Inez, sitting, leaning forward. Serious readers will understand when Inez has more to say.

Page 86: a passion for gambling—card players. That was about Richard and his sickness. This too will be understood.

Page 216 is a reminder that it is all about fear and desire and trying to keep the balance, to sleep through it, waking up refreshed.

Page 232 represents the end of a nightmare, and it points toward the end of the book, "In a small house in the countryside the author was dying at an early age then he recovered and nobody knew why or how."

Happy reading!

from *Emergency Exit*

Night life in Inlet is for the birds topless joints and that's it what else can I tell you chicks hang out in doorways. Then when you are not looking for that, when you're not vulgar, the museum is closed. They lock the doors and throw parties for bigshots.

Men with their hair cut short fall drunk in chairs without bottoms. This happens a lot at Ned's Eatery. Ned is dead his son makes hamburgers and frenchfries and malts with a knife lying alongside the cashbox.

The Salvation Army woman keeps singing all these silly songs in my ear then retreating to the safety of her windswept doorway.

"Flashes of people—not even *real* people," he said, "responding to a complex situation where a certain motif is persistent . . ."

I went under the bridge Jim walked across it. This *can* go on.

Following the prayer there was a news show. The screen closed out everything else happening in the world.

I wash my clothes and water the plants. The Holy Ghost lives next door. Down the hall the Threshold Law writer has a secret apartment where he brings his mistresses. He's married to a fat woman way across town who is good to him. She reads him the Letters of Paul. They open doors in his head. But the Good Samaritan opens *her* eyes!

The word spreads. In Darien and Bridgeport in Canaan Woodbury Stamford Monroe Fairfield the word spreads fast: the trains are late: in Silver Spring there are no trains. There are shopping centers full of places with glass doors you can see through glass doors. The Circumcision of The Gentiles took place yesterday in the doorway of a shop in the shopping center across the street. The Whore of Babylon slept next door. The trumpets of doom are heard constantly down the hall. Doors closed or not.

The killer slept in the sauna waiting for Deborah to arrive. Roaches crawled into his mouth.

The Ingram family is exploring the mountains nearby. Camping equipment attached to their backs. Clouds move swiftly overhead.

During the summer I see from the streets of inlet people in windows looking down on other people. Boys sitting in doorways. In one window only the tip of a face. An elbow. An arm. A leg. A small portion of somebody's back.

Small raggedy Indian children are chasing Barry Sands on the beach. They're barefoot it's fun. Barry drunk stumbles and falls and rolls in the sand laughing. The kids climb on his chest and walk up and down. They can't stop giggling they stuff shells and pebbles into his mouth. Seaweeds sprout from his ears.

Julie is speeding along an isolated country road in a light blue Dodge, current model. Pavement hot grey. I'm watching her. Trees grass bushes a thick dark green splash of earth on the far side. She is going upstate to . . . at the gas station she stops, asks the attendant, how do you . . .

Robot Repair Shops, Inc., have sprung up all over Inlet. A chain of them owned by two brothers who live in Florida. Business is fantastic robots break down more often than cars.

As though driven by a state of madness Barry is making a list of words starting with the letter Z: Zombie Zlokobinca Zen Zener Zendavesta Zozo Zlito Zabulon Zapan Zardust Zlata Zeus Zohar Zollncr Zoether Zodiac Zugen Zwaan Zuccarini Zola and Zekerboni. He yawns as he loses interest in the Z's. He falls asleep there on his couch. Julie appears in his sleep. She speaks: Through the Z you have connected to the underworld of the snake. And since I am a creature of the water and the sky you have greatly reduced your chances of possessing me. Too bad for you sucker!

Fiction Collective Two

Jeffrey DeShell

I've been trying to remember some clever anecdote about my life with the Fiction Collective for some time now, and I really can't come up with much. I never lunched with Marianne Hauser at Gundel, nor played catch with Steve Katz in Prague, nor got drunk with Mark Leyner in Soho, although I would certainly love to do all of these things. I do recall having big fun with Cris Mazza and then later Cris and Elisabeth Sheffield when we edited our anthologies, but I'm not sure how interesting that would be to anyone else. When the Congressional flap about the anthologies and *S & M* broke, I was out of the country, so I can't even talk about that. The experiences I do remember, the experiences that have stayed with me and become part of me, are the experiences of reading the books. Brilliant books, important books, books like *98.6*, *The Talking Room*, *Matinee*, *From the District File*, *The Alphabet Man*, *Double or Nothing*, *Straight Outta Compton*, *F/32* etc., books that wouldn't have been published, that WOULD NOT BE AVAILABLE, if not for the Fiction Collective. It's not been easy: like any collective, we don't always agree (a collective of writers is a

contradiction in terms), but some way, somehow, the books appear in print (and sometimes
you can even spot one in a bookstore). This
writing, this literature, part of which you now
hold in your hands, *this* is our legacy. I'm
proud to be a part of it.

from *S&M*

It was certainly afternoon early or late it was hard to say the curtains were partially open but the light was grey indeterminate they both had been trying to catch their breaths for some time and were just now settling into some regular respiratory rhythm the air was sweet and thick Chandler lay on her side her arms bunched up under one of the pillows S— nestled her face in the nape of Chandler's neck one hand lazily splayed just beneath Chandler's navel fingers entangling with the sparse pubic hair the other absentmindedly scratching her own now dried hip while her breathing and heartbeat were beginning to calm her mind was racing between recently acquired memories of tastes smells caresses sounds etcetera and questions fears and anxieties about what all those sensations might signify.

In her more her more what upbeat hopeful optimistic sane those words no longer had the same meaning those words no longer meant what they did before she and Chandler had made love those words had been contaminated by too real kisses had been polluted by genuine whispers each of those formerly positive words was now infected by a virus of fear because whatever could be actually experienced could also be truly lost but anyway in the best of those impure tainted corrupt positive upbeat hopeful moments S— almost felt like she could lie with Chandler forever their breaths smells juices and even skin all mixing and blending together combining to form some as yet unnamed substance some secret material it was as if they had discovered a strange new element by a curious alchemical experiment mysterious even to them she felt Chandler's warm ass press closer against her belly and she responded by immersing her face deeper in Chandler's neck and hair.

What was she doing what the fuck was she doing it was much too soon to think about what this new thing might be or what it should be named it was much too soon to think about any of that this would be over quickly enough as it was S— could feel a slight chill on her back and ass that she hadn't noticed before soon she would have to move get under the covers or change positions and perhaps the spell would be broken perhaps the magic would disappear that was the trouble with magic either it was over much too quickly poof gone before you got a good look at it before you knew what was happening or else it overstayed its welcome becoming worse than banal rotting in the refrigerator like some once wonderful dessert she closed her eyes and began to gently suck the skin that covered one of the knobs of bone on Chandler's spine determined not to think yet about what any of this meant.

That was what sex was for shutting down the mind escaping memories making any future other than the next orgasm irrelevant but nobody could fuck forever S— wondered why she felt so cynical and so sad the silence was beginning to bother her she wondered what Chandler was thinking feeling whatever she who was used to silence who cultivated quiet who thrived in it was now beginning to get spooked by it What are you thinking she asked Chandler who began to speak in an unusually throaty voice It's amazing isn't it how different it is between two women than between a man and a woman there's really no comparison not that one is necessarily better than the other but having sex with a man and having sex with a woman seem almost like two totally separate gestures don't they I mean other than the geography you might say they really don't seem to have much in common some of the sensations are the same and some of the actions and reactions too but they don't seem to belong to the same universe do they that was really nice what we were doing really gentle and wonderful and it can be gentle and wonderful with men too but it's a different kind of gentle as well as a different kind of wonderful I don't know I'm not making much sense S— was surprised Chandler had proven herself no novice at either evoking or experiencing feminine pleasure she wasn't nearly as awkward in bed as she seemed in real life so what was she doing now why was she playing this naive innocent role and for whom or was it in fact a role at all sometimes habits were difficult to break especially sexual habits perhaps she wasn't as comfortable with this as she had seemed perhaps it wasn't a part she was used to assuming S— had made love with enough neophytes to know that many of them needed to talk about it afterwards sometimes to be reassured that it was okay sometimes to explain their motivations and attractions and sometimes to surround what they had done with words to attempt to verbally strip the strangeness the novelty off of what could be a rather overwhelming and possibly disturbing experience she liked that about new women liked the way most of them enjoyed talking after fucking.

S— remembered something Steph used to say about men used to call them all surfers when asked to explain she replied simply that men were superficial S— whispered into Chandler's ear I think men are something like surfers Chandler laughed Surfers why Because their rhythms are so quick and so light they can only ride on the surface each wave a separate entity men have no concept of the big picture it's not totally their fault it has to do with their physiology but they're so goddam linear they're always moving towards some goal always riding that wave in to shore Awesome dude S— laughing continued Women are more spatial we're more like divers exploring something we know quite well she moved her right index finger down to the top of Chandler's labia with men it seems like they always only skimmed my surface even when their cocks were inside of me she inserted her finger into Chandler's wetness Chandler's body stiffened ever so slightly they were still somehow on the outside do you know what I mean she withdrew her finger completely with women on the other hand I always feel as if my body is being reminded of something my mind had forgotten long ago she began to caress the fold of skin directly above Chandler's clit something important my own mortality perhaps whereas with men even men I've been quite fond of loved even I've always felt this tremendous gap separating us an abyss that only seemed to grow larger once we were in bed until the distance became so great we were finally indifferent to it she could feel Chandler's breathing begin to quicken and her muscles tensing then relaxing I never felt closer to any man after fucking him it just made me feel really alienated I think it's because our rhythms are so different men have the predictable rhythms of life in them she began to fingerfuck Chandler with two fingers they're born they work they come they shrink up and then they die but women we have the primordial rhythms of death in us she folded her thrusting fingers and ever so gently rubbed the hood covering Chandler's clit with the tip of her index finger much more ancient much more difficult to figure and impossible to compare it's like the difference between a stopwatch and a sundial Chandler made a noise that was half giggle and half moan then S— began to lick the back of Chandler's neck.

Chandler took S—'s wrist and removed her hand from her crotch S— felt slightly rebuffed then turned to face her her eyes were incredibly erotic jesus christ S— had to look away continued talking into the pillow it's like those art projects we did in grade school S— thought of that smell of wet paper towels in the bathroom of the museum where they had first met you know when you would get a sheet of paper and stretch it over a coin or some other relatively flat object like a bracelet or a key and then with your pencil you would rub the lead over the object until you could see it come into relief it was almost magic I would close my eyes and try to get one of my friends to put something secret under my paper so when I rubbed it with my pencil I would be surprised I loved that I loved the way it seemed like we were making something appear out of thin air when in reality we were only showing what was there underneath the paper the whole time when we made love just now it felt like we were unveiling something that was already there it's sort of a stupid metaphor but that's what it felt like to me I see what you mean Chandler replied with women there's this sort of unspoken patience we start from the same place and so we're in no hurry to get anywhere because there's really no place else to go S——'s heart fluttered a bit that was very well put there was really no place else to go she dropped her head and searched out Chandler's right nipple with her mouth But by staying here we've already begun to leave she almost said but caught herself now wasn't the time to be sad this still wasn't tragic not yet if there was going to be a time for pain and hurt and S—— couldn't help herself she thought that the pain and hurt phase was inevitable then it would surely come at its own pace its own rhythm there was no need to rush it would come much too soon as it was S—— wondered if she were the only person in the world who had to remember to enjoy what she desired probably not.

Although her earlier self consciousness had to a large extent evaporated into the dense air of the bedroom the fear was never far away although she was now convinced that Chandler was at least somewhat interested in her she had no idea of knowing exactly what kind of interest it was or just how far it extended mysteries once solved immediately replaced by others they lay there quietly for a few moments S—— kissing and sucking Chandler's left nipple until Chandler moved back and elevated herself on her left elbow I want to look at you she said S—— smiled she was happy dropped her eyes and leaned forward to kiss Chandler's neck but Chandler's slight motion of retreat froze her forward momentum and deflected it into the opposite direction so that she stretched yawned and turned over on her back again S—— felt slightly rebuked but this was okay this was okay maybe this explained why Chandler always appeared so stiff and awkward maybe it was a reaction to her own forward curves that was okay she could be cool too while keeping her shoulders flat and horizontal on the bed she turned her neck and head to look at Chandler who was staring down at the interval of bed between them S—— thought back to her first boyfuck a mercifully quick moment in someone's car with a pimply faced thing who smelled of beer cigarettes and Brut for men what was his name she couldn't remember she did recall that she was terribly disappointed and that it hurt quite a bit she decided to ask Chandler about her own first experience she raised up on her right elbow Do you remember the first time you did it Chandler looked up You know its funny but only sort of I do remember these incredibly intricate fantasies I constructed around this guy who played sports I even forget his name now anyway I used to spend hours daydreaming about fucking him in his car on the football field on the high-jump mat at school in my parents bedroom on the couch downstairs I read a lot so I sort of knew what it might be like and we did go out a couple of times but to tell you the truth I'm not quite sure either that I really fucked him or that he was the first but for some reason he is the one that I always remember.

Chandler stared down at the bed between them and began to draw circles on the sheet with her forefinger S— looked at Chandler then at the ceiling she was curious about Chandler's previous experiences with women but that question might be a bit too intimate for this first encounter S— remembered how incredibly strange yet extraordinarily natural it felt when she first kissed and then made love to another woman she knew that it wasn't the same for everyone for some there were boundaries to cross for others no boundaries at all she wanted to know if there were boundaries for Chandler and how and when she had crossed them and she wanted to keep the conversation going she wanted to keep Chandler in bed with her for as long as possible she hesitated and remained silent her eyes following Chandler's fingernail as she outlined circles on the sheet. She looked at Chandler's face and figure her posture made it seem as if she was poised over the edge of something suspended between two different extremes for some reason this made her suddenly think of Steph crying on this same bed after a horrible fight S— had brought her a glass of water set it on the floor and quickly left the room went to a movie the first one she had come to she had never forgotten the echo of those sobs as she walked down the hall and out the door but what had made her think of that now and why was she so eager to risk hearing those echoes again maybe it was the light it was funny wasn't it the one thing that could help her forget what she had just been through was the one thing that created possibilities of repetition once again S— felt acutely afraid of her own desires Chandler stopped her finger movements and smiled cheerfully almost teasingly at her as if she were mocking that fear You look like you want to say something S— smiled back she did want to say something she wanted to say two things at once do you like me and please leave but the words that came out were When did you first sleep with a woman.

Oh jeez it's a long story are you sure you want to hear it Of course Chandler rotated her shoulder towards S— to lie on her stomach her hands and arms at her sides S— resisted caressing her back for a few moments but then couldn't help herself she gently ran the palm of her right hand up over Chandler's shoulder blades and upper spine to her neck then down her spine to her lower back then back up again she could feel her diaphragm vibrate through her back as she spoke I remember that in high school all of the boys intimidated me really scared the hell out of me like most other girls I hung out with I didn't have much self esteem back then I was so sure that none of those boys would have me I didn't want to take any chances of wanting them and then having them reject me so every night before I went out I used to masturbate to take care of myself that way I wouldn't let what my need want lust or whatever it was show I didn't know much about girls back then when I was growing up I had this hazy notion that lesbians were all old and ugly and that they slept together only because no men would have them I figured I was in enough danger of that as it was but anyway in high school I was my own lover because I didn't think anyone else wanted me.

But at college things changed male sexuality became less mysterious to me and therefore less desirable What college did you go to I went to Bennington my first years at Bennington I still masturbated all the time but in college it was for a different reason it was because I couldn't stand any of the boys there they were all so goofy so silly and pretentious it was easy enough to be radical and punk with daddy's gold card I was still really horny but my lust wasn't directed at anyone in particular it was sort of a generalized desire maybe my standards were too high but after a while the thought of fucking another one of those stuck up pomo boho artfags really turned my stomach anyway like I said before I still masturbated constantly two or three times a day sometimes but then it was for a much different reason then it was so that I wouldn't be tempted to get involved with any of those assholes looking back on it I guess it was something like self defense but it was funny the less interested I became in them the more interested they became in me after a while they wouldn't leave me alone after I stopped fucking my social life skyrocketed I used to go out with a few of them I remember many times lying on my bed trying desperately to get myself off before one of them would come to take me to some stupid performance art piece video show or concert I went everywhere wet spent and probably reeking of my own come I'm not sure what that all means except that I learned not to depend on men for anything I guess I was lucky it's not that I hate men quite the contrary I just have never needed them and that has always felt good.

I used to be really cruel to some of them I was sort of cranky for a while so I used to experiment I would try to see just how unattractive or rude I could be and still have them want me I began by not returning phone calls which quickly progressed into making plans then not showing up but that got boring too so I decided to take a more active approach sometimes I would wear the stupidest musty old bag lady polyester clothes to a formal evening I remember once at this fancy wedding reception Chandler began to giggle I left a small piece of cake smeared on my face for the entire night just to see when and if someone would mention it when one of the guests did say something I would smile and say Yes I know this one guy was really persistent so I rewarded him by having the worse possible breath and body odor every time he came to pick me up I wouldn't brush my teeth or take a shower that morning and then I'd eat some onion and garlic right before he arrived it's amazing how free you can be when you don't want to fuck How long did you carry on so Only until the end of my sophomore year I guess all that masturbating made me a little crazy for a while.

Well anyway to get to the point that spring break some girl-friends and I went to New York we stayed at one of my friend's parents' apartment on the lower east side one night we went to this women's bar The Lavender Door it was fabulous dark seedy slightly dangerous and so elegant and erotic I had never seen anything as beautiful as those women in there dressed in breath-taking gowns dancing cheek to cheek with other women some in competing dresses and others in expensive men's suits hair cropped or slicked back one even had a little moustachio pen-cilled in on her upper lip it was so wonderful and literary I felt like I was in Paris in the twenties I felt adventuresome that night felt like trying something new I suddenly wondered what it would feel like to dance with one of those women to touch a sophisticated shoulder to feel the heat of a cultured thigh through the sequins and silk there was this one woman stand-ing alone by the bar jesus how cliché this is sounds like a Play-boy fantasy she was about my height but skinnier long linen cigarette pants matching jacket black silk blouse I was a little drunk a little scared too but I thought what's the big deal I'm just going to ask her to dance women do that all the time dance with each other it's nothing so I asked her to dance and she says yes and we're dancing close and she's very pretty has these terrific green eyes we dance a little more have a little more to drink she kisses me on the cheek and caresses my back again this is nothing we're just being friendly I can stop go back to my table anytime I still haven't done anything not really I'm still in control and then she kisses me on the mouth I let her I mean I wanted her to kiss me I was very attracted to her it was a nice kiss but again I'm thinking this is no big deal so we kissed so I tasted another woman's tongue and lips this doesn't mean anything by now I'm pretty excited by the nov-elty and the transgression kissing a woman represented to me my friends are watching and I'm thinking to myself when will I actually be bisexual at what moment will my identity change from hetero to bi women can dance together they can caress one another they can even kiss no big deal it's really nothing so at what exact point will I have crossed that line and do I want to cross that line do I want to have sex with this woman do I want to acquire a new identity so she asked me to go home with her just for a nightcap I hesitated but finally agreed told my friends I would see them tomorrow and I'm thinking now even though I'm going home with a woman I picked up in a bar and my friends know it I still haven't done anything I can still back off at any time I'm getting closer to that line but I haven't yet done anything irrevocable we make out a little in the cab and we get to her loft she did have a nice place Sydney was her name and we're kissing and stuff and I'm still thinking I can stop this I am in control she took her clothes off and I'm kissing her breasts and nipples thinking two things so this is what sucking a woman's nipples is like no wonder men enjoy it so much and again this is nothing I can leave at any time this is just an experiment even with her tongue inside of me I still thought I could stop get up put my clothes back on and walk away I said to myself you haven't come yet so this is still nothing it wasn't until just after I came that I thought okay this is what you did you have had a lesbian experience you have crossed the line and I guess it did change me in some way anyway I lived with her the following summer and then in the fall I went back to school met a man and never saw Sydney again.

S— shuddered slightly she was beginning to get chilled and Chandler's story sounded like a warning a warning S— knew she wouldn't heed Chandler turned on her side her back toward S— with her ass and feet against S—'s hip and calf she turned and pressed her body against Chandler's this was too weird too much too soon she needed to detach to back off relax instead she buried her face even deeper into Chandler's hair and neck as if she could be safe there safe from what she wasn't sure she closed her eyes and tried to breathe Chandler into her lungs Chandler said something she couldn't understand What I asked about you what was your first sexual experience Male or female Female even though Chandler couldn't see her S— inadvertently frowned to make her response more heartfelt more weighty and profound It wasn't nearly as romantic as yours it was my first year of college and I had a boyfriend mostly because everyone else did he was someone to do things with I was really angry with him one night for some reason I don't even remember why I went to this party I didn't know anyone there but this guy started talking to me about photography turned out we were in the same studio or something he was a painter anyway so I'm lonely and still grouchy and this guy starts coming on to me he was gorgeous but I'm not sure if I'm interested because I'm mad at my boyfriend or if I'm genuinely attracted to this guy anyway he asks if I want to go smoke with him upstairs and I guess I was still pretty pissed so I said sure so we go upstairs to smoke this joint and this girl follows us I thought she was a friend of his or something and I think it's probably a good thing she's here because now he won't try to put the moves on me or anything like that anyway we're smoking this joint the three of us and I finally get a good look at her she's pretty in an athletic way looks like a runner or something long blonde hair rather nordic with ruddy skin so we're sitting around smoking and all of a sudden he starts kissing her and they start making out on the bed on top of the coats fuck this I think I'm getting out of here but as I get up to leave the girl springs up apologizes and asks if I'd like to go to their apartment for some more smoke music and to look at some portrait paintings this guy her boyfriend had done yeah right I think I may be a freshman but I'm not stupid so I shake my head maybe some other time but then this girl Sara was her name kisses me on the cheek and then begins to pout pouts can go right through me you have a nice pout too and I was a little high from that jay so ok let's go.

We went to their place drank a few beers smoked some more dope and listened to music then looked at his pictures he had about eight or nine full-size canvasses of Sara he told me he never painted anything else anyway the paintings were okay not great sort of impressionistic a lot of dark blues reds and browns but then he showed me a work in progress the portrait was nothing special but he was working from these wonderful fifteen by fifteen black and white nude photographs Sara was gorgeous without her clothes there were four or five of them and I think I embarrassed him by being much more interested in the photos than his paintings I stared at them for a while I wasn't looking at the pictures I was looking at her S— giggled they made me really aroused almost weak in the knees this had never happened to me before or at least never so dramatically after looking at these prints I wanted to fuck her so badly I could hardly speak I finally managed to tell her that she photographed extremely well and that I would love to have her pose for me sometime to which she replied by removing her shirt and kissing me hard on the mouth I'll never forget that kiss it was as if a whole new exquisite world had opened up it was so natural so perfect the perfection of it makes it hard for me to put into words I remember wondering what had taken me so long we all went to the bedroom and the difference between Sara and her boyfriend was absolutely amazing to say the least it was like night and day after we made him come it didn't take very long we asked him to leave I guess that was rather mean of us but he just didn't fit.

The quiet soon enveloped them fixed suspended them S— stared at a mole on Chandler's upper spine what is she thinking what does she think of my story after some time Chandler sat up drew a sheet around her and leaned back against the wall Can I see some of your work S— looked up swallowed hesitated the only prints at the apartment were the pictures of Steph buried away in her closet she didn't know how eager she was either to look at them or to have Chandler see them she could easily lie tell her she didn't keep anything at home it was all in her studio at work but for some reason maybe it was the sex or the stories they had just told or something but she nodded climbed out of bed removed the two gray portfolios from the closet and placed them almost like an offering on a pillow in front of Chandler's lap.

These are mostly of Steph she explained as she sat down against the wall next to her and I haven't looked at them for awhile If you don't want to show me that's okay No I think these pictures are good and I would like you to see them I guess I'm just not sure how I'm going to react that's all S— can I ask you a favor before we start Chandler looked directly into her eyes S— nodded I don't want you to ever photograph me okay Why not are you a criminal Chandler laughed No nothing like that I just don't like to be photographed that's all will you promise me I don't see what the big deal is it's not like you're ugly or anything I bet you're quite photogenic It's not that it's not that at all but please promise me that you never will take my picture okay Okay if it means that much to you S— added a jesus christ under her breath It does mean that much to me they sat on the bed for a moment neither moving until Chandler said Let's look at the pictures when she opened the first portfolio a couple of postcards from hell fell out they looked at them on the bed why did she want to do this why did she want to put herself through this maybe to see if she was over Steph she would never be over Steph or maybe to prove to herself and to Chandler how strong she was but she didn't feel particularly strong at the moment I forgot about these What are they Postcards from hell Steph sent them to me after she left S— stared at the postcards Chandler looked at S— until she gathered them up and reached over Chandler and placed them in the drawer in her nightstand then sat back down on the bed Chandler opened the portfolio and removed a print S— winced internally there she was black and white sitting at some bar an old shot taken when they first started going out not one of either model's or photographer's best she had really hoped the first picture they saw would have been in color color was less real to her somehow black and white was more painful closer to her memories more mythic perhaps Canon F-1 50 mm lens Kodak Tri-x 400 ASA Steph staring straight at the camera a beer bottle in her right hand her chin resting in her left elbow on the table the bar and the backs of two men in the background she didn't want to look at Steph's face which was framed a bit to the right of center her eyes were wide open her hair was wild and there was something in her frown that made her look drunk and lascivious whorish almost no that wasn't it S— swallowed hard noticed Chandler move her gaze from the picture up to S—'s face then back to the picture she looked frightened that was it scared just like S— was now christ this wasn't easy Chandler brought out another print one of the nudes she had done in the studio she winced again That's beautiful said Chandler fuck it who did she think she was she couldn't do this she wasn't that strong she sat up and swung her feet and legs off of the bed her back toward Chandler What's wrong I can't look at these right now you can look at them by yourself if you want to Are you okay I'm fine it's just too early to look at her again that's all I'm sorry I shouldn't have insisted after a while S— felt Chandler's arms encircle her shoulders and her fingers stroke her hair it felt very nice they sat there for few moments like that then S— suddenly felt very tired she got up to splash some cold water on her face and get ready for a nap when she returned from the bathroom Chandler was lying on the bed surrounded by a gallery of black and white photographs of Steph.

R. M. Berry

The novel *Leonardo's Horse* tries to answer the question, why is anything art? It approaches that question from two directions, one in which art's power is revealed but no one seems to care, another in which everyone seems to care but art's power is suppressed. In both cases I'm seeking an answer of more than merely theoretical interest. I want to know what draws anyone, Leonardo da Vinci or a semi-literate redneck, to art in the first place. What I'm after is self-knowledge.

Francesco Melzi wasn't part of my original design. I discovered him while researching the novel and got interested in him because he didn't fit. As the scion of an aristocratic family, he had nothing to gain and a good deal to lose by associating with an artist. Moreover, there's little evidence that he was either very talented or devoted. So for me he came to represent a test case. If I could imagine how Melzi became involved with Leonardo's art, then I could imagine how anyone could become involved.

"In Which Francesco Melzi Discovers Fiction" occurs in the novel just after the dying Leonardo stages his "last dimostrazione," a kind of mad psychology experiment. The experiment leaves two characters, Leonardo's assistant Battista de Vilanis, and his servant, Mathurine, lying unconscious on the floor. Melzi, who has witnessed it all, comprehends nothing.

This excerpt originally appeared in *Apalachee Quarterly* and received "special mention" from the 1991-1992 Pushcart Prize.

In Which Francesco Melzi
Discovers Fiction

Francesco Melzi is still standing at the foot of Leonardo's bed where amid prone bodies and a profusion of paper lilies we abandoned him two minutes and countless digressions ago. A washbasin rests on the floor beside his slipper. In it floats a kidney bean. He's been sufficiently impressed by the madness he's witnessed—the proliferation of color, the tiny military engines, all the shouts and banging—to recognize the last dimostrazione as Leonardo's doing, but he has no earthly idea what he was supposed to have seen. Worse still, he suspects that whatever it was, it had to do with whatever Battista was privy to during the night Melzi passed against the studio door-jamb scrunched up muddy and wet from trouncing through the marsh northwest of town escaping the brigands who attacked him on his way back from the hovel of Hadjani, the infidel alchemist, who in addition to smelling to high heaven of tumeric and crawling with purple vermin the likes of which Melzi has never before seen in his life, also drove a damn hard bargain—a fine gold earring with the Melzi family imprint on it for a pouch of dirt Leonardo never even used!—still dripping mud and swampwater from this adventure, shivering in the cool night air, listening to the clatter within the studio and waiting resolutely for nothing more glorious than a task. Melzi's always known Leonardo was beyond him, but the degree of his own inconsequence just now assails him like a mosquito.

To have been born with neither facility nor prowess is very vile, but it's altogether intolerable to be stuck with an imagination.

Of course, Melzi has been given a task. Fate and Leonardo's last will and testament have selected him to carry the 6,000 plus pages of all the Maestro meant to accomplish—as well as a suitably dignified narration of his demise—back across the Alps to Milan where what currently passes for civilization awaits it. Although the task doesn't require heroics, Melzi expects to fail. King François Premier, who brought Leonardo here in the first place, is no fool. He has already claimed the *Gioconda*, the *St. Anne*, and the really disgraceful *St. John*, and Melzi figures he'll confiscate the manuscripts as soon as the body's cold. Will schmill. And as if this weren't enough, Leonardo's taking so long to die—displaying ever more convincing evidence of senility along with an astonishing repertory of physiological indignities—that Melzi's begun to wonder if the one scene he's going to get to narrate will turn out to be a farce. All in all, his present predicament resembles the sort he's been mired in his whole life, and he longs for newness with the sharpness of a puncture wound. Every step he's ever taken has been slightly awry, and now he suspects this will always be the case, that nothing he learns will make any difference. It's not really his fault, of course, anymore than plague or drought is. Still, they kill you.

Watching the kidney bean wriggle toward the basin's lip, Melzi decides that his disappointments began with the Margrave of Tarvisio, Paolo Zanetta di Cristoforo da Sestri, count of Tyrolo, Bressanone, and God-knows-where-all, widely known as the Sky. About the time he was first becoming acquainted with Leonardo, while still only a boy, Francesco got himself embroiled in an affair of honor with a lord thirty years his senior and no inconsiderable figure. How exactly it happened no one at the time could say, but there had been slights, words, clumsy jostling, two slaps, someone's cup of punch splashed on a doublet and, of course, a lady—Francesco's youthful aunt whose commonplace flirtations he'd misinterpreted much as the Margrave had misinterpreted the skinny, whiskerless fellow standing at her elbow. It would later be rumored—as partial excuse for the unseemly mismatch—that the Sky was in truth a cast-off son of a disgraced doge's younger brother, no margrave, hardly even a count, possibly a merchant, ill-bred, bumptious, left-handed, certainly the pox-infested diddler of all things concave—but no matter, for when startled into overhastily challenging the lady's young escort who, he soon learned, was a *young* escort indeed, the Margrave was still much favored by the Castello demi-monde, widely sought for masques and cicirlanda, and very nearly the latest rage. All agreed that for the fifteen-year-old Francesco it was a marvelous opportunity.

No sooner had the two antagonists spun on their heels than the Melzi cousins, Amalfi, Andrea, Arturo, were proclaiming Francesco's prodigious manhood in the Piazza del Duomo. In her parlor Francesco's mother wrung her hands over the slovenly points of her son's dueling hose and declared to Eleanor da Sanseverino that the condescension had been entirely on the Melzi's part. In the Giardini Pubblici Francesco's youthful aunt was overheard sighing into her handkerchief that, yes, it was fine to be fought over but what a pity no one played the lute. Only Francesco's father seemed sensible of any danger. Throughout the afternoon he fretted in his library, terrified that the Margrave, having contracted a match so far beneath himself, would call upon the French regent to intervene and force a retraction, or worse, would simply disdain to acknowledge Francesco's rights in the affair, would dispatch his man— or ghastly thought! a mere hireling—to declare his scorn for the boy's insolence and refuse him satisfaction. What everyone in the Villa Melzi was celebrating as a coup might result in their family's humiliation! But to his unspeakable relief when the awaited message arrived it was delivered by the Margrave's amanuensis and personal companion, a comely youth widely rumored to be the Margrave's bastard-bloodkin in the maternal line, and joy of joys, rather than renege, the Margrave announced himself eager for the meeting. Never had a family's hopes for its son been confirmed so early! Paolo Zanetta di Cristoforo da Sestri, Margrave of Tarvisio, count of Tyrolo and Bressanone, popularly called the Sky, had recognized

Francesco as his rival. Between the boy and glory only gangrene stood in the way.

The appointed morning arrived slowly. The Melzi family were unprepared for so spectacular an undertaking in their son's youth and so had to barter some of Francesco's strategic advantages—choice of weapons, ground, hour, number of passes, etc.—to gain additional time. An entire wardrobe of figured nether socks, brocade jerkins, short-capes, doublets, and clasps had to be ordered for Francesco, for Amalfi his second, for their three attendants, half a dozen witnesses and all those family members who considered themselves personally implicated. Who could have anticipated that a still-growing boy might have to intimidate a middle-aged lord with the cut of his waistcoat or that such an honor would arrive so unexpectedly? As the days passed, negotiations turned subtle. The Margrave insisted on a specific vintage of Spanish sherry to be served between passes; Francesco's mother finagled for the angle of sunlight on her son's fil d'or; both sides had an opinion about the aunt's missal, motto and veil. There were officials to bribe, of course—dueling being strictly illegal— and a host of Melzi younger brothers in ecclesiastical positions set about the tricky business of indulgences. Kinsmen and well-wishers poured in from outlying towns. Meals became complex, multiple-stage affairs, and every night skirmishes broke out between the retainers of the factions. Milan was a party.

And yet through it all Francesco remained calm. Inside his head a rich humming sound, like viola d'amore strings, vibrated day and night. There was a new ease in his movements, a manliness and joviality, as if the part of family champion had been created for him in a lost moment before the earth was formed. Nature itself carried him along. So this was glory, he thought, the reason he'd been born. Its nearness lifted his spirits, kept his thoughts tranquil amid the hubbub. For the first time in his life he and the world seemed a single thing.

When on the morning of the ninth day Francesco and Amalfi finally saw the sun leak through the aspens outside the Roman gate and so began to lead the nineteen horsemen, seven coaches, innumerable lackeys and noisy coda of tag-along cretins, lepers, amputees and consumptives down the narrow lane of the French regent's mulberry grove, the weather had already turned hot and sultry. The ostrich plumes hung from the men's caps at a noticeably less jaunty angle than when sewn in place, and moisture could be seen on the horses' nostrils. No one spoke. At the end of the lane was a clearing bounded by willows and a shallow pool. The Margrave liked it, his man explained, for its youthful air—a remark Francesco's father suspected of impudence. As the Melzis entered the clearing they could see their rivals waiting across the field, silent as doom in their bright blue cloaks. The mist obscured details, but Francesco assumed his enemy was the horseman riding slightly taller than the rest, plumed, erect, head turned blithely askance. For several minutes he tried to glimpse the man's face—all the while affecting indifference—but each time his eyes passed in the Margrave's vicinity all Francesco saw was the amorphous drapery of a riding cloak. This unnerved him. How could someone on a spirited horse manage always to have his back toward you? The distraction caused by this enigma could be strategic, Francesco realized, and so he tried to concentrate on the nearby chatter instead. Amalfi was complaining that their adversary had used Flemish tailors. Someone had neglected to bring the trumpets, and a serving man was being dispatched to get them. Everyone agreed the Margrave was a splendid foe.

Thinking back on this moment years later, Francesco would suspect that it was then that the first hint of his life's inscrutability had come to him. As everywhere around him figures started leaping to the ground, abusing servants, lifting ladies from coaches and congregating in little wads of gesticulating kinsmen, Francesco realized he didn't know how to dismount. It wasn't a lack of training. He had, in fact, mastered five ways: the hoist, the escalier du cavalier, the leg-over, the rump vault and, of course, toppling, but he knew of no way for a family champion with viola d'amore strings in his head to do it. His former ease had vanished. His legs were planks. Large portions of his body had filled with cold water. Part of the problem seemed to be that everyone else had something to do. And while Francesco could imagine a family champion seething inwardly, or gazing off abstractedly, or pronouncing doom in his grave baritone, or doing almost anything, so long as he was the focus of attention, he really couldn't imagine a champion trying to look inconspicuous or wiping the sweat from his lip or whistling or scratching or doing virtually any of the things that, if truth be told, until nine days ago Francesco did a great portion of the time. It seemed astonishing how inept he'd suddenly become. And all that saved him from a debilitating attack of self-knowledge was the sight of his father, Uncle Baldassare, Amalfi, and four retainers marching authoritatively across the field just as someone clutched his thigh. He looked down into his cousin Arturo's somber face. Don't worry about the hood, Arturo reassured him. We've decided on the stratagem of La Croix. If this fails, there are diversions. All is being managed. The advantage is ours.

Now, if there was anything that seated on his horse like a cigar store Indian, struggling to maintain his poise for the benefit of onlookers who hadn't noticed him since the Roman gate, and trying desperately to come up with a way to sneak over behind the carriages and relieve his screaming bladder . . . if there was anything Francesco wasn't worried about just now, it was the hood. Mainly because, until Arturo's remark, Francesco hadn't known there was one. So that was how the Sky kept his cloak turned towards you. His head was draped! This realization brought with it eight seconds of relief followed by the most paralyzing sensation of public nakedness Francesco had ever known. How, for God's sake, had he wound up seated out here in this sizzling, yellow light, unhidden, unbearded, unbejeweled—as prosy as a length of string—while across the clearing lurked his enemy shrouded in Olympian blue? No wonder no one was paying Francesco any mind. Every member of the Melzi contingent was preoccupied with one question: What was the enemy concealing? There might be deceptions here, depths, mistakes. What if Francesco were about to sacrifice his limbs and flawless complexion to a joke? But when Francesco tried to confide these fears to Arturo, he was chided for cowardice. Didn't he trust his kinsmen to know what they were about? Surely, having behaved so well until now he wasn't going to embarrass them with unmanly qualms. Francesco decided to mind his bladder and stay put.

Three hours passed. It was soon apparent that the Margrave's disguise was a more elaborate obstacle than Arturo's jocular tone had let on, and accusations of stalling were beginning to be heard on both sides. Several neutral observers had earlier noted an air of the executioner about the draped head, and now the Melzi spokesmen denounced this allusion as indelicate, if not grounds for further umbrage. The threat of a chivalric chain-reaction culminating in a geometrically expanding series of new challenges loomed over the negotiations and was only dissipated when Francesco's mother labeled the whole disagreement a ploy to drive the Melzi women back into the Castello. Many were persuaded of the reasonableness of the Margrave's circumspection by an eloquent foreigner's citation of the notorious case of Bardolini and the Englishman, and Francesco's cousin Andrea was kept busy compiling counter arguments: Men should know whom they are murdering, retaliatory prosecution lacks style, true spectacle requires the exposed visage, etc. In the midst of the clearing the negotiators beseeched one another, snickered and shook their fists in the air. Twice Francesco's father marched back to the horses, instructed the party to remount and was riding away when a blue-cloaked messenger arrived to whisper a concession in his ear. The servants set tables of eats and wine out under the willows. A handful of bedlamites attacked the coaches with mudballs. Francesco's youthful aunt succumbed to heat prostration. It began to look like rain.

By the time the Margrave was persuaded to remove his hood, revealing thickly rouged cheeks, a garish yellow wig, purple lines spreading from the corners of what looked like blue lips, and a paper ball-mask—the blatant hokeyness of which seemed a confirmation of Francesco's worst fears and should have been more than sufficient warning to everyone else involved but wasn't—the viola d'amore strings vibrating in his head had subsided to a buzz. The sweat trickling down his spine and accumulating in a squishy wad of linen between his buttocks had at one point very nearly provoked him to gallop right out onto the field of conquest in a last ditch effort to look like the champion he knew himself to be, but when in a fatal instance of good sense he'd confided the impulse to Arturo who forthwith entrusted it to Uncle Baldassare whose ears belonged to Francesco's dad, he'd learned that such tactics sacrificed in sagacity what they gained in panache and besides, he was just fifteen, what did he know? Melzi would never understand that what he was confronting was the modern genius for replacing conflict with organization or that his difficulty was merely that of everyone else since the Renaissance—how to resist anything so amorphous, rational, and outwardly benign as bureaucracy. However, he did understand that what had gotten concealed underneath the Margrave's hood had been glory, and having been taught since birth that it was the most exciting thing in the world, he recognized as deeply significant the fact that he was feeling bored. He tried to continue waiting, grew drowsy, started to daydream and pretty soon didn't want to die. An awkward development under the circumstances but one that at least loosened him up enough to dismount. And as the spectacularly clothed gentlemen in the midst of the clearing continued hefting, scrutinizing, and deprecating the Margrave's Swiss rapiers, thus instigating a contrapuntal fracas within the ongoing squabble over whether the rouge, wig and ballmask constituted a disguise within a disguise and so were liable to the same objections as the hood, Francesco scooped up a fistful of veal from the serving tables and wandered past the coaches where two footmen were whipping back an onslaught of squealing urchins. Behind a dray he discovered his youthful aunt sitting on the grass, her skirt hiked up above her knee, sharing a bottle of chianti with the French viscount's blacksmith, Slipknot de Gruyere. She cocked an eye at Francesco, demanded just what did he think he was doing here when his duty so plainly lay on the field of honor? And as Francesco stumbled towards the willows to relieve his agonized bladder at last, he marveled that her voice had spoken the very question that was his own.

And on and on and on throughout the remainder of the afternoon. So for Francesco it wasn't much of a climax when the steadily developing drizzle finally ran the Margrave's cheeks, wilted his ballmask and made unavoidably obvious the insult that, suspected far too late, had already provoked Francesco's father to frantic searching for some technicality that would extricate his family from the miserable affair. But no luck. For on the Margrave's horse sat, not the Sky of course, but a *woman*—the gigantic, slovenly vixen from the trattoria of Chiaravalle, Sour Maria as she was commonly known. And surrounded by guffawing blue-cloaked horsemen, she galloped about the soggy clearing, challenging the Melzi champion to combat, deriding his reluctance to meet her, and wondering that such a noble family had no offspring to defend its name. Francesco's father retired to his coach without a word, pulled the drapes, and declared that he wouldn't show his face again until safely within—not just their palazzo in the city—but the Villa Melzi seven hours journey hence. Uncle Baldassare re-grouped the nineteen horsemen, tried to quiet the riffraff who, having picked up Sour Maria's taunts, were now dancing around Francesco's father's coach hooded in flour sacks, chal-lenging him to martial contests and insinuating various irregu-larities in his masculine parts. Someone pushed Amalfi into the mud; Andrea got punched in the eye; no one could find Arturo. And as the cooks and lackeys sprinted about gathering up the waterlogged hambones and linens, and as Francesco's mother keened loudly within her sister's carriage, and while the horses squealed and reared and the wheels sucked noisily at the soft ground, without a backward glance, the soggy band rattled out of the clearing on its long way home.

For Francesco little seemed to have changed. Straggling along with the other riders and coachmen—not really behind or beside anyone, hardly connected, merely drawn along by the fastidiously maintained hiatus between his horse and ev-ery other—he felt as extraneous now as he'd felt all day. It was, of course, apparent that the whole undertaking had been a masquerade, not just for Sour Maria and the Margrave, but for himself. He was no rival of a high-born rogue; he was a boy—

promising student of elocution and ballroom dancing, hope of his family's future, but in point of fact, no great shakes. However, what did seem to have changed was the rest of the world. There'd been a disaster. And although he'd had no hand in it and couldn't participate in the family's grief and viewed this ignominy as if from afar, Francesco knew himself the cause of all. No longer solitary and negligible, he was now isolated—something done *to* him. And as the rain matted his hatbrim to his forehead and mud from the carriage wheels splattered his chest, he felt drawn to the lepers and cretins cavorting nearby. Even their filthy anonymity was preferable to such importance, and Francesco had to stifle an impulse to leap down among them. A wretch with no nose spat loudly in his direction; a shapeless creature—so mudcovered Francesco couldn't distinguish male from female—showed him its arse and gave a screech like cats fighting. And as the procession continued on past black fields and mulberry groves until at darkness it reached the twisting road beside the Adda, Francesco gave himself over to fancies of gore and mayhem, horses stampeding, metal crashing down, the perverse fellowship injury brings.

At last the dark walls of the Villa Melzi appeared through the storm, and the whole band of drenched travelers drew together in a corporate shudder of relief. Here were dry clothes, protection from laughter, forgiving sleep. But as the carriages approached the outermost gate, their passengers were startled to discover the vilest turn of all in this vile, vile day. Blocking the entrance was a mound of ox manure as high as a man's head, whole cartloads of it dumped into the path and heaped so that not even a solitary rider could pass. You could see its black shape from a furlong's distance, see the rain streaming in shiny rivulets down its sides, a sliver of moon glistening in the moist folds. A dueling foil protruded from its front pinioning a missive written in Latin quadrimeter, something about decorum, catastrophe, the lesser lights' sphere. As the riders and horses stopped, a hush fell, and Francesco felt himself drawn in. The day had begun as a summons to him, the chance to enact his character and fate. His only mistake had been to misconstrue what part he'd play, to vastly underestimate the strangeness of the thing. Dismounting from his horse Francesco strode over to where three exhausted coachmen were rolling their eyes, shuffling their feet, each more determined than the rest to shirk this chore. One of the men warned: The young lord! There were some coughs, a stir, then nothing. Francesco took a deep breath and the odor was like a plunge into dying. He could hear the patter of raindrops on the mush, watched the offal oozing around his toes. So this was it, he thought, the reason he'd been born. He edged a foot into the stew. An old retainer beside him protested weakly, and when Francesco replied, he was surprised to hear the sound of his own voice—as rich and soothing as viola d'amore strings! He waved the servants back, waded in up to his knees. It would be slow work, he knew, but he felt strong, ready, as if nature had prepared him for this challenge long ago. And as his mother and cousins and aunt peered out from their carriage windows, Francesco thrashed and shoveled and scooped with his bare hands, until at last the Melzi champion cleared a way so his family could go on.

After this, it was generally acknowledged that Francesco would always be wrong. The civilized hypocrisies that everyone else recognized from childhood, he'd blunder through life believing, and he'd doubt only those inevitabilities no one else paused to consider. Faith in him was screwed a turn too tight, suspicion left uncapped altogether, and so instead of shooting for virtue's pinnacle, he'd habitually aim just above it. His most recurrent vision would be of his inferiors gazing upward, laughter spilling from their mouths, as he glided in a perfect arc just over his heart's desire. Even in the most ordinary undertakings there would always be a pile of manure blocking his way. Because he alone saw it, his actions struck others as peculiar. His parents hardly knew what to think. They might have reconciled themselves to a commonplace son— Francesco's father was himself pretty commonplace—but a commonplace son determined to act like a champion was indistinguishable from a fool. His mere presence could make villainy fashionable, nobility clownish. There seemed no alternative but to turn him into an artist. And so when Leonardo da Vinci next dined at the Villa Melzi, Francesco's father dropped the necessary hints, and Leonardo—who was by no means averse to accepting money if he didn't have to work for it—figured a rich idiot in the studio could cause no problems if you gave him nothing to do. So Francesco Melzi became Leonardo's apprentice, and though the liaison with a common guildsman was an insult to the Melzi name, it kept the family embarrassment out of harm's way.

Throughout his youth Francesco knew that this was his family's reasoning, and now eight years later in a foreign land he has often imagined that Battista da Vilanis, the weasel Salai, all the courtiers in the chateau, even the maids and stable hands—in short, the entirety of the imaginable universe knows, too. Wasn't the lord of this very same Amboise regent in Milan when the Margrave humiliated Francesco? Who would expect the French to keep a secret? Gazing at Leonardo's splotched and hairy head poking out from underneath the mountain of bedclothes just now, Francesco feels a flutter of rage rise in his throat. Disdain, disdain. Never has he known glory except as a joke. He's terrified that the present situation is just another set-up, that Leonardo's manuscripts will turn out to be gobbledy-gook. Francesco's read them—pages of triangles and half-moons, sketches of cow innards, about a thousand drawings of pulleys, water-screws, tie-beams, masonry, some wildflowers and horseheads, all surrounded by inscrutable remarks written backwards in a mixture of Tuscan, hideous Latin and phonetic spellings of Arabic and Greek . . . well, honestly now, is this what genius looks like? Melzi's brain is a tangle of conflicting plots; he feels like a character in some malevolent author's play. Out of a thousand farces how to conceive even one satisfactory ending? It's hopeless. And yet, doesn't he seem to be confronting at this very moment the unlikeliest phenomenon of all—a second chance? He watches Leonardo's dry lips twitch in silent argument with God-knows-what specter. His whiskers are matted with broth and onions, his forehead a glob of age spots, peas, worry-lines. If not from such old and homely stuff, from where do better worlds come?

And so, knowing that Leonardo has already willed him his squiggles, laundry-lists, nightmares, mistakes, but amply aware that if France wants them Leonardo's notebooks will prove less sacrosanct than a kidney bean, and feeling for the first time that ignominious success might be preferable to almost any kind of defeat, Melzi is just beginning his life as a scoundrel when Battista moans, No more flowers! Melzi glances down at the figure lying spread-eagle at his feet and, with one toe, up-ends the water-basin. Battista comes off the floor sputtering. You win, Melzi tells him. Have at the paintings, desecrate the studio, leave your mark wherever you choose, France will probably confiscate everything anyway. Melzi smiles just to let Battista know Melzi doesn't take him for a fool and adds: I'm bribing you. Which amounts to an understanding, and in seconds Battista's skipping down the stairs.

Melzi next brushes a paper crocus from the bed where Leonardo appears to be swearing at no one and, seating himself on the pig's-bristle throw-rug, appeals to the Maestro for understanding. History is a difficult task. How unfair that weariness can demean life's climactic moments, that neither doom nor triumph ever arrives on time. Truth is, only in retrospect is anything thrilling; even in the midst of conquests you're mostly bored. How well Francesco understands this now. Much of Leonardo's own life has suffered this defect—no offense intended—and here at the conclusion his death's making a poor spectacle. How wrong to dwindle into anti-climax! Left to itself has nature ever contrived a satisfying show? Melzi pauses, moved by his own eloquence. At last he means to strike a blow with his own arm, to punish the world for countless disappointments. Briefly, he enumerates the maxims, regrets, gestures and facial expressions appropriate for Leonardo's final moments. He recalls Leonardo's heartfelt penitence for wasted opportunities, the discharging of his faithful servants, the tender parting of the Maestro and his beloved disciple, Francesco Melzi. He runs through the story of how King François Premier collapses sobbing when he hears the news, mentions the castle eulogies, processions through the streets of Amboise, anguish in Florence, Venice, Rome, and concludes with the triumphal return of Leonardo's works to Milan under the protection of his spiritual heir, commentator and learned apologist,

Francesco Melzi. He does not mention Battista's overpainting of the *St. John*, the disappearance of half a thousand scribbles detrimental to Leonardo's reputation as a sane man, or the succession of folk Melzi expects to pay off, be sodomized by, or hire some thug to bludgeon in order to make this scam work. In a really swell peroration he touches on the perpetuation of Leonardo's memory through the publication of his treatises and founding of the Academia Leonardi Vinci, both under the supervision of the internationally renowned Leonardo publicist and patron, the esteemed heir to an esteemed house, the immortal Francesco Melzi. And then patting Leonardo's knee, Melzi adds: Trust me. Leonardo gazes out the back of Melzi's head, makes an unintelligible snort. And with a quick sigh, Melzi's on his way back down the stairs, already wondering how he's going to get himself and 6000 pages across the Italian Alps before King François cuts him off with an army from Marseilles. There's a heavy feeling in his chest, and he thinks it's penitence, vows to confess when he's safe in Milan, but he must already know it won't do any good. He'll live with it his whole life long. For Francesco Melzi has discovered fiction.

──── Richard Grossman ────

By the early eighties, I had given up on being appreciated by poetry people, who were definitely not from my planet, and had stopped writing poems in disgust at how inbred, shallow and inept the world of verse had become. Ultimately, this hiatus proved impossible to maintain, and in 1991 I decided to write a novel that would not only embed poetry but also would describe what poetry ideally should be. Hence, *The Alphabet Man*, in which I used one medium of expression as the model for another.

The plot came about as the result of a conversation that I had with a former CIA assassin when I was flying into Los Angeles. He was a man in his seventies, trim, dapper and amiable, who took a liking to me and confessed that he had killed American soldiers in three wars. I thought to myself, "What if he were also trying to kill me?" From there, I worked things out. I have now placed this person on airplanes in all the novels of my *American Letters Trilogy*. In all three books, his aim is to destroy the person sitting next to him.

The Alphabet Man took approximately six months to complete. I wrote it in a ten story castle next to the Hollywood sign. I was suffering grievously from sciatica at the time, so the pain of Clyde Wayne Franklin and his killer clown was in some sense real.

I wish to take this opportunity to say that my experiences with FC2 have been nothing but pleasurable and supportive. Many people told me that my novel was too risky and difficult for anyone ever to publish. If it weren't for Curt White and Ron Sukenick, my fiction manuscripts would, in all probability, still be moldering (or smoldering) on a shelf.

from *The Alphabet Man*

when you peeped through that door and you saw mike you saw
mike you saw mike opening her up you saw his swinging butt and
like a halo around the butt you saw his flaming hair and you saw
the rectal opening there like a lug nut and the milky pants were
on the floor and you saw his butt swinging in and out of her and
you couldn't see his teeth and you couldn't see her belly but from
where you were watching it seemed that he was eating it looked
like he was at a trough gnawing and feeding on her and she was
screaming and milkman have to get their milk and eggs where
they can where they can where they can and she sang mike don't
open me up like this oh baby please don't open me up mike
please don't open me there's someone at the door o mike baby so
good so good oh mike it's so good there's someone at the door
baby someone there oh mike baby please don't open me up like
this she sang mike don't open me up like this oh baby please
don't open me up mike please don't open me there's someone at
the door o mike baby so good so good oh mike it's so good
there's someone at the door baby someone there oh mike baby
please don't open me up like this she sang mike don't open me
up like this oh baby please don't open me up mike please don't
open me there's someone at the door o mike baby so good so
good oh mike it's so good there's someone at the door baby
someone there oh mike baby please don't open me up like this
she sang mike don't open me up like this oh baby please don't

open me up mike please don't open me there's someone at the
door o mike baby so good so good oh mike it's so good there's
someone at the door baby someone there oh mike baby please
don't open me up like this it's true that I can do things to you
now that I could never do to you before I can now be the thing
I need to be and get myself ready for the feast cuz the blood
will spring from its loop and enter me for you are the oracle but
I am the auricle and I am not a figment but reality you always
thought I was only a dream something to stick in an anus something to crap on and restrain you thought that I ripped apart your
mom you thought I killed the milkman I did neither your mother
hung herself and the milkman split he had his fuck and split he
had no reason to hang around a madwoman a woman who sang
in her apron and staggered around that sickhouse and some
fucking sicko snotty kid because you could tell walking in the
door the place was sick but you said I ate your mom which was
OK with me because any sin will do the real and unreal in hell all
amount to the same thing they do because sins are bodiless there's
no such thing as a sinner or a sin there is no such thing as suffering or loss in hell you see the only hell in the universe exists inside
of me Clyde the only thing that matters are the vows we make the
only thing that matters are the contracts all the dumbshow of the
universe all the actions from the center to the edge is essentially
meaningless and quiet and all the humor amounts to the same
thing which is why all comedy and religion were created at the
very same time because only a comic fool would ever make a fatal
vow and I created your laugh and I created your prayers and my
intentions were always clear I was the one who made you fall in
love and I was the one who hired the priest I was the one who
bought the nails that nailed you in your diapers to your destiny
that nailed you to your sickening cross I am not a clown my name
is not Sinbad I have not been in your book but I lived inside the
clown who lived inside you as you will now live inside me and I
was the essence of your suffering your mother sang to me she put
me to sleep with her songs your mother made a deal with me to
be born for you and teach you poetry the curse the contract
extends back through history from generation to generation your
mother loved her songs and made me sing them to you which I

did while you were jacking off in your bedroom dreaming your
mother knew she knew everything she knew you would kill
Charlie she told me all about it she told me you would do it when
you were born she told me you were her clown she told me you
were her clown she told me you were her clown she told me you
were her clown she told me exactly how you would kill him and
unzip him she told me every fragment of his brain that you would
coldly eliminate and she told me the memento you would cut she
told me you would unzip and cut she told me the memento you
would cut and unzip and cut and unzip and cut him and throw it
in the corner she told me you would take your memento she told
me you would cut at your hatred cut cut cunt rubbarubba cut cut
cut cut cut cunt rubbarubba cut cut cut cut cut cut cut cut cut
cut cut cut cut cut cunt rubbarubba cut cut cut cut cut cut cut
cut cut cut cut cut cut cut cut cut cut cunt rubbarubba cut cut
cut cut cut cut cut cut cut cut cut cut cut cunt cut cut cut cut
cut cunnnnnnnnt rubbbbbbbbbacut cut cut cut cut cut cut cut
cut when she sang her final song it wasn't to you it was sung to
me she sang it out it wasn't really what you heard it was another
melody her mind was already gone among the flames she saw the
flames rising out of the basement she came babes she had the big
fucking death orgasm she came and came and came she was my
lover Clyde she came as I fucked her she came for me she came to
me she came when you shot your Daddy she came when you cut
him she came when you touched her she came when you shot
your Daddy she came when you touched her deep down deep
down deep Down Down Down between the apronstrings she
came whenever you touched her thing that Daddy made you
touch while he was whipping he made you kneel between her legs
and touch her there as he beat you and beat her and screamed like
a beast that PRIMAL SCENE with you kneeling and her coming
and his screaming like a conquering beast and swinging his whip
and the small clink of chains and her singing and then she
touched you Clyde it was then she touched you you poor pathetic
thing it was then she stroked your hair it was then and only then
she stroked your thing she was my lover Clyde she came as I
fucked her she came for me she came to me she came when you
shot your Daddy she came when you touched her she came when

you cut cut cut him she came when you shot your Daddy she came when you touched her deep down deep down deep Down Down Down between the apronstrings she came whenever you touched her thing that Daddy made you touch while he was whipping he made you kneel between her legs and touch her there as he beat you and beat her and screamed like a beast that PRIMAL SCENE with you kneeling and her coming and his screaming like a conquering beast and swinging his whip and the small clink of chains and her singing and then she touched you Clyde it was then she touched you you poor pathetic thing it was then she stroked your hair it was then and only then she stroked your thing she was my lover Clyde she came as I fucked her she came for me she came to me she came when you shot your Daddy she came when you touched her she came when you shot your Daddy she came when you cut him when you cut off his thing she came when you touched her deep down deep down deep Down Down Down between the apronstrings she came whenever you touched her thing that Daddy made you touch while he was whipping he made you kneel between her legs and touch her there as he beat you and beat her and screamed like a beast that PRIMAL SCENE with you kneeling and her coming and his screaming like a conquering beast and swinging his whip and the small clink of chains and her singing and then she touched you Clyde it was then she touched you you poor pathetic thing it was then she stroked your hair it was then and only then she stroked your thing she was my lover Clyde she came as I fucked her she came for me she came to me she came when you shot your Daddy she came when you touched her she came when you shot your Daddy she came when you hacked and hacked at his V and slashed his thing and bit it and threw it in the corner and screamed she came when you touched deep down deep down deep Down Down Down between the apronstrings she came whenever you touched her thing that Daddy made you touch while he was whipping he made you kneel between her legs and touch her there as he beat you and beat her and screamed like a beast that PRIMAL SCENE with you kneeling and her coming and his screaming like a conquering beast and swinging his whip and the small clink of chains and her singing and then she touched you Clyde it was then she touched you you poor pathetic thing it was then she stroked your hair it was then and only then she stroked your thing she was my lover Clyde she came as I fucked her she came for me she came to me she came when you shot your Daddy she came when you touched her she came when you shot your Daddy and cut him she came when you touched her deep down deep down deep Down Down Down between the apronstrings she came whenever you touched her thing that Daddy made you touch while he was whipping he made you kneel between her legs and touch her there once he beat you hard you touched with your lips once he made you touch with your lips with your lips and your tongue with your lips you ceased to count with your lips with your lips with your lips and your tongue and your tongue once once and you ceased to count and your tongue with your lips with your lips with your lips and your tongue and your tongue and your tongue and your tongue and your tongue with your lips with your lips with your lips as he beat you and beat her and screamed like a beast that PRIMAL SCENE with you kneeling and her coming

ONLY ONCE

ONCEONLY

ONLY ONCE

ONCEONLY and

his screaming like a conquering beast and swinging his whip and the small clink of chains and her singing and then she touched you Clyde it was then she touched you you poor pathetic thing it was then she stroked your hair it was then and only then she

stroked your thing she was my lover Clyde she came as I fucked
her she came for me she came to me she came when you shot
your Daddy she came when you touched her she came when you
shot your Daddy you cut cut cut and she came when you touched
her deep down deep down deep Down Down Down between the
apronstrings she came whenever you touched her thing that
Daddy made you touch while he was whipping he made you
kneel between her legs and touch her there as he beat you and
beat her and screamed like a beast that PRIMAL SCENE with
you kneeling and her coming and his screaming like a conquering
beast and swinging his whip and the small clink of chains and her
singing and then she touched you Clyde it was then she touched
you you poor pathetic thing it was then she stroked your hair it
was then and only then she stroked your thing but I owned her
she was part of me and you saw clown but she saw Devil she saw
me the lover of the dawnlight come and sigh and I wasn't drinking you were drunk but I was sober I'm always sober I have
nothing to prove I have nothing to do I have nothing to say I
have nothing to accomplish I only have to make my claim which
I am about to do you see it doesn't make a difference what you do
you were damned from the moment you entered the womb you
entered it from above on your way to below you fell like a meteor
through the milky darkness because life is a tumble the ceiling
trap is birth the floor trap is death and you just tumble through
cuz you are not suffering for any reason you never did anything
wrong and all your words were good and you went down and
split apart and let me enter your cell and your soul and your spirit
split and let me in as a result of an ancient Jewish curse handed
from mother to son and I flew on leathern wings and planted a
comedian and the comedian grew and grew and grew and now
it's time for the final scene in which I make my claim your
mother knew what she was doing when she refused to touch you
cuz one of the rules in hell is that the damned never touch each
other except in satanic rituals and you were born in hell cuz the
damned give birth to the damned and your prayers mean fuck
and you were the child of two devils as you always knew they
weren't human they were evil spirit vipers and you're not going
anywhere you haven't been you're just going to be my food that's

all there is to it you are going to become me you are going to
enter me you are going to become part of me you are going to
become my microbe and you will become my slave you will
become my eternal slave my piece of bacterial shit and you will be
forced for all eternity to obey my commands you will never sing
again and you will never write another letter and the letters on
your skin will disappear and your poems will disappear and you
will no longer stalk or pray or sing you'll just become my shapeless thing my damned internal slave a slave of evil swimming in
my chyle a calm part of me a part of a larger evil body Clyde so
go ahead and finish your book and put aside your pen and open
for me open up your misery remember remember remember it
doesn't take much effort to join me Precious Sweetheart darling
Clyde fall into the flames burn forever sizzle green in my gut

What are the hidden costs of the digital revolution? When I was researching part of the baggy tome from which the following is lifted, I turned to the library located in the American Embassy in Paris, just off the Place de la Concorde. (Be sure to call a day ahead to get a pass; otherwise, nyet.) Once upstairs—past cumbrous limestone, charmschool-flunkout guards plucking passports, and, natch, the Monumental Staircase—I found a library as yet uncomputerized.

To the card catalogue we go. I opened the combined subject/title "E" drawer (I was searching for my Environment) and started to flip cream-colored cards. First flip took me to a card carrying details of an opus entitled "Those Enterprising Americans." Flip two provided same for "America: The Entertainment Machine." I gulped, then slammed shut the slight, deep drawer.

Inefficiency be blessed. How else to get so sharp a snapshot of our great nation—or at least how it represents itself to the world? Here's my vote for a digital counterrevolution, where the digits in question are our own tripping fingers.

from *The Lost Scrapbook*

... because I was right at that juncture when, every day, I turn selfish: blindly selfish, shamelessly selfish, *will*fully self-pampering; I do this not only because I believe it good, and salutary—I endorse the notion of applied self-indulgence—but also, at bottom, because I believe that I deserve it; after all, it had been a good and productive day; in the long quietness of the afternoon, as the shadows from my yard's birches slowly slipped off the corner of my desk, I had finished line-editing three long chapters of an odd, repetitious book on massively parallel processing systems, written by a UC Santa Cruz professor who seemed to have read a little too much Raymond Queneau; the manuscript had been typed on a manual, which, as usual, had left the text somewhat dodgy, but the writing was relatively clean and, blissfully, triple-spaced; distractions had been few, and I had emptied my coffee cup only twice; so it was the kind of afternoon in which I had taken real satisfaction from my wriggling red pencil, performing its poky arabesques among the crawly rows of black type; tightening the good professor's readable text had been a fine first outing for my luminous new birthday pencil—a birthday gift that I had bought for myself despite the fact that yesterday, which was when I purchased the proud number 1 3/4, was not my birthday; mine, in fact, is in October; but I had reasoned that it isn't just every day that my daughter, Rebecca, turns 5 1/2 months old, and so the day certainly warranted considerable commemoration; further, why not appropriate the day's goodness for myself, I reasoned; as I have said, I subscribe to the doctrine of concerted selfishness; yet whether it had been more selfish for me to buy the pencil-present or to receive it, I had not yet determined . . .

. . . So there I was, at 5:30 PM, pampering myself preposterously: pouring a deep cup of apricot-flavored decaf, plopping down at the kitchen table, stretching my feet onto the adjacent chair, and flipping open my *Redbook*—best arts coverage of all the monthlies, no doubt about it; then, to cap things off, I took the walkie-talkie from my skirt pocket and placed it on the table, in front of the napkin rack; now *this* is indulgence, I thought, this is what is called for; it was pleasant to feel the walkie-talkie physically removed from me—its tug-weight in my pocket often grew tiresome; and it was just as pleasant to see it stretched out on the table before me: the constancy of its dense gray hum meant that Rebecca was sleeping peacefully; and so, too, I could be at ease; Rebecca was a difficult sleeper, fitful and cranky during her passage out, but, thankfully, almost unflappable when she was under, and that was nice: I cherished her company when she had achieved her quietness, perhaps feeling—again selfishly—that I had helped provide her with this ardent repose; occasionally, in fact, I would read to her while she was asleep: I would sit by her crib in her low-lit room and, taking my time, share one-way words with her; this tenuous act of communication was, of course, no more than a sanction for my remaining with my daughter a little longer; but I adored the experience, principally because Rebecca's silent response was, to me, incomparably expressive and moving; when I read to her, her quietness, her peacefulness, was what I sought to hear, and it echoed in me as if in an expanding cavern, and often left me trembling with love; and so, then and there, after taking a final gulp of my decaf, I decided to indulge in even more self-pampering: I lifted my legs down from the chair, and, with lightness and celerity, stole upstairs . . .

—Darling, I said, in my low dusk voice: we got a letter;

. . . I approached the crib and saw her apple face and voluptuary's lashes; she seemed warm within her bulky bedclothes; her breathing was regular, and her lips gnashing; gently I pulled the brown corduroy chair closer to the crib and settled into it; being closer meant that I had to speak even more quietly—precisely what I was after:

—Yes, we did, I said: in fact, *we* didn't get a letter—*you* did; look—she even addressed it to you . . .

. . . Amidst the dense quietness I showed her the envelope, where Rebecca's name, and only her name, was written above the address; I had been thrilled to pull it from the letterbox that afternoon; it was just like Robin to do something like that:

—You see?; so, here's your letter;

. . . I withdrew the envelope's several pages and unfolded them, careful, though, not to make too much rattling noise; as always, the letter was handwritten, in Robin's angled script; I cleared my throat, quietly, and settled in to read:

—So, here we have it . . . Dear Rebecca—Hey, how do you like that?—so . . . Dear Rebecca . . . O tiny tykelette, o noble neonate, let us now talk of transformations . . . not grammatical, of course, no clause for alarm *here*, but personal, ezymatical, sociobiological . . . for your faithful correspondent, your penning epistler, AKA your Auntie Robin—she spells it a, n, t, i—has found something that makes anti—spelled a, *u*, n—matter! . . . O 'tis true, 'tis true!—and, my darlin', I'd better take a break already!—

. . . In fact, I had forgotten how rollercoastery the gal could get; I put the pages in my lap and, in the tenebrous quietness, stretched my arms and shoulders, readying myself to dig back in; flighty Robin, how busily she worked to achieve the expressivity that came inevitably, inescapably, to Rebecca, just sleeping and warm; the counterpoint could not have been more telling; and yet, I thought, looking over towards my system's second walkie-talkie, which was taped to the railing of the crib, it would only be Robin's expressivity, as I read it, that would be conducted by the walkie-talkie to its sibling in the kitchen; only her words would be burbling to the shiny appliances downstairs, while Rebecca's infant eloquence would not come through; the instrumental world, it occurred to me, inhibits certain kinds of communication; absent the right kind of listener, all sorts of essential signals are lost; still, it seemed funny, as I envisioned the scene downstairs: the stillness, the walkie-talkie, the words; and I wondered, perhaps, what a burglar might think, coming in upon the chattering room:

—OK, then, here we go again . . . ; so: 'tis true!—*so*—And what would so newly enthrall your pen-y Auntie?—oh, just figure it out—Nothing but a regenerative slap of worthwhile work . . . Yes, 'tis a project, projecting me into modes of research, modes of inquiry, modes of understanding, and modes and modes of fun . . . sorry . . . but really, as the latest of his delvings beneath the frozen sea of official reality, Chomsky, my ongoing guidewire, my lifely thrillmaster, has asked me prepare a report on events at Al Yarmouk University, in *your* favorite city, Irbid, Jordan, where, several muddled months ago, the Government slipped the pink slip to more than a dozen professors and half as many U administrators just, make that unjustly, because they came out in support of some student protesters . . . in other dicta, 'twas a nasty bit a business, squelching students and their academic inspirers, who would believe anything like that ever happens . . . ne'ertheless, for me, it's a hugely engaging and galvanizing gig, though for Chomsky, of course, it's just anti-business as usual, as he continues writing and talking and generally crusadering about all his other unstoppable passions . . . abuses of democracy in bosom-ally Costa Rica, America's backing of Indonesia's invasion-cum-massacre in East Timor, the selective blindnesses and biases of the allegedly free press . . . I've started calling that ragged institution the *de*press . . . the sorry circumstances of the pal-less Palestinians, and many Chomskian moral more . . . and he continues with all his work and support despite all the fat-catcalls and obloquy, great word, that Chomsky should hie back to noun-town, as in Things'll be great when you're . . . where all the blights are right—Oh, God—that is, that the little academic linguist should stick to tending his grammatical garden, where he has some expertise, and not if, and, or but into affairs that he can not possibly comprehend . . . but such is the genuineness of Chomsky's greatness that he can not help speaking out when the world requires the word, when wrongness has become the only surface structure in sight . . . Tha 'tis, the Chomp's deep, universal concernedness excludes nothing but indifference, and his totally generous essence springs from a democratic instinct so passionate that, hearthlike, it warms you, it incites you, if you be around . . . I know that I have certainly stolen my fire from him . . . even though, a course, the fire was freely given . . .

. . . And *whew*: time for another intermission; there was only so much of this my poor tongue could handle in one take; I then rose and stretched and went to the dresser behind me, where I pulled the cord on the little lamp, whose burlap shade was decorated with a big clown face; as I had been reading, I had been racing, somewhat, against the room's increasing darkness; then, while settling back into my chair, I thought of the Oxbridge don who, night after night, would read Herodotus to his sleeping son, to see if the child would have an especial facility for learning classical Greek later in life; it had been an interesting experiment—although I wondered what skills Rebecca might acquire after but one evening of Robin-exposure:

—So, my dear: Round three; *so* . . . But the connection, a course, between Chomsky's linguistic researches and his political activism is as plain as pre-petrochemicalized day . . . Tha 'tis, as you must recall from when yo mamma slipped this into your chest pressé—Thanks, Rob—that it was Chomsky who, in the supple Sixties, reached back to the linguistic tradition of hardy old Professor Humboldt and championed the necessity of distinguishing between linguistic *performance* and linguistic *competence*, and then chose to climb up the latter . . . Tha 'tis, Chomsky said that linguists should devote the utter most of their attention not to faulty, fractured, floozied speech, but to the cerebral structures that *enable* language activity . . . because he saw, you see, that everywhere, every time, everyhow, everywhen, people develop astonishingly complex and versatile language capabilities, capabilities that allow them to produce and understand a literal infinity of perfect sentences,

even though they have only been exposed to limited and usually imperfect linguistic input . . . and that what he be meanin'
about innate competence . . . Tha 'tis, in Chomsky's perfect
words, the subtlety of our understanding transcends by far what
is presented in experience . . . or, once again, in my imperfect
rewording, from shattered shards we reconstruct the crystal . . .
how did we learn to do it? . . . I mean, I didn't go to shard-
school, did you? . . . and Chomsky *marvels* at this, at our miraculous linguistic competence, he *glories* in it, rather than
rifty-fixating on the shortcomings of corrupt, imprecise,
wheezy speech . . . and what's more, my diapered dreamboat,
this is also true at the level of phonetics, of physically producing speech-sound, where we also exhibit what can only be
considered a kind of miraculous competence . . . Tha 'tis, just
think about the glories you are growing into, my pre-verbal
princess, just take a moment to consider the accomplishments
that await you when you arrive unto the Age of Articulation . . .
effortlessly producing endless streams of luscious sounds . . .
affricates, fricatives, glottal stops . . . all those saucy snippets
of sound and meaning, each of whose physical production represents no less than an astonishment of movement and coordi-
nation . . . performed on a microscale so exquisite that, if you
think about it, it should leave you speechless . . . but 'tis true,
'tis true: even the process of articulating so simple a phrase as
"I am not worthy of your consideration" entails a dexterity
and physical finesse that outstrips Irina Kolpakova's entire
career at the Kirov, and Ivan Lendl's every move at the net . . .
and this Chomsky saw, and felt, and was moved by, and was
overtaken by, and has now, also, articulated in me . . . and it's
been so fun, so transportive, so remaking, my good gurgler, to
have found within myself so rich a palate of possibilities . . .
sorry . . . real, real bad . . .

    . . . In fact, I was rather glad that the phone had begun to
ring: by that point, I welcomed an external prompt to jump off
the joyride of the letter; so, hearing the second ring, I nudged
my chair away from the crib, put the letter down on the seat,
and pivoted to leave, lightly bunking my foot on one of the
crib's legs as I turned; then I slipped out, after confirming that

Rebecca was still asleep; I crossed the hallway into my bedroom; there, I sensed the dense, silencing presence of the mattress and linens almost as an atmospheric change; this was evidently a site of repose; I decided to keep the lights off:

—Hello, I said, picking up the phone;

—Hello, said a masculine, somewhat metallic-sounding voice, before the line lapsed into silence:

—Hello?, I tried again: hell—?

—Now in your neighborhood, the voice cut in, before the line again settled into scratchy silence:

—I'm sorry; who is—?

—A service new to your community, and now available—

. . . Ah, I thought, pulling the phone from my ear and hearing the bright voice continuing on: it's one of those machines that electronically dial phone numbers and make solicitations; I had read about these devices—in fact, more than once—and had wondered if I would ever receive such a call; curious, I decided to listen for a bit; but I already suspected that this wasn't the kind of thing that I would welcome regularly:

—Difficult-to-get-at eaves and overhangs, without exception, without risk; statistics show that 70% of all homeowners overlook the necessity of adequate gutter maintenance, even though clogged or insufficiently cleaned gutters can be breeding grounds for unwanted pests, while the slow corrosion of gutter metals can—

. . . And enough, I thought, placing the handpiece down: more than enough; the call was funny, and ironic just now, but it was also kind of eerie: the call had been made at random, but the pitch held such purposefulness; it was an odd combination; thus I was glad to return to Rebecca's room, where the calm and the muted lights were unperturbed; I bent over the crib and saw that she was there—just beautiful and there, sleeping peacefully; but then, while looking down at her, my selfishness flared volcanically and I could not resist picking her up—just for a moment, to feel her warmth and solidity; and so, for a second, I luxuriated in the tactile sense of her, her warm, articulated physicality; then I put her back and tucked her in, and laughed once to myself when she hiccuped slightly:

such small, unexpected eruptions I always found heart-rending, thrilling, the littleness of their urgency; I stroked her once on the chest and watched warmth and peacefulness retake her:

—So, then, where were we?, I said;

. . . I settled back into the chair; the letter's several pages had been disheveled in the move, but I found my place with little rattling, little difficulty:

—OK; so—right here; *so*—And there is much much more to be gotten from all this, my little listener, once you come over to applying a competence criterion, as you do already, I might add, for a lilly, or a tabby, or a child—good ole Rob, still at it—Thus, in short, in sum, in all, it was but a baby-step for Chomsky, graced with this understanding of the ineffable richness of our bio-abilities, to become the universalist that he be, to extend his understanding to the political realm . . . and to leap, by bio-necessity, into his political work—

But enough: that had been Rebecca's third hiccup; the rest of the letter, and there wasn't much, could wait; placing it on the chair, I rose, found the pacifier in the crib, and gave it to Rebecca, who was by then awake: her arms and legs had already taken on the waggly insistency of wakefulness; this transition remained, for me, a pleasure—to see how she changed gears, from sublime quietude to flappy agitation; but for some reason she did not take the pacifier, plopping it out in a froth of saliva; I tried again, but again it came tumbling over her cheek; so OK, I thought: we'll just wait this one out; I got close, and smiled broadly, and kissed her cheek; then I pulled away and, with one finger, started stroking her chest; such little disturbances, I thought, yet so total, so automatic, are our responses; we were made large and strong to come to the service of smallness; I continued stroking and smiling, then started humming—a tuneless something, in lower tones, that just passed through me and limned the air; it would help her, I sensed; and, in fact, before long, Rebecca became calm, and settled back into drowsiness; then she hiccuped again; I picked her up:

—Yes, dear one . . . you just took in too much of Robin's letter, now, didn't you? I said;

I placed Rebecca's quilted warmth against my shoulder and again applied the pacifier; but still it was not taken: Rebecca twisted her head to keep it away; so then I simply held her and stroked her back, and this, thankfully, seemed to work; her left hand crawled relaxedly down my chin, and her breathing became fine and regular; then she hiccuped again; but it occurred to me, this time, that what I had heard had not been an ordinary hiccup: coming close to my ear, it seemed deeper than usual, closer to a full cough; and she seemed to linger with it for a little longer: it took greater possession of her system than was customary, and didn't finish as decidedly as did other such bursts; I began to walk around the room with her, slowly:

—Yes, my darling, yes; we'll get this one out of you one, two, three;

I strolled her about the room and heard, before long, that her breathing was settling into its usual huffy sibilance: evidently, she was slipping back into sleep; There, I thought: that's what was necessary; then her hand relaxed at my jaw, and she exhaled deeply; it was working; but when she spurted into wakefulness again, with a thundery cough, I then sensed, clearly, that something was a little off; there had been something in that cough—it wasn't a hiccup, but a cough—that was not right; there had been an extra presence of wrenching, of chokingfulness; and as I began to bobble her at my shoulder, she began to cry—or to attempt to cry, for at intervals a cough would rush up and dislodge the crying, cut it off and supplant it; so I concentrated my attention on her breathing, and heard that she seemed syncopated, out of rhythm with herself; I put her back down in the crib:

—OK, now, sweetness; just let this pass; just leave it go;

I reached to the washstand for her bottle of apple juice, but found it empty; so I gave her the knuckle of my index finger, because it seemed right, as if it would work—perhaps it would open her up to some air; but she could not take it; she was, by then, crying and coughing rather fitfully, difficultly alternating between the two: her crying would reach up in volume until it was knocked back down by a spluttering cough; and while standing above her, and looking down, holding her small shoulders with my hands but feeling very far away, suddenly something within me began to feel a little decentered, or confused and lost; I began to get the sense that I was out of my depth, that some sort of unknown threshold had been crossed, beyond which I, as a mother, despite all my reading and preparations, would not be at my best; her crying was not normal crying, everyday crying, which I knew how to minister to; her coughing was also uncustomary, an invasion from somewhere else; there might be, it occurred to me, something genuinely wrong; and then I became aware of a voice, a low, dull voice, drilling within me: Please, Rebecca, please; please stop coughing; please just stop; but then, right then, she coughed again, and I, unthinkingly, pulled my hands away from her; I didn't know if I should move her, if I should even touch her at all; I became afraid of the possibility that the slightest jostling might compound the problem, interfere with the natural processes of self-correction; but I had to, I had to touch her, and I did: I picked her up, and heard her breathy struggling, and felt her jumping, and took her downstairs . . .

In the kitchen I placed Rebecca on the table, softened by a placemat; then I smoothed my skirt with the flat of my hands and went to the refrigerator for some apple juice; I got one of Rebecca's bottles from the cupboard and, after nervously spilling cold juice over my hands and the counter, filled the bottle to the half-way point; but Rebecca would not take it: she shook her head from underneath the nipple, she could not organize herself to suck; I put the bottle aside and, brushing my hair from my face, noticed that the child's crying had grown somewhat subdued; but at the same time her coughing seemed to have worsened—to be coming from more deeply within her, to be happening more frequently, and to be jackknifing her belly slightly up with each one; and now, after each cough, she would lather or gurgle for a moment, then wrench her chin up, which tensed her neck; at the same time, the hot-and-cold drafts that were then coursing through me, and the flashing stiffness besetting my arms and forehead, all left me stuck—immobilized, lost, uncertain of what to do; and again I became aware of the voice drilling within me: Please, no;

Rebecca, please; please stop coughing; yet my inability to act on these pleadings, to do anything to help her, splashed through me like wet fire, an inward bludgeoning of doubt, of panic, of fearful complicity: my daughter was suffering, possibly grievously—I could feel the difficulty that her body could not specifically express—but I had hit the end of my capacity to respond effectively; I saw her distress, I was in the very presence of her ordeal, of her little body jolting, but I did not know what was happening within her, I did not know what to do, and was terrified of doing the wrong thing; all I could do was grab and release the cloth of my skirt; all that was delivered to me was Please, Rebecca; please stop coughing; and dark clouds, fire-clouds, like the black clouds of an oil fire—wind-tumbled and billowing—gathered in my peripheral vision, fire-clouds of disbelief, of impotence and rage; fearing to be consumed by the clouds, I pulled away, hitting my hand on the sharp corner of the counter; but from that distance, the phone mounted on the wall by the refrigerator came into view; I rushed to it, picked up the handpiece and dialed Clovis High Plains Hospital, whose emergency number I had taped to the fridge . . .

Quickly, immediately, there was someone on the line; but I could not wait: I rushed past the formalities, the technicalities:

—Hello, I said: *hello*; please, as quickly as you can, an ambulance over to—

But they were still talking, they were insisting on talking first; so I stopped; if I had to, I would listen, I would hear out their formalities:

—And while the strength and durability of copper will guarantee many long years of use, the lighter and more economical Teflon gutters allow for decorative touches that—

And with a sudden *whump* the fire-clouds swelled and eddied around me: this could not be true, I thought, this could not be happening; this is a movie; and then I stumbled, almost falling, against the kitchen wall; but I immediately regained myself, and rushed back to the phone and crashed the handpiece back into place, making sure that the connection was severed, that I had hung up; then I brought the handpiece to my ear again:

—For instance, our new Palm Beach Green, in scalloped trim—

Again I crashed the phone back down; and not knowing whether to leave or to stay—but what could I do in the kitchen, with my heart drumming, my heart blithering—I bounded past Rebecca and mounted the stairs, taking two at a time; running into my bedroom I clicked on the light and saw, with horror, that the other phone was also hung up; but still I ran and picked it up, to double check, and when I heard the same metallic man-voice I pressed and pressed the disconnect button, down to its bottom, forcing my fingertip into the button's little sharp hole, and then I held the rounded button down for an unendurable five, six, ten seconds; but still the crawling voice was there—every time, unstoppably, cutting through the fire-clouds continuing to engulf me, and I screamed Damn you *Damn you* as I ran out and back down the stairs; but back in the kitchen, before I could get to the phone again, I saw, ecstatically, that Rebecca was coughing much more slightly, and was hardly crying at all, and had diminished in movement; but when I came closer, I saw that her face was brownish and strained, and that her lips seemed coated with phosphorescent-seeming off-white; and then the fire-clouds tumbled in on me, enveloped me, leaving me thinking No; no; this can not be; things like this just do not happen—this is impossible in a million ways; and I bent and grabbed Rebecca and brought her to my shoulder, and I pumped the small of her back with the heel of my hand, over and over, then harder and harder; but she was not responding, she was barely moving, her hand was a chill against the top of my neck; and I could not strike her any more, I could not hit her again, so I put her back on the table and petted her temple, and felt a frightful, scalding flame flare within my shoulders and face and chest, and I knelt down beside her, and made myself promise that I would not faint, and I thought No, this is impossible, it could not, it could never happen so quickly, then I heard myself begin to intone, to say:

—Please, Rebecca; please; *please* . . .

And I leapt up and ran to the kitchen phone:

—*Hello*—!

—So why not take advantage of—

—Hello—*hello!*, I continued, repeatedly pressing and punching the disconnect with the flesh of my hurting index finger, making the plastic clatter and the bell ding:

—Hello!, please . . . *someone!*, *please*, pick up the phone!; *hello—please—this is an emergency—!*

—New to your community, and now available—

And I crashed the phone down and returned to Rebecca, and again knelt by her side; and as the fire-clouds swarmed across me, and crested above me, to unsensingness, to closure, I again started stroking her chest, her shoulders, her cold and unmoving hand; and I felt a surge of liquid crying rushing up within me, and overrunning me, and my knees were hurting, and it was becoming difficult for me, too, to breathe; the fire-clouds were eclipsing me, invading my access to air, I was struggling to keep a sip of breath coming through the clouds' blackness; but I knew that I had to fight back, that I had to fight them off; so with my elbows and arms I forced them away, I buffeted the fire-clouds from me, pushing them, I was jostling and shoving, feeling their massy billowiness resisting my arms; and in the clearing, past the clouds that I was struggling to force away, through the slight remaining aperture of light and air, I saw, behind Rebecca, on the table, in front of the napkin rack, the walkie-talkie, lying on its side, perfectly quiet . . .;

Eurudice

Early in 1990 a fly-specked yellowed telex arrived in India from, of all places, Normal, Illinois, a town I would have guessed, had I heard it mentioned in conversation, to be an ironist's fiction. From Normal the message had traveled to Providence, R.I., an equally ominously named spot, had been forwarded to Heraklion (Hercules) in Crete, and from there to Bombay, then on to Jaipur, the pink capital of the state of Rajasthan, to the home of the maharaj of Dundlod, whose secretary sent it on to Dundlod's castle in the remote upstate province of Shekhavati, in the heart of the desert, where it was delivered by a rotund Sikh who rarely left his lotus position in the front of his cardboard-and-thatch store and who served as the village pharmacist and postmaster, to another Sikh, a ramrod-straight stern fighter who was the maharaja's driver and bodyguard and who presented it to me on a silver dinner tray along with three freshly shot and curried gaunt pigeons. The telex from Normal changed the course of my life. The maharaj was glittery-eyed, swarthy and shy, and his name was Bonnie. The engulfing desert was blinding and brilliant and strangely rich. The palace was hand-painted with aging floor to ceiling frescoes of goddesses, beasts and feasts. The marble courtyards were covered in sand which barely mobile servants were paid to sweep. Our days were filled with laziness and innuendo, chats and folk lessons, location scouting and preparations for a documentary on local 'possessed' women I was planning to shoot, and little could have shaken that delicate balance of escapism, surrealism, and daily life. The telex informed me that my manuscript, f/32, had been selected winner of the Fiction Collective Two annual fiction contest and the prize was publication within the year. I'd never submitted any manuscript to any publisher in my life. *f/32* had been my thesis for an M.A. in creative writing in Boulder in 1987. Ron Sukenick and Robert Steiner had been my committee advisors. Providence had worked it out so that the reader-writer judging the award for 1990, Fred Tuten, deemed no submission suitable for publication and, rummaging through their archives, my committed ex-professors discovered my text, fixed it up, and presented it to Fred who approved of it (it did after all chronicle the toils of a cunt) and I thus became, to my shock and terror, pride and shame, a published author. That novel brought on offers, translations, journalistic gigs, and I swam with the flow and have never looked back and never lived in a palace again; and that's life functioning at its best, I believe.

from *ƒ/32*

Mixing their semen with that of previous and future lovers in one highly idealised cunt is aphrodisiacal for men. Ela's cunt is a homosocial, mildly homosexual bond, a conduit that joins all men who come into it but also measures them up against one another. A natural selector.

•

The stories of men chasing Ela through thick and thin make other men chase her also. If she agrees, she replies: "OK, let's have sex. If we fuck, I will forget you." This frightens men. They blubber: "But you don't understand me." Ela: "We fuck or not. Choose." As men rise to the task, eager to write history with their cocks, they feel like pilgrims and crusaders setting out on a rocky course towards the great miracle awaiting them at the end.

•

Simultaneously, thousands of thoughts cross men's minds: Will I survive? Succeed? What if I lose my erection when I am so near the goal? I'd better use my *Kama Sutra* reading. I can surprise her by performing all 369 positions with acrobatic agility and without a safety net, progressing from the Chinese wheel to the Indian reversed aeroplane to the elephant-on-bird posture and back.

•

Ela orders them: "Spread your body." She puts silver or

pink lipstick on her cunt. "Get ready, go!" she calls. She urges: "Do one for the mirror!" Soon she comes with a war cry.

•

Sometimes she directs them to undress, grab the bed posts or hug their knees, and be still. She admires their curves, moans and lifts the hissing whip. She enjoys their determination to stifle their cries, the timidly offered buttocks that turn red, and her own exhaustion. She comes even before the first strike. Ela sees flagellation as an overcoming of boundaries, outside the realm of common sensations, free and exhilarating. Scars highlight the beauty of flesh, for all things obtain value against a background of death. When men complain: "I am at the end of my emotional rope," Ela takes it as a request for S & M. She gets out her handcuffs, thread and needle, pincers, nippers, pliers, ski equipment, gladiator costume, and replies; "I've never been suicidal; I suffer from the opposite syndrome." She whips her lovers with their belts. She prefers belts that have large metal buckles, such as the VW logo. When they relax, men enjoy it as the first sign of her love. She never whips the same man twice.

•

Meanwhile, men are always busy thinking ahead: The detail is what matters, just like in the movies . . . the long masculine curve of my thigh in the chiaroscuro . . . I'll take her on a grand tour of the furniture: to the armchair, the sink (preferably full of dishes), washing machine (best if it's working), fridge, the broom closet (like a jail for juvenile delinquents), the balcony. Then what?

•

Am I the opposite sex? Ela asks, in mid-rhythm. Or am I the sex?

•

I am not doing enough, men think in terror; I should now do a rain dance, 30 knee-bends and 30 push-ups while inside her, flailing my muscled arms hither and thither, then run out and bring back the guy from the upstairs apartment and perform a Bermuda triangle (both men on her), then Ben Hur (one rider, two chariots), then end with a vicious cycle (one behind the other).

•

After sex, Ela sleeps while men narrate to her their unassorted childhoods till dawn. They peer into her post-orgasmic face that glows with heavenly peace and suddenly know that they can never be One with her. This thought torments them, and they interrupt their monotonous stories ("when I was nine, my Dad got drunk, pulled down my pants and chuckled"); their voices crack, their blistered cocks fade and they shout: "How frightfully fulfilling love is!"

•

Ela thinks: I envy the stylites (Christian ascetics living on pillars). I would love to live alone on a vibrating pillar.

•

Then suddenly men notice that simply looking at the sleeping Ela is enough to conjure up their favorite melody (*Nanna's Lied, Und was bekam des Soldaten Weib?, Tango habanera, La donna e mobilé, Cielo e mar!*), and now that they so enjoy the music, they don't lift their eyes from her again. When the intensity of the music forces them to shut their eyes, men hear from within them a rising murmur: words spill forth from them again, as if sprung from the very air. They still want her to know everything about them; they need to empty themselves out into her. It is as if their instinct for survival leads them to vivisect themselves, to wrench from themselves their innermost core and drop it at her feet.

•

Men feel equal and intimate with her when they speak. Their own prattle reassures men. Their sexual performance alone leaves men threatened. They prefer the warmth of language.

•

Ela resents men for using sex as an excuse for confession.

•

Ela often blind-folds herself during her everyday fucks to avoid the sight of men self-consciously stroking and poking her with gummy reverence. "This is the Test," men think, "the big time, I can't fuck up, my honour is on the line: suppose I make a mistake, suppose I fuck like an actor or a secretary?"

So Ela ties her panties over her mocking eyes and exposes instead the pure eye of her cunt, which loosens men up. When they don't feel watched, men perform better. Besides, Ela prefers not to see what she desires. She dislikes the visions of human panic that surface during sex.

•

Every man who finds himself inside Ela wonders: How is she rating me? Men fuck in the terror that another man has surpassed them; they fuck as if they were being judged by God.

•

For Ela, a blind fuck is as courageous as any other gamble. A one-nighter provides an intensity created by the mystery of the stranger and the ensuing suspense that transcends the two individuals and that is impossible to sustain for long. Any lasting relationship contains the seeds of its own pedestrianism. A flying fuck cannot be dominated. Anonymous sex is weightless.

•

"My life up to now was spent with caution, and what happiness have I gained?" men confide in Ela. "Why should I plan? Why should I work? Things come and go without my planning, in spite of my plans. So I come, into you, Ela, wherever you take me," men avow. Ela mistakes the tears on their faces for sweat.

•

Ela wishes she were a hermaphrodite. Her inquiries into sex-change remain disappointing: science cannot add on to her pelvis a functional cock that could penetrate her own cunt in solitude.

•

Men feel grateful to be allowed into Ela. They think: a cock is insensitive and crude. I must try not to become a hammerhead. Ela thinks: men are vulnerable inside a cunt, and at its mercy. They plunge into something they have never seen. So both sides relish what they imagine to be the weakness of the other.

•

For that moment when they enter Ela, men feel in control,

for it is their erection which excites her. That glory evaporates as they get busy deciding what tempo to follow, which parts of her body are most sensitive, how to use their muscles, weight, skin and memory to satisfy her, how to time their orgasm to coincide with hers. They blank out their pleasure to concentrate on hers. They turn into hard-working greasers slogging in the mines.

•

Ela plunges into sex head-on like a gleeful dolphin. She doubles up into loops, rises into a pyramid, unravels like a flowing ribbon, contorts into yogi formations. She grunts, gurgles, gulps, giggles, twitters, squeals, shrieks, sobs, laughs, whistles, mews, clucks, crows, claps, chants and wheezes until she is hoarse. She twitches, quivers, kicks, nods, ruffles, rises and thumps on to the ground like a dying queen. She sings tremulous Egyptianite pitches like a muezzin's call, and produces endless operatic combinations of vowels, foreign euphoric sounds that compose an indecipherable discourse of hedonism. It is rumoured that she speaks in phrases from a forgotten holy tongue.

ELA'S EX-LOVERS' OBSERVATIONS ON ELA'S WAIL:

A: "Ela's orgasms are a symphony titled 'Death of a Tragedienne'. Her wail makes every metaphor literal: it reveals the unknowable in the familiar, the impossible in the possible, death in life."

B: "Ela's wail is the missing link. It is a catharsis, the Ideal Happiness. Unaffected by the world. I no longer feel nauseated by all the people who want her, or afraid that they may take her away, because I now know that she can never be possessed."

C: "She doesn't come, she prays. Better than those choruses of Buddhist monks and Bulgarian priests . . . People who say she mistreats men have not heard her wail: it is the greatest gift a man could hope to receive in life. It is anything but funny."

D: "No institution, no knowledge, no family, no cultural heritage could prepare me for this. It is the impenetrability of nirvana."

•

Ela's response: All I did was come.

MEMORIES OF A VOYAGE THROUGH ELA'S BODY DURING HER WAIL:

A: "For the first time in my life I was the Other. I lost my cock. It felt complete, effortless. There was no decapitation, no slicing off, just sliding into a dissolve. I was fused into her. Her cunt, superimposed on my groin, was my cunt, allowing me to physically be her. I was amazed how natural and fulfilling it was to be a woman. I felt so close to her then."

B: "Inside her I see large boulders, through which move strange red vehicles that could be bedouins on camels under a small blue sky. Atomic particles and metallic structures circle here and there. Pink searchlights and white light beams fly around. It is a biological spaceship. It is the soul performing for humans."

C: "A circular door of light slides open, and I step into a busy chamber: an astral pinball machine with shaking walls. Over my head I see a glass-domed atrium: the outer layer of Ela's stomach. I proceed deeper into this silver warehouse; I want to locate the wail. The pinball alley shoots up firecrackers of energy around me that fall into a gutter. The gutter is made of slimy organic tissue and drifting pieces of sediment. It has the beauty of a swamp; it destroys every cliché of beauty. I stand amidst the most incredible lubrication of everything I see by a continuous torrent of bodily fluids. The texture of the walls is living; it is akin to the grey matter of the brain, with blistery wrinkles, unlike the hard shapes of familiar creation. The timeless unity of this bacterial fungal formation overwhelms me. I feel my eyes have been opened physically and I witness true beauty at last. The prevalent colour is raw pink. I notice on my side a throbbing red bicycle seat that may be her liver.

I look up and realise I am under her heart: her breast curves upward like the dome of a church, and through it I can see a bubble-city. It's where I want to be. I move up through a corridor of rings like inside a dinosaur skeleton. A stifling presence gathers around me. It's pitch black. I walk sideways through two huge floatable gas balloons that press on my body. I feel like a trespasser. I can't see to turn back. I shouldn't be here, I think. There is no oxygen . . . !"

•

Am I causing all this ecstasy? men wonder. They think it is her love that gives to their embraces this potency and a meaning they never dreamed of before, so they hug her madly and believe: "She loves me so much she can die; I am more than a transient cock." Transported by her rapture into the highest echelons of manhood, secure in their sexual genius, feeling as finalists of the world championship for the best lover, men now want Ela to focus her eyes and acknowledge them; to tell them that she loves them.

•

Ela thinks: Being owned and being fucked are opposites. Possession is erotic only for that second when I hold a man tightly in me; the annihilation of the self is not itself erotic. An orgasm is the outcome of a vague, deadly danger that forces me to reach beyond my capacities. It is a crime against the mind.

•

"Don"t you see," men ask, pounding themselves into Ela, "don't you know me?" "I am your slave, I am here!" they pant. "I am your prehistoric lover, I am back!" "Say yes!" "Am I making you happy?" "Do you like it?" "Do you love me? Say it!"

•

In fact, Ela responds to the sensations in her body, and not to what causes them. In this way, she is both erotic and chaste.

•

Ela slaps, caresses, tickles, hugs, relishes, sucks and excites herself, gasps in an impetuous rage of joy, drowns in a solitary singing madness that confounds her lovers. She rolls off the bed or the bench or the ledge and, holding them tightly inside her, drags them along on the ground, leaving behind her a phosphorecent trail of cum, like an extraterrestrial crawling slug.

•

Her lovers puff, gush, fret, thrash, reel, grope, climb and heave as if struggling with the ocean after jumping ship; they shove their flustered cocks into her last niche, agonise to hold on to the rudder and steer, to bear the brunt of her lust, break her trance, force open her heart and shackle it. They clutch their eyes to escape from the sights of her flame that bring them to the verge of coming; lights flash in their brain, they turn black in the face, blinded by sweat, but refuse to go down. They knead, rotate, swing, ride, plough, smother, sling and manipulate her like a rodeo horse or a Chinese gymnast. Their breaths whistle through clenched teeth, their tongues bloat with pounding blood, their cocks sail on lost to them for ever, but they cling to Ela even more tightly, and can still blubber: "I am planted in you," "I am a sword piercing you," or again, "Call me: My love!" They storm the fortress of her cunt for days, pound the breath out of her, beat ugly grunts from her throat, press for what now they live for: to reach her very centre, her inaccessible soul; to hear Ela bleat: "This has never happened to me before!"

•

Ela's orgasm* is a visit to the Other world. It is an endless piercing fall into empty space. The floor falls down from under her. Her innards push to jump out. But a tremendous centrifugal force keeps her body pinned to the spinning drum of the world.

•

While she comes, Ela chokes, convulses and faints. Some rookies become perturbed: they stop short, cover her with blankets, dab her with water, weep and call the police. Then she comes to.

---

* Ela's clitoral orgasm is a whole new book.

•

Sooner or later the men smell the pungent stench of a duel taking place, the foul odour of their own burning nerves: they are being devoured by her, and they become enraged. They envision every man whose marks have been effaced from the walls of her cunt, every fanatic who played deadly games with his cock in flames. It dawns on them that no man has ever broken into her: she is voluptuous death. So they feel exuberant, like men who face a doomed struggle. They blurt out: "This will kill me. Do you want a corpse in you?"

•

But loss pleases Ela. She loses or abandons anything she owns. It gives her freedom. Good sex is sex she cannot control.

•

The men refuse to give up. This is their time in the lights, their chance on stage, when they must break her into recognition. They fuck against hope. They implore God to send them more cocks, one in her mouth, one in her ass, two in her ears; teams of fresh cocks to replace the tired players. For they know that her cunt could open under them at any moment and hell would show through.

•

Sex is apocalyptic. An orgasm is a shocked, stunned recognition: "God exists!" Each orgasm is a divine unmasking, Ela believes.

•

All these hours Ela rises and falls and laughs with awe at the pandemonium of her flesh, the whipping maelstrom in her cunt. She gives men everything but the words they need. She wails, comes, faints, comes to, comes and faints again, until she loses consciousness for so long that she could be declared legally dead, and she no longer feels even through her cunt.

•

Men are suddenly shocked to feel their own pleasure: it comes over them as a quick, sharp joy that is out and gone. Then they have come to the edge of the cliff. They lie spent. Some jump off. Some calculate how far they must go for it to happen again. Some want to talk about it. Some ask to be held.

Some shout: "I came like a woman!" Ela believes men suffer from vagina envy.

•

So after Ela's pupils have not been seen for hours and her body is jerked by spasms from head to toe, and men no longer know where their cocks end and her cunt starts, after they have cried enough tears and have poured into her their last lifedrops, men groan with stunned, paralytic grief, dash forward in paroxysm and shrivel inside her. But they refuse to withdraw and face the deflated world outside of her. Instantly, her wondrous cunt swells around them, so that even after the men droop dizzy from defeat, they still fit tightly in her cunt and can sense it resurrecting them; and then they hear her deep reverberant laugh.

•

Sometimes Ela feels she has exhausted her cunt's inventiveness that previously unlocked her as a wind into the world. The sex that gave her freedom seems old. She feels doomed to repeat herself. But only sex can contain her inner seismic turbulence and make the anxiety of being herself something she can laugh at.

4. DEATH: EPILOGUE

People behave outrageously with Ela, for they need to give themselves to her, but also to find a respectable reason for their spontaneous subjugation. They treat her everyday actions as proof of her love for them. "Don't be afraid of your love! You can fool yourself, but you can't fool me!" they claim.

•

Ela counsels her followers: "I am not necessary to you. I am the light from a thigh suddenly revealed under a lifted dress." When Ela tells her followers that they stifle her, they offer to take her away from this world that drains her. The idea of her rescue, of saving her from others, becomes the centre of their lives.

•

As Ela lacks common sense, she needs friends or servants to look after her. But being served by people who love her is exhausting and keeping those who serve her from loving her is impossible. That is the deadlock of Ela's quotidian existence. It explains the high turnover of all the persons who are connected to her.

•

Men don't think Ela is subject to need, disease or growth; they don't believe she had a past, or a childhood. In her presence, words become cumbersome and meanings fall apart. She seems like a vision that may vanish at any moment. Men blab: "Women like you turn up in literature, they can't sit across the table and eat dinner with me!" "You are life to me, but it's strange to be near you!" Ela responds: "How sad that I am everything to you."

•

No one knows who Ela is. So everyone wants her. "This is the real thing," men think, and want to rise up to her standards. She embodies everyone's ideals and pretences, for she is arbitrary, like a dream-condensation; that is her freedom.

•

Ela's freedom is mere indifference. She lives well on her indifference, for people love her freely and easily because her own affections are not involved. They feel proud to possess her unpossessed spirit and to buy her all that she can do without.

•

People exist as fiction for Ela. The world is a second language for her. She contemplates: People can't see that I am normal. No one presumes that I am a subject. I need a sign on me.

•

Men endlessly develop florid theories about Ela. They assume she contains more than meets the eye and undertake to unveil her. "Behind Ela's confidence beats a heart wounded by a fatal love for a man," some judge. "If you solve me," Ela contends, "I am not a mystery. If I am a mystery, do not solve me; make up your mind."

•

Ela thinks: Love is a curse. Don't be loved and you'll be happy.

•

"Oh, Ela," men babble, "I'd be happy if I could just look at you across the table for the rest of my life!" Every man whom Ela meets advises her: "You must become the real you. No one knows you like I do. You must get to know yourself. The real you is sensitive, sweet, insecure. Let me impregnate you."

Alan Singer

When I began to write my first novel, I wanted to insist on a radical suspension of beliefs, a disruption of those conventions that bind a culture in the cocoon of habitual practice. Language is of course the starting place, the breeding ground for conceptual novelty. Therefore, I was, and I remain, committed to a language energized by rhetorical rather than plot complexity. I take rhetoric to be that feature of style which holds the language open for new possibilities of sense. Metaphor, for example, exerts a skeptical leverage on all forms of intelligibility by which we make the world recognizable to ourselves. Metaphor belies the familiar, presents us with a world that coheres only in the necessity of its incoherent moments, unlike plot which is bound to naturalize its incoherent moments. Consequently, metaphor bears much of the expositional burden of my fiction. It goes without saying that the only obligation I set for myself as a writer is not the making of an image of the world, so much as the remaking of the reader—in the sense that we always come to the world through our ways of constructing it. The older and more accepted idea that a writer needs to find an audience begs the question of where the audience itself comes from. It takes the reader and the reader's world as givens which of course spells the end of possibility. The idea that the invention of a fiction is the remaking of the reader is not, I think, an unseemly presumption, particularly if we remember that in its most potent forms—I think of Sterne, Conrad, Joyce, Kafka, Beckett, Blanchot—fiction has always been a ruthless dislocation of all those self-certainties that comfort us with the knowledge of who we are.

from *The Charnel Imp*

Such was the shock that detonated Moertle's gunmetal eyes when I delivered the news of his daughter's demise. I spoke in my most deliberate voice of hypothesis and conclusion, mounting symptom upon symptom until the architecture of fatality rested upon his arched brow as an awesome edifice.

But my most patient numbering of the signs of illness was in fact only intended to gain time for myself to fill my own eyes with comprehension of what I saw before me. For as easily as I had read the symptoms of the disease on the daughter's small person, so it would be that much more difficult to tell the vast story of this Moertle's destruction from the appearance he presented to me there.

The injunction issued at the slaughterhouse gate must have struck him with the severity of the nail that held it above his questioning eyes. Perhaps at that moment he even heard the urgent ring of my voice in the bold-faced word—**QUAR-ANTINE**—like the insect buzz already putting sticky legs on the membrane of an ear unable to distinguish the hearing from the motion of the head shaking it off. The word held him on its tether. His head hung on the heavy yoke that specified the terms of the quarantine: "No one shall enter under penalty of law."

He stamps his feet four times, blows through his nose, nods toward the industrious hive of the sawblade, which he does not hear behind the split boards of the slaughterhouse gate. The narrow stall of his comprehension begins to hiss with the sound of a secret bodily expulsion. His sour breath squirms in the projectile of spit that he leaves sizzling on the curled leaf of the quarantine document. I would have needed my microscope to know whether the printed word could culture the germ that stained it.

And then there was not another sound to trample the slow, lumbering avowal that he released from his barred lips. I know everything he said, though he was speaking to himself. For me the words are like drops of water-bellied image that makes them hang and sway and plop. And though the drops are as clear as eye-water, everything revealed in that glistening surface tension will burst like a bubble in the blink of an eye. Each ripening reflection falls the moment of its fullest ingestion of imagery. So the vision of Moertle at the gate comes to my eyes with the urgency of a world awaiting destruction.

He had approached the locked doors of the slaughterhouse. He had read the terms of the injunction. He had departed.

Then he returns. But it is not to be a reconciliation with the leaded shot of print—**QUARANTINE**—which richocheted from his credulity.

He returns, yanking the leash of a tottering steer, aiming himself at the locked gate, the steel point of his concentration gleaming out in front of him like the knifepoint touching the center of his brain. The beast in tow is as dry and as brittle as any we find piled up on their own bones at the end of an empty street or lying on their sides, collecting sunlight in the declivity of their sunken hides and swimming with maggots. The shivering haunch is as thin as an edge of paper smacking the wind, and as sharp.

The gate is no obstacle for a man who has the key. The doors to the slaughterhouse flap wide wings against the lowering bosom of sunlight when they are opened. There is a rush of breath from the cellar darkness that has been pickling within. Under the wide lintel of the entranceway, the hide of the steer is blown like still water into ripples over its back. A low moan is squeezed from the thinness of the animal girth as though

Moertle's foot were playing the pedal of a sour organ. Simultaneously, the fumes of some furtive, gastric combustion rush upon Moertle as though he had trodden through a field of rotten vegetables in the darkness that is deepening with every step he takes into the empty building. But his sense of direction is unimpaired. Though he cannot find the breaker switch to make all before him visible, he has only to reach into the blind depths for the crucial implements of the task he has undertaken. He is confident that the darkness itself will conform to the shapes of his beckoning hands, like fistfuls of warm clay already wriggling to the rhythms of the labor he has in mind for them. That is how memory works.

So he accepts the blinding darkness as the torch of his other senses. He lights his lungs with the wick of a long breath. He thrusts his nose lanternlike out in front of each darkening step. He lets his ears burn to hear the paces of the animal in tow. For he has entered the long dark tunnel of pursuit that is as coiled with metamorphosis as the wet labyrinths of digestion.

The burnished light of reason is my only witness to what the darkness will not admit to sight.

Holding the shortened rope with one hand, Moertle finds the animal's jumping blood with the other. The warm haunch is still. But the pulse runs with a fury from under the long jaw to the depth of the chest, where he seizes a fold of loose skin as thin as the detachable tail of the elusive salamander panting safely under its rock. He marks the place with the strength of his twisting fingers. He will feel for it again as a bruise when he takes the animal's heart.

And from this moment, everything else seems to be swept along on the current he has traced with sensitive fingers to the place of the animal's heartbeat. Without a sense of direction, Moertle walks forward, finds the mouth of the narrow corridor that will swallow the animal whole and deliver it beneath the short metal bridge where he will be waiting.

There the blunt hammer weighs in Moertle's hand as though he were standing below his victim, submerged in a depth of rancid water rather than above, choking on the explosive air of the animal's fright. A coarse hair tickles his nose when

Moertle takes his last breath. And then the contact of the hammerhead with the nodding skull begins a telepathic communication that will reverberate in every successive motion. It will carry Moertle toward an understanding of what pains his own head with such crystalline memory that he can execute in the dark what is usually possible—even for professional butchers—only under a strictly regulated wattage of searing light.

The handsaw flickers a little light to help him find his mark on the neck. The animal's head weighs with the shifting weight in Moertle's shoulders, permitting him to reach for it with aplomb when it drops from the tooth of the saw. The vibrations of the saw remain alive in Moertle's hand, though he has lost the instrument itself to the slippery mire at his feet. Then the head slips too on his greasy fingertips, and he is suddenly aware that the blackness all around him is merely a kindred sensation to the cold, ocular jelly where his thumb is stuck in an aghast socket of the animal eye.

He is glad to replace the head with the hook in his open hand. But the hook floats at his own eye level when he stands. It will not be lowered to the floor on its cold chain without a jolt from the electric generator, which will not warm to this enterprise.

Therefore Moertle must carry the weight of the carcass on his own back before it will dance above his head in the light of brandished cutlery. If the hook will not move, he will move to the hook. With the shoulder of beef draped over his shoulder, legs and hooves dangling the length of the human torso like straps of a preposterous knapsack where he takes his grip, Moertle is kneeling in the fetal position. It is the only position which gives the requisite leverage to catapult the headless carcass onto a point of steel as small and concentrated with invisible light as the undilated pupil of hate. But perhaps because this side of meat has already been shaved so close to the bone by shimmering blades of sunlight, Moertle's human frame, slightly canted forward, then seesawing in small movements beneath the length of its burden—somehow converting the inertia of the seesaw into swift and tightly sprung vertical motion—is able to lift and project the ponderous motions of mammoth animal life, though the carcass weighs only as a phantom of its lumbering prairie existence.

Moertle's first exertion is ended. The splayed carcass swings from the gibbet by a tenuous noose of gristle pulled out from the hide like a bleached shirt collar. Wiping his brow, Moertle realizes that he is soaked through with the juices that gurgle around the pit of the fruit, even though he is only just now ready to pick up the knife and section the pulp.

Now the sensations of the spurting artery are coming from the sweaty hairs of his own chest, and the cloth of his trousers is bunching between his legs with every strenuous movement, as though he were perspiring with the animal's exertions, substituting his feeling for the animal's flesh.

"Memory is a leash tied at both ends. Nothing must be permitted to rest in its form of life or it is lost. The foot in the shut door is the one that fits the bruised slipper of our most miraculous transformations," are the words he splatters the walls with, working now in close quarters at the end of the alleyway, everything echoing against a metal trough where his feet are beginning to slip.

Long, curving and bitten with the toothmarks of a fiercer metal, the serrated knifeblade sends a shiver through the steer's underbelly when it is pierced, opening lips of conviviality that sigh, are licked with iridescence and finally gush forth with all the closely packed organs, like a bough struck off by lightning in the orchard, redolent of sugar and smoke and dripping long after it reaches the ground. Moertle's hands smear everything they touch. He no longer wants the knife handle and its solid grip on things. He would rather know the feathery kiss of the wounded lip on his elbows. He would rather know his hands buried deep inside the abdominal cavity and feeling for the root of things, the ducts knotty as chicken necks that he can snap between two fingers, the network of tubes branching without source or destination but deepening his entanglement until he cannot refuse the impulse to hold up a bowl-shaped organ—liver or third stomach—feeling for the buoying sensations of another world, puckering its lips, opening its gills, floating within.

And the uplifted chalice overflows, spilling gulping portions with each concussive syllable that Moertle projects, like a man heaving stones up the sides of a pit: ". . . rather . . . let everything be different . . . what is recognizable has already irreparably altered the eye persuaded of its familiarity . . . and the wistful sensations . . . the scattered . . . the restrung moments . . . when they are close as bees in the hive, then memory is a honeyed thing . . . but you cannot swallow it . . . its thickness occludes the throat . . . the tongue tells a different story then . . . the vanity of making whole pricks the eye as a shard from the mirror if you get too close . . . let the image seep from its cracks . . . not the mirrors . . . look again only if your face is hard enough to break that glass . . ."

And what was a welter of hiving life in the animal's belly is now a seething depth where Moertle's feet have sunk, making the lapping sounds of the ruined pier. But now the hatchet raised above his head—and despite the leather hood of darkness—shows that he has not found what he is looking for. So the head of the hatchet falls too, to the search.

The ribcage sounds like a wooden chest when it is broken open. Bones splinter too, intimations of light that prick the eager fingers guided along their curving paths. The animal lungs burst from their cage. The invasive touch of the atmosphere sweats the more intimate tissue beneath to a cluster of raisins clutched in a sodden fist. And far beneath the lungs, the heart twisted with its overgrowth of arteries like fattened leeches, is an indefatigable root that will not be pried loose until the hatchet's cold lip is sunk upon the thick shaft of the aorta. Finally, everything falls from the ribs of the carcass as dying fish to the unsteady bottom of the boat, slick, curving back into the air, briefly thrashing, slowly flattening beneath the pressing palm of darkness.

When the carcass is completely scooped out, and the long segmented spinal column and perpendicular shoulder bones are shining through a taut film of crimson saliva, then the slack hide and legs hang as if nailed to a crosstree, as if the armature of crucifixion were these very bones themselves from which the animal's life has always leapt at the world. Headless victim, its tail hung with weights to the floor, the carcass dangles without a shiver left like a curling hair to its chilly flank.

Moertle's upward gaze hangs too from the only light dredged out of this long immersion in darkness, winking from the tip of the steel hook. Now, and by that fiercely honed fight, I can see what has been obscured by the feverish activity of this slaughter. I can see that the slow uncovering of layer upon layer of membranous tissue, which had first appeared to be the compunction of a meticulous search, was in fact only the brusque clearing of space for what is now fully discovered and restless to be free in all the tensile anatomy of Moertle's own body.

He stands on the last rung of a stepladder. It must have been there all along like the cliff edge on a moonless night. He stands as if ready to embrace the full length of the stripped carcass or else to receive it with its ribs splayed out like the flared coat of the exhibitionist. It offers only the pale stiffness of the hook, lower than eye level to Moertle's eye, but pointing up.

His is the grey fish mouth poised for the silver hook. He sees nothing else because he has deliberately hung the drying steer. He has beheaded the carcass. He has split the hide and carved out the walls of the animal girth only to make a place for himself there (especially where the animal head roars its absence), to replace the horns, the shocked eyes and rippling nostrils with the frenzied mask of his own fright. Moertle wants to hang his own head on the hook. And because he has relieved the carcass of the weight that hung within it like a second life, he believes that the hook will support them both.

Only a gentle kick at the ladder, a fanciful trapeze motion of flying arms and legs to cross three steps of pitch air, head pointed high and he will feel the frozen tip of the hook rising in the back of his own throat stiff with the alarum of a screaming tongue.

But Moertle has forgotten that the darkness is a cloak thrown over the scene of all such imaginings. So, with his head thrust out and bowing into the mouth of destruction, he merely falls upon the shoulder of the carcass and does not even whisper to the hook in passing.

The glancing blow is enough to cause the hook to bite

completely through the gristly collar where it held its prey, landing the carcass on top of the man and both into the pit of offal.
The naked hook swings above them like a windblown moon.

The contact of the two bodies resounds with a splash.
The sound is indistinguishable from the motion with which
Moertle spews from the stagnant center of the well, drenched
in outrage, speechless because his mouth is clamped upon a
crapulous curd, holding it with his teeth so it doesn't touch his
tongue, but unable to propel it over the squeamish lip without
a nudge from the back of his throat. He cannot use his hands
quickly enough to wring out the wetness binding him in his
own clothes. And the frantic movements that have put him
unsteadily on his feet and tipped him forward in the depth of
darkness until he is swimming furiously toward the light of
the open door—it has dilated over his shoulder since he entered—exhale the final breath of the animal's existence, because with each step forward Moertle feels the animal breath
suspiring over his skin with the sour stench of digesting grasses,
spoiled hays, fermented pollen, pursuing him into the open
corral on wider and wider wings of ghostly odor.

Moving in full stride out of the slaughterhouse gate,
Moertle is leaving bloody footprints like boiled kidneys in
the sunlight. Yet they are camouflaged over an expanse of
ground already blooming with crimson flowers, sprouted so
closely to the earth that it might be soaked with them. Had
Moertle eyes for anything but the path beating down my door,
he would have lost them amid the cresting grasses grown
long enough to wave at a passing fugitive on the road, but
thrown back like a wet head of hair over the aroused body of
land he crossed.

Moertle touches me when he sees me. He is trying to
pinch himself out of the dream by getting a better grip on his
surroundings. He is smearing my clinical lapel as though I
had been brusquely pulling the heads of chickens across my
chest. He is fairly bursting with the color he imparts to me. It
is in his clotted hair no less than on his bobbing dimples. It is
dripping from the inside of his shirt cuff no less than from
the pinched corners of his eyes. He is himself the picked fruit

already crushed between impatient fingers where they are breaking it off its stems.

Knowing full well everything he had to tell, I waited to hear it from his own lips.

Don Webb

In 1983 I moved to Austin, Texas. The Half Price bookstores were full of trade paperbacks distinguished by an ugly colophon (of a stylized chicken) and very cheap prices. I bought many books by writers I had never heard of like Sukenick and Major. (I was a broke game-designer in those days, not to mention college drop-out.) I loved the world they opened for me. I found out that the Fiction Collective had a fiction contest. In between writing dungeon play modules and being screwed over in a five book fantasy deal, I did the little prose poems that became *Uncle Ovid's Exercise Book* and won me a tip to Normal, and a pasta dinner from Curt White that I threw up (nervous at the thought of my second public reading). *Ovid's* was well received—and helped inspire Richard Dorset and Bruce Sterling to coin the word "Slipstream." I hope that others reading these words now, especially if they bought this book third-hand at a garage sale, have similar Doors open in their own inner worlds. That was why the Collective was Dreamed up. So It Is Done.

Metamorphosis No. 80
The Pyramid Builder

CHAPTER I

In this chapter John Rothe is revealed to be all things to all men. To Charlotte Ubu, leading Denver feminist, he is a genial uncle. To the Chamber of Commerce, he is Denver's leading banker. To the Diocese, he is a financial and spiritual pillar. He is even a patron of the arts. At the end of the chapter he receives a call from his lawyer Yage Thomas. The gig is up.

CHAPTER II

In this chapter young John Rothe is born in the silk stocking row of Carson City. His family's money protects John from the harsh realities of the Depression. In 1938 he receives a camera and a wirerecorder. With these he is able to supplement his income through blackmail. After the first blackmailing scheme, his uncle Abramelin Rothe denies his nephew access to his (Abramelin's) gardens. John will wonder how the old man knew for the rest of his (John's) life. As an amateur reporter for the *Carson City Tattler*, John learns the importance of publicity. Throughout his life there will be many, many photos. He stares hard at the camera, willing himself to be remembered. See? Here he is now.

CHAPTER III

In this chapter John meets Father Sustare. John's folks are glad John is so interested in the Church. Father Sustare introduces John to sodomy. John graduates from high school. Rumors begin about John's "religious life."

CHAPTER IV

Yage Thomas, a third-year engineering student at the University of Cairo, is initiated into the mysteries of the dark side of the Tree of Life. In the Anti-World he gains a glimpse of John Rothe and the fate lines glimmering around him.

CHAPTER V

Don Trampier, young homosexual millionaire from Boulder, Colorado, arrives in Cairo to make *Passion Among the Pharaohs*. He gathers *gali-gali* men, snake charmers, and plump belly dancers for "color." Anti-American sentiment sweeps Cairo with the arrival of Rommel's army. Yage Thomas enables Don to narrowly escape, but all the film equipment is lost. In an obscure ritual in Malta, Yage and Don place a curse on Don's wealthy grandmother. They return to the States—Don to Boulder, Yage to Yale Law School.

CHAPTER VI

John becomes a male nurse. During the day he works at Our Lady of Sorrows Charity Hospital in Boulder—at night he's a private nurse to Mary Trampier. Don arrives from Egypt.

CHAPTER VII

John becomes a procurer of underaged boys for Don. There are larger and larger parties. There is a raid. John posts a twenty-five dollar bond and leaves for Denver. Don leaves for Europe on V-E Day. Yage begins his practice in Boulder.

CHAPTER VIII

Mary Trampier dies, leaving all her wealth to Don in a "spendthrift" trust. He'll be able to live opulently, but never get his hands on the capital. Yage Thomas lends John enough money to begin an X-ray lab. On August 6, 1945, Father John Sustare is consecrated Bishop of Denver.

CHAPTER IX

Two years pass. The world recovers from war. The Marshall Plan. John's clinic flourishes. John buys a restaurant and the Starlight Motel. An incredibly emaciated Don Trampier turns up at Denver General Hospital. By means of the folding green passport, John spirits him away to the Starlight.

CHAPTER X

John assumes control of Don's life as "business manager." The drinking is curtailed. The parties begin anew. John buys Don's trust for Don's "own good." Sister Mary St. John becomes Bishop Sustare's private secretary. Don's physical and mental health return.

CHAPTER XI

John begins dipping into the trust with the aid of Yage Thomas. Money is stored by Bishop Sustare in tax-free Church funds. John and Yage become fiduciaries for the Bishop's Trust. Sustare visits Rome and is honored by the Pope.

CHAPTER XII

Don's mansion is raided. Seven counts of contributing to the delinquency of a minor and two counts of sodomy are leveled against Don. John is able to buy up all the pictures, including those of himself and the Bishop. Don flees to California. A tacit agreement is reached with the D.A.'s office. Don will stay in California.

257

CHAPTER XIII

John claims that expenses incurred because of the raid have almost depleted the trust. Don's checks become smaller—his drinking gets greater. He dissolves in vodka. Months later he is admitted to a Charity Hospital. He expires in three days. The body is shipped to Boulder. It disappears mysteriously. An empty (closed) coffin is provided for the funeral. John does not attend.

CHAPTER XIV

Twenty years pass. John gets richer. Yage gets richer. The Bishop gets richer. John builds a huge golden bank in downtown Denver. The rectangular skyscraper is topped by a pyramid. Yage gives John some stolen Egyptian art to decorate his office at the apex. John becomes known as "Pharaoh John I."

CHAPTER XV

Bishop Sustare retires. Bishop Keel, his successor, demands that the trust which Bishop Sustare has so long held "for the Church" be turned over to the Church. The directors of the trust, John and Yage, refuse. There are suits and countersuits. The framework, built by Yage Thomas years before, stands. John and Yage control the trust. Sustare fears for his soul and decides to hand over the money. Yage runs down the elderly Bishop with his black Lincoln Continental.

CHAPTER XVI

Sister Mary St. John, unaware that the Bishop's death was not an accident, cleans out his safe. She discovers pictures of the Bishop and young boys from the raid twenty years ago. So the Bishop didn't secretly love her after all. She resolves to go to Bishop Keel with the documents and testimony that will break up Bishop Sustare's private trust. Yage Thomas, horny from killing the Bishop, picks up a young boy.

Extract from Chapter XVI

. . . to the Presidential suite of the Starlight. But first a kiss from those gumdrop lips. Yage turns to look at the boy in the blue light of the International House of Pancakes sign. The boy's face shimmers in the blue, he turns into someone or something else. Surely Yage can't expect otherwise. America is a media democracy—a land of shifting identities Where You Can Grow Up To Be President, a Heisenberg land. The face is steady now. It's the alcoholic face of Don Trampier. Strong dead hands close on the lawyer's neck. There has been a miscalculation.

CHAPTER XVII

Bishop Keel is able to retrieve the Church's money as well as all of the Trampier trust, which Bishop Sustare had been bagman for. Sister Mary St. John is shrived of her sins and retires to an old nun's home. John Rothe is publicly discredited and leaves Denver for his hometown of Carson City. There John discovers that he is the heir to Abramelin Rothe's estate.

Extract from Chapter XVII

. . . fit the gate, John wonders what the second key is for. A long heavy old-fashioned brass key, its barrel is decorated with kabbalistic signs . . . the garden is lovely. Rocky Mountain wildflowers abound. Fountains. The fruit trees haven't budded, though. John moves to inspect them more closely. At the base of the first, a peach, is a small keyhole. John inserts the second key and begins winding the tree. When the spring feels taut, he pulls the key out. The tree buds, then blooms within a minute. John begins to walk to the next tree. Don taps him on the shoulder.

Deborah McKay

My being a writer is impossible. I am mentally ill, I have been a single parent for twenty years and have a daughter at Brown and a nine year old son, who is a wild and wonderful child who was an orphan in Romania for the first two years of his life, I am 51 years old, I work six days a week, including many evenings, and I have no energy or time to write. But I also have a disease, which has come very close to being fatal, the hideous disease of having to write. I have tried every known cure. Nothing works. My first book, EVE'S LONGING, took me twenty years to write. It took that long because of the above and because I have led such a ridiculous life devoted to following my heart's desires, doing what I have been told to do in dreams and visions, and ruthlessly seeking the truth. My second book I have been working on since EVE'S LONGING was published seven years ago. It is an impossible book to write. It claims to be not only my own autobiography but that of the reader, to tell the absolute radical truth like no other book in the universe has ever done, and to be about those things for which we all long in our moments of greatest lucidity. I have no time to work on the book and I don't want to work on it because it makes me crazy. I work on it daily.

from *Eve's Longing*

Chapter One

Eve opens her eyes and sits up in bed, clutching the bed sheets up around her neck with one hand, while she leans over and opens the window with the other hand. She grabs the birds, one by one, from the window ledge and stuffs them into the wide-mouthed jar on her bedside table, poking them down into the jar with the eraser end of a pencil.

"Get in there, you little brats!" she snaps at them as she jabs their round heads with her pencil, packing them down tightly, while still clutching the sheets up around her neck.

By the time she has filled the jar to the brim, she is out of breath, yet she manages to screw the metal lid on and then pound it down with her fist, until her hand aches and the lid is tight.

Now that there is no chance of the birds escaping, she leans back on her pillows and takes a deep breath. She keeps her eyes fixed on the glass jar, watching the birds trying to move within its confines.

They are squirming around in the jar, trying to breathe, but Eve has figured out that she has packed them so tightly that they are now limited to two possibilities:

1. They can move, and risk injuring one another, or
2. They can not move.

She herself was reduced to the same two possibilities a week ago, and had chosen to remain motionless in bed.

The birds, on the other hand, decide to move, and, therefore, the wing of one of them pierces a hole in the stomach of another, their feathers knot and tangle, until they begin to become indistinguishable from one another, and then, finally, it is impossible to tell where one bird ends and the next begins. Their movement has woven them together, glued wing-on-wing by their own white paste. They are smashed up against the jar in bleached patterns.

Eve waits until their motion has ceased altogether, and then she reaches one hand down into the jar. She pulls out the contents, which, to her delight, have been woven into one, large, pasty bird-shawl. She releases the bed sheets from her grip and wraps the shawl about her shoulders. The room fills with the smell of dead sparrows.

The shawl is lovely: the way three bird's eyes have been glued down the front like shiny buttons, with talons creating a delicate embroidery along the edges. Eve relaxes back into her pillows, snuggling in the shawl.

Her brief moment of peace is interrupted by an overwhelming desire to analyze the birds, to figure them out, to arrive at a theory as to their ontological status. But the scraping she hears out in the hallway is even more compelling.

She presumes there are more birds out in the hallway, pecking at the faded, yellow-flowered wallpaper. She listens attentively. Yes, she can distinctly hear more birds out there, although the door to the hall is closed, so she can't see them. She hears them beckoning to her.

"Get up, you bum!" they whisper to her through the keyhole of the door. They are breathing *her* air and eating *her* wallpaper and yet have the nerve to hurl insults and challenges at her!

"Planning to sleep for another week, you slut?" they ask her, in snide tones, through the crack of the door.

Finally, she pushes herself up from the bed, neatly buttons the shawl down the front, and opens the door to the hallway. Her legs are weak from lying in bed for so long. They buckle and she lurches forward, catching herself with her hand on the opposite wall. She feels something slippery, lifts her hand and finds a detached wing, greasy as if buttered. It sticks to the palm of her hand, and she tries to shake it off, but it clings. She pries it off with her foot, but then it sticks to her foot, so she has to hop on the other foot down the hallway, toward the kitchen.

The hall is filled now with birds, sickly specimens, unhealthy, city birds, ramming against the walls in aborted flight, thudding onto her back, dead weights, feathers up her nose, a talon holding one of her eyes shut, wings scraping across her, opening little, bleeding slits in her skin.

But she persists in making her way, slowly, down the hall, hopping, stumbling, and, finally, crawling. She is sweating under the shawl, making her way toward the kitchen, inch by inch. Then, suddenly, she bursts out laughing. She gets up on her knees and grabs one of the birds in mid-flight, holds it tightly in both hands and kisses it smack on the top of its head. Then she tosses it up into the air again.

"Get the hell out of here!" she yells at all of them. She is actually beginning to feel grateful they have come, since this is motion after a week's damp stillness. Their wings have smacked her awake.

Chapter Two

It has taken Eve over half an hour to get down the hallway from her bedroom to the kitchen. Even after the birds had finally flown off, it still took her fifteen more minutes to crawl on her hands and knees, over slippery mounds of feathers, until she made it into the kitchen.

Now she pulls herself up into a chair at the kitchen table and looks around the room. An acidic taste rises in her throat, but she swallows it back down. She makes a decision to do something appropriate. But it's hard to think straight, with these bird feathers sticking out from her nightgown pocket, a few stuck in her hair, two glued to her legs. But she is determined, closes her eyes, takes a deep breath, and forces herself to concentrate. She formulates the basic question:

"What would be the appropriate behavior of a woman sitting at her kitchen table?" she queries.

Of course, as is true in all philosophical inquiry, once the question has been formulated, the answer follows easily. Clearly, one appropriate act would be to eat something.

So Eve begins to look for something to eat. She notices, for the first time in a week, that she is hungry. She can't recall eating at all during the week she has been in bed. Yes, she is beginning to feel quite hungry now. In fact, she can't remember ever being this hungry before.

After searching through the refrigerator and all the cupboards, she has finally arrived at the perfect thing. It is a can of baby peas. She realizes, with a surge of joy, that if she could chose *anything* in the universe at this moment to eat, it would be this very can of peas.

She takes the can and carefully opens it, so as not to spill any of the juice, and pours the whole can into a bowl in front of her. Without a doubt, she has never in her life seen a more delicious meal before her. How delicately the color of the peas is echoed by that of their pale green juice! Her mouth waters for the peas and the liquid bathing them so tenderly.

She sits staring at the bowl with growing appetite, but nothing else happens. There seems to be some problem, something causing the chain of events to have halted.

"What happens next?" she questions.

She states the problem out loud:

"Number One: I am hungry.

"Number Two: There is something wonderful to eat in front of me.

"And Number Three: I do not seem to be eating."

It should be so simple, she thinks to herself. She recalls having eaten nearly every day of her life, and yet this morning she seems to have lost the knack.

She decides to further assess the situation and define the problem. She thinks for a moment in silent meditation. Ah! she has it. She needs a way of getting the peas up from the bowl and into her mouth. She needs a *means of transportation* for the peas. She is determined to figure this out.

"The first element," she reasons to herself, "we shall call 'A' (my mouth), desperately needs a direct way of relating to the second element, call it 'B'(the peas). Clearly, the middle link is missing. There needs to be an overall design, in which both 'A' and 'B' can function mutually together. Perhaps if I made a diagram of this? I used to be able to solve these problems so easily."

Eve has been sitting in front of the peas now for forty-five minutes, growing increasingly frantic, conceptualizing every possible solution for how one might relate A to B, and yet she has not tasted so much as a *single pea*! Her eyes keep darting about the room, looking for a clue. She is trying to be patient, trying to be calm and reasonable, trying to recollect how she has done this in the past.

Then, finally (as if not by her own reason, but by divine inspiration) she discovers the missing link: the *spoon*! She leaps up from the chair, snatches a large soup spoon from the dish drainer, and scoops the peas into her mouth. In her haste, some of the juice sloshes over the edge of the spoon and slides down over her wrist and then on down her arm. After she has finished every pea, she lifts the bowl in both hands and pours the rest of the juice into her mouth and then licks the bowl clean.

Chapter Three

After licking the bowl clean, Eve looks up to see spinning grey wings encircling her head. She feels dizzy, closes her eyes and puts her head down on the kitchen table and falls asleep. A few minutes later, Eve's sister, Clare, with whom Eve shares the apartment, arrives home, carefully balancing three full bags of groceries and a bouquet of white carnations in her arms. Clare smiles with pleasure at seeing Eve up out of bed. There have been times when Eve's retreats to bed have lasted far longer than this one.

Clare tiptoes over and puts one of the bags of groceries

down in the sink, one in the dish drainer and one in the other chair at the table, so as not to disturb Eve. Then she goes over to Eve and feels her forehead. It feels normal. Clare quietly puts away all the groceries, goes into Eve's bedroom and changes her sheets and closes the open window. Then she goes back into the kitchen and gently strokes Eve's head.

Eve blinks and looks up at Clare, still not quite awake.

"You're up!" Clare says cheerily.

Eve makes no response. She just stares around the room, blinking, with a puzzled expression, as if she didn't know where she was.

"I'm so glad you're up because Dad's in town, " says Clare. "He was hoping you could join him for lunch today. I can't come because I have to work the lunch shift."

Eve nods her head without saying anything.

"You probably should start getting ready if you want to go," says Clare. "You'd have to leave in about an hour."

Eve bolts upright in her chair and gasps. "In an *hour*?" she says in disbelief. "I'll never make it!" She looks at Clare, her face panic- striken.

"Yes, you will," says Clare. "I'll run a bath for you." She takes Eve's hand and leads her into the bathroom.

After Clare goes back into the kitchen, Eve shuts the bathroom door and locks it. Then she turns off the cold water and fills the rest of the tub with just hot water. Her hands are trembling so badly she can hardly undo the buttons on the bird shawl. The shawl is slippery and slides out of her hands and falls into the bathtub. A stain emerges from it in the hot water. Eve reaches in and pulls it out, scalding her hands. She wrings the shawl out in the sink, wraps it in a huge bath towel, drains the tub, scrubs it out with Ajax, puts in more hot water and finally climbs in.

The submerged part of her body aches and turns bright red, but she hardly notices. She scrubs herself very hard with a rough sponge and lots of soap, beginning at the top of her forehead and moving down her body systematically, so as not to miss a single spot, concentrating especially on her arm where the pea juice has hardened. Then she washes her hair, scrubbing her scalp vigorously, in little circular motions, digging her nails in, rinsing and shampooing over and over. Then she lets the water out of the tub, but the drain is clogged with feathers. She frantically pulls the feathers out and flushes them down the toilet.

She turns on the shower and stands up. She takes a clean washcloth and repeats the previous process, in exactly the same sequence, but with a different soap and shampoo. She stands for a long time letting the water pound on her head. Then she gets out and dries herself carefully with six different towels and brushes her teeth for twenty minutes, using up the toothpaste four times and adding more, spitting out blood where she brushes too hard on her gums.

She looks at herself in the floor-length mirror, sees a hair on her breast, so she turns on the shower again, gets back in and rinses the hair off, this time checking to make sure all hairs, pea juice, and feathers have been removed before getting out. Then she sits on the edge of the tub and clips her fingernails and toenails into the tub.

As she washes the nail clippings down the drain, she remembers one time when she and Clare were on their way to meet their father for dinner. Just as Eve was putting a token into the slot at the subway station, she found herself paralyzed and knew something was drastically wrong with her fingers holding the token. She looked down at them and noticed that she had neglected to clip her fingernails. So she had grabbed Clare's arm and made her come back up into the street with her and wait while she ran into a drugstore, bought a pair of nail clippers, and clipped her nails carefully over a trashbasket.

Eve is staring at the water swirling in a spiral down the bathtub drain. She feels a chill come over her body and sees a tiny image of her father spinning in the water. He is only the length and width of her thumb and is wearing a neatly pressed, grey summer suit, a perfectly starched white shirt and a navy blue tie with very tiny white dots on it. She stares at the white dots, thinking about how evenly spaced they are on his tie. She hates those dots and reaches down to pry them off with one of her fingernail clippings, but too late, he has swirled down the drain.

Now she pictures her father looking at her across the table in the restaurant. She can smell his wonderful, freshly-starched shirt and his after shave, Aqua Velva. She wants to put her head on his shoulder to rest, to smell him better. She leaps up and looks in the bathroom mirror. She pulls her long, wet hair back into a tight rubberband, smoothing every strand of hair down flat against her head. Then she sprays deodorant on, waits for it to dry, and sprays it on again, three times.

Clare knocks tentatively on the door. "You better get dressed," she suggests. Eve desperately wants to take another quick shower, but she resists, and goes into her room to get dressed. Clare has laid out some fresh clothes for her on the bed. Eve changes her blouse four times and her skirt twice. Nothing looks right. She grabs more clothes from the closet, even winter clothes, although it is mid-August. There is something wrong with everything she puts on: broken zippers, missing buttons, rips and stains. Clare comes to the door of Eve's bedroom.

"You look fine," she says encouragingly. "You just buttoned it worng." She unbuttons Eve's blouse and re-does it. Then she hands Eve her purse and a piece of paper with the name and address of the restaurant where Eve is to meet her father. Then she leads Eve to the front door. Eve sighs and reluctantly hurries uptown to meet her father.

Chapter Four

Eve approaches her father as she always does, stumbling toward him, heart trembling, blood rushing to her head, not seeing anything on the street, but, instead, imagining herself waving enormous palm fronds and bowing before him. She imagines she has burnt offerings for him in her purse, in a small bag made of red velvet: chunks of whole frankincense and myrrh. She trips on the curb, catches herself on one knee, tears her stocking, jumps back up and runs on, afraid to be late.

As she hurries toward him, though he is still sixty blocks uptown, she begins chanting to herself, as she often does, chanting a passage from some philosopher or theologian in her head, repeating it over and over again, like a mantra. She must keep it in her head so that it is ready, should she need to toss it out as a barrier between them. Today the passage that has popped into her head is from Wittgenstein:

Whereof one cannot speak, thereof one must be silent.
Whereof one cannot speak, thereof one must be silent.

She says it over and over while she waits impatiently for the subway, tapping her foot to the rhythm of the words.

Whereof one cannot speak, thereof one must be silent.
Whereof one cannot speak, thereof one must be silent.

She is afraid, as always, that her father will find out that she doesn't understand this passage, so she tries another.

Cogito ergo sum.
Cogito ergo sum.
Cogito ergo sum.

But after saying it three times, the words start sounding strange and she can't remember what they mean. They stick in her throat like a lump of phlegm. She gags. She can't remember what it means! She tries chanting another phrase, this time very slowly. In fact, she is chanting it so slowly, it sounds like a record on the wrong speed:

To be is to be perceived.
To be is to be perceived.

But this phrase sounds all wrong too. She wonders if it is backwards and tries it the other way around: "To be perceived is to be"? She pictures her father looking at her in disappointment. She knows full well that he's always been the brilliant theologian and she his clumsy apprentice, unable to handle even the most elementary philosophical truths (although she

271

always pretends to understand them perfectly). The best she can hope for is that at least he won't find out *today* that she knows nothing. She will agree with him and nod her head, as always, and pray, her hands clasped under the table, that he won't ask her any questions she can't answer.

When Eve gets out of the subway, the heel of her sandal gets caught on a grate and rips off. She bends over and picks it up, puts it back in place and stamps her foot furiously. She wonders if perhaps she should run into a store and buy some glue to glue it back on, but she is afraid of being late. What to do? What if the heel should fall off as they walk to the table in the restaurant? She couldn't bear it. Well, the heel seems to be staying on for the time being, and with each step she stamps down hard on it, limping along the sidewalk like a cripple, hoping the little nails will hold it on, even without the proper glue.

When Eve arrives at the restaurant, her father is waiting just inside the door. They give each other a quick hug and sit down at the table he has reserved. They make a handsome pair, both very tall and thin, with a striking resemblance to each other, especially in the forehead, cheekbones and nose, clearly father and daughter. He looks distinguished as always, in his grey suit, his navy blue tie with the white dots on it, and, of course, his slim leather briefcase under his arm. Even Eve looks respectable, wearing a tailored, white blouse with tucks in the front and a grey, pleated skirt. No one would suspect from her appearance that the hem of her skirt is unsewn and is being held up by a piece of masking tape.

As is their habit, they leap headlong into a shared catechism, which they recite each time they are alone together and are forced to make conversation. The catechism consists of questions and answers concerning various members of the family and anything else safely benign. This catechism has as its essential property the fact that its questions will never delve beyond the level of harmless inquiry. The catechism circles over the same material in increasing detail, like a spiral, until the time has been filled and they are allowed to stop. That tedious spiralling pushes her shoulders over into their habitual slump, humping her back out, her head hanging over her plate as if in prayer. She succeeds in mumbling appropriate responses until, at the last minute, just as their time together is almost up, Eve surprises both of them by blurting out,

"Dad, what do you think of Anselm's ontological proof?"

For a split second just after she asks the question, she imagines her question leaping out from her mouth and wrapping around her father like an arm, drawing him closer to her, drawing them into an intimate embrace of words, a sharing of their heartfelt secrets: him confessing those hidden thoughts he has never told to anyone, confessing how special she is to him, his first-born, the apple of his eye; and she confessing to him how beautiful and perfect he is to her, how desperately she has always wanted to be exactly like him, how much she wants him to approve of her, to think she's smart, how much she wants to be his confidant, how much she loves the smell of his Aqua Velva.

Suddenly she remembers the question she has just asked him and looks up at him.

"Anselm was definitely on the right track," he says, "despite the fact that his argument is obviously tautological."

His face looks as it so often does to her, when she has the courage to look at him directly, as if he were braced against some secret pain, as if there were dozens of straight pins sticking into him, one under each dot in his tie.

"And what do *you* think of the proof?" he asks her, always turning the question back on her as soon as he can, like all good Socratics.

She sighs. "You're right," she says, wanting to continue the conversation, but too afraid that her words will rush out like spurts of blood or spit, staining his tie. She just shrugs her shoulders and smiles awkwardly at him. As she smiles, she notices that the left side of her mouth is higher than the right, so she coughs as an excuse to cover her crooked mouth. Her father hands her his handkerchief, as she knew he would. She breathes in his familiar smell and secretly wipes away a few tears while he studies the check.

They wait in endless, painful silence, while the waitress takes her father's credit card and comes back. Finally, they go out into the street and he hails her a cab. They exchange safe, *pro forma* hugs and she hastily leaps into the cab. The heel of her sandal drops into the gutter as the door slams, but neither of them notices.

Rosaire Appel

On My Writing More or Less How I Write

First fellow doesn't meet, pry the lock. Practice without him. Polarize. Pulverize. An example emerges from the wrong base, right and wrong begin to talk and talk back. It is tight: confusion restricted. A second fellow follows. This is back-room thinking. It stalls. I toy with the fellow until he admits to problems of common conformity. But distractions occur. Getting to the root implies digging. Digging suggestive of dirt or gold—what emerges reflects, breaks wind, stalls. I apply force in waves. Straight lines are replaced with curves. Anything that you call a system begins to talk back if you listen. $U=I$, if $2c=x$. Once a trajectory can be plotted, claustrophobia develops. To counter this I go into the dark, which is open and silent as actual dark. I strike a match. Visibility occurs as a gradual sentence, shapes begin to coagulate space. Another fellow appears at the back—but the match by this time, if it's real, has gone out.

from *Mabel in Her Twenties*

Now Mabel looked both ways before crossing. Although caution at that hour meant nothing. Was a brief success more disturbing she wondered than no success at all? One or two other assumptions provided and troubled her more than she could afford.

She crumpled the pages he sent her. Once was enough she had told him twice—which had proved she wouldn't be who he wanted. She advised him that she would no longer be that and that he was not invited.

Most women wouldn't say this while others were listening, all kinds of laughter were mimicked. If no one wanted to tell her about it, it was best to assume that she knew what had happened. Everyone wanted to be invited especially when it was hot. Which it was.

"Hammond," they whispered, "has met someone else."

But Hammond had only seen her once, with oblivious opinions and crucial precaution. Nobody mentioned her name. The way Mabel moved made everyone curious—why didn't she want to know that name? She would not allude to anyone directly including the man she had met at the station.

"Till now it's been very amusing," she told them, as if she had seen a movie of it and not the real things that had been.

To say this at the earliest moment when anything happened, she managed. A phrase that contained what had happened to them, a stamp a seal a hammer for Hammond.

And he in turn had one for her.

Her long arms had been bare to the shoulder. When he'd stepped aside she'd gone in.

Of course she had been invited to visit or would she be satisfied now? Several kisses were passed with success. Such kisses so brief must hardly be noticed, the weather and so forth and then they went out.

Hammond uncorked a new bottle. This was the moment to hear what she said if she said it most clearly to him. For the moment with efforts not fashionably pending—the rest of story erasing the ending. Mabel was starting too slowly.

Each time she came back with somebody else she'd prefer to forget him it seemed to Hammond.

Each time she came back with a candle a card a hole in the wall of white icing.

Though she might as a rule though without seeming closer—a scene was replaying itself in her mind. Quick scenes, many seasons replaying.

"How does it end?" he demanded.

If he were quicker this kiss and the knot—and yet she preferred to ignore what she heard when Hammond put words in her mouth. A card at the entrance main course. A fork in the flesh of the goose that was cooking.

She was quickly tired of that course of that cooking and said she would rather before he had finished.

If he hadn't the heart to restore his own name—if he threw his arms up or put them around her, if Mabel would surely return. Though some would linger without seeming weaker to those who used force it would seem. Some sticks were meant to be crossed. Others were meant to be cut and buried. If chairs were brought forward for closer inspection a room was more nearly emptied.

"Hammond!" exclaimed Mabel at the sight of him.

He drew away from the window.

There was no label to stiffen his collar, to slow and the quicksand and there by the bed. A privateer who made things by hand, somewhat limp, but just for the satisfied now.

Alert or asleep or disguised their houses, Mabel would always remember those rooms. She would always remember success in the evening, no hint of deletion and honorable mention.

For Hammond might often be mentioned.

"Won't you come in?" someone asked right away.

"I am waiting for Hammond," she told them.

An honor no less accessible to her was guarded at the appropriate angle. To reach through the shield to finger that angle, her lips for himself because she'd been willing. Thus Mabel ignited a spark which appeared to spark everyone else that she met. She was easily balanced on a strong point advancing, the outcome was everything else.

Mabel because she was young.

Because it was useful and she was young, she wanted both sides of a conversation, both sides of a shell and whatever within—all of it hers for the taking. If she were pale she corrected her color and though others would try to put words in her mouth, Mabel refused to swallow.

Neither was Mabel bolder however by a pond with what pleasure turned sharply. Something that could not be anything else in another part that looked like itself. In a part that had several occasions.

Hammond said, "Why are you stopping?"

Spread on the grass in one location—the location was entirely disrupted. He had taken off his watch and his jacket. He had put down the cup she was holding, saying nothing, it was different on every occasion.

The part however where her laugh was haphazard, she had never predicted the rest of her life. She straightened the blanket, she was stalling.

Other times there was nothing to do. "I'm not the only person am I?" Hammond asked. She said he was wrong.

"I'm only the person I am?" he tried.

He could see she was not really listening.

Face to face she concealed the fact that she'd come here with others occasionally from somewhere else who had wanted what others observed.

No doubt he'd been fond of trees also. A tree could be subject an obstacle or attraction as well as itself any time.

Now Mabel began to consider the day, the first day that nothing seemed true. Most people would like to be liked she believed, and those who are liked may stop where they are while the others have to keep moving.

Hammond said nothing too soon. When he was lazy on Saturday morning he had that position and extra pillows. For someone like him to insist on convenience though moving to some other place every time.

For someone like Mabel to set the table—this would be most convenient.

Sometimes she thought he was testing his future. Sometimes he was teasing, sometimes she couldn't tell. Sometimes she thought and didn't say. At such times she thought that a stranger would smile and saw fit to open the windows and look. Didn't anyone caution her against this? The way her skirt was green, her umbrella. That Saturday morning she said something generous and nothing extraneous stopped her. They had gathered enough for both taste and spirit, which sent them toward the future again.

For anybody else would she cry?

Perhaps she might cry on another occasion—this was the chance he was willing to take that some other location would yield something else. And of course if it did he would offer no less than the saying, saying what he was doing.

Mabel would remain to be seen.

Mabel said she was perpetually amused.

When evening finally was falling behind them he brushed off his annoyance and tried to console her. He tried to console her how ever she wanted, it was the least he could do.

He could see she was counting moreover. He could see she was brushing her hair.

Shouldn't someone tell her what he was doing and what it meant, he wondered.

The issue was this she was certain. There were several plots he was moving among as he pleased without any assurance. Above the scene lightning extended. His hands were free to support the props and her hands were free for the taking.

No one gives lessons all day like his mother, in spite of what they could save, she was thinking. This made a scene for the background for her while Hammond was brushing away his annoyance.

For Mabel was apparently warming. This was something he didn't want to mention the fact of the force of anyone winning. False starts should be crumpled and strewn in the grass. Second place was no peace without hurrying.

One hurried and didn't want to cross. One hurried and did, yet could not.

A position one way or another was built and he didn't have the right to unhinge it. He still had to be her best test. But Hammond put on his coat and stood up and in this way went on with the rest.

Mabel telephoned, Hammond was out.

She tried again uninvited to do so. He went his own way whenever he wanted. Then she shook out her pockets, she was finished.

But Hammond telephoned back. Once he was back and didn't want to stop, he used what he knew and didn't press when she cried. He was better because he didn't press.

He had found a new way a new weight, he believed. "Shall I tell you something else?" he asked. He could talk to her at the back of his mind and when he was pleased he was warm. Though the heat wasn't on he was warm. Certain sounds that had sounded to her like demands were nothing but pleasure he assured her.

"This is more pleasurable than anything else," he concluded walking and talking beside her.

"Mabel," he said simply, "Mabel."

She knew what he meant, he meant her.

"Once there was someone like you," he started but Mabel would not let him finish.

——Black Ice Books——

Cris Mazza

I have a short story that's a magazine-killer.
In the mid-eighties, on two separate occasions,
this story was accepted for publication then
the journal folded before the story appeared
in its pages. If a person experiences not one
but two flights to Paris in which the plane loses
an engine and has to land in New York or
Boston, the ill-fated passenger, who still hasn't
seen Paris, should nevertheless feel safe during all future air travel. Similarly, I was fairly
certain I wouldn't kill any more magazines,
but then it seemed I almost killed Fiction Collective. My first book, *Animal Acts,* was accepted for publication by Fiction Collective
in early 1987. Two full years later, text was
set and proofread, the cover was designed,
blurb copy was written, but no book yet existed. Instead of those long-awaited copies of
my book, in April 1989 I received a letter in-
forming Fiction Collective members that the
press would cease to exist unless we all con-
tributed to an emergency collection. I have no
memory if I ever knew what the specific problems were, nor do I know if any other members were moved as quickly as I was to put a
check in the mail. I was saving my first book's
life, not its publisher. But as if my meager con-
tribution could help buy a reprieve, within

weeks Curt White and Ron Sukenick had com-
pleted a reorganization and the Fiction Collective became FC2. A scant month later a box of
crisp, shiny red copies of Animal Acts arrived
at my doorstep, one of the last titles to use the
original publisher name "Fiction Collective."

Between Signs

**Living Legends of the Enchanted Southwest
Watch Authentic Indians,
Handmade crafts, Leather,
Pan for Gold with Real Prospectors**

He'll drive with one hand. With the other, unbuttons her shirt.
Then when trucks pass, close, going the opposite direction,
he'll drive with no hands for a moment, waving to the truckers with his left hand, his right hand never leaving her breasts.
She'll arch her back, smile, eyes closed. The wind of the
passing trucks will explode against the car like split-second
thunderstorms.

*Swim
Ski
Relax
Play
In Lostlake City*

**DO NOT PARK
IN DESIGNATED
PARKING AREAS**

Someday she'll return, using this same road, and it will be late spring, and the migrating desert showers will wash the windshield of collected bugs and dust over and over, and the smell of wet pavement will lift her drooping eyelids, and she'll not stop until she's knocking on his door and it's opening and he's standing there. She'll feel the explosion of his body or the explosion of the door slamming.

15 Restaurants
11 Motels
Next 2 exits

RATTLESNAKE-SKIN BOOTS
TURQUOISE BELT BUCKLES
BEADED MOCCASINS, SNO CONES

They took nothing. Credit cards bought gas and food, plastic combs, miniature toothbrushes, motel rooms, tourist T-shirts, foaming shaving cream and disposable razors. She watched him shaving as she lay in the bathtub. Then he shaved her. Rinsing her with the showerhead, soaping her over and over again. Shoved a blob of jelly, from a plastic single-serving container taken from the diner, far inside her, went to retrieve it with his tongue, drop by drop, taste by taste, but there was always more where that came from.

See Mystic Magic Of The Southwest...THE THING?

While she takes a turn driving, he'll lay his head in her lap and watch her play with herself. The sound is sticky and sweet like a child sucking candy. The sun will appear and disappear. A band of light across her bare knees. She'll hold his hand and his fingers will join hers moving in and out. The seat wet between her thighs. A cattle crossing will bounce his head in her lap and her legs will tighten around their joined hands. Air coming in the vents is humid, thick with the warm smell of manure, straw, the heat of bodies on the endless flat pasture under the sun. He'll roll to his back and her wet fingers embrace his erection.

VISIT RUBY FALLS

Make a Bee-Line to ROCK CITY

Don't Miss CATFISH WILLIE'S RIVERBOAT
Restaurant, Lounge, Casino
Fresh Catfish & Hushpuppies
Beulah, Tennessee

Rip Van Winkle Motel just 35 miles

He has no sunglasses. His eyes are slits. Bright white sky and blinking lines on the road. Touches blistered chapped lips with his tongue. Digs into his pocket, sitting on one hip and easing up on the gas. Crackle of paper among the loose change. He unwraps the butterscotch and slips it into his mouth, rolls it with his tongue, coats his mouth with the syrup. When he passes a mailbox on the side of the road, he looks far up the dirt driveway beside it, but can't see where it leads. At the next mailbox, five miles later, he stops for a second. The name on the box says Granger, but, again, the driveway is too long to see what it leads to.

Triple-Dip ice cream cones
Camping, ice, propane
Truckers Welcome

SLIPPERY WHEN WET   FALLING ROCK

They weren't allowed to rent a shower together, so they paid for two but when no one was looking she slipped into his. Someone far away was singing. They stood for a while, back to back, turned and simultaneously leaned against the opposite walls of the shower stall, then slid down and sat facing each other, legs crossing. She told him he looked like he was crying, the water running down his face, but his tears would probably taste soapy. She said once she'd put dish detergent into a doll that was supposed to wet and cry. From then on it had peed foam and bawled suds. He reached out and put a hand on each of her breasts, holding her nipples between two fingers. A door slammed in the stall beside theirs. Water started and a man grunted. He rose to his knees, pulled on her arms so she slid the rest of the way to the floor of the shower, the drain under her back. He eased over her, his mouth moving from breast to breast. Then he lathered her all over, slowly, using almost the whole bar of soap, her ears and neck, toes, ankles, knees, lingering between her legs where the hair was growing back and sometimes itched so badly while they drove that she had to put her hand in her pants and scratch. She was slick to hold. He didn't rinse her before pushing his cock in. The sting of the soap made them open their eyes wide and dig their fingernails into each other's skin. Staring at each other but not smiling.

Taste Cactus Jack's Homestyle Cookin

Relax in Nature's Spa
CHICKEN HOLLER HOT SPRINGS
Sandwiches, Live Bait

ROAD CLOSED IN FLOOD SEASON

Finally she stops and buys half a cantaloupe at a roadside fruit stand. After eating as much as she can with a plastic spoon, she presses her face down into the rind and scrapes the remaining flesh with her teeth. The juice is cool on her cheek and chin. Part of a tattered map, blown by the wind, is propped against the base of a telephone pole. He had laughed at her for getting cantaloupe Marguaritas, but then he'd sipped some of hers, ordered one for himself, said it tasted like her. She breaks the rind in half and slips one piece into her pants, between her legs. The crescent shape fits her perfectly.

MARVEL AT MYTHICAL RELICS
INDIAN JEWLRY
VELVET PAINTINGS

TEXMEX CHICKEN-FRIED STEAK
TACOS, BURRITOS
FREE 72 OZ STEAK IF YOU CAN EAT IT ALL!

When the dirt road gets so bumpy he has to keep both hands on the wheel, she'll take over using the vibrator on herself. He'll watch her, and watch the road. The road always disappears around a bend or beyond a small rise. The car bounces over ruts and rocks. She won't even have to move the vibrator, just hold it inslde. She'll say he chose a good road, and her laugh will turn into a long moan, her head thrown over the back of the seat. One of her feet pressed against his leg. Her toes will clutch his pants.

View of Seven States from Rock City

Poison Spring Battleground
next exit, south 12 miles

PIKE COUNTY DIAMOND FIELD
All The Diamonds You Find Are Yours!

For three days he's had a postcard to send home, but can't find the words to explain. It's a picture of the four corners, where Colorado, New Mexico, Arizona and Utah meet. He hadn't gotten down on hands and knees to be in all four states simultaneously. But he had walked around them, one step in each state, making a circle, three times. When he arrives at Chief Yellowhorse's Trading Post and Rock Museum, he buys another postcard, a roadrunner following the dotted line on highway 160. This one's for her, wherever she is, if she left a forwarding address. The rock museum costs a dollar. A square room, glass cases around the edges, dusty brown pebbles with handwritten nametags. Some of the rocks are sawed in half to show blue rings inside. A bin of rose quartz pieces for a nickle each. Black onyx for a dime. Shark's teeth are a quarter.

HOGEYE, pop. 2011
Hogeye Devildogs Football
class D state champs 1971

Behold! Prehistoric Miracles! Indian Pottery, Sand Paintings Cochina Dolls, Potted Cactus

Found Alive!
THE THING?

They'll toss their clothes into the back seat. Their skin slippery with sweat. She'll dribble diluted soda over and between his bare legs. Tint of warm root beer smell lingering in the car. She'll hold an ice cube in her lips and touch his shoulder with it. Runs it down his arm. It'll melt in his elbow. She'll fish another ice out of her drink, move it slowly down his chest. When she gets to his stomach, the ice will be gone, her tongue on his skin. She'll keep his hard-on cool by pausing occasionally to slip her last piece of ice into her mouth, then sucking him while he slides a finger in and out of her. The last time she puts the ice into her mouth, his hand will be there to take it from her lips. He'll push the ice into her, roll it around inside with a finger until it's gone. The road lays on the rippling desert like a ribbon. Leaving the peak of each of the road's humps, the car will be airborn for a second.

292

Cowboy Steaks, Mesquite Broiled

Black Hills Gold, Arrowheads,
Petrified Wood, Chicken Nuggets,
Soda, Thick Milkshakes, Museum
WAGON MOUND TRAVELERS REST

He had to slow down, find a turnout, pull her from the car and half carry her to the shade of a locked utility shack. She dropped to her knees, then stretched out full length on her stomach. He sat beside her, stroking her back. Her body shuddered several more times, then calmed. When she rolled over, the hair on her temples was wet and matted with tears, her eyes thick, murky, glistening, open, looking at him. She smiled.

INDIAN BURIAL MOUNDS NEXT EXIT
GAS, FOOD, LODGING

RATTLESNAKE ROUNDUP
PAYNE COUNTY FAIRGROUNDS
2ND WEEKEND IN JULY

DUST STORMS NEXT 18 MILES

The waterpark is 48 miles off the main interstate. He's the only car going in this direction and passes no others coming the opposite way. The park was described in a tourbook but wasn't marked on the map. Bumper boats, olympic pool, 3 different corkscrew waterslides, high dive. The only other car in the lot has 2 flat tires. Small boats with cartoon character names painted on the sides are upside down beside an empty concrete pond, a layer of mud and leaves at the bottom. Another layer of dirt at the bottom of the swimming pool is enough to have sprouted grass which is now dry and brown, gone to seed. The scaffold for the waterslides is still standing, but the slides have been dismantled. The pieces are a big aqua-blue pile of fiberglass.

Ancient Desert Mystery...THE THING? 157 miles

Land of Enchantment
New Mexico T-Shirts

BULL HORNS
HANDWOVEN BLANKETS
CACTUS CANDY
NATURAL WONDERS

She'll look out the back windshield. The earth is a faint, rolling line against a blue-black sky. His hair tickling her cheek. She'll be on his lap, straddling him, her chin hooked over his shoulder, his cock has been inside her for miles and miles. Sometimes she'll rock slowly from side to side. Sometimes he'll push up from underneath. Sometimes they'll sit and feel the pulse of the engine, the powerful vibration. The air coming through the vent, splashing against her back before it spreads through the car, is almost slightly damp. Smells of rain on pavement, clean and dusty. Out the front windshield, both sky and land stay so dark, there's no line where they meet. No lights and no stars.

If we go west fast enough, will it stay predawn forever? We can try.

Did you ever pester your parents, When'll we get there, daddy?

And I'd've thought it was torture if he said *never*.

GOSPEL HARMONY HOUSE CHRISTIAN DINNER THEATRE

MERGING TRAFFIC   DEER XING   SHARP CURVES
                                                             NEXT 10 MILES

They started walking toward the entrance of the WalMart store, but she turned off abruptly, crossed a road and climbed a small hill where someone had set up three crosses in the grass.

They were plant stakes lashed together. Kite string was tangled on a tumbleweed. When she got back to the parking lot, five or six big cockleburrs were clinging to each of her socks. She sat on the hood of the car picking them off. When he came from the store with two blankets, toilet paper, aspirin and glass cleaner, she said, There weren't any graves up there after all. He put the bag in the back seat, turned and smiled. Kiss me, she said.

Meteor Crater and gift shop, 3 miles

WARNING:
THIS ROAD CROSSES U.S.
AIR FORCE BOMBING RANGE
FOR THE NEXT 12 MILES DANGEROUS
OBJECTS MAY DROP FROM AIRCRAFT

BIMBO'S FIREWORKS
Open all year

He spreads a map over his steering wheel. This road came 45 miles off the interstate. He pays and follows the roped-off trail, stands looking at the cliff dwellings as the guide explains which was the steam room, which compartment stored food, which housed secret rituals, where the women were allowed to go and where they weren't, why they died off before white settlers ever arrived, and the impossibly straight narrow paths which connected them directly to other cliff dwelling cities and even now were still visible from the sky, spokes on a wheel converging on their religious center.

Bucksnort Trout Pond
Catch a Rainbow!

Krosseyed Kricket Kampground

» » »

Two Guns United Methodist Church
Sunday Worship 10 a.m.
Visitors Welcome

She doesn't even know how long she's been sitting by the side of the road. The car shakes when the semis go past. Sometimes she can see a face turned toward her for a split second. The last time she went behind a rock to pee, she found three big black feathers with white tips. Now she's holding one, brushing it lightly over her face. Her eyes are closed. Somehow the scent of the feather is faintly wild. When she returns—in a year, two years, five years—in heavy sleep long past midnight but long before dawn, he'll never know any time passed at all. Like so many nights before she left, her footsteps will pad down the sidewalk. The nurse who shares his life will long since have put on her white legs and horned hat and gone to the hospital. Using the key he made for her, which she still carries on her chain, she'll let herself in. Move past the odor of hairspray in the bathroom. Drop her clothes in a heap in the doorway—simple clothes she'll easily be able to pull on in the moments before she leaves him. Then she'll stand there, listen to his body resting. Watch the dim form of him under the sheet become clearer. She'll crawl to the bedside, lean her elbows and chin on the mattress, his hand lying open near her face. She'll touch his palm with the wild feather, watch the fingers contract and relax. Until his hand reaches for her, pulls her into the bed and remembers her. She opens her eyes and squints although dusk has deadened the glare on the road. Slips the feather behind one ear. She doesn't remember which direction she'd been going before she stopped here to rest.

BRIDGE FREEZES IN COLD WEATHER

The Unknown is Waiting For You!
See The Thing? just 36 more miles

STATE PRISON
Do Not Stop For Hitchhikers

Yield

The music channel hadn't had any music for a while. She sat up, stared at the screen, counted the number of times either the interviewer or musician said *man*, lost track quickly, changed to the weather station, turned the sound down. She massaged his shoulders and back, each vertebra, his butt, his legs, the soles of his feet, each toe. He said, I'm yours forever. Said it into the pillow. Anything you want, he said. She lay her cheek against his back and watched a monsoon, palm trees bending to touch the tops of cottages, beach furniture thrown through windows. He had rolled over and was looking at her. His eyes looked almost swollen shut. Anything, he said. She looked back at the screen, yachts tossed like toys, roofs blown off, an entire pier folded sideways along the beach. She said, I've never been in something like that.

He pinned her wrists in just one of his hands, hurled her face-down. She was open and ready as though panting heavy fogged air from her cunt, and he slammed himself in there, withdrew completely and slammed in again and again. With each thrust she said, Oh! And he answered when he came, a long, guttural cry, releasing her wrists to hold onto her hips and pump her body on his cock.

They lay separate for a while. Now, she said, hold me . . . with both hands. Hold me like something you'd never want to break. Tomorrow I'll drop you off at the nearest airport.

SPECIAL PERMIT REQUIRED FOR:
Pedestrians
Bicycles
Motor Scooters
Farm Implements
Animals on Foot

Home of Johnny Johnson
Little All-American 1981

Ice Cream, Divinity, Gas, Picnic Supplies
Real Indians Performing Ancient Rites

He'll set the car on cruise control and they'll each climb out a window, pull themselves to the roof of the car, to the luggage rack. Their hair and clothes lash and snap in the rushing wind. Dawn has been coming on for hours. The sun may never appear. The sky behind them pink-gold on the horizon, bleeding to greenish, but like wet blue ink straight above them. She'll unbutton her shirt and hold her arms straight up, lets the wind undress her. They'll take turns loosening their clothes and feeling thin, cool rushing air whip the material away. Bursting through low pockets of fog, they come out wet and sparkling, tingling, goosebumped. They'll slide their bodies together, without hurry and without holding back, no rush to get anywhere, saving nothing for later, passing the same rocks, bushes and fenceposts over and over. As the car leaves the road, leaping and bounding with naive zest, they'll pull each other closer and hold on, seeing the lovely sky in each other's eyes, tasting the sage and salty sand on each other's skin, hearing the surge of velocity in the other's shouted or breathless laughter, feeling the tug of joy in their guts, in their vigorous appetites. The sky still deep violet-black, the dawn still waiting, the car still soaring from butte to pinnacle to always higher peaks.

John Shirley

I don't remember any specific origins for "Jody and Annie" (which was originally published way before the movie *Natural Born Killers*, by the way) other than having been in various rock bands, including bad ones, and having spent time puzzling over the specific center of gravity of Generation X to Z kids as I knew them in rock clubs and in shopping malls and from encounters on, say, Hollywood Boulevard where I was absorbing the cruising scene . . . And in my having puzzled even further over the fascination with serial killers, noting the actual existence of the only partly-ironic serial killer trading cards, comic books about them, and movies like *Henry: Portrait of a Serial Killer*—that is, the glamorization of random murder. Trying to get at the root, the cause of what, to me, was a repugnant glamorization. And having observed a growing syndrome among people who were obviously willing to humiliate themselves or otherwise destroy themselves to get into the media. A sense of the lack of inwardness, in all modern people, the lack of an axis of relationship between the individual and society, the individual and the living world itself.

The puzzling sense that everyone felt they were heirs whose fortune had been stolen somehow; that they were to have been the annointed and someone, while they slept, rubbed off the ointment. The general feeling in the air that an undefined birthright had been stolen—and that much is quite correct—and they identified that missing birthright willynilly where they could, usually with pitiful wrongheadedness. People who think themselves glorified only pitiful, mindless, lost. Yet weirdly capable of evoking our sympathy. This is just as much a story, really—though it was written long before the incident—about that young man who stood by and watched his murderous, empty-hearted college-frosh pal rape and murder a little girl in a Vegas casino bathroom. About them both. And postmodernists tell us that there are no real values—and yet when we do without values, without any kind of inward presence, without an inner axis of right-relationship to the world, this is what results. Jody and Annie get themselves on television however they can, and little girls are murdered in Vegas bathrooms.

As for dealing with Black Ice—it was just like dealing with a small press associated with a University; little pay, little distribution. They used the illustrator I wanted, though, which a large press would not have done.

There are, you see, at least some advantages to writing for the small press (I make a living writing for TV and movies so I can focus on the advantaged side of small press publishing). Bigtime contemporary publishing is more than ever before concerned with the bottom line. I've had books accepted by editors but then rejected by the marketing department. Not categorizable enough, or something. We're now writing not for the public per se, but for Barnes and Noble's perspective on the public. Hence the sudden vitality and value in small, delightfully eccentric presses like Mark V. Ziesing and the newer ones (check out Night Shade books) or Black Ice. They answer a need. They articulate special things for people; they answer special tastes. They publish for individuals—not for demographic surveys.

Jody and Annie On TV

First time he has the feeling, he's doing 75 on the 134. Sun glaring the color off the cars, smog filming the North Hollywood hills. Just past the place where the 134 snakes into the Ventura freeway, he's driving Annie's dad's fucked-up '78 Buick Skylark convertible, one hand on the wheel the other on the radio dial, trying to find a tune, and nothing sounds good. But *nothing*. Everything sounds stupid, even metal. You think it's the music but it's not, you know? It's you.

Usually, it's just a weird mood. But this time it shifts a gear. He looks up from the radio and realizes: You're not driving this car. It's automatic in traffic like this: only moderately heavy traffic, moving fluidly, sweeping around the curves like they're all part of one long thing. Most of your mind is thinking about what's on TV tonight and if you could stand working at that telephone sales place again...

It hits him that he is two people, the programmed-Jody who drives and fiddles with the radio and the real Jody who thinks about getting work...Makes him feel funny, detached.

The feeling closes in on him like a jar coming down over a wasp. Glassy like that. He's pressed between the back window and the windshield, the two sheets of glass coming together, compressing him like something under one of those biology-class microscope slides. Everything goes two-dimensional. The cars like the ones in that Roadmaster videogame, animated cars made out of pixels.

A buzz of panic, a roaring, and then someone laughs as he jams the Buick's steering wheel over hard to the right, jumps into the VW Bug's lane, forcing it out; the Bug reacts, jerks away from him, sudden and scared, like it's going, "Shit!" Cutting off a Toyota four-by-four with tractor-sized tires, lot of good those big fucking tires do the Toyota, because it spins out and smacks sideways into the grill of a rusty old semitruck pulling an open trailer full of palm trees...

They get all tangled up back there. He glances back and thinks, *I did that.* He's grinning and shaking his head and laughing. He's not sorry and he likes the fact that he's not sorry. *I did that.* It's so amazing, so totally rad.

Jody has to pull off at the next exit. His heart is banging like a fire alarm as he pulls into a Texaco. Goes to get a Coke.

It comes to him on the way to the Coke machine that he's stoked. He feels connected and in control and pumped up. The gas fumes smell good; the asphalt under the thin rubber of his sneakers feels good. *Huh.* The Coke tastes good. He thinks he can taste the cola berries. He should call Annie. She should be in the car, next to him.

He goes back to the car, heads down the boulevard a mile past the accident, swings onto the freeway, gets up to speed— which is only about thirty miles an hour because the accident's crammed everyone into the left three lanes. Sipping Coca-Cola, he looks the accident over. Highway cops aren't there yet, just the Toyota four-by-four, the rusty semi with its hood wired down, and a Yugo. The VW got away, but the little caramel-colored Yugo is like an accordian against the back of the truck. The Toyota is bent into a short boomerang shape around the snout of the semi, which is jackknifed onto the road shoulder. The Mexican driver is nowhere around. Probably didn't have a green card, ducked out before the cops show up. The palm trees kinked up in the back of the semi are whole, grown-up palm trees, with the roots and some soil tied up in big plastic bags, going to some rebuilt place in Bel Air. One of the palm trees droops almost completely off the back of the trailer.

Jody checks out the dude sitting on the Toyota's hood.

The guy's sitting there, rocking with pain, waiting. A kind of ski mask of blood on his face.

I did that, three of 'em, bingo, just like that. Maybe it'll get on TV news.

Jody cruised on by and went to find Annie.

It's on TV because of the palm trees. Jody and Annie, at home, drink Coronas, watch the crane lifting the palm trees off the freeway. The TV anchordude is saying someone is in stable condition, nobody killed; so that's why, Jody figures, it is, like, okay for the newsmen to joke about the palm trees on the freeway. Annie has the little Toshiba portable with the 12" screen, on three long extension cords, up in the kitchen window so they can see it on the back porch, because it is too hot to watch it in the living room. If Jody leans forward a little he can see the sun between the houses off to the west. In the smog the sun is a smooth red ball just easing to the horizon; you can look right at it.

Jody glances at Annie, wondering if he made a mistake, telling her what he did.

He can feel her watching him as he opens the third Corona. Pretty soon she'll say, "You going to drink more than three you better pay for the next round." Something she'd never say if he had a job, even if she'd paid for it then too. It's a way to get at the job thing.

She's looking at him, but she doesn't say anything. Maybe it's the wreck on TV. "Guy's not dead," he says, "too fucking bad." Making a macho thing about it.

"You're an asshole." But the tone of her voice says something else. What, exactly? Not admiration. Enjoyment, maybe.

Annie has her hair teased out; the red parts of her hair look redder in this light; the blond parts look almost real. Her eyes are the glassy greenblue the waves get to be in the afternoon up at Point Mugu, with the light coming through the water. Deep tan, white lipstick. He'd never like that white lipstick look, white eyeliner and the pale-pink fingernail polish that went with it, but he never told her. "Girls who wear that shit are usually airheads," he'd have to say. And she wouldn't believe him when he told her he didn't mean her. She's sitting on the edge of her rickety kitchen chair in that old white shirt of his she wears for a shorty dress, leaning forward so he can see her cleavage, the arcs of her tan lines, her small feet flat on the stucco backporch, her feet planted wide apart but with her knees together, like the feet are saying one thing and the knees another.

His segment is gone from TV but he gets that *right there* feeling again as he takes her by the wrist and she says, "*Guy*, Jody, what do you think I *am*?" But joking.

He leads her to the bedroom and, standing beside the bed, puts his hand between her legs and he can feel he doesn't have to get her readier, he can get right to the good part. Everything just sort of slips right into place. She locks her legs around his back and they're still standing up, but it's like she hardly weighs anything at all. She tilts her head back, opens her mouth; he can see her broken front tooth, a guillotine shape.

They're doing 45 on the 101. It's a hot, windy night. They're listening to *Motley Crue* on the Sony ghetto blaster that stands on end between Annie's feet. The music makes him feel good but it hurts too because now he's thinking about *Iron Dream*. The band kicking him out because he couldn't get the solo parts to go fast enough. And because he missed some rehearsals. They should have let him play rhythm and sing backup, but the fuckers kicked him out. That's something he and Annie have. Both feeling like they were shoved out of line somewhere. Annie wants to be an actress, but she can't get a part, except once she was an extra for a TV show with a bogus rock club scene. Didn't even get her Guild card from that.

Annie is going on about something, always talking, it's like she can't stand the air to be empty. He doesn't really mind it. She's saying, "So I go, 'I'm *sure* I'm gonna fill in for that bitch when she accuses me of stealing her tips.' And he goes, 'Oh you know how Felicia is, she doesn't mean anything.' I mean—*guy*—he's always saying poor Felicia, you know how Felicia is, cutting her slack, but he, like, never cuts me any slack, and I've got two more tables to wait, so I'm all, 'Oh right poor Felicia—' and he goes—" Jody nods every so often, and even listens closely for a minute when she talks about the customers who treat her like a waitress. "I mean, what do they think, I'll always be a waitress? I'm *sure* I'm, like, totally a Felicia who's always, you know, going to be a *wait*-ress—" He knows what she means. You're pumping gas and people treat you like you're a born pump jockey and you'll never do anything else. He feels like he's really *with* her, then. It's things like that, and things they don't say; it's like they're looking out the same window together all the time. She sees things the way he does: how people don't understand. Maybe he'll write a song about it. Record it, hit big, *Iron Dream*'ll shit their pants. Wouldn't they, though?

"My Dad wants this car back, for his girlfriend," Annie says.

"Oh fuck her," Jody says. "She's too fucking drunk to drive, *any*time."

Almost eleven-thirty but she isn't saying anything about having to work tomorrow, she's jacked up same as he is. They haven't taken anything, but they both feel like they have. Maybe it's the Santa Anas blowing weird shit into the valley.

"This car's a piece of junk anyway," Annie says. "It knocks, radiator boils over. Linkage is going out."

"It's better than no car."

"You had it together, you wouldn't have to settle for this car."

She means getting a job, but he still feels like she's saying, "If you were a better guitar player..." Someone's taking a turn on a big fucking screw that goes through his chest. That's the second time the feeling comes. Everything going all flat again, and he can't tell his hands from the steering wheel.

There is a rush of panic, almost like when Annie's dad took him up in the Piper to go skydiving; like the moment when he pulled the cord and nothing happened. He had to pull it twice. Before the parachute opened he was spinning around like a dust mote. What difference would it make if he *did* hit the ground?

It's like that now, he's just hurtling along, sitting back and watching himself, that weird detachment thing...Not sure he is in control of the car. What difference would it make if he *wasn't* in control?

And then he pulls off the freeway, and picks up a wrench from the backseat.

"You're really good at getting it on TV," she says. "It's a talent, like being a director." They are indoors this time, sitting up in bed, watching it in the bedroom, with the fan on. It was too risky talking out on the back porch.

"Maybe I should be a director. Make *Nightmare On Elm Street* better than that last one. That last one sucked."

They are watching the news coverage for the third time on the VCR. You could get these hot VCRs for like sixty bucks from a guy on Hollywood Boulevard, if you saw him walking around at the right time. They'd gotten a couple of discount tapes at Federated and they'd recorded the newscast.

"...we're not sure it's a gang-related incident," the detective on TV was saying. "The use of a wrench—throwing a wrench from the car at someone—uh, that's not the usual gang methodology."

"Methodology," Jody says. "Christ."

There's a clumsy camera zoom on a puddle of blood on the ground. Not very good color on this TV, Jody thinks; the blood is more purple than red.

The camera lingers on the blood as the cop says, "They usually use guns. Uzis, weapons along those lines. Of course, the victim was killed just the same. At those speeds a wrench thrown from a car is a deadly weapon. We have no definite leads..."

"'They usually use guns,'" Jody says. "I'll use a gun on your balls, shit-head."

Annie snorts happily, and playfully kicks him in the side with her bare foot. "You're such an asshole. You're gonna get in trouble. Shouldn't be using my dad's car, for one thing." But saying it teasingly, chewing her lip to keep from smiling too much.

"You fucking love it," he says, rolling onto her.

"Wait." She wriggles free, rewinds the tape, starts it over. It plays in the background. "Come here, asshole."

» » »

Jody's brother Cal says, "What's going on with you, huh? How come everything I say pisses you off? It's like, *any*thing. I mean, you're only two years younger than me but you act like you're fourteen sometimes."

"Oh hey Cal," Jody says, snorting, "you're, like, Mr. Mature."

They're in the parking lot of the mall, way off in the corner. Cal in his Pasadena School of Art & Design t-shirt, his yuppie haircut, yellow-tinted John Lennon sunglasses. They're standing by Cal's '81 Subaru, that Mom bought him "because he went to school." They're blinking in the metallic sunlight, at the corner of the parking lot by the boulevard. The only place there's any parking. A couple of acres of cars between them and the main structure of the mall. They're supposed to have lunch with Mom, who keeps busy with her gift shop in the mall, with coffee grinders and dried eucalyptus and silk flowers. But Jody's decided he doesn't want to go.

"I just don't want you to say anymore of this shit to me, Cal," Jody says. "Telling me about *being* somebody." Jody's slouching against the car, his hands slashing the air like a karate move as he talks. He keeps his face down, half hidden by his long, purple streaked hair, because he's too mad at Cal to look right at him: Cal hassled and wheedled him into coming here. Jody is kicking Cal's tires with the back of a lizardskin boot and every so often he kicks the hubcap, trying to dent it. "I don't need the same from you I get from Mom."

"Just because she's a bitch doesn't mean she's wrong all the time," Cal says. "Anyway what's the big deal? You used to go along peacefully and listen to Mom's one-way heart-to-hearts and say what she expects and—" He shrugs.

Jody knows what he means: The forty bucks or so she'd hand him afterward "to get him started."

"It's not worth it anymore," Jody says.

"You don't have any other source of money but Annie and she won't put up with it much longer. It's time to get real, Jody, to get a job and—"

"Don't tell me I need a job to get real." Jody slashes the air with the edge of his hand. "Real is where your ass is when you shit," he adds savagely. "Now fucking shut up about it."

Jody looks at the mall, trying to picture meeting Mom in there. It makes him feel heavy and tired. Except for the fiberglass letters—*Northridge Galleria*—styled to imitate handwriting across its offwhite, pebbly surface, the outside of the mall could be a military building, an enormous bunker. Just a great windowless...*block*. "I hate that place, Cal. That mall and that busywork shop. Dad gave her the shop to keep her off the valium. Fuck. Like fingerpainting for retards."

He stares at the mall, thinking: That cutesy sign, I hate that. Cutesy handwriting but the sign is big enough to crush you dead if it fell on you. *Northridge Galleria*. You could almost hear a radio ad voice saying it over and over again, "Northridge Galleria!...Northridge Galleria!...Northridge Galleria!..."

To their right is a Jack-in-the-Box order-taking intercom. Jody smells the hot plastic of the sun-baked clown-face and the dogfoody hamburger smell of the drive-through mixed in. To their left is a Pioneer Chicken with its cartoon covered-wagon sign.

Cal sees him looking at it. Maybe trying to pry Jody loose from obsessing about Mom, Cal says, "You know how many Pioneer Chicken places there are in L.A.? You think you're driving in circles because every few blocks one comes up...It's like the ugliest fucking wallpaper pattern in the world."

"Shut up about that shit too."

"What put you in this mood? You break up with Annie?"

"No. We're fine. I just don't want to have lunch with Mom."

"Well goddamn Jody, you shouldn't have said you would, then."

Jody shrugs. He's trapped in the reflective oven of the parking lot, sun blazing from countless windshields and shiny metalflake hoods and from the plastic clownface. Eyes burning from the lancing reflections. Never forget your sunglasses. But no way is he going in.

Cal says, "Look, Jody, I'm dehydrating out here. I mean, fuck this parking lot. There's a couple of palm trees around the edges but look at this place—it's the surface of the moon."

"Stop being so fucking arty," Jody says. "You're going to art and design school, oh wow awesome I'm impressed."

"I'm just—" Cal shakes his head. "How come you're mad at Mom?"

"She wants me to come over, it's just so she can tell me her lastest scam for getting me to do some shit, go to community college, study haircutting or something. Like she's really on top of my life. Fuck, I was a teenager I told her I was going to hitchhike to New York she didn't even look up from her card game."

"What'd you expect her to do?"

"I don't know."

"Hey that was when she was on her Self-Dependence kick. She was into Lifespring and Est and Amway and all that. They keep telling her she's not responsible for other people, not responsible, not responsible—"

"She went for it like a fucking fish to water, man." He gives Cal a look that means, *no bullshit*. "What is it she wants *now*?"

"Um—I think she wants you to go to some vocational school."

Jody makes a snorting sound up in his sinuses. "Fuck that. Open up your car, Cal, I ain't going."

"Look, she's just trying to help. What the hell's wrong with having a skill? It doesn't mean you can't do something else too—"

"Cal. She gave you the Subaru, it ain't mine. But you're gonna open the fucking thing up." He hopes Cal knows how serious he is. Because that two-dimensional feeling might come on him, if he doesn't get out of here. Words just spill out of him. "Cal, look at this fucking place. Look at this place and tell me about vocational skills. It's shit, Cal. There's two things in the world, dude. There's making it like *Bon Jovi*, like Eddie Murphy—that's one thing. You're on a screen, you're on videos and CDs. Or there's shit. That's the other thing. There's no

311

fucking thing in between. There's being *Huge*—and there's being nothing." His voice breaking. "We're shit, Cal. Open up the fucking car or I'll kick your headlights in."

Cal stares at him. Then he unlocks the car, his movements short and angry. Jody gets in, looking at a sign on the other side of the parking lot, one of those electronic signs with the lights spelling things out with moving words. The sign says, *You want it, we got it...you want it, we got it...you want it, we got it...*

He wanted a Luger. They look rad in war movies. Jody said it was James Coburn, Annie said it was Lee Marvin, but whoever it was, he was using a Luger in that Peckinpah movie *Iron Cross.*

But what Jody ends up with is a Smith & Wesson .32, the magazine carrying eight rounds. It's smaller than he'd thought it would be, a scratched grey-metal weight in his palm. They buy four boxes of bullets, drive out to the country, out past Topanga Canyon. They find a fire road of rutted salmon-colored dirt, lined with pine trees on one side; the other side has a margin of grass that looks like soggy Shredded Wheat, and a barbed wire fence edging an empty horse pasture.

They take turns with the gun, Annie and Jody, shooting Bud-Light bottles from a splintery gray fence post. A lot of the time they miss the bottles. Jody said, "This piece's pulling to the left." He isn't sure if it really is, but Annie seems to like when he talks as if he knows about it.

It's nice out there, he likes the scent of gunsmoke mixed with the pine tree smell. Birds were singing for awhile, too, but they stopped after the shooting, scared off. His hand hurts from the gun's recoil, but he doesn't say anything about that to Annie.

"What we got to do," she says, taking a pot-shot at a squirrel, "is try shooting from the car."

He shakes his head. "You think you'll aim better from in a car?"

"I mean from a moving car, stupid." She gives him a look of exasperation. "To get used to it."

"Hey yeah."

They get the old Buick bouncing down the rutted fire road, about thirty feet from the fence post when they pass it, and Annie fires twice, and misses. "The stupid car bounces too much on this road," she says.

"Let me try it."

"No wait—make it more like a city street, drive in the grass off the road. No ruts."

"Uh...Okay." So he backs up, they try it again from the grass verge. She misses again, but they keep on because she insists, and about the fourth time she starts hitting the post, and the sixth time she hits the bottle.

"Well why *not*?" She asks again.

Jody doesn't like backing off from this in front of Annie, but it feels like it is too soon or something. "Because now we're just gone and nobody knows who it is. If we hold up a store it'll take time, they might have silent alarms, we might get caught." They are driving with the top up, to give them some cover in case they decide to try the gun here, but the windows are rolled down because the old Buick's air conditioning is busted.

"Oh right I'm sure some *7-11* store is going to have a silent alarm."

"Just wait, that's all. Let's do this first. We got to get more used to the gun."

"And get another one. So we can both have one."

For some reason that scares him. But he says: "Yeah. Okay."

It is late afternoon. They are doing 60 on the 405. Jody not wanting to get stopped by the CHP when he has a gun in his car. Besides, they are a little drunk because shooting out at Topanga Canyon in the sun made them thirsty, and this hippie on this gnarly old *tractor* had come along, some pot farmer maybe, telling them to get off his land, and that pissed them off. So they drank too much beer.

They get off the 405 at Burbank Boulevard, looking at the other cars, the people on the sidewalk, trying to pick someone out. Some asshole.

But no one looks right. Or maybe it doesn't feel right. He doesn't have that feeling on him.

"Let's wait," he suggests.

"Why?"

"Because it just seems like we oughta, that's why."

She makes a clucking sound but doesn't say anything else for awhile. They drive past a patch of adult bookstores and a video arcade and a liquor store. They come to a park. The trash cans in the park have overflowed; wasps are haunting some melon rinds on the ground. In the basketball court four Chicanos are playing two-on-two, wearing those shiny, pointy black shoes they wear. "You ever notice how Mexican guys, they play basketball and football in dress shoes?" Jody asks. "It's like they never heard of sneakers—"

He hears a *crack* and a thudding echo and a greasy chill goes through him as he realizes that she's fired the gun. He glimpses a Chicano falling, shouting in pain, the others flattening on the tennis court, looking around for the shooter as he stomps the accelerator, lays rubber, squealing through a red light, cars bitching their horns at him, his heart going in time with the pistons, fear vising his stomach. He's weaving through the cars, looking for the freeway entrance. Listening for sirens.

They are on the freeway, before he can talk. The rush hour traffic only doing about 45, but he feels better here. Hidden.

"What the *fuck* you doing?!" he yells at her.

She gives him a look accusing him of something. He isn't sure what. Betrayal maybe. Betraying the thing they had made between them.

"Look—" he says, softer, "it was a *red light*. People almost hit me coming down the cross street. You know? You got to think a little first. And don't do it when I don't *know*."

She looks at him like she is going to spit. Then she laughs, and he has to laugh too. She says, "Did you see those dweebs *dive*?"

Mouths dry, palms damp, they watch the five o'clock news and the six o'clock news. Nothing. Not a word about it.

They sit up in the bed, drinking Coronas. Not believing it. "I mean, what kind of fucking society *is* this? Jody says. Like something Cal would say. "When you shoot somebody and they don't even say a damn word about it on TV?"

"It's sick," Annie says.

They try to make love but it just isn't there. It's like trying to start a gas stove when the pilot light is out.

So they watch *Hunter* on TV. Hunter is after a psychokiller. The psycho guy is a real creep. Set a house on fire with some kids in it, they almost got burnt up, except Hunter gets there in time. Finally Hunter corners the psycho-killer and shoots him. Annie says, "I like TV better than movies because you know how it's gonna turn out. But in movies it might have a happy ending or it might not."

"It usually does," Jody points out.

"Oh yeah? Did you see *Terms of Endearment*? And they got *Bambi* out again now. When I was a kid I cried for two days when his Mom got shot. They should always have happy endings in a little kid movie."

"That part, that wasn't the end of that movie. It was happy in the end."

"It was still a sad movie."

Finally at eleven o'clock they're on. About thirty seconds worth. A man "shot in the leg on Burbank Boulevard today in a drive-by shooting believed to be gang related." On to the next story. No pictures, nothing. That was it.

What a rip off. "It's racist, is what it is," he says. "Just because they were Mexicans no one gives a shit."

"You know what it is, it's because of all the gang stuff. Gang drive-bys happen every day, everybody's used to it."

He nods. She's right. She has a real feel for these things. He puts his arm around her; she nestles against him. "Okay. We're gonna do it right, so they really pay attention."

"What if we get caught?"

Something in him freezes when she says that. She isn't supposed to talk like that. Because of the *thing* they have together. It isn't something they ever talk about, but they know its rules.

When he withdraws a little, she says, "But we'll never get caught because we just *do it* and cruise before anyone gets together."

He relaxes, and pulls her closer. It feels good just to lay there and hug her.

The next day he's in line for his unemployment insurance check. They have stopped his checks, temporarily, and he'd had to hassle them. They said he could pick this one up. He had maybe two more coming.

Thinking about that, he feels a bad mood coming on him. There's no air conditioning in this place and the fat guy in front of him smells like he's fermenting and the room's so hot and close Jody can hardly breathe.

He looks around and can almost *see* the feeling—like an effect of a camera lens, a zoom or maybe a fish-eye lens: Things going two dimensional, flattening out. Annie says something and he just shrugs. She doesn't say anything else till after he's got his check and he's practically running for the door.

"Where you going?"

He shakes his head, standing outside, looking around. It's not much better outside. It's overcast but still hot. "Sucks in there."

"Yeah," she says. "For sure. Oh shit."

"What?"

She points at the car. Someone has slashed the canvas top of the Buick. "My dad is going to kill us."

He looks at the canvas and can't believe it. "Mu-ther-*fuck!*-er!"

"Fucking assholes," she says, nodding gravely. "I mean, you know how much that costs to fix? You wouldn't believe it."

"Maybe we can find him."

"How?"

"I don't know."

He still feels bad but there's a hum of anticipation too. They get in the car, he tears out of the parking lot, making gravel spray, whips onto the street.

They drive around the block, just checking people out, the feeling in him spiraling up and up. Then he sees a guy in front of a Carl's Jr., the guy grinning at him, nudging his friend. Couple of jock college students, looks like, in tank tops. Maybe the guy who did the roof of the car, maybe not.

They pull around the corner, coming back around for another look. Jody can feel the good part of the feeling coming on now but there's something bothering him too: the jocks in tank tops looked right at him.

"You see those two guys?" he hears himself ask, as he pulls around the corner, cruises up next to the Carl's Jr. "The ones—"

"Those jock guys, I know, I picked them out too."

He glances at her, feeling close to her then. They are one person in two parts. The right and the left hand. It feels like music.

He makes sure there's a green light ahead of him, then he says, "Get 'em both," he hears himself say. "Don't miss or—"

By then she's aiming the .32, both hands wrapped around it. The jock guys, one of them with a huge coke and the other with a milkshake, are standing by the driveway to the restaurant's parking lot, talking, one of them playing with his car keys. Laughing. The bigger one with the dark hair looks up and sees Annie and the laughing fades from his face. Seeing that, Jody feels better than he ever felt before. *Crack, crack.* She fires twice, the guys go down. *Crack, crack, crack.* Three times more, making sure it gets on the news: shooting into the windows of the Carl's Jr., webs instantly snapping into the window glass, some fat lady goes spinning, her tray of burgers tilting, flying. Jody's already laying rubber, fishtailing around the corner, heading for the freeway.

They don't make it home, they're so excited. She tells him to stop at a gas station on the other side of the hills, in Hollywood. The Men's is unlocked, he feels really right *there* as she looks around then leads him into the bathroom, locks the door from the inside. Bathroom's an almost clean one, he notices, as she hikes up her skirt and he undoes his pants, both of them with shaking fingers, in a real hurry, and she pulls him into her with no preliminaries, right there with her sitting on the edge of the sink. There's no mirror but he sees a cloudy reflection in the shiny chrome side of the towel dispenser; the two of them blurred into one thing sort of pulsing...

He looks straight at her, then; she's staring past him, not at anything in particular, just at the sensation, the good sensation they are grinding out between them, like it's something she can see on the dust-streaked wall. He can almost see it in her eyes. And in the way she traps the end of her tongue between her front teeth. Now he can see it himself, in his mind's eye, the sensation flashing like sun in a mirror; ringing like a power chord through a fuzz box...

When he comes he doesn't hold anything back, he can't, and it escapes from him with a sob. She holds him tight and he says, "Wow you are just so awesome you make me feel so *good*..."

He's never said anything like that to her before, and they know they've arrived somewhere special. "I love you, Jody," she says.

"I love you."

"It's just us, Jody. Just us. Just us."

He knows what she means. And they feel like little kids cuddling together, even though they're fucking standing up in a *Union 76* Men's restroom, in the smell of pee and disinfectant.

Afterwards they're really hungry so they go to a Jack-in-the-Box, get drive-through food, ordering a whole big shitload. They eat it on the way home, Jody trying not to speed, trying to be careful again about being stopped, but hurrying in case they have a special news flash on TV about the Carl's Jr. Not wanting to miss it.

The Fajita Pita from Jack-in-the-Box tastes really great.

While he's eating, Jody scribbles some song lyrics into his song notebook with one hand. "The Ballad of Jody and Annie."

» » »

They came smokin' down the road
like a bat out of hell
they hardly even slowed
or they'd choke from the smell

Chorus:
Holdin' hands in the Valley of Death
(repeat 3X)
Jody and Annie bustin' out of bullshit
Bustin' onto TV
better hope you aren't the one hit
killed disonnerably

Nobody understands em
nobody ever will
but Jody knows she loves 'im
They never get their fill

They will love forever
in history
and they'll live together
in femmy

Holdin' hands in the Valley of Death

He runs out of inspiration there. He hints heavily to Annie about the lyrics and pretends he doesn't want her to read them, makes her ask three times. With tears in her eyes, she asks, as she reads the lyrics, "What's a femmy?"

"You know, like 'Living In Femmy.'"

"Oh, infamy. It's so beautiful...You got guacamole on it, you asshole." She's crying with happiness and using a napkin to reverently wipe the guacamole from the notebook paper.

There's no special news flash but since three people died and two are in intensive care, they are the top story on the five o'clock news. And at seven o'clock they get mentioned on CNN, which is *national*. Another one, and they'll be on the

NBC Nightly News, Jody says.

"I'd rather be on *World News Tonight*," Annie says. "I like that Peter Jennings dude. He's cute."

About ten, they watch the videotapes of the news stories again. Jody guesses he sould be bothered that the cops have descriptions of them but somehow it just makes him feel more psyched, and he gets down with Annie again. They almost never do it twice in one day, but this makes three times. "I'm getting sore," she says, when he enters her. But she gets off.

They're just finishing, he's coming, vaguely aware he sees lights flashing at the windows, when he hears Cal's voice coming out of the walls. He thinks he's gone schizophrenic or something, he's hearing voices, booming like the voice of God. *"Jody, come on outside and talk to us. This is Cal, you guys. Come on out."*

Then Jody understands, when Cal says, *"They want you to throw the gun out first."*

Jody pulls out of her, puts his hand over her mouth, and shakes his head. He pulls his pants on, then goes into the front room, looks through a corner of the window. There's Cal, and a lot of cops.

Cal's standing behind the police barrier, the cruiser lights flashing around him; beside him is a heavyset Chicano cop who's watching the S.W.A.T. team gearing up behind the big gray van. They're scary-looking in all that armor and with those helmets and shotguns and sniper rifles.

Jody spots Annie's Dad. He's tubby, with a droopy mustache, long hair going bald at the crown, some old hippie, sitting in the back of the cruiser. Jody figures someone got their license number, took them awhile to locate Annie's Dad. He wasn't home at first. They waited till he came home, since he owns the car, and after they talked to him they decided it was his daughter and her boyfriend they were looking for. Got the address from him. Drag Cal over here to talk to Jody because Mom wouldn't come. Yeah.

Cal speaks into the bullhorn again, same crap, sounding like someone else echoing off the houses. Jody sees people looking out their windows. Some being evacuated from the nearest houses. Now an *Action News* truck pulls up, cameramen pile out, set up incredibly fast, get right to work with the newscaster. Lots of activity just for Jody and Annie. Jody has to grin, seeing the news cameras, the guy he recognizes from TV waiting for his cue. He feels high, looking at all this. Cal says something else, but Jody isn't listening. He goes to get the gun.

"It's just us, Jody," Annie says, her face flushed, her eyes dilated as she helps him push the sofa in front of the door. "We can do anything together."

She is there, not scared at all, her voice all around him soft and warm. "It's just us," she says again, as he runs to get another piece of furniture.

He is running around like a speedfreak, pushing the desk, leaning bookshelves to block off the tear gas. Leaving enough room for him to shoot through. He sees the guys start to come up the walk with the tear gas and the shotguns. Guys in helmets and some kind of bulky bulletproof shit. But maybe he can hit their necks, or their knees. He aims carefully and fires again. Someone stumbles and the others carry the wounded dude back behind the cars.

Five minutes after Jody starts shooting, he notices that Annie isn't there. At almost the same moment a couple of rifle rounds knock the bookshelves down, and something smashes through a window. In the middle of the floor, white mist gushes out of a teargas shell.

Jody runs from the tear gas, into the kitchen, coughing. "Annie!" His voice sounding like a kid's.

He looks through the kitchen window. Has she gone outside, turned traitor?

But then she appears at his elbow, like somebody switched on a screen and Annie is what's on it.

"Hey," she says, her eyes really bright and beautiful. "Guess what." She has the little TV by the handle; it's plugged in on the extension cord. In the next room, someone is breaking through the front door.

"I give up," he says, eyes tearing. "What?"

She sits the TV on the counter for him to see. "We're on TV. Right now. We're on TV..."

─────── Mark Amerika ───────

March 30, 1992

Archival Memo-Fiction:

To: All FC2 Director-Dreamers
From: Mark Amerika (Zine Publisher)

After having processed the idea of calling the
new series Black Ice Books, I really think
we're onto something. Here's an opportunity
for the direction of fiction to change yet again,
this time in the Post-Cold War era where
Amerikans, hoodwinked by fancy terminol-
ogy, try desperately to out-survive psychic and
economic Depression. The release of Black
Ice Books, the immoral equivalent of our
founding fathers (not to mention our found-
ling mothers), would indicate the emergence
of a new anti-depressant drugtext that is guaranteed to make you forget why you hate living (by overdetermining what living-in-Hate
effectively does to YOU, the sensitive body-
type leaking an estranged Identity). Who will
buy these new books? Black Ice Magazine
readers, but Fiction Collective readers too, and
(potentially) a whole shitload of "Others"

who, seeking eternal rewards by opening the Doors of Perception, go Naked Ape-Shit over the possibility of reading something that has that "crazy, decontextualizing effect." The context is Literature. The effect is and has been to numb the reader into high-brow complacency. Now, the grimy hardcore grunge of Amerika ("special interests" with a mission to discover what a decaying country is all about), have a reading option. These people (actual human readers desperately struggling to curate an imaginative DMZ so as to ward off all potentially benumbing propaganda wars—Ha!) are out there. They have NO DISPOSABLE INCOME. They will STEAL our books off the shelves in the thousands and the system (everybody except US) will LOSE MONEY. The decay will accelerate. We will, single-handedly, undermine the entire world! (and if you think it's been undermined by State Capitalism up to this point, lemme tellya, YOU AIN'T SEEN NOTHIN' YET!). Black Ice Books will take its avant-pop grunge-mechanism ("the writing, babe, the writing!") and terrorize the free-market system in such a way as to assure us our place in the Smithsonian. History will create our meaning for us! And if that's not enough, we can wordbomb the mass media with unending rounds of tactical nuclear writing, scrambled missives whose

energy and unpredictable auras will cause
millions of people all over the world to deto-
nate an internal oblivion-device guaranteed to
force the totalitarian dick-energies who rule
the airwaves to cave-in on their own antiquated
mindsets! Spawning netcasts will forever distribute our victorious cause! We are unbeat-
able! Impenetrable! Anarchistic! Mind-
blower! WE ARE TREACHEROUS! INVIS-
IBLE! WATCHING THIS WORLD LOSE
ITSELF IN ITS OWN TRACKS! END OF
STORY! NO MORE ANYTHING! NO
MORE CONTROL!

Village Tripping

niceties niceties   nice cities (don't exist)   meanstreets
                                                          meanstreaks
                                                           means&ways

falling headfirst into the pavement our buoy of boys
    cracks his numskull and turns more nonsensical
derivation   inside/out & backwards   (summer
salt   wintry peppering)

Tuesday was okay   Thursday he had a plan   Friday
  he was out roaming the meancitystreets   Saturday
he slept late   Sunday he wrote a little   Monday he
woke up feeling like blowing it all away   Monday
night's marginalia took him over   soon he was
Tuesday morning looking for a new gig   the plan
had decentered   too bad for our buoy of boys   his
  nuclear family holocaust was hollow and cost a
bundle to repair   the damage was irreparable or so it
turned out   so he began shooting stars with
speed   pretty soon he had a gig as bagman for a
CBGB shitband everything was going supergroovy
I thought I saw him dead on Astor Place but that
was some space chick from Missouri   Amber was

her name   she had been dumped near the great
cube   the rolling spinning turning statuesque
personification of a geometric gentrified neighborly
  transmogrification   her heart was stone   her mind
was stoned   Lois E. Sider and her kid sis Apple Sider
say that Amber used to whore around Saint Mark's
Church   it's really too much   I'm gonna forget
it   Saint Marx was a bad man or so I hear them
calling

brain fried and scrambled maybe sunny side up
sweet disposition   honey can you take out the
garbage   so I go for a walk   where to take this shit
(I wonder) if only words could recycle   Too late for
a bold cure   gotta face reality   The Ecocycle Truck
rides by I start chasing it Here   take this   I throw
myself into the truck it turns me into blueprint

now I'm feeling architectonic   I go to a bar   The
Grass Roots   drink a tonic   grease my hair with yet
still more tonic   all I need now is a relatively mild
form of detoxification   I can hear them calling me
by name   Saint Marx they yell   I'm not a Marx   I
yell back   *I'm an animal*   well Mark   the truth
comes out   Saturday creeps into the bedroom like a
nun in a bikini asking me where do I find Saint
Charles Place   I say New Orleans   you can't miss
  it   all the parades go down it on Mardi Gras   the
trolley rides up and down it   you can't miss it   but
I *do* miss it   and now it's late March   one month
too late   never enough Sundays   Friday was the
beginning of the workweek   I wrote a nuclear
education piece called "Unclear"   Saturday I took
off for a little eco ramification principal player in the
ensuing garbage scene was Me   plus   Apple Sider
and oh yeah a cameo by our buoy of boys   what's

his name   I forget   doesn't matter   fact is he slept
  late   overslept   yes   so very much unlike him
usually the kind to get up on time   eat a good
breakfast   make it to the workspace   start honking
on the tele   tele-ing everybody that he's alive and
well and doing the dirty deed and dog eat dogging
and do or dying and driving The Big One home
jeez I can't wait for Wednesday

Alkaloid Boy meets The End Is Nearing and reevaluates his
current position. Flinging out long scroll he goes over the balance sheet mesmerized in its condition. Movement ratio un-
touched unencumbered transient feedback loop outside the
vicious circle no hawks to ward off no chastity belt to slow
him down. Meanwhile the growing Big Death hid away inside
The Death Terminal's central location computer virus spreading facts sheet distorted "just when you thought you had your
program under control you find out that it has a mind of its
own." Somewhere in the neutral column lay Blue Sky. She's
more than the Indian selfadhesive facility that keeps your body
broken in and mind mattered. She's the loose canon free whistle
love hassle-free blowjob nuke warm tomb mama womb mama.
It all spreads out everlasting hope peace love care. You can see
it in her face. The way she does her hair.

Ancient rock star from other planetary consciousness in a time
still not known to Man. Alkaloid Boy growing into the rough
discursive passages of The Black Death and its Terminal Blues
perception. No gloom and doom here boys. Just blatant disre-
gard for mutual laughter easygoing pyrotechnics love's ala-
baster wings serenade symposium. *None of it.* The upper of
the Upper feigning heroics getting rich. The lower of the Upper poorly performing cheap imitations of their hierarchical
master geniuses. Then the vast middle of Everybody losing it
slowly wondering how in the hell slave labor technology turned
into the heavy burden. Many clothes draping the monster new

technology. Many fashions dining the plates of the masters. Many new plates of pictures shining on the dead reel of the Platonic masters. The genius overload fortified to kill. Blue Sky looking into the Big Sky seeing The Black Death hovering spiritually resounding throughout the heavens. Her motor desiring The End Is Nearing while Alkaloid Boy tries to make a comeback. Music videos show the old man balding. His voice whispers soundtrack backlash: "alkaloid boy / he's very nervous / alkaloid boy / you can see it in his delivery..."

You're here for Youth. Youth is eternal until The Black Death does its final number. Until then it's Youth. Either that or die a slow death of usury. Use. Use and re:use. Re;use and re/fuse. Isometric exercises compounded by daily withdrawal into isotopic future's realignment clause. Why? Because because because because. Because The Death Terminal's central bank location has videotape information leading to the facts. Never mind the computer virus slow death takeover. Never mind the terrorist indoctrination full liability comprehensive plan. Never mind the collection agency's pedantic perusal of your bodily flesh. Excise your sin taxes and levy the poisoned language juice in their artless direction. Turn strong social impacts into natural make-up compacts and see how they run like peegs from a numb see how they fly.

Blue Sky calls me over the intercom to say she's all lost in the secret agent boiling bubbling hot love lava of last night. Easy happy going coming. Super stroll in the autumn bowl. Leaves of her ass strumming electric blue guitar notes against my despotic numbed musculature. Freedom tongues rolling hot saliva sweat over the creamy dew drop madness moisture. Heaven and Earth. Wild lustful forestry energy. Trees on the horizon in a natural burn. The moral equivalent of our founding fathers. Eating clear Blue Sky heaven juices cleansing insides reeling years morning dreams thundered pleasure lightning happiness eyes wide open. Summer shower tar pits kneel. The feel of plunder.

» » »

More Black Death resounding throughout the skies above little twitches in the face responding humanly despondent responding. "I'm gonna run for The House...change some things...turn back the clock to Eden..." : easy going open heart mind electric blue sky numb hope peace care flesh free

BLAST!!
BLAST!!!!!!!!!!!!!!!!!!!!BLAST!!!!!!!!!!!!!!!!!!!!!!!!!!!!!!!BLAST!!!!!!!!!!!!!!!!!!!!!!!!!!!!!!!!!
the lower of the lower of the lower of the lower of the lower
of the lover of the loner of the lower of the loner of the lover
of the   B !!   L !!!   A !!   S !!!   T !!

The shack shakes and rattles. Smacks of independence(?). The shits are coming!! The shits are coming!! Before we can put on our excess clothing drapery refinements fashionable chic motif in a new wave nightclub pretentiously portraying the scene of our lifeless generation the feds bust in ::: Bureau Chiefs (says The Big Wig). Are you Alkaloid Boy?

I was Alkaloid Boy until you guys gentrified the world. Now I'm occasionally employed by the Jacksonville Public Library. Dealing with the indigents. Our growing traffic problems are a direct tribute to you and your oft spoken of leader The Great Producer. Is he still alive?

Never you mind Alkaloid Boy you're under arrest. Who's the babe?

I'm no babe you pig shithead I'm Blue Sky and I represent this too harassed heavy metal genius of other-worldly consciousness.

No such thing as an other-worldy consciousness sweety better get yer facts straight (she looks at him / her face is swollen and full of my cummmm). We got it all on the fact sheets. Spread dead and ready to go. We can put out your story faster than you can dream up a new name sister. Hey. Wait a minute. Don't I know you? Weren't you Sister Slew in that ear droning nightmare demonstration we bombarded back in 92?

Look pig shithead you may be The Great Producer's loyal Bureau Chief but that doesn't dismiss the fact that my client and I have our god given rights as unalienated beings doing our own thing here in...

Fuck the facts sweety you've got two minutes to get your shit together or we're taking you as you are. Okay boys. Start burning...

Symbiotic conflagrations burning persisting desiring the mode made contagious and spreading all over the facts sheet balance sheet clean reading sheets slowly preambling a long and ever needed silence. Yours is Youth I can hear a voice whisper to me. Yours is to make up the despondent truce and then break out free swinging reluctant renegade. Keep the fires burning. Toil in the making and give for the taking. Rake in the mind some extra sensitive leaves of flesh and intermesh with the golden locks of the linked Blue Lady. Terminal dysfunctional regional start-up. Slow expansion of the peripheral phases on the edges moving *in*. Satellite superstardom promiscuous selling of the idea in the form of fleshy things!! What perfect timing!! Just as the tyrants finally got hold of something real and useable the switches blew and the hub heeded progress. More storms later. Many more. Writing's sweet revenge on the numb. The num is out there

Village Tripping

                    1 or 0
                    afford
                    o lord
                    ignore
                    abhor

arbor equals tree.
it's official.
The troops are climbing high in pin-stripes army stripes marines.
The upper of the Upper.
resounding in the heavens.
Blue Sky laughs eye dying
piercing stinging madness.
civilization

at a standstill

standing
                    falling
standing
                    falling
standing
                    falling
still
         still
                    life

Decharacterization: first and foremost / high on the list of things

To Do

1) evil eyed optimist
2) puritanical pessimist
3) retrograde renegade
4) easygoing numskull
5) taxing interest
6) megalomaniacal monsterman
7) persevering wanderer
8) sunshiny souvenir
9) sovereign veneer
10) venereal vegetarian
11) pornosophic filmmaker
12) college student
13) bank president
14) beatnik historian
15) girl watcher
16) punky playboy
17) diseased dyslexic
18) monkey grammarian
19) existentialist outlaw
20) linguistic statesman
21) early riser
22) effervescent eunuch
23) egghead eavesdropper
24) neoconservative butcher
25) egotistical holyman
26) harmonic hegelian
27) continue the discontinue
28) still crazy after all these years
29) butcher the butcher
30) wearisome whacker
31) where art thou waterfall?
32) butcher the butcher

333) dead meat   dead meat   dead meat   dead meat
421) off to the boonies
5X1r#217) name   address   social   security   perforation
·dis
int
egr
ati
on!

final mishapover
B L O W N
pro ./ por ./ tions

eros intensification

Alkaloid Boy and Blue Sky meet up with another couple who go by the names Hair Monster and Rose Hips. Hair Monster looks kind of like the protagonist in the film ERASERHEAD although his persona and presence remind you more of Sergy Eisenstein. His light eyes shine in the dark and you'll often feel the weight of his prolonged silences as they surround and eventually control the action being generated in the scene you share with him. Rose Hips is a She-Ra love goddess who has something for everyone. Her energy *adds* to Hair Monster's energy and together the fields of force go whacko. You get the feeling you're going out on your first eco-anarcho double date. There's no Weatherman-like bomb-exploding going to go on here, no Black Panther rabble-rousing. Just energy shock waves sending electric love currents all throughout the mise-en-scene. A major motion picture. A creature feature starring friction and static with a cameo by mystical genius.

Alkaloid Boy is telling Hair Monster about the unexpected wake-up call he and Blue Sky received from The Bureau Chiefs.

"They were lost in the mid-twentieth century, man, I mean you wouldn't believe it. They had it all covered in one major crackup: breaking and entering, illegal search and seizure, unwarranted arrests and, of course..."

Hair Monster raised his index finger to his lips and said Shhh.

Rose Hips made an expression like I know, we've already been there.

Blue Sky whispered that she thought the page was being bugged.

Big Artist Man appeared out of nowhere and said Hey, watch out, they'll throw you in the pit for resisting slave labor technocratic nightmare.

Isreal Disreal threw up his hands in passive disgust and said Win some Lose most.

M/F an old friend recently taken out of the pit and put back on the contaminated soil said Don't kvetch it's worse down there.

Willa Thrilla sold out. She's buying tutti-fruity gunshot for the kids at war.

New Anima is now Nude Arsenal. S/he is busy inventing a religion that wipes out supply/demand via autosuck restitution full money back guarantee.

Open your eyes and tell me what you see.

Samuel Delany

I first began to realize the troubles I would have with *Hogg* when the London copy shop, where I took it to be Xeroxed, phoned me to say that they would not make copies of the text. The office manager had looked at it, read a page or two, and told them to return it to the customer.

A year or two on, I picked up a young, stocky Irish-American (complete with red hair, very thick glasses, and freckles) near the city's downtown waterfront, who took me back to his apartment in the industrial streets west of the Village. Our after-sex talk turned to books. At one point, getting up from the futon and putting on a paisley robe, he said: "Do you want to see the weirdest, most outrageous thing I've ever read? Just a second." He went to a drawer, pulled it open, took out a manuscript in a black spring binder, and brought it back to me. "Read five pages of that—any five pages. It doesn't really matter which ones—go on!"

I opened back the black cover and began to flip through what was obviously a Xerox of Xerox of a Xerox—I could only guess how many generations. There was no title page. It began simply at page one.

It was the manuscript of *Hogg*.

Somehow, to say, "Hey, you know, actually I wrote this . . ." seemed absurd.

So I read a few pages. Yes, it was my novel.

"That's . . . pretty amazing," I told him. "Where'd you get it?"

He'd gotten it from a friend who'd gotten it from a friend who'd gotten it from a publishing company, where the manuscript, on arrival, had created a small furor in the office. Before returning it, someone had made a quick and unauthorized Xerox . . .

"I'd like to read the whole thing," I said. "Could I get one . . .?"

"I guess so. Although it's pretty dim to copy once more..."

Unfortunately, we never ran into each other again. But I didn't really need one.

At this point, Larry McCaffery became aware of the recent interest in the novel—and the controversy it was causing. I'm not sure whether he actually heard the discussion tape. (At one point, Ron said he was going to send it to him.) Larry asked to see *Hogg* and took it to Ron Sukenick and Curt White at Fiction Collective 2, who were just putting together a new line, Black Ice Books. Did I want to see *Hogg* published? Yes.

from *Hogg*

"This is Edward Sawyers, and I'm at the Crawhole waterfront tonight, walking through a crowd of people who have gathered behind a loose police line to watch the investigation of the day's latest—and we all hope the last—act of mindless slaughter. There are searchlights set up on the barges around the docks. There's an ambulance here—it arrived only seconds before me. But, from what police have already told me, there isn't much need for one—except to take the bodies to the morgue. Thankfully, there are only two known victims this time—Harry Bunim, twenty-nine, and his common-law wife, Mona Casey, thirty-four. Right now the police are searching for a missing year-old child, the Bunim's little son, Chuck. And we are all hoping here, as I know you are all hoping out there, that he was not been . . ."

Through the police car window "American Pie" finished, and over the sound of Mr Sawyers in front of me, I heard from the police car's radio speaker: "This is Edward Sawyers, and I'm at the Crawhole waterfront tonight, walking through a crowd . . ."

I listened about half a minute, then looked back. Sawyers was beckoning to one of the shirt-sleeved men. The assistant led over a fisherman from the ring of spectators—a barefooted, bullet-headed nigger. Up in front of his plaid shirt, he clutched a harmonica.

Sawyers was gesturing with one outstretched hand and saying: ". . . that's right, over here: You want to tell us what it's been like down here today?" He held out the mike to the fisherman.

Beside me, the radio was saying: "Thankfully, there are only two known victims this time—Harry Bunim . . ."

Still clutching his harmonica, the fisherman leaned over Sawyer's microphone: "This is a pretty peaceful place, like, mostly. After a little fightin' and a little fuckin', there ain't really—"

"Come on, now." Sawyers pulled the microphone back sharply. "Let's watch the language. We're on the air. Teddy, cut! Okay, pick it up . . . from: Why don't you tell us something about what it's like down here?"

"Eh . . . well," the fisherman said, much more slowly. He'd lowered his harmonica about to his belt. "People fight some. Sometimes they . . . you know, mess around. But usually it's pretty peaceful."

"Until tonight?"

"Well, this here tonight is just terrible."

"And can you tell us where you were when the screaming started?"

"Down on my boat, playin' on my mouth harp." He gestured with the instrument, caged in ten dark fingers. "And I heard Miss Mona scream. And then the shootin'."

"What did you do?"

"I was scared as a—" He looked at the microphone. "Well, I was real scared. You know, you don't hear nothin' like that around here much."

Beside me, the car radio said: ". . . are hoping out there, that he has not been hurt. We're going to talk now with Mr Andy Prescott, who works on a boat not far from the barge on which the most recent multiple slaughter took place. Mr Prescott told me earlier that he comes from Mitchuan, Kansas, but that he's been a fisherman out of Crawhole for the past seven years. We're going to be talking to Andy in just a moment now. Come right on, yes, that's right, over here: You want to tell us what it's been like down here?" Somewhere in there was a little click, but it went by pretty soft.

"Eh . . . well. People fight some. Sometimes they . . . you know, mess around. But usually it's pretty peaceful."

"Until tonight?"

"Well, this here tonight is just . . ."

But the assistant was leading Andy from the man with the microphone, while another was escorting up a black policeman. Sawyers was saying: ". . . you, very much. We're going to talk now with Officer Horace Pelham, who was the first police officer at the scene of the crime, who was, indeed, the first person to enter the barge cabin: Without getting too gory, Horace, can you tell us what you saw when you went in?"

"I wasn't the first one in," the cop said. He looked pretty sober. "It was another guy, one of the dock cops—one of the guys who works Crawhole regular. I told him that."

The man with the microphone grimaced at the assistant. Behind the cop's shoulder, the assistant shrugged.

The cop started to glance back, and Sawyers practically followed him around with the microphone. "Well, you were *one* of the first ones in, then—"

"I was the second," the cop said, turning back. He pushed his cap up and scratched his forehead. "I don't think I *can* describe it without gettin' gory. The woman had been all hacked up. First we thought the man was just shot, but when we turned him over, it looked like he got hacked up too. It's just a *mess* in there! I mean, I've seen killings before, but this is about the worst one I *ever* . . ."

The fisherman with the harmonica, and the first assistant, had come over to watch from near the police car. They stopped about three feet from me. After a few more moments, the fisherman said: "I thought he was gonna let me play my mouth harp. You said before, I was maybe gonna get a chance to play my mouth harp on the radio." He turned the instrument around in his horny black hands, frowning. "That's what you said." Suddenly he lifted it to his mouth and blew a clutch of bending blues notes, loud and twisting—they ended squawking: the assistant had grabbed the harp away and was making *Shushing* motions.

Sawyers, the policeman, and the second assistant glanced over. But they went on talking.

And from the radio, Andy's voice: ". . . because Harry always liked my music, you know. I'd see him, sometimes when he'd come by, just stop and listen. Miss Mona too. It's just terrible. An' she gonna have another baby—"

And, from the radio, Sawyers': "Thank you, Andy. Thank you, very much. We're going to talk now with Officer Horace Pelham . . ."

I looked back into the center of the circle of spectators. Officer Pelham was saying: ". . . no, but I was at the Webster's gas station. I didn't have anything to do with the Stevens' place, so I don't know what it was like there. But I tell you, I just never seen anything like that inside, here. We're just hopin' now that the baby is all right, or maybe just hurt a little. What everybody is afraid of, of course, is that he's been killed, or that the Harkner kid—"

"The alleged Harkner kid," the man with the string tie said, then frowned when that didn't sound right. "Allegedly it might be Dennis Harkner . . ." He frowned at that too.

"Yeah," the policeman said. "Anyway—we're just hoping that he didn't go and kidnap the baby. That's a pretty terrible thought. I mean, you don't even know which one would be worse, the kid being killed, or being carried off with someone like that. We're lookin' all around, hopin' that we can find it while it's still—"

From the car radio came a blast of harmonica music.

The man with the string tie glanced over again.

The assistant beside Andy gave an immense shrug, then pointed into the open car window.

". . . um, alive," Officer Pelham finished.

"Yes," said the man with the string tie. "Of course. And we're all, all of us, the listeners and all of us here on the mobile unit, praying with you that little Chuck will be found in time, before . . ."

Andy looked down at the mouth harp in his hands. He had a vague smile. He glanced in the car window, then back to his harmonica.

From the car radio, Officer Pelham's voice came on: ". . . because it gets all thick—the blood. You bleed that much and it don't run no more. It makes like a jelly, you know? And it gets—but you said not to get too gory, huh? Describin' things like that, that's pretty hard."

Sawyers' voice: "And you were at the Stevens' house, earlier?"

And Pelham's: "Oh, no. I didn't have anything to do with that—no, but I was at Webster's gas station . . ."

I wandered away from the car and Andy and the assistant, and made my way out of the circle of fishermen and police who had come up to hear and watch the man with the string tie. I went down to the water a little ways along the dock.

A big, split beam was set into the gravel edge. Below, sludge, thick and dull, slopped the rocks. I walked along the beam, looking down.

It was floating near a piling. Its back, a muddied island, with four small islands around it, bobbed in the oil, wood chips, and algae. The head must have been hanging straight down— if it still had one.

It bumped the pile, floated a few inches away, was carried back, and bumped again. I watched it awhile. Then I looked back at the crowd.

Four policemen were circling the gathering.

One was Whitey.

He glanced at me, saw I was watching him—suddenly he left the others, with a gesture to keep on going, and came over. "Hey, boy." He nodded, put his hand on my shoulder and said, real quiet: "Look, I don't got time to mess with you now. But after they finish up with this thing, if they don't put me on no special detail—" His pale eyes flicked back to the other policemen, then swiveled, like small lights, to me— "I'll meet you right there where we was foolin' around before, okay? Then I'll really throw some dick into you and you can have you a—"

While he was talking, I looked down at the water.

Whitey glanced too—and his eyes got bigger, and brighter; suddenly, they got real small. Then they opened up again.

345

"Jesus—!" He dropped his hand. Three times as loud, he said: "Oh my God . . . !" Then he whirled, calling: "I found it! Hey, I found it, right here!"

People in the crowd turned.

About six of them hesitated, then—one was the nigger orderly with the shaved head and the round glasses—started over.

From the barge, the gray-haired man in the rumpled suit called: "What you got?"

"I found the goddamn baby!"

The whole crowd started for us. Other cops were coming too. People reached us, pushed around us. In the crowd, the director was making large semaphore gestures at the assistants, who were trying to keep the cables from underfoot. The man with the string tie was coming forward too, talking into his mike the while. But you couldn't hear him because other people were shouting too much. A lot of niggers got in my way and somebody else—it was the white orderly; I looked down and saw his red socks flash below his jean cuffs—pushed me back.

And while I was trying to keep from falling, another person grabbed my shoulder and spun me around, hard: I stared up into the face of an angry black, in a blue workshirt with the sleeves torn off. I didn't even recognize him till he bellowed: "Where the hell you run off to, you motherfuckin' little son of a bitch?"

It was Big Sambo.

"You *get* your pink ass back down to the tug there with Honey-Pie, or I'm gonna bust your yellow-headed self all to *hell!*" He raised his hand to hit me. I cowered back. "An' if I *don't* find you there when I come, you better not *never* let me see you again, or it's gonna be me and you! You hear me?"

His fist fell—caught me on the shoulder, because I ducked. I dodged through the two fishermen pushing up behind me, and ran. I ran until I got to the tugs.

Then I stopped.

I looked back at the crowd. I looked at the squat, rust-hulled tug at its dock. I looked over the roadway that Nigg and Hawk had brought me down on the motorcycle.

I looked at the tug again.

I walked out on the dock, crossed the sagging plank, went to the cabin door, pulled it open, and went inside.

At the galley table, Honey-Pie sat on a chair with her bare feet wrapped behind the rungs and her fists in the lap of her dress. She looked at me, blinking.

On the window sill, the radio was still going: ". . . have been other mass murderers—indeed, man has committed atrocities against man, even in this decade, that render the terror here insignificant; yet the concentration of all this violence into a single day, in a single town, coupled with the alleged youth of the assassin—" Sawyers' voice was interrupted by another, further away: "Oh my God!" Then, louder: "I found it! Hey, I found it right here!" There were murmurs, whispers, shouts; then, one shout among them: "What you got?" And Whitey's bawling reply: "I found the—" *Bleep!*—"baby!" Sawyers' voice returned in an intense whisper: "Wait a minute . . . Wait . . . ! I *think* they've found something. Yes. I think they've got the . . . Everyone is running toward the water. I'm moving with the crowd. I'm moving. Fishermen, policemen, and those who are simply curious onlookers are clustered at the water's edge, crowding onto the docks to see, staring down into the . . . ! What? No, we're trying to find out for you if he's all right. Hello? Hey . . . ? Is he all . . . ? One of the orderlies has just pushed by me, making for the ambulance. Now he's getting out the stretcher. People are making so much noise, you couldn't hear the sound of a baby crying even if—What's that . . . ? Two of the policemen now, with grapple-hooks, I can see from here, are reaching down into the—Yes . . . ? Oh my God, folks, the poor thing is . . ."

The cup of coffee sat in front of Honey-Pie. I thought she was going to pick it up and drink it. But when I walked around the table, I saw there was a ring inside it, half an inch above the liquid, on which gray skin quivered and wrinkled. It was maybe two, three days old.

There was a mattress, folded over on itself once and stained over the narrow blue and white stripes. I went to it and sat down.

Honey-Pie watched me as I hunkered back against the wall. I pulled my sneaker heels back against my ass and wrapped my arms around my knees. One knee was coming through. I was breathing hard, and my belly, pressing again and again against my thighs, felt funny. I shook back hair that was tickling my forehead; it fell again, still wet.

Sawyers was saying: ". . . makes at least thirty-one people dead today: by gunshot, rifle and pistol; by stabbing—knife, screwdriver, broken fire poker; by clubbing, with a rifle butt, with a pair of wire-clippers; by strangulation, with jumper cables, bailing wire—and now the latest victims include a pregnant mother and her year-old child. That thirty-one does *not* include Michael Rhomer, tragically killed in the street because someone mistook him for the murderer. There are over half a dozen people in severe condition at Frontwater District Memorial Hospital. This city, I think it is safe to say, has never seen a day like this before. And we all pray it never sees one like it again. I'm going to be talking to Police Inspector Haley in a few seconds. Inspector Haley is going to explain what the police will be—Oh, yes. That's right. Yes, this is Inspector Haley. Inspector?"

"Yeah? Well, we're all agreed this has been pretty terrible." It was the voice of the man in the rumpled suit. "Anyway, we're sure he hasn't gotten too far away. He's only had minutes to run, this time. And the place is surrounded with just about everything we have. We got it from a couple of people at the bar where he did the first bunch in—people who knew him there—that the kid don't even know how to drive. We've already done some checkin' on him. We're gonna catch him, soon now."

"Can you tell us why you're so sure the capture is imminent, Inspector?"

"Well, there's that thing he always writes . . . Is that all right to talk about? Do they know about that?"

"If they've been listening to their radios, Inspector. Ladies and Gentlemen, Harkner—or the killer alleged to be Dennis Harkner—at the scene of each crime has written 'All right,' somewhere on the floor or a wall or a window. This time, it's on the front of the barge cabin where the murder was committed. Would you tell us something about how he writes it, Inspector?"

"Huh?—well, in these big . . . Eh, with blood . . . Eh . . . blood. The murder victims' blood. That's pretty—you know—grim."

"Yes, Inspector. And you were saying?"

"Oh, yeah. Well, he didn't get a chance to finish it this time. He wrote 'All' and the first four letters of 'Right.' Then there's this smear—you can see it over there on the cabin wall of the barge."

"Yes, I do, Inspector. Ladies and Gentlemen, the spotlights are illuminating the front wall of the barge's cabin where the victims, Harry and Mona Bunim, with their year-old son, Chuck, worked and lived. Next to the door, across the torn tarpaper, you can read, plainly and clearly, the gruesome words the Inspector has described."

"Well, see," the Inspector repeated, "he didn't have time to finish. So he must not have had time to get too far away." In the background whispers and talk, someone playing a harmonica passed close to the microphone. "Somebody, Inspector, just told me . . . I just was handed a note that the officer who, minutes ago, discovered the mutilated body of little Chuck, floating in the water, was also the first to hear the gunshots and shouts of the victims and to come running to their aid, apparently scaring Harkner—the alleged killer—away. And that it was he, *not* Officer Pelham, who was first to enter the cabin, to be greeted by the horrendous sight."

"Yeah," the Inspector said. "He's one of the regular Crawhole fellas. Whitey's a good old boy."

"Thank you, Inspector. Ladies and Gentlemen, this is Edward Sawyers, and we've been talking to Inspector Haley, here at the Crawhole docks, not thirty feet from the barge on which, perhaps half an hour ago, occurred another in the series of slayings that have branded this day as one of the blackest in the annals of mass murder. The Inspector has assured us that the capture of the killer, alleged to be seventeen-year-old Dennis Harkner, is imminent. A net of police has been set around and throughout Crawhole. From evidence at the scene

of the murder, we have been assured that the killer is somewhere in the—"

Then the door crashed back.

Honey-Pie's fists jumped onto the table and she jerked
her chair half a foot, without standing.

"Aw, shit," Hogg drawled. Grinning, he lowered his
booted foot to the floor, and let go of the jambs. His bare foot
was gun-colored with filth, to the frayed cuff. On the sill, his
club-like toes, the nails picked back like they were bitten bad
as the ones of his dirty, sausage-thick thumbs, flattened. The
workboot, crusted with dirt, flexed with the foot inside. He
grinned, wide enough for me to see, as well as his big, yellow
front teeth, some of the side, rotten ones. His close green eyes
were bright in his grimy face. Greasy hair clawed his forehead. Chin, cheek, and upper lip were dark with stubble like
sand. He looked around the galley. When his eyes went from
me to Honey-Pie and back, his grin got even looser.

Hogg stepped inside, real slow. The slab of his hand slid
up to his belly. He furrowed the matted yellow around the
creased pit of his navel, between the hanging shirt edges. Then
he dropped it, to hook the scuffed belt with his thumb, pulling
the brass buckle down his gut. Things inside the hammy, hairy
forearm moved. "Cocksucker, you wouldn't believe the shit I
just been through, tryin' to find your ass." He barked out one
syllable of rough laughter. "You know them two cocksuckin'
bastards, Nigg and Hawk, had the nerve to come back to the
bar? Well, like I was goin' up to save them a run-in with all the
police that was still hangin' around after all Denny's shit—I
mean, I seen 'em hustlin' you out the goddamn door; they
must've thought I was asleep or something—anyway, I just
took 'em back around in the alley, you see, explainin' to them
why all the cops was there and all about what Denny had done
and then, soon as I got 'em out of sight of anybody—well, I
began to bang heads. Couldn't bang Nigg's too hard 'cause he
works with me too often and probably will again, but I did in
the white boy! He told me where you were."

From the radio, Sawyers said: ". . . loading the sheet-cov-
ered bodies into the ambulance for that final . . ." and outside,

along the docks, a siren made Hogg glance toward the window; red light swept the bottom corner of the screening. ". . . while the tiny, towel-covered figure—one of the orderlies nearly dropped his side of the stretcher, but now he catches it up, and they move on to the ambulance's open doors. Yes, the tiny, draped figure is now inside. The orderlies are climbing in. Inspector Haley is over, talking to the driver. One of the orderlies looks out the back door—has he forgotten something? No, he's just taking a last look at the scene here, as we shall be doing shortly, with its floodlights, its police cars, and the dozens of police officers still checking the barge for evidence. Now the door is being locked. The ambulance, starting slowly at first among the crowd of fishermen and other locals who are wandering around it, is beginning to drive off." And from the radio speaker came the sound of the siren—thirty seconds old. "Momentarily, we'll be switching you back to the studio for a final rundown on the search for Dennis Harkner, a wrap-up of the local and national news, and music till midnight with . . ."

"Hey—!" Hogg jammed a thumb at the window sill— "how you like that shit, huh? I guess Denny's just about the most famous person we know, hey, cocksucker?" He scratched his belly again and ambled forward, like a huge blond ape. "I'd a' thought the goddamn infection would a' laid him too low for that kind of mess. But I guess there's some spunk in the little jackoff yet." He scratched down under his belt. "I guess tomorrow we gonna hear about how twenty or thirty big, brave pigs done finally smoked him from some outhouse with mace and what-all and machine-gunned his ass down. But, shit, the cocksucker ain't no more'n seventeen!" Hogg laughed. "I just sort of wish I'll get a chance to see him once more and maybe shake his hand 'fore they kill him. Man, you should've seen him in the bar, there, clubbin' them bikeys and shootin' old Ray in the belly— *Wham!* The wop and his old lady and me was just a-laughin' and applaudin'—dangerous? My syphilitic left nut! Before he cut out of there, he give me a big grin. I gave him one right back. 'Go on, motherfucker,' I told him. 'It's all right. Go on!'" A puzzled look broke, here and there, through Hogg's grin to pull together on top of it.

"I don't know why he's doin' it. Don't expect I ever will. But it sure is something, huh?" He pulled his hand out from his belt and reached down to dig at his crotch. Down on his greens where the head of his dick would be was a wet spot the size of a water-glass bottom from the drip his work got him, I guess.

Thinking about it in there, thick as my wrist and long as a flashlight, with an inch of foreskin swinging off it (I was still breathing hard), I felt my own dick move in my pants.

Hogg turned to close the door—the latch didn't quite catch and it drifted open an inch as he turned back. Once more he looked around the room, at Honey-Pie, at me, at Honey-Pie. "Motherfucker," he said. The grin was back on his face. He moved his feet apart and, at his thighs, flexed his hairy hands. "Well, looks like we got some nigger meat here." Hogg shook his head a little. "Hey, baby . . . Ain't nothin' *like* sweet young nigger meat! Maybe you didn't land yourself in such a bad place after all, cocksucker. Come here, nigger meat."

Honey-Pie stood up so fast the chair overturned. She stepped back, looking serious and blinking.

"Come here . . ." Hogg stepped forward.

She took another step back.

"Come on, honey. Lemme see some of that chocolate pussy. Go on, pull up that skirt and let me see some sweet, brown, nigger pussy." Mouth wide open, Hogg stuck out his tongue and wobbled it like a wet fish. A drop of gray spit hung from his lower lip. "Hey, cocksucker, you gonna help me fuck this little black bitch . . ." One hand got into his fly; on the other a single hairy finger bent, beckoning. "Come here, nigger meat. Lemme see some pussy . . ."

Her next step back, Honey-Pie's heel landed on the mattress. I wasn't sure, from behind her, but it looked like she started to bunch her skirt up.

"Shit . . ." Hogg whispered, came around the table, pushed her. "Lay down—!"

She grunted when she hit the mattress, rocked back against me; I caught her from hitting her head on the wall.

Hogg's hand did something inside his pants; another fly button hit the floor, rolled under the table, clicked against one of the iron braces, and fell over.

His wormy cock came out, hard as a pipe, dangling its rag of skin. His knees hit the mattress, and I caught his stench. I tried to remember how many times his clothes had been soiled since I'd met him. With his thumb, he jabbed at the fleshy petals of Honey-Pie's cunt. She jerked against me.

I let go and scrambled around to get my face between them. I licked her pussy around where his thumb dug—she didn't have much hair. Then I tried to get at his cock—the rim of his fist beat at my mouth—but he wanted to get it in her. Hogg shoved forward and my head got caught between his fleshy gut, his wrinkled jeans, her bunched-up dress and smooth brown belly. I pulled out. Hogg was already humping her, hard. His knees were on the floor and he was grunting like a pig. She was gasping like one.

I crawled down his legs, and for a while I gnawed on his bare, black, cracked heel.

Then I got up again, crawled onto the mattress again, and pulled at the back of his pants. They came down over his heaving ass; coming up, the buttocks opened, shit-stuck either side. They fell, clamping, then rose, the hair pulling apart the half-dried paste. The sphincter, discolored and wrinkled, suddenly puckered, then bubbled. I stuck my tongue in it. His buttocks ground my face. "Yeah," Hogg growled, "you finally eatin' shit, you little bastard." His hand came back and pushed my head further down. With a palm on one cheek, I ate out his asshole. I put my other hand between his legs. Sweat ran down his balls. When I fingered the fat, sliding cock and the rolling edges of Honey-Pie's pussy, he humped harder. I licked and thought about the way, when he finished fucking a woman or a girl, right afterward he would sink his scummy pole into my mouth and loose another load or fill my belly with pee. Thinking about that and eating out his asshole while he fucked Honey-Pie made it better than eating shit out of—

—Big Sambo bellowed: "MOTHERFUCKER!"

The door crashed back.

I heard Big Sambo's boots bang across the floor; the nigger roared, "What the *fuck* you—!"

Hogg came up off Honey-Pie, rising in one movement—
I got pushed aside onto the mattress—to turn, crouching, his
cock still up and gleaming. He was grinning like a yellow-
headed gorilla.

Honey-Pie rolled against the wall, terrified. The way she
curled up made me think of a brown beetle somebody had
stuck with a pin and then just pulled it loose.

"Oh, man," Big Sambo said, beside the table, real low.
He was crouched too. "Oh, man, you fuckin' on my *daughter!*" His fists came up like slow cannonballs. "I'm gonna kill
you, motherfucker . . ."

"Aw, shit," Hogg drawled, in the same tone as when he'd
come in. He hefted up his trousers, enough to close the top
button. His belt still swung. His cock still hung out, glistening. But it was pretty much down. "Try, nigger."

Big Sambo's face snarled up like a prune. One black
workboot stamped forward. One of those cannonballs swung
by his hip. When it stopped, there was a knife in it; I'm damned
if I know where he'd hidden it.

Hogg grabbed the edge of the galley table. It came up,
the clamps on three legs yanking loose nests of splinters. The
fourth leg just broke. Hogg brought the table back with both
hands and heaved.

The cup crashed, splashing tan and splattering pieces.

The table corner hit Big Sambo's chest. The nigger
grunted and went back. Both fists hit the wall over his head—
he didn't drop the knife, though. The table landed upside down.
The nigger came forward, among the upright legs (and one
stump), stumbling against the brace across the underside.

Hogg was already at the sink, though. He snatched the
ten-inch skillet from its nail—the nail pulled loose, clinked on
the stained aluminum drainboard, rolled into the basin—lumbered around, fast, and swung.

It gonged the left side of Big Sambo's head. Clutching his
face, Big Sambo staggered right and right into the pan as Hogg
brought it back again. This time the knife fell on the floor.

Three seconds later, so did Big Sambo.

Feet wide—the bare one in spilled coffee—Hogg rubbed

at the arm from which the pan dangled. It looked like he'd wrenched it. Then the pan clanked to the floor and wobbled around with a sound like somebody swallowing it. Breathing hard, Hogg looked first at Big Sambo, then back at the mattress.

Honey-Pie sat, her cheek pressed to the wall, one wrist against her mouth, one hand spread on the wood. She was blinking at Big Sambo.

"Come on, cocksucker," Hogg said. "Let's get outta here 'fore somebody comes around to see about the noise."

He wasn't even thinking about Honey-Pie at all, now.

I got up but, as I stepped over the nigger, I looked back at her. She was staring at me . . . I felt my face trying to mimic hers, as though that would let me know what was going on inside her.

"Come *on!*" Hogg's hand just caught my ear; it stung so hard I almost fell. If he'd caught me full in the head, he might've knocked me out.

I got to the door—scraped my shin against the broken table leg, but not bad—and pushed it open. I looked back at Hogg, who was rubbing his arm again. He wiped his mouth on his shoulder, kneaded his bicep, bent his elbow a couple of times, then kneaded his forearm.

Behind Hogg, taking her hand from the wall now, Honey-Pie was still looking at me.

"Go on, go on," Hogg said.

I crossed the deck. Hogg came on behind me. I heard him laugh. "Shit, cocksucker—" I glanced back. Stuffing his meat back into his pants, immediately he gestured me to go on—"but I sure like to beat up a nigger. Can't beat on old Nigg too much 'cause we always on jobs together." I heard him buckling his belt. "Beatin' on the bikey was fun. But it ain't like a nigger." At the head of the gangplank, Hogg stopped me with a hand on my shoulder.

From the deck we could see down where the police cars were still parked by the barge. The red light was off now. The van from the radio station was pulling out. Police were all up and down the dock. There was still a crowd. There were still spotlights.

On the barge beyond, a figure, arms out for balance (from here I couldn't tell if it was Red or Rufus) walked to the top of the pile and turned to look. It was joined by a second (Rufus, or Red . . .). After a few seconds, they went down the other side.

"Come on—!" Hogg started. "No . . . wait'll they go by."

The radio van was rolling up, very slowly. Some of the assistants, the director, and Sawyers walked beside it. A guy with a roll of cables over one arm came running up and, jogging along, handed them up to somebody in the open back door.

The director looked behind her, saw him, and called, "Hey, hurry it up. You guys were supposed to have that all packed before we took off." She turned back to her clipboard and, still walking, got out a pen and made a mark. "Well, let's just hope we don't have to do anymore of *those* tonight!"

"It went okay," Sawyers said. "It seemed to me like it went okay."

The guy who'd handed up the cables into the van grabbed the van door and tried to vault inside. He didn't make it, and some of the assistants laughed.

"What'd you think about it, Mary?" Sawyers' earphones were around his neck now. The wire looped across the blood-red strings. "You think it went okay?"

The director turned up another paper on the clipboard. "I guess so. Maybe that part where you were getting Pelham to describe the inside of the cabin was a little much."

"Aw," Sawyers said, "this is a liberated age! And Martin'll love it—you know I really thought he was the first cop in there. That's what I *asked* for. That's what I thought he was."

The director looked up and saw the guys horsing around at the back of the slowly rolling van. "Hey," she called. "Cut it out, huh? I don't want to have to do an on-the-spot coverage about one of you breaking a leg." She turned back to Sawyers. "Babes, have you got a cigarette? I'm out."

"Sure. Here you go."

She took one from the pack he offered, but made a brushing gesture when he started to pat himself for a lighter. "No, that's okay. I got matches. It's all right . . ." She put the clipboard under one arm, bent her head; flame flared on her chin and cheeks.

She'd stopped about seven feet in front of us. When she looked up, she suddenly frowned. She was looking straight at us, too—no, not straight at us: between us.

Without thinking, I pulled back a little bit. I heard Hogg take a breath; almost as though he was getting out of the direct line of her stare, he stepped back too.

I glanced behind us.

What she was staring at was Honey-Pie, who stood in the doorway, one hand high on the door frame, the other on the doorknob, one foot inside the sill, one foot out. Her dress was all torn. Her head was all low between her shoulders, her mouth was sort of loose, and her eyes were wide. She was watching, not intense enough to call it a stare, back. She didn't look all that much like she was hurt or anything—maybe she looked like she was sick. Or maybe just funny.

I looked back at the director. I could tell her eyes had just flicked back and forth between me and Hogg, and back to Honey-Pie.

I looked at Hogg. He'd just glanced at Honey-Pie too; now his eyes went to fix on nothing in particular in the general direction of the director. He wasn't looking *at* her, I could tell. But his jaw was clamped so hard it almost looked like the muscle was about to shake.

The director lowered the still flaming match. Her frown got deeper. Sawyers was walking on. Again she looked at me, at Hogg, at Honey-Pie. I could see her start to turn away; and I could see her not do it. Her own jaw clamped, loosened. She shook the match suddenly, tossed it away. "Hey," she said. "Little girl? Are you okay . . . ?" Hogg still wasn't looking at her. "Is everything all right?" (There were police all over the place, so I guess there wasn't too much Hogg could do.) "What's the matter?"

Honey Pie wasn't looking at either me or Hogg. She blinked a couple of times at the director. I don't even think she was thinking particularly about me or Hogg. She moved her head a little, blinked again, and in a low voice answered: "Nothin'."

The director, her frown become all questioning disbelief,

raised her cigarette slowly. At this point, I don't think she was thinking about Hogg or me either. I thought she was going to march up across the plank.

She didn't.

She turned away, took a couple of steps, looked back, frowned again—even then I thought she might come back—went off half a dozen steps more, glanced back at us again, then turned away.

Hogg let out his breath.

She glanced back a couple times more.

Hogg looked at Honey-Pie. She still stood in the doorway, looking down at the deck now. Once she looked up at us both, then let her eyes drop again.

The director had caught up with the van. She grabbed the side of the door, vaulted up—brushed away one guy who tried to give her a hand—and turned, holding onto the side, and looked back again, her cigarette a pinprick in the gauze of shadows that pulled across them.

"Come *on,* cocksucker," Hogg whispered, "let's get *going!*"

He glanced at Honey-Pie once more, then lumbered over the sagging plank. I hurried after him.

We went by two policemen talking to about six fishermen. None of them even looked at us.

Rob Hardin

I first learned of Black Ice Books in the fall of 1987, in an uplifting missive from a chronically benevolent friend. After scanning the latest armload of my writing—three poems, an essay and my first short story, "Still," which appears in this anthology—novelist John Shirley wrote to report he'd forwarded everything to Professor Larry McCaffery of SDSU. McCaffery, he explained, was on the editorial board of Black Ice Books.

I'd had doubts about "Still" because its design and execution had had little to do with any fiction I'd ever read. After studying music composition at Maryhurst College, I fretted that I'd grown too interested in the music of prose. I worried that the prose was perhaps too poetic: I had been writing in poetic forms since I was a little boy and was accustomed to thinking in stanzas. (That's why "Still" begins with seven paragraphs of seven lines each.)

Writing teacher Dennis Cooper had advised me to "write about sex" because "then you can't write for your parents." Fair enough—but I mistrusted the grid of wish fulfillment. To avoid it, I'd chosen a sexual situation that would embarrass but not excite me. (Weeks later, I questioned the perversity of my choice.)

Most of all, I'd wanted to present artistic imagery in scientific language. To describe soft things in a hard way. To develop the dream-image of an exploding torso as if it were a subject in a fugue.

All of these factors gave "Still" the feel of an indecent experiment. Even so, at least one reader liked "Still," as I soon learned: McCaffery responded with a letter I ought to have framed. He offered to publish "Still" in *Fiction International*, my essay in *Postmodern Culture* and my poems in *Mississippi Review*. "Unlike anything I've ever read," he enthused—thus redeeming my sense of my purpose.

Just to make certain I'd question my sanity, the esteemed editor asked if I knew any "weird writers" who were "having difficulty getting published." Dumbfounded, I told him I'd limit the list to a hundred and dubbed McCaffery a damned peculiar godsend. Ten years later, McCaffery edited my collection, *Distorture*, for Black Ice Books. When *Distorture* won the Firecracker Award, I thanked him for the extra sulfur.

Still

He wasn't drunk or paralytic, and no one had put him under hypnosis. The X-K seemed to have fooled around with some dangerous strain of boredom, then wandered into a trance through a door that locked automatically. Motionless from his tensed shoulders to his gangly legs, he was the image of an ollie hanging out. Some photo-realist might have sculpted his look of lobotomized bliss.

Like the windshields of showroom cars, his eyes merely framed the absence of the owner. They were wading-pool blue and glimmered above his small, sunburnt nose. His lips were thick, chapped, the color of scarlet model paint. Long ash-blond curls fell to the ridged neck, just touching the over-developed deltoids. The chest and groin were striped with shadow under half-drawn venetian blinds.

The white room was big, empty. It contained only black furniture. The blinds, metal chair and cubed coffee table gleamed with streaks of sunlight. The black-sheeted mattress reflected nothing. Stage center, it drooped over a board mounted on some concrete blocks. The X-K sat on the mattress. He was still except for his legs, which rocked slightly as they dangled over the bedboard.

The man who lived there slanted against the doorpost, his frame a limp diagonal. He couldn't understand how the kid had gotten past two dead-bolt locks and a steel door—

a tall order, especially for someone whose mind was missing. Fortyish, slight, the man pushed sharpened fingernails through silver-black hair. His eyes curved to inverted U's as he sized up the X-K's oblivious body.

In the hallway, mounted on vinyl-coated steel rods: a compact disc player, turntable and cassette machine. In the bedroom, discreetly wired above the windows: thin white speakers. Mahler's *Kindertotenlieder* poured from them, filling the room with its *fin de siècle* necrophrenia. Next to the amplifier, various records and tapes: SPK, Gesualdo, *Deploration On The Death Of Ockeghem.*

The man walked to the window, drew the blinds, then moved to the closet. Parting the rack in the middle, he pulled out lace-up leather pants and a shirt of cherry-red silk. He slid into them, then slipped into black boots of soft Italian leather. Last of all, he chose a black medieval waistcoat. He ran two fingers along its raised pattern of scythes, stopped at the breast pocket, and reached in.

He dragged out a cigarette and held a match to it, staring at the X-K the whole time. Like storerooms that once contained important negatives, the eyes led to an absence. The X-K's Body seemed a better canvas than the eyes: its musculature had been eccentrically developed. So much wreckage lay under the surface that it was as if a breastplate of spears threatened to rise from the Body's skin.

The man studied the Body for a few seconds, approached it, and dropped to a kneeling position.

Tilted between thumb and forefinger, butt of the filter pushed forward by the thumb, the cigarette drew zigzags of smoke across the chest. The (visual) process implied deeper operations: the cigarette was *evocative*, a light pencil tracing wave-forms on the screen of a Synclavier. Afternoon chilled to evening; as if in response to the cigarette's floating graphics, the Body began to shudder.

The man pointed his cigarette at the xiphoid process. He considered burning a mark there, then dismissed the idea. There was no reason to disfigure the Body with a grid that would rise in welts. The thought of inflicting pain left him indifferent:

any damage to the skin would prove too literal for the imagination to distort. The Synclavier screen would freeze under the Medusa-gaze of Violence, and discoloration would be the only added dimension in place of numerous subtractions.

The jagged lines began to straighten and intersect. A moment of extreme pleasure took him over as the grid of smoke tightened against The Body. The tautening lines resembled laces that were slowly being pulled through a series of obliquely-positioned holes. He blew smoke rings against this—one for the hollow of each violin-soundboard hip—and the rings complicated the lattice-work to Art Nouveau.

As the window's square of sky dimmed, the glow of the cigarette ash grew brighter: it became an arrowhead of raw meat under the violet lamp of a science exhibit. Trembling slightly, the Body paled to black-light-poster garish as bands of smoke rose to restrain the shoulders. At last, it was encased in a suit of ghostly white bondage gear.

The Body shuddered in the draft. Bumps rose in patches on its chest and stomach, streaks reddened across the white shoulders. Tiny slash-marks appeared where the sleeping skin smarted most under the fumes.

Lesions formed between the costal margin and the linea sublunaris. The lesions widened and spread below the xiphoid process; they spat threads of black smoke which climbed the thorax, deserted the Body at the upper deltoids, and gathered into blurred bars. The bars crumbled into black dots which formed shadowy, Seraut-like representations of nucleated cells. The cells were bound into spirochetes, and these gathered into whorls. The smoke had become a pointillist's animated cartoon of the morphology of multi-cellular animals.

The skin surrounding the nipples cracked and healed repeatedly, as in a case of fast-motion eczema. The area soon resembled a cartographer's map of layered transparencies.

The sunset was of epic duration. Lingering streaks dangled in the mirror like an homage to Calder. In contrast, the Body's scars healed in the tangerine light as in a fast-motion film, until the cartography of lesions and ruptured tissue smoothed to uninflected white.

The man exhaled sharply. He could not account for the series of Herschel Gordon Lewis mutilations he had just performed. He calmed himself, lit another cigarette, and returned to the Body.

As before, the chest writhed under blurred restraints. Roman X's bound the torso, and a mesh of fine ash tightened around the tremulous frame.

Particles of red smoke seemed to magnetize lit cigarettes inside the Body: red tips pressed through its smoking skin.

The space between the ribs and stomach, and another directly below the navel, filled with pus until they began to swell and pulsate. Bumps appeared on these areas; the bumps darkened, blistered, opened. The muscles and tissue below these began to bulge. The upper chest and navel were invisibly pulled in opposite directions until the waist and ribs were twisted open.

Pieces of the Body began to fly around the room.

The man trembled with release. Fissures opened in his chest, spuming with ejaculate until he was completely drained. His lids closed slowly, like power windows. Through them, he saw the yellow of oncoming headlights. The yellow intensified to white until, when sleep came down, even that empty color had been erased.

As the *Kindertotenlieder* ended, the two Bodies slumped to the floor. Integuments lifted themselves slightly from the lacerations and veins wriggled out. These flew to the center of the room, knotted themselves into an arabesque, and hardened into a green partition, which stood between the Bodies.

The partition was divided into two halves. Its design revealed droll figurations which, seen at a distance of a few yards, proved to depict an unusually violent masque.

The organs featured in the masque were impaled on an arabesque that, in the style of Art Nouveau at its most excessive, represented a kind of serrated circuitry.

At the center of the arabesque, trefoil components outlined the disfigured body of Origen. Two keyholes formed the stylized wound in his side. Drops of blood hung in a chain from each keyhole, and each chain extended laterally to an antipodally positioned object. The right chain led to a burning trilobite, the left, to a brain sealed in fire. The pointed flames which surrounded each object terminated in a band of smoke that curved diagonally to the top of the arabesque. There, both bands joined in an ogee and, at its vertex, spelled the word *PASSIVITY* in skywritten characters.

The room dimmed.

The delicate lineations of the arabesque drooped, then tore, until the partition came apart in ragged halves.

The two veinless Bodies flattened like deflating beach toys, molding themselves to the wood-grain of the floor. Only the man's head remained erect. It swelled to hydrocephalic, and its lips began to move.

Invisibly, a phonograph stylus clicked against a record label. Forced by the record's spiral groove, it endlessly repeated this action at the interval of a double-dotted quarter note.

The man's mouth twitched in time with the clicking stylus. The ticcing was violent, parodistic, and was soon accompanied by a periodic bulging of the eyes.

A string section see-sawing between two unrelated chords—C major and E-flat minor—and bassoons and tympani answering each other with absurd trills, grew faintly audible between clicks.

As the light continued to dim, only the twitching head moved. Even the monotony of its ticcing suggested a kind of stasis.

The room went black, but the noise persisted like an after-image.

D. N. Stuefloten

I was wandering around Australia in the late seventies, writing a novel about dreams. I had long since consigned myself to obscurity. My life had itself carried me down obscure roads, through obscure countries, I enjoyed obscurity, preferred the arcane, I liked to hide in corners, skulk in shadows, slip off into nether-lands. Nevertheless, somewhere in Australia, I read an account of the Fiction Collective. I can no longer recall what magazine, what newspaper, carried this account. I filed the reference in some dark recess of my mind. Many years later I was returning to California from Manzanillo, Mexico, with the manuscript of a new novel stowed in the panniers of my motorcycle. I recall the implacable heat of the northern deserts. I slept one night in a streambed, hidden from view, and watched a full moon rise out of a canyon. How long can one continue thus, hidden from view? I soon discovered that the Fiction Collective— dredged from my mental cubbyhole—had become FC2. The manuscript—the first I'd sent anywhere in twenty years—caught the attention of Curt White and Ron Sukenick. FC2 is a kind of obscurantist venture, Quixotic perhaps, a lapidary gleam in some exotic jungle, an arcane growth, a sore, a goad, a bloom, a reproach to the timid. I am glad to have found it.

from *The Mexico Trilogy*

1

One lizard eye stares up at her. She lies on a sack bed—burlap stretched over a wooden frame—in a dark corner of the room. There seems to be a lizard at her breast—specifically a swollen iguana, or ppuppulni-huh, its chitinous teeth fastened at her teat. One exophthalmic eye, with its translucent lid, stares up at her face. Her face sweats, and sweats. Her lips are swollen, bruised. A gecko runs up the wall beyond her. Elsewhere in the room the priest—the man who plays the priest—sits with his face in his hands. The "husband" sits in another corner, a cigarette glowing between lips. A twist of blond hair lies lankly on his forehead. There is an oily sheen to his face. All of them—all three of the people in the room—are illuminated by the ochre glow of the napalm that flows softly over the hills outside. This glow pulses as each canister of gelatinous petroleum splits open and ignites, one after another. An F-4 Phantom—the smiling pilot is visible through the plexiglass cockpit—banks away from the line of horsemen descending the defoliated hillside. We marvel at the beauty of the scene: the sky to the east a deep purple, the sun rising through the smoke that rises from the ruins of Saigon. Or is it Quang Tri? Or Hue, that ancient city? In any case the horizon is swirling with a smoky, purple glow. Another plane banks away. The pilot, goggled and masked behind his plexiglass, makes a gesture: thumbs up. We watch the line of horsemen descend the blackened slope, threading their way, wearily, between the ochre blossoms of napalm.

The woman pushes the swollen iguana from her breast.

"Are we going to breakfast?"

"We're going to the museum."

"I could use some tea."

"The tea here is terrible."

"So is the coffee."

"At least it's drinkable."

"Just a cup—first—"

"First?"

"Before the museum."

"What difference does it make?"

"I'd like just a cup—"

"The coffee is bad enough, but at least it's drinkable."

"Coffee, then."

"We'll go to the museum first. If you need to drink—"

"Then afterwards—"

"We'll see."

The swollen iguana crawls back to her breast.

2

Along the tiled floor of the building scutter scorpions. Occasionally the man who plays the husband takes off a shoe and slaps at one. He swears using short, guttural words. Perhaps he is German, or Dutch. We can't be certain. There is no discernible accent when he speaks his lines in English. A good actor, of course, is a good mime. He may be a German actor mimicking American speech patterns, or, equally, an American mimicking a German's profanity. He is blond enough to be a northern European—or an American of northern European descent. His lips are thin, but fleshy. That is, they are not thick lips, but they protrude from his face. They are red and slick, as though perpetually wet. This may be more a characteristic of Germans than Americans. He wears a white T-shirt, as many

Americans do. His belly seems soft. It falls over the belt of his pants. His shoes are supple brown leather, moccasin-type. He smokes Gauloises—the pack is in the rolled-up sleeve of his T-shirt—but this may be an affectation. The Gauloises are not necessarily an indication of his nationality.

The scorpions enter the room from the cenote, along with other animals and insects which will be named. The actor lights another Gauloise and blows the smoke towards the woman.

"Let's run through it again."

"No, it's too hot."

"I want it to be perfect."

"I can't concentrate—"

"Just start. Are we going—"

"Are we going—to breakfast?"

"We're going to the museum."

"I could use some tea."

"The tea here is terrible."

"So is the coffee. God, I could use some iced coffee."

"You have no discipline, do you?"

"It's so hot—"

He roughly stubs out his Gauloise. He turns to the window as napalm bursts nearby. For a moment his eyes glow orange.

"Discipline. That's what you lack—what all of you lack.".

"All of us?"

"You are too soft."

"It's this heat—"

"The heat has nothing to do with it."

There is a scorpion on the sill. He takes off one shoe. He fondles it. He runs his fingers into the shoe, where his toes would go. Then he turns the shoe around and slaps the heel onto the scorpion. He scrapes the carcass off the sill and pushes it along the floor to the foot of his bed. He pushes it into a pile of other dead scorpions.

"The heat," he says, "has nothing to do with it."

He unrolls his pack of Gauloises from his sleeve. He shakes one into his hand. After a moment he puts it between his thin, wet lips. He doesn't light it, however. He continues to sit there. Finally he leans back against the wall, and shuts his eyes.

3

A single eye glares at her. He has, of course—the man who plays her husband—two eyes. But it is his affectation to lower the lid of his right eye while staring at the woman. We believe this is a conscious act. He must be aware of the unsettling effect this stare has on her, and on others. His left eye is stern, even mad. It seems paler, a paler blue, than his right eye. Is that possible? The woman turns away from this stare. The iguana, the ppuppulni-huh, crouches on her belly, which is otherwise bare. His tail switches once, twice between her legs. With each switch she gasps, and her face turns further away. Her face is so oily with sweat we are not sorry to have it thus averted. When she speaks her words are muffled. The husband has to lean forward to hear her.

"I heard screams last night," she says.

"Screams?"

"I'm certain of it."

"I heard nothing."

"I was awakened—they awakened me—"

"Awakened?"

"I don't know the time."

"You were possibly dreaming."

The priest, until now silent in his corner, lifts his head.

"I heard them too," he says.

"You?"

"Distinctly. Quite—distinctly—"

"Sound effects."

"What?" says the woman.

"Sound effects," repeats the husband. "If you heard anything at all."

The sun glows through the window to his left. There is a softness to the air that occurs only in the tropics. In this light—especially when augmented by the bursts of napalm—the man seems recognizable. That is, we imagine we have seen him before, perhaps similarly illuminated. He bears a certain resemblance to the film noir actors of another time—Dan Duryea, perhaps, or even Alan Ladd. But their time has gone. If this man is an actor like them, he is an anachronism. It may be he actually appeared in films during the dying days of film noir, or perhaps in the later European films influenced by film noir. If so he must be older than he looks—at least fifty. He would be out of place in modern American comedies about adolescent boys or horror movies filled with plasticized faces and rubbery monsters. Nor would there be a place for him, or for his rapacious glare, in the cineplex boxes which have replaced the grand movie palaces across the American landscape. Perhaps he is aware of this. His soft belly and sallow skin suggest the dissolution of dreams. His thin, wet lips curve into a sardonic grin. Even his presence here, in what must be the lowest of low-budget movie making, is an admission of dispossession. He is dispossessed. He grins, sour, sardonic, sallow, at the sweat-stained body of the woman who plays his wife.

She seems familiar also. We have seen a poster which may be a portrait of her. It achieved some fame during the American-Vietnam War. If it is her, she was both younger and happier then: the skin of her face, in the poster, is tauter, the eyes livelier. Her arms are raised above her head in an attitude of triumph. From her waist to her ankles she is sheathed in white latex pants. Clearly outlined at her crotch are the swelling shapes of her labia major. Because the pelvis is thrust forward, these labia are not only clearly defined by the thin, tight latex, but seemingly *offered*—thrust forward, presented, exposed, delivered to the hungry men of the 9th Marine Expeditionary Brigade and the 173rd Airborne and the 1st Air Cavalry who, at that time, slid through the jungled valleys and denuded back alleys of Vietnam, M-16s cocked, M-60s shouldered, grenades hanging, pockets stuffed with K-bars, C-rations, infrared night sights, packets of C-4, phosphorus bombs and 9mm pistols. How many of these teen-aged lips—most of the American soldiers seemed to be teen-agers—how many pressed hungrily against those printed, proffered labia limned there in those white latex pants? Men jerked off in ditches and foxholes, behind crates of ammunition and in flapping tents. Semen flew through the air like shrapnel, precious seed spilled like blood, bodily fluids exulted, whooshed, blasted like rockets into the thick Vietnamese air. During her tour of Vietnam—it was her apogee as a starlet—she wore the white pants at every stop. She wore them at Da Nang, she wore them at Cam Ranh Bay, she wore them—or a pair exactly like them—at Bien Hoa and An Khe and Phu Bai, even at Bong Son and Nha Trang and, one famous night, at Phuoc Binh. At Phuoc Binh, cheered on by GIs still glassy-eyed from mortar attack and a fire fight, she—according to rumor—took off the white latex pants: *peeled* them off, peeled them down her hips, peeled them down her thighs, peeled them down her calves, removing and re-tieing her high-heeled, black patent, ankle-strapped shoes, and danced—perhaps for an hour, perhaps *all night*—on a raised platform in front of these desperately hungry men, some still bloody, heads and arms wrapped in mud-stained gauze, uniforms stained, faces stained, bodies thickened and stained with lust, blood, sweat and tears. Is this true? Which battalion, which company, which platoon witnessed this event, which became famous throughout Vietnam? The story, the rumor—true or not—preceded and followed her everywhere she went in that dark, blasted country, like a miraculous vision: labia glossy, engorged with blood, red and slick and swollen—the night brazen, unleashed, still smelling of cordite and death, swollen with the odors of crushed flowers and rotting fruit, swollen with her perfume soured with their sweat, swollen with musky semen, swollen with her dark, effulgent secretions, her black shoes brilliant, beating on tables, beating on counters, beating on platforms, beating on backs, beating in the air, beating while raised high above her head while her white legs flashed in the black, swollen, thick night, the black night which gave way to a thin red dawn, to thin roosters crowing, thin children crying, thin faces emerging, sallow, yellow, exhausted, from bamboo huts, from tin shacks, from holes in blasted walls, from craters in the blasted ground, the ground turned red by the thin, silent sun, and black by the thick, silent, drying blood which stained the earth from border to border to border.

» » »

4

The building is shaped like a fat cross. It has been, we are given to understand, constructed—at some expense—as a duplicate of the original building, which is somewhere on the Yucatan Peninsula of Mexico. There is a cenote there, which is a kind of natural well, formed when the peninsula's limestone shelf—a limestone shelf covered by mere inches of soil, a scant country, earth pungent but flimsy, as easy to rip apart as tissue paper—formed, we say, when this limestone shelf is undermined by an underground stream. This limestone then collapses, exposing the water underneath. At the site with which we are concerned, and at many others in Yucatan, the cenote is considered sacred. The most famous example of this, at least to foreigners, is the cenote at Chichen Itza. In some cases—in our case—a temple was built around the cenote. When Francisco de Montejo swept through Yucatan in the service of the Spanish king, this Mayan temple, like many others, was torn down. The limestone blocks, plus additional stones and adobe, were then used to construct a Catholic church on the same spot. This was not seen by de Montejo and the other Spaniards as a desecration, but as proof of the power and rightness of their religion. During the Mexican Revolution, and particularly during the regime of Plutarco Elias Calles, Catholics were persecuted and many of their churches—including the one of which we speak—were closed. It was not confiscated, but neither was it allowed to reopen. Over the years artifacts were brought to it, including some which had adorned the original temple. It thus became, by default, a kind of museum, and remained one until well into the present century, though largely ignored: it was too far from Merida for convenient day trips, and not close enough to any major sites to attract tourists. A hotel was built in the 1930s in a nearby village, but it drew few guests and by the time of our story was largely inhabited, on the upper floors, by relatives of the original owner—primos and tios, hijos and hijas, abuelitos and cuñados—and on the lower floor by chickens and goats. This hotel has not been reconstructed for this film.

It was a long journey for the three actors to reach this site. They met for the first time in the Hotel Don Jesus. They flew in separately. The woman was disoriented. She staggered down the hotel corridor. "Where am I? Where am I?" Her room was anonymous. It told her nothing. Her luggage was piled all around her. Outside, buses without mufflers snarled past like angry beetles. Everything was hot. Even her air-conditioned room seemed hot. The airplanes, however, had been cool. The airplanes, like the hotel room, had been anonymous. She got on the first one in Iowa. The ticket specified dates and times but said nothing about weather. In Iowa it was always cold, except for the summers, which sweltered. In the airplane the air was thin and chilled. She flew for hours, for perhaps thousands of miles. Clouds passed beneath her at incredible speeds. Yet she sat still. She exerted no energy. When she changed planes she felt expelled—expelled down one chute, into another chute, jostled by strangers who tugged at her purse, who plucked at the sleeves of her mohair coat, whose hands—fleetingly, anonymously—brushed her hips, her fanny, and even her breasts. The caresses were casual, and vanished as soon as she experienced them. Soon she entered another plastic compartment. The seat was comfortable. There was a strange rumble, a kind of pressure, and then silence. People murmured softly around her, as though they were in church. Finally a child began to cry. It cried, perhaps for hours, for thousands of miles, across frontiers, across continents, past ruined civilizations, past third world countries and second world countries and first world countries in the throes of insurgencies and bankruptcies. On the earth far below muggers mugged, judges judged, coups couped, cars lurched off assembly lines, and giant machines stamped out millions of plastic cups. Yet within the plane was audible only a slight hiss, perhaps a faulty air-conditioning vent, and the lonely cry of a single child.

At the hotel she asked the blond man where he was from. He grunted something incomprehensible in reply. It did not sound like the name of a place. They were in the room of the man who looked like a priest. He had instructions, vouchers, tickets spread over a table, but he seemed confused by the whole display. The blond man pouted, and kept muttering his incomprehensible words. A map was spread on the table also, but none of it was recognizable.

"Wow," she said. "Did you see those men? At the airport?"

They turned their faces towards her.

"In the blue uniforms. They were cute. You know, sexy. But they had these funny guns—all black, like pistols, but big—"

"MAC-10s."

"What?"

"MAC-10s." It was the blond man, whose single eye now transfixed her. "Machine pistols, my dear. A slight pressure on the trigger—and you are cut in half. Verstehen sie? But you are right. Very sexy."

"Ugh," she said—to herself; the two men had turned back to the map. "No one told me they were real."

Bayard Johnson

When I wrote *Damned Right* I'd already written about five novels. I sent them to one or two places and when they were rejected I decided I should quit wasting time and write a better novel. Then I wrote *Damned Right* and Lyndal said she would handle the post office if I would just get the manuscripts ready and manila folders addressed. So I made a big push and we sent out twenty-five. *Damned Right* went out to FC2 on Valentine's Day.

Some big presses suggested I try smaller presses. Some smaller presses suggested big presses. After a year and half the book had been rejected at twenty-four places. I was working as a ship captain when I got the message that FC2 had called. I got to shore and called them back and they said they had my manuscript titled *Damned Right* and wondered if it was still available for publication. I said hell yes. They said, "Good, well, we just wanted to check, because it's been a year and a half, and we apologize for the delay, and as long as the manuscript's still available we'll go ahead and read it."

from *Damned Right*

How can you be sure you're really in Los Angeles when you finally get there? A double-walled fortress defended on all sides by false cities. Rogue cities. Ghost-L.A.s with the real city hiding somewhere behind a screen of deceptor-cities. How many people come aiming for the center, only to bounce off? Or bog down and get shunted off to some secondary satellite city. Stuck on the periphery of what's really real. Exiled to a frontier town.

But it's right in a way. It makes sense. Of course it wouldn't be hanging right out in the open for any casual nerd to yank on. Real truth and true beauty don't operate that way. They lie concealed. Hidden away for the few, for those of us who know what we're looking for. Who know where it is and what it's for. That's how purity operates. Nothing's so clear-cut. You have to dream it first. Then maybe—maybe—you'll know it when you see it.

We fly through dark canyons and up hills and down. Our freeway is three lanes now. In the distance we begin to see scatterings of light. Promising, maybe even seductive. But we won't be fooled again. Straight on then. We'll know when we know, and not before. I feel more urgency than ever before. Desperate almost. I feel a tightness in my chest and throat, almost a choking. I have to fight it down. I have to try to think about something else, and push down a little harder on the gas.

Finally coming down an endless grade we merge with a four-laner feeding the city. We're six lanes each way now and together we make twelve. The cars and trucks slide roaring down and forward and below us spread all the billions of twinkling lights of the city. Well, maybe not. I'm not making any assumptions but what else could it be? Twelve lanes more or less, who's counting? We're in the thick of it now. Blasting across the flats, crossing and ducking under wide freeways with names I've never heard of—five lanes each way to someplace called the Simi Valley! Incredible. This has to be it.

Only it isn't. The green overhead freeway signs are still pointing out the lanes to take to get to Los Angeles. Five lanes feed that way. We're not there yet. I cross over just in time to catch the freeway leading onward, inward. We were nearly shunted off onto some other route. There's no going back on a freeway. It's always one-way. The signs only tell you which exits lie up ahead. They never say a word about the ones you passed. You keep blasting onward, inward, and the chances are good that you'll never pass the same interchange twice.

I've never been crossed up on a freeway in my life. I came this close just now. It rattles me. I step down on the throttle, to ease back up toward ninety and settle my nerves. There are so many cars. We can't get it up to ninety, even with lane-changes. They keep clogging things up, ahead, behind, to either side. It's sometime in the middle of the night and the jerks are clogging up the freeway! We're pinned in, held down to 65 and 70. Only an occasional burst toward 80. Then, boxed in again. Swerving, switching lanes, twisting your neck off.

What the hell is this? It's not supposed to be like this. We keep following the wide green signs for Los Angeles. We start up a grade and the whole freeway is slowing down. We can't have this, anything is better. We'll scream down the shoulder. I work over to the fast lane but there's no shoulder. You can see where they moved the lanelines over, gobbling up the inside shoulder and narrowing the widths and getting an extra lane out of it without widening the pavement.

What is this chintzy shit? This is the world capital of freeways, what the hell do they think they're doing penny-pinching on one miserable little lane? This isn't what we came here for. There's no hitting 200 on this assembly line. Christ. It must be rush-hour. My sense of timing must be screwed up. I've been in such a hurry. I've always been but lately, more so. Much more. There's no slowing down. Not for a second. I guess I stopped to eat but I can't remember when, or what I ate. I guess I slept but I can't remember sleeping. Oh well. Life's like that sometimes. Something must have thrown my timing off. It has to be rush-hour. Bad timing. I've always had the greatest sense of timing. Naturally, without ever having to think about it. I'll get it back. It's just a question of getting in synch. We'll have to come back when the timing's right. We'll hit this stretch sometime in the middle of the night, when the nerds are at home in bed and we got six lanes to weave through and wander across at gliding speeds that bring motion almost to a state of crystalline immobility.

The freeway is slowing down again. We're under forty and almost bumper to bumper. It feels like a standstill. The slowest this car ever went when it wasn't speeding up from a stop or slowing down to a stop. I can't take it. The thought of gridlock. I swerve to the right, cutting across lanes. From behind me comes honking and screeching. We never bothered to put in blinkers or brakelights, who needs that shit when you're whistling past at a hundred miles an hour faster than the slugs you're passing?

I angle toward the right shoulder. They haven't gobbled up the shoulder on this side for extra lanes yet. Oh, wait'll we come back at 2 A.M., we'll show you the blazing unleashed potential in this clogged broad desecrated swath of concrete. We'll set it right. We'll atone for this rush-hour obscenity and we'll cleanse our minds and clear our eyes and pay some homage, at 190 and beyond.

We swerve to miss the scattered pieces of a rusted tailpipe strewn along the shoulder, then crank it up a little and fly down the shoulder at close to eighty. I feel better already. The sea of geeks is frozen in a solid grinding mass on our left. An endless strip of sweating and crystallized humanity. Criminals! Blasphemers! They think this is reality—

until, suddenly, Who's this now, what in the hell was that, streaking past in a reddish blur down the right shoulder? You can't drive on the shoulder! It's—it's—uh, it's not fair! That's what it is. Come back here, you. Sorry, heathens. God's on my side. I'm in motion. Isn't that proof enough? Come on, join me in Paradise. What's stopping you? The WASP-mafia cop-puppets are all jammed into the gridlock with the rest of the infidels. What are you afraid of? We can all be Jesus on the 405, or the 101, or the six-oh-whatever.

I'm laughing and letting her loose. Let her go, let her run. We hump and soar down the blacktopped shoulder, crunching over the light dusting of busted safety glass. I'm blind with speed and freedom and I miss the signs and they nail us. The shoulder goes branching off suddenly. We go with it, walled off by a solid column of the creeping dead. They're bumper to bumper with the headlights of each lighting up the insides of the car ahead, like they do in funeral processions. Gawd! No way through. We brake hard and keep veering right with the curve of the shoulder. The raised divider is between us and the freeway now. We keep braking and swerve left to try to force an opening, and have to swerve back. They stand their ground, they're unflinching. They have solidarity. It's a wall and there's no getting through. No giving way for some erratic swerving hick with no blinkers and no brakelights and license plates with drawings of some grizzled prospector panning for gold. I should've switched to California plates before hitting the bigtime. To blend in, like a chameleon. The guardrail is between us and the freeway now. There's no backing up on the freeway. That's rule number one. Not that there are any rules. But when we built the transmission we didn't bother putting in a reverse gear. Who needs the extra clutter? We aim to go ahead.

The offramp keeps narrowing and curving right. Finally we force an opening in the slow line and wedge our way in. We slow, and stop. We're one of them now. We wait. Wait! Does anyone know what for? We're off the freeway.

Nothing like this ever happened before. The freeway was my show, my arena. It's always been home to me. I never knew an instant of doubt or confusion or fear on the freeway.

I was king. And before I was king, I was the crown prince. I was born and bred for it. I'm an American. I love the freeway.

And now it's dumped on me. We're stuck here, we're waiting. Just like all the rest. Nobody knowing what for. Waiting to die. God. Don't forget to take a number.

I screwed up. It wasn't the freeway. Grow up and face it. It's me. I'm the one who blew it. The freeway's your tabula rasa. What you going to write there? I just drew a scribbling line right off the edge of the damned page. It was up to me. I'm the one who got us into this. It's up to me to get us out.

Actually, it makes sense. Of course I blew it right off the bat like this. Here's the bigtime. Here I come, blowing in from the sticks. I'm a hick, I mean, I'm from Seattle. We got one freeway going up and down and one shooting off to the right. A few ancillary twists and swirls and feeder lines. Sure, I got a message, I got a gift. You think they want to hear about it, here in the mainstream? Come on. What the hell did you expect. Wise up, dumbshit. You're a god damn provincial. You come blowing in to the bigtime and expect to blow 'em all off the road at 200+ the first time out? And at *rush-hour?* Jesus. What's the matter with me?

We stop at many stoplights. They're machines that hang in the air and show colored lights that tell you when to stop, go and watch it. Right, stupid. We all know that. Even people in Iran know that. Never mind that they have the lights upside down over there.

Ok. Only it's not so obvious. There's more to it than meets the eye. They tell you when to go, but they're not called golights. Here's why. It's about control. You can always go. Straight ahead, that's the American way. It comes to us naturally, it's an instinct we got. You don't need a light to tell you when to go. That's the default mode for an American. Always has been. Get going and keep going. We never got over the shock of running into the damned ocean. That was nearly a death-blow. We never recovered.

And then hot on its heels came stoplights. When our resistance was down. They're unnatural, like a stillbirth. All that arrested potential. Frozen possibilities. Twenty years earlier they never would've took. Stoplights were a big step backward for America. Hitting the ocean and stoplights were a one-two punch. We're still reeling. We're dazed and staggering with no guard up. They're closing in for the knockout punch. See that's what this is all about. My life I mean. Bobbing and weaving. And blasting, straight ahead. Blurring past before they can lay the glove on you. I'm in the clear out here. I slipped through the ropes and I'm not even in the ring. Out here, we fight by my rules. No gloves. You should feel what you're hitting. In fact, no rules.

It was a black day in Cleveland in 1903. They put up a stoplight. That's no surprise. Lots of stupid things have been done over the centuries. I mean, think of all the millions of people who went through life thinking God didn't want them to fuck. It's twisted. It's almost as stupid as putting up a stoplight. But it would have been tolerable, if someone just put it up. A weird footnote in history. Get this, in 1903 some nut in Ohio put up this weird tower with three lights called a stoplight.

Only it didn't stop there. This is the bad part. Don't drive on if you don't have the stomach for it. Nobody'll hold it against you. It's not easy for an American to think about the virus that feeds on the American dream. The night of the walking dead wasn't a movie, it was last night. And tonight, and tomorrow. Hopefully, not the night after that. I'm working on it. I'm working on the driving dead. Don't you think it might wake you up some, when you're doing 60 on the southbound 405 somewhere around Hawthorne or Downey and someone or something blurs past you in the fast lane somewhere on the far side of 210 miles an hour? You'll feel the heat of my wake burning your cheek as it washes over you and for the next few miles you'll take an extra glance in the mirror before changing lanes. Maybe, gradually, you'll fall back asleep. That's your problem. I won't.

What happened in Cleveland wasn't that some nut propped up the colored-light tower and plugged it in and everyone laughed and the lights burned out and it was a joke in the footnotes of history. See, somebody paid attention to it. They *minded*. Who the hell was it? The first dipshit who sat waiting at a red light when nobody was coming should have been taught to bow and shipped to Japan. He'd like doing calisthentics and singing company songs before starting work each morning. He wasn't an *American*. Don't blame it on a woman, they didn't let women drive cars in those days. It was a macho thing. And some macho dirtball sat there waiting until this light with no brain told him it was safe to cross the street. Oh my God! It just doesn't make sense. I've never waited at a red light when nobody's coming. I never will. It's a question of life and death. I'd choke and die. Who could breathe? Some twit with a badge and a motorcycle aiming his electric blow-dryer at you doesn't make it right either. If you can go you got to. Life isn't long enough to live any other way. If you might make it you have to try. That's the way Lewis and Clark saw it. Heroes don't go asking for guarantees and 5-year/ 50,000-mile warranties. And Americans are heroes. Every last one of us. It's the nature of the critter. Love it or leave it. Go back to Europe. The Old Country. Wise up and learn something about yourself. Don't you know your ancestors were miserable peasants who came here because they wanted something more out of life? So quit settling for less. God damn it, quit settling. This is America. Step on the gas. The light turned green half an hour ago.

The Nilon Award

Ricardo Cortez Cruz

I always/already said that art is a weapon. A note reminding me of rapper Ice T, named after poetic licenser Iceberg Slim, who sang an old school jam on his crazy album/vinyl *Power* sending the message that you could push art like dope to people en masse. Well, I wasn't sure about that, but I yearned to revolutionize the masses, get niggas high on life.

Unfortunately, I learned that selling phat-ass stuff from the ghetto to mainstream isn't easy. Gotta do it right. And, if a brother's or sister's heart ain't in it, he or she shouldn't try, yo. Dig? Lucky for me, *Straight Outta Compton* got done at the speed of light and came out really fresh. However, with *Five Days of Bleeding*, it took a lot of verve to make Zu-Zu Girl strong. She was a body of (s)language; there were pieces of her all over the place. Eventually, the process of putting the whole thing together conjured images of "Love on the Rise" (I mean, the way Kashif and Kenny G tirelessly spent the night producing that 12-inch cut/version, recursively going over the same stuff). "Cool," I finally said to myself, when the groove was done. "Tadow, how you like me now?"

Initially, it seemed almost campy when my bleeding begun getting attention. Before I could spit or shout "Fubu (For us, by us), baby," I had rocked the house, yaw, with two raw, badd, mad, funky compositions replete with riffs—"we can think of composition as a bundle of parts," I quoted in *Compton*. As a writer, I was creating program music, race music. And I was gone, folks tagging me the first major "rap" novelist, that term blowing up (and in my face as well), trying to claim/own me like a new wave of graffiti. Critics swore that my lyrics were/wore like lines from the soul/sole, man. People began hailing me, Youngbleed, as the raging voice and energy of the ghetto. And I was eating it all up, like candy.

I will never forget, with everything being everything, how FC2 and Black Ice Books helped put me out there. I'm a cultural worker focusing on issues of Otherness, and indeed I have a dream. If I ruled the world (imagine that), I'd want people to see me as a new sound/thing, an overnight sensation, living for the city. "I'd be clubbing," I thought, cause even now I like the idea of being "about it about it," a bestseller in Oprah's/Girlfriend's Book Club or something.

Every night, I thank God for FC2: Back in the day, they (my homeys there) was the one with the nerve to hype me; they gave everybody a chance to vibe and jibe with me. They launched my career, my journey into sound. And it was all good.

For the record, I continue to mix shit up, bringing the noise, trying to move the crowd. To quote the late rapper Tupac Shakur, "That's just the way it is."

More Mental

Rooster quietly sat on somebody's stoop watching Yolanda she hit the steps looking up cotton above her big head LeRoi Jones' or Amiri Baraka's *The Slave* in her black hands. She wore embryonic eyes and a flower dress Drop waist out on the porch late night as repairmen came by and smiled with snakes crawling near her feet Then they threw cable off their shoulders like it was chain or thread for stitches and went to work in front of her. Rooster bled under a tree chomping candy hard and noisily Tuning out the world switching back and forth between present and Past a bottle of Campho Phenique for infection.

Rubber repairman Rubber repairman Rubber repairman. Rooster realized that one of the repairmen wasn't wearing any rubber But/butt didn't seem to care as His back was turned to Rooster and he was playing with his cable.

Strong safe sex theme in the Los Angeles Times compelling a bloody Rooster to read in order to find out how to get AIDS. First-aid. Band-Aids. Etc.

Los Angeles Times
CIRCULATION: 1,242,864 daily/1,576,425 Sunday
THURSDAY, MAY 23, 1991, 204 pages
DAILY 25¢ (Designated Areas Higher)
Rooster thought about what-might-have-been:

Girl, 2 1/2, Stabbed to Death; Man Killed

A 2 1/2-year-old girl was stabbed to death and her mother was seriously injured Monday night. Police said a man who knew the woman was also stabbed to death in the incident at an apartment building on Alameda Street, Compton. The names of all three were withheld pending notification of family members. According to police, the man entered the woman's apartment to use her phone, but drew a knife and attacked her. All three were stabbed during the struggle. "He just accosted her for reasons that are unclear," Sgt. Brad Bennett said. "He was an acquaintance of the woman. The accosting may have been of a sexual nature."

"The newspapers reported an inaccuracy," Rooster said. "The murder weapon was a nigger flicker." Rooster smeared blood all over his face and hands, his big head wobbling like a dented globe set with millions of people. Half-dossing in a blue funk, he thought about his daddy, the menace of the nigger flicker. Rooster sweated blood. He saw a long line of violence Little Black Man and The Devil. Like father Like son Like hell.

Imagine being stabbed by your own nigger flicker. Fun? Impossible? Bizarre? Asinine? Rooster cracked up.

He was livin' large Gaudy Gold chains linking/tangling swinging around his neck like rope touching silver on the sidewalk No Copper.

Suspect in 10 Rapes Arrested After Chase

By DAVID FREED, Times Staff Writer

A 24-year-old man suspected in a string of at least 10 rapes in three cities was arrested early Tuesday after running from a residence in southwest Los Angeles and leading police on a brief car chase, authorities, said.

» » »

Yolanda looked disgusted/frustrated regretting this day fighting back the tears beating the rocks thinking wondering hoping that Billy Bugle Boy has disguised himself as one of the repairmen Mr. Fix-it Handy Man. The aftermath Terrible storm. Lights out & a lover to turn her on.

Rooster laughed under the tree, his eyes shaded, his face ajar, his mouth chewing gum, dinosaur teeth acting playful. Stealing looks Rooster the robber Rooster a thief gaining insidiously Sitting deviously in the dark showing his horns. Bleeding Grinning Tripping. She would probably throw up at the sight Squeamish weak battered bruised Feeling the funk left by the Boogie-man but Seemingly Sensing the mimicry of a Devil.

Rooster planned to get her and then end it all. He knew how to get away with murder, now that Billy Bugle Boy was gone.

Shots Fired at Set of Gang Film; 1 Hurt

By STEPHEN BRAUN, Times Staff Writer
A movie company completing a film on gang life in the El Sereno area of Los Angeles got a taste of the real thing early Saturday when shots were fired at the set during a drive-by incident, injuring an actor, police said.

Police were unsure of a motive.

"It could have been anything," Sgt. Robert Gruszecky said. "There were some officers there. Maybe they were the targets. One of our big concerns was the number of actors roaming around the area dressed up in gang clothes. It could have been that, or any of 100 different reasons."

Rooster could do anything. Be anything. Fuck anything. The drugs were a cop-out an excuse a license to ill a Spike Lee joint a trip a Kool breeze a mulatto heroine bitch like Yolanda a bomb in Bob Marley's mouth a fix a drive to Colorado (Suicide) Bridge in Pasadena a quake a fallout a clod of blue grass a firebug a sucker MC a freak out a bag of candy a house party a red Devil.

LOS ANGELES COUNTY—Rooster California dreamin'.

Shit happens. Old wounds never heal. Blood is thicker than tequila, Rooster attested. Rooster as weak as water. High as a kite. Ego-trippin'. Stabbed by a nigger flicker sharp as a tack. In the prime of his life. A squirrel trying to get a nut. Thought he had nothing to lose but was dead wrong. Problem child. Being Black his whole life's story. A victim of circumstance. They all look alike anyway, packed like sardines inside a Metro. Poor and disadvantaged. No excuse. No offense. But, poor and disadvantaged. Eventually, they got on each other's nerves. Starting dogging each other out. Finally, Rooster got sick and tired of the ain't-yo'momma-on-the-back-of-the-pancake-box jokes.

That's just my theory.

Community caught in Back-and-forth Battle
By PAUL SMITH, Staff Writer

LA PUENTE—There's good news and bad news in one statistical trend reported from the notorious Laura and Valley area where flagrant rock cocaine dealing is an everyday fact of life, authorities said.

The good news is that narcotics arrests in the area fell 27 percent from 1989's total of 1,015 arrests to a total of 739 arrests in 1990, according to the Sheriff's Department.

The bad news is that street dealing, virtually eliminated from the area for several months last year during intensive 24-hour-a-day sweeps by deputies in the the densely populated, four square-block area, has slowly returned, said Lt. David Betkey.

» » »

Rooster used the grapevine to find Yolanda. Trash in the streets, Rooster a regular Jack traveling a beanstalk for the golden goose. Yolanda fair skin Black woman unsuspecting unwinding unreserved unmasking herself to a wayfarer, Rooster bleeding revenge. Bad blood. Rooster leaning over on his side dripping dying dyeing Muddy Waters his face changing from brown to red. Murder and rape in cold blood.

Everything premeditated Yolanda grabbing the repairman's cable wanting to do it with Billy Bugle Boy but taking anything she can get. She stopped everything too crude too cheap too easy But he kept going pulling down on her panties eating flowers begging her to give it to him.

"Quit," she said. She smacked him in the face.

"Fuckin' cunt around-the-way bitch slutty dumb-ass freak!" he called her. "Turn on yo' electricity by yourself!"

Rooster thought she'd cry like a white woman in the movies on television Liz'beth Taylor etc. but Black women don't play that shit.

"Shoot, it's obvious to me you can't turn me on," Yolanda said One Black hand on her hip the other pointing at his face Head moving up and down as she talked. "I've seen more meat on a cheese stick. Now take yo' Black ass home."

The other repairmen Clapped Laughed Patted Mr. Right on his back and they all left Cable between their legs. Yolanda Questioned the fairness of life the Reason Billy would rather fuck a white woman Why he hit her Broke her Crushed her heart Yolanda left wondering why caged birds sing.

LETTERS TO THE TIMES
Britain's Queen Elizabeth II

I couldn't help noticing the sad juxtaposition of two stories on your front page (May 15): "Queen Eats Soul Food in Los Angeles" and "Winnie Mandela Is Sentenced to 6 Years in Prison."

EVETTE KING
Watts

» » »

Rooster bled more freely under a tree chomping candy hard and noisily Tuning out the world switching back and forth between present and Past a bottle of Campho Phenique for infection Yolanda in full view.

How to Write Us
The Times welcomes expressions of all views.

Brutal (Stabbing is)...Rooster Hurt and Hiding on Somebody's stoop in Compton Yolanda thinking She Miss It or Miss Fine swinging on the porch past the bars that cover her front door and window.

Accountability in the LAPD
I agree...that we need to heal the wounds of this city. But wounds do not heal unless they are treated.
COUNCILMAN MICHAEL WOO
Los Angeles

Bleeding Rooster looked on with bitter repulsion sore burning Causing him to slump over But he planned to get her and then end it all so he made his move Crawling through the wet grass like a snake (Yolanda swinging) Crawling through wet blades (Yolanda swinging) Crawling and hurting like a snail coming out of salt (Yolanda swinging) Creeping up to her side Grabbing her leg Dragging her down to the ground Throwing blood up against her Yolanda screamed.

Tussle. Street fight. All-star wrestling. Rooster licking the flowers wanting a virgin like father Like son. He pulled down Yolanda's panties slid on top of her making sure she could feel it Stinging Burning She screamed.

"Quit!" she yelled. "Stop!"

Nobody could hear The neighbors in Compton blasting Loud music Yolanda squeezing the tracks in Rooster's arms.

» » »

Gang Life Contains Short Life Span

By CINDY RANSOM, Times Staff Writer
As a teenager growing up in a San Pedro hous-
ing project, Lionel "Little Train" Taylor
thought being a gang member was cool—until he and his friend, Leon Jackson, were fa-
tally shot as they climbed the stairs to crash a
house party.

Yolanda screaming. "Please stop! Oh God!"

Rooster threw her dress into a T-shirt Feeling the climax
Coming Yolanda wiggling underneath him screwing herself
hitting the steps.

Oh God a terrible headache Yolanda's screaming reminding Rooster of the little children running around at The Swap
Meet on Manchester South Central Los Angeles:

"You like?" an oriental woman in the booth asked
Rooster, showing him a By Any Means Necessary T-shirt.

"Hey, if you don't stop running I'm going to bust you in
the mouth!" a Black woman cried.

"You like?" asked the Chink, holding up a shirt of Bay-
Bay's kids. "Only three for ten dollar."

"Stop it!"

"How about this?" she asked.

"What is it?" asked Rooster.

"Get over here before I whip yo' ass!"

"From the movie," the oriental woman answered.

"Get yo' fingers off of that!"

"How much is it?" Rooster asked.

"Alright, don't make me get up!"

"3.50 apiece."

"Leave that man alone before he goes off!"

"$3," said Rooster.

"Three for 10 dollar," said the woman.

"Sit yo' little ass down!"

"How much for one?" asked Rooster.

"Did you hear me?"

"3.50."

"I said sit yo' little ass down!"

"Look how much I've spent!" shouted Rooster.

"Quit showing out!"

"Free pair of sock," said the woman.

"Free shirt," demanded Rooster.

"What's yo' damn problem?"

"OK, three dollar."

"Give me extra-large," demanded Rooster.

"No extra-large," she said.

"You want yo' daddy to come beat yo' ass?"

"Shut up!" Rooster shouted Dripping a Stream of Consciousness Yolanda stained with Blood.

"Get off me!" cried Yolanda. "You through!"

"Goodnight," said Rooster. "You about to be dusted. I'm the sandman."

He cackled like it was nothing Lying in the grass.

Diane Glancy

I wrote Broken Spell because I visited a nursing home in Tulsa and the voices I heard in the hall haunted me. Personal frustrations, disappointments and family squabbles were open for everyone to hear. But in spite of it all, I wanted to show how the entanglements of this life transcended to some ultimate understanding or release. Or the possibilities of them anyway. I like to mix those elements of realism, and the spiritualistic, if there is such a word. If there is such a mix. Life is difficult for the Native American, yet there is another world to inhabit—one of imagination and strength. I like the thought of Anna's wings unfolding. I like the thought of her becoming the forgiving as well as the forgiven. I think I believe in a compassionate hereafter.

Broken Spell

Trees leaned toward the sidewalk like a hand shoved them down. The wind stampeded across the road. Then rain rushed at an angle past the window under angry bites of lightning.

"Cay mah nok tah." Anna America sat in her chair. Her cotton, flowered robe was stiff. She'd sweated during her nap that afternoon, then dried. "Maybe this will break the hot spell." Anna held her cane on her lap. Her head rested against the back of the tall chair, two fingers across her mouth. The rain coughed over the roof, splattered on the ground in puddles.

"Into the nineties & it's only turned June." She summed. "The summer'll be in the hundreds before it gets started."

But this storm would cut into the heat. For a while, anyway, Northeastern Oklahoma Cherokee County Shelter would be cooler. Anna America could doze & remember when she'd been in school long ago. She could remember her woven shawls, seed-bowls, the moon as heavy as a horse blanket. She could think of nights the heat held on like children clawing at their mothers when they came to the shelter. She tried to turn away its smell & the eyes in the chairs out in the hall disappearing into wrinkles. The horror of some of them crying out.

"Push me that stool. I need to get this old stump up off the ground." Anna made her arm fly. Bird with five wings.

"You got your sash wrapped around your foot," an old woman said at the door. "Don't fall when you get up."

"I got nowhere to go."

The rain made nasty splats on the steps. Anna remembered the angry nurse when the old women made puddles. She must have dozed again. For a moment she was in her house with its bed & chest of drawers, the table & one chair. She chopped the other chairs for firewood late last winter. She startled herself awake with the memory of her son, William America, carrying her out of her house like a bride. Surely the veil of death on her. She'd never go back. Why couldn't she die?

A lightbulb flickered in the hall. The thoughts in her head drove her farther into memory. Her daughter & two of her sons in alcoholic stupors. She had been there herself several times before she got ahold of the cross. Drinking her way across the country. She had years she couldn't remember. Her head fell forward a moment in her chair. She slept off & on all day, then spent hours awake in the night, angered that she couldn't sleep. Doting on war chants. Buckaroo Braves. Indians in rodeos. The nurse came in & hushed her, tied her to her chair as though the hand of the storm pushed her down too. The nurse said she would stuff a sock in Anna's mouth if she didn't shut up.

Her head felt like a hundred pounds & hurt the back of her neck. She rallied. "Heck chaw nah maw."

"You can't scream in the middle of the night. There're some who sleep." The nurse was always grouchy.

"I can't sleep!" Anna shouted at her with a gritty voice. "The storm!"

If only she didn't doze all day. But what else was there to do? When she slept, little children came into her dreams. She imagined she was on the prairie again running to the mission school, riding her pony later to the consolidated school, baking bread & cakes with her mother. Loving her husband until he got so drunk she couldn't tolerate his presence. Then she'd wake a moment. The Shelter for Aged Indians was better than the memory of him.

It seemed the animals growled sometimes at night, especially when she was back in her house with young children & her husband on the rampage. He'd stay out in the bushes raking the house, walking on the roof just to scare her & the children.

Sometimes she still saw the red eyes, the electrical cord going up to the moon. On clear nights its milky light shone through the curtains at the window. Her chants cracked under her old voice. She could not hold them back. The nurse tied a rag around Anna's face, covering her mouth. She hummed the tune that rose from her heart. Visions the old Indians had were usually calm affairs. No one could raise their voices, but croaked like toads that came out after rain.

The warning siren eeked from the corner of the greenish sky, slobbered over the edge of Cherokee County then shut off. Wind storms came all the time. Anna was not interested in them. She was tied to her chair. Maybe she would fly with the roof to the edge of town, if all the noise was about a tornado. Maybe she would drown in a downpour if all they were getting was rain. Then her life would end in water as it had began in the womb. Yes, she had liked that lesson in school.

Her skin felt puckered & thin. Would the Great Spirit recognize her as the creature he had once made? Didn't the minister say that God looked on the heart & not the outward part? In the light that came in the door from the hall, she could see the snarl of veins just under the surface. Her joints were swollen, aching. Her head forgetful, cranky, afraid.

In the old days the fathers died easily. Now everything seemed out of whack. Maybe the whites mutated death also, once quick & glorious, easy as corn bread. Now it contorted before her in screams, cries, agonies she heard all around her, even sometimes she guessed from her own mouth. A prolonging of it all. How many had she sat with? Grandmothers who went on to the hunting grounds, humming in joy to rise from the earth. Her thumb twitched against her side & woke her a moment. She thought someone touched her, shoved her slightly like the trees calmer now after their tremors. Had the storm already passed? Had they left her in her chair all night or had she been in bed & forgotten? Maybe the storm came in the early evening & they had not put her to bed yet. Maybe they'd simply forgotten her on their rounds.

Anna thought often of her children. How she'd put them in bureau drawers to sleep when they were babies because there was no place else for them. How she'd been stupid with drink, sometimes probably falling asleep as she fed them & they must have crawled & wandered around the house picking up crumbs to eat, crying, their noses always running. Maybe they had bumped against her until they woke her & she, sick with drink, probably whacked them in the head to shut their mouths. They had learned silence & pain. Had always known it. How had it fallen apart? How had they survived? She remembered the mission school when William & the other children painted wigwams & teepees & wore tribal costume & sang as their fathers & grandfathers had. & she, drying out, watched them until years later, her heart grew warm & she heard the prayer-hum within herself. She sang it again, even though the rag was around her face. What fluttered then in her chest? The Great Spirit offered forgiveness & new life. She knew that if she knew nothing else on this flat earth.

Yes, the rain had already slackened, sputtered off toward the east. "Let them have it," she said. What day was it? What month? She couldn't think anymore. It all shattered before her. Who cared what time it was anyway? Did her grandfathers have clocks?

Let the heat flush out everyone's bad temper. She was through with the earth. The treacherous place. Electric horse-blanket for a moon. What a waste it had been. Her husband no longer on her. No, Anna had not remembered that in a long time. She felt a flush for a moment between her legs as she thought of him. Why did it come back in her old age? She touched herself in her robe, then took her hand away. The nurse would tie her hands to the sides of her chair if she saw her. His love had turned yellow as whiskey anyway & the pleasure he gave her didn't last.

The siren retched with spasm again. She heard a roar pass over. Maybe she would rise into the storm & pass out of this civilization. She'd never been part of it anyway. She would be glad to leave the lumps of her legs in their purple houseshoes with blue veins popping out everywhere. She felt her sagging breasts, the wrinkled skin inside the flowered robe. Even her mind played tricks. The trickster, coyote.

She woke up young again until she looked down at her arms & saw the robe fallen open while a woman washed her, folds of skin on her narrow belly. Was it morning? Where has the storm gone?

"Come on, Anna America," the gross nurse said. "You can wail all night, but in the morning, not half of you comes back."

Anna's robe was stained with food. Death was a kicker. The nurse talked about a limb from the tree across the porch. The storm was gone, but no, not the heat. She'd been wrong. The wind came back with the heat & tricked her.

The storm had come & gone & Anna had known little of it. She was taking care of the children, chasing off her husband, then another man had come, & she had to watch out for him too. She didn't want him on the place. A man was just another child to take care of. She threw rocks at him.

Anna couldn't remember the day if they told her a hundred times, pinned it to her nose. She didn't know her children sometimes when they came. She'd think of them playing in the mud by the house & they'd come in dirty & she'd tell them to wash, & it would be William America standing there saying it was her grandsons. She'd tell them to go away, but they screamed their names in her face so she could understand. Why didn't they shut up? No, she put her two fingers across her mouth. She wanted them to come.

Her head fell forward, lost somewhere in her thoughts. The red eye of the sky looked in the window, the land toward which she moved but couldn't get to for some reason. She always felt held back. That hand again.

Life was enough to kill hundreds & thousands of buffalo. It could put Indians in jets & real estate. Bombs away. Now death was another life in itself. "He sheck aa." Anna choked out her prayer-language.

She had begun life as a polliwog in the womb. She remembered the lesson in school again before she had quit. Then she turned animal, breathed the air of this world. She had gone through every stage but the wings. Maybe they weren't left out after all. No, the Great Spirit knew what he was doing.

She had borne the wings in her spirit all her life. She remembered now they had carried her along. That's what she had felt in her chest. The wings were coming to her now in death. Maybe they were already on her back. Wouldn't she love for the gross nurse to find them. Anna tried to feel her back, but couldn't reach it. One day soon she would walk to the sky. Yes, she nodded to herself. She would pull the blanket moon over her, nothing behind her but a moan or a whimper.

Fiction Collective / FC2 / Black Ice Books
Complete Bibliography

(To purchase any of the books listed below, or to view the complete FC2 backlist, visit our website, http://fc2.fsu.edu)

Second Story Man; Mimi Albert, 1975
Althea; J. M. Alonso, 1976
The Kafka Chronicles; Mark Amerika, 1993
Sexual Blood; Mark Amerika, 1995
Degenerative Prose; Edited by Mark Amerika and
　　　　Ronald Sukenick, 1995
The Fifth Season; George Angel, 1996
Mabel in Her Twenties; Rosaire Appel, 1992
transiT; Rosaire Appel, 1993
The Mind Crime of August Saint; Alain Arias-Misson, 1993
Searching for Survivors; Russell Banks, 1975
Babble; Jonathan Baumbach, 1976
Chez Charlotte and Emily;
　　　　Jonathan Baumbach, 1979
D-Tours; Jonathan Baumbach, 1998
The Life and Times of Major Fiction;
　　　　Jonathan Baumbach, 1987
My Father More or Less; Jonathan Baumbach, 1982
Reruns; Jonathan Baumbach, 1974
Separate Hours; Jonathan Baumbach, 1990
Seven Wives; Jonathan Baumbach, 1994
Statements 1; Edited by Jonathan Baumbach, 1975
Statements 2: New Fiction; Edited by
　　　　Jonathan Baumbach and Peter Spielberg, 1977
From the District File; Kenneth Bernard, 1992
Leonardo's Horse; R. M. Berry, 1997
Plane Geometry and Other Affairs of the Heart;
　　　　R. M. Berry, 1985

The Talking Room; Marianne Hauser, 1976
Holy Smoke; Fanny Howe, 1979
In the Middle of Nowhere; Fanny Howe, 1984
Mole's Pity; Harold Jaffe, 1979
Mourning Crazy Horse; Harold Jaffe, 1982
Straight Razor; Harold Jaffe, 1995
Sex for the Millennium; Harold Jaffe, 1999
The Great Taste of Straight People; Lily James, 1997
Damned Right; Bayard Johnson, 1994
Moving Parts; Steve Katz, 1977
Saw, Steve Katz, 1998
Stolen Stories; Steve Katz, 1984
Find Him!; Elaine Kraf, 1977
The Northwest Passage; Norman Lavers, 1984
Life of Death; Philip Lewis, 1993
I Smell Esther Williams; Mark Leyner, 1983
American Made: New Fiction from the Fiction Collective;
      Edited by Mark Leyner, Curtis White and
      Thomas Glynn, 1986
Modern Romances; Judy Lopatin, 1986
Emergency Exit; Clarence Major, 1979
My Amputations; Clarence Major, 1980
Reflex and Bone Structure; Clarence Major, 1975
Punk Blood; Jay Marvin, 1998
Four Roses in Three Acts; Franklin Mason, 1981
Animal Acts; Cris Mazza, 1988
Chick Lit: Postfeminist Fiction; Edited by Cris Mazza
      and Jeffrey DeShell, 1995
Chick-Lit 2: No Chick Vics; Edited by Cris Mazza,
      Jeffrey DeShell and Elisabeth Sheffield, 1996
Former Virgin; Cris Mazza, 1997
Is It Sexual Harrassment Yet?; Cris Mazza, 1991
Revelation Countdown; Cris Mazza, 1993
Avant-Pop: Fiction for a Daydream Nation;
      Edited by Larry McCaffery, 1993

Eve's Longing: The Infinite Possibilities in All Things;
    Deborah McKay, 1992
The Secret Table; Mark Mirsky, 1975
Encores for a Dilettante; Ursule Molinaro, 1977
When Things Get Back to Normal;
    Constance Pierce, 1987
Rope Dances; David Porush, 1979
Little Sisters of the Apocalypse; Kit Reed, 1994
Blood of Mugwump; Doug Rice, 1996
Napoleon's Mare; Lou Robinson, 1991
Broad Back of the Angel; Leon Rooke, 1977
Nature Studies; John Henry Ryskamp, 1998
Spectator; Rachel Salazar, 1986
Valentino's Hair; Yvonne V. Sapia, 1991
The Common Wilderness; Michael Seide, 1983
Aviary Slag; Jacques Servin, 1996
Mermaids for Attila; Jacques Servin, 1991
City in Love; Alex Shakar, 1996
New Noir; John Shirley, 1993
The Comatose Kids; Seymour Simckes, 1976
The Charnel Imp; Alan Singer, 1988
Memory Wax; Alan Singer, 1996
Fat People; Carol Sturm Smith, 1978
Crash-Landing; Peter Spielberg, 1985
Hearsay; Peter Spielberg, 1992
The Hermetic Whore; Peter Spielberg, 1977
Twiddledum Twaddledum; Peter Spielberg, 1974
Broadway Melody of 1999; Robert Steiner, 1993
Matinee; Robert Steiner, 1988
The Ethiopian Exhibition; D. N. Stuefloten, 1994
Maya; D. N. Stuefloten, 1992
Mexico Trilogy; D. N. Stuefloten, 1996
Doggy Bag; Ronald Sukenick, 1994
The Endless Short Story; Ronald Sukenick, 1986

Long Talking Bad Conditions Blues;
    Ronald Sukenick, 1979
Mosaic Man; Ronald Sukenick, 1999
98.6; Ronald Sukenick, 1975
Up; Ronald Sukenick, 1998
Meningitis; Yuriy Tarnawsky, 1978
Three Blondes and Death; Yuriy Tarnawsky, 1993
Close Your Eyes and Think of Dublin: Portrait of a Girl;
    Kathryn Thompson, 1991
Griever: An American Monkey King in China;
    Gerald Vizenor, 1987
Agnes & Sally; Lewis Warsh, 1984
A Spell for the Fulfillment of Desire; Don Webb, 1996
Uncle Ovid's Exercise Book; Don Webb, 1988
Cares of the Day; Ivan Webster, 1994
An Illuminated History of the Future;
    Edited by Curtis White, 1989
Anarcho-Hindu; Curtis White, 1995
Heretical Songs; Curtis White, 1980
The Beginning of the East; Max Yeh, 1992